THE STRANGE ONE

Fred Bodsworth

THE
STRANGE
ONE

Dodd, Mead & Company · NEW YORK

For my wife, Margaret

I hope the characters of this story *appear* to be real, but I hope no reader will be so convinced as to believe them *really* real. It is a work of fiction and all of its cast are fictional people—except the goose, which is a fictional goose.

F.B.

PART ONE

Alice

CHAPTER ONE

THE barnacle goose was instantly awake, for even in sleep his senses had detected the change in the behavior of the sea. He had been restless and more than normally alert since the last of the flock moved out the day before on the flight to the Greenland nesting fiords. Alone now, he missed the security, the relaxation of vigil that was possible in a flock that always had a few individuals awake and on guard, and he awoke the moment the first big smooth-topped Atlantic swell hit him.

Unlike most geese, the barnacle is not a bird of the wet fields and marshes, but a bird of the sea and of the salt-rimed cliffs and tideflats close to the sea. This one was a male of the previous year's nesting, and though less than a year old he was already intimately familiar with the ways and patterns of wind, waves and tides. It was this acute familiarity that had wakened him now. For he recognized, even in sleep, that the sudden swell, so similar superficially to any ocean roller, was intrinsically and ominously different.

It had surged in from the west with no warning across a previously calm and quiet sea. Now more swells came, in smooth and orderly succession. They were thirty feet high, long and gently sloping ridges of blue-green water with flattened glassy tops instead of sharp foam-flecked crests.

The goose had spent most of his life breasting Atlantic swells such as these but now a strange uneasiness seized him, because these swells rising unheralded out of a waveless sea had no wind driving them. The air was heavy and still. The rollers, seemingly unpowered, were moving with a tremendous and mysterious power of their own, as though the sea itself was fleeing from some distant and violent mid-ocean disturbance.

Each time the goose was lifted to the top of a swell, a long hummocky blue mound reared like a sleeping sea monster along the horizon to the east. Then it sank into the sea again as the goose slipped down into each trough. It was the Outer Hebrides, a closely knit chain of islands which spatter out from north to south like beads of a shattered necklace—a massive breakwater of sand and rock which shields the northwest coast of Scotland against the full fury of the sea. Westward for two thousand miles to Labrador no land rises to break the somber monotony of ocean, and the long heaving swells that thunder against the isles' western beaches have the tremendous power of the entire Atlantic behind them.

Near the southern tip of the island chain is Barra, a lonely rugged isle honed down by wind and rain and by the tides of a sea that never rests. It is a small isle, not ten miles across at even its widest point, yet the restless waters that lash its shores become a gathering point every autumn for the world's largest wintering flock of barnacle geese.

They are medium-sized geese, about two feet from tail to bill, and boldly marked with black, white and gray. The breast, neck and head are black except for a large round face patch of contrasting white. The back is gray, the sides and belly white. Their identification badge is the striking white face patch, visible for long distances.

But more striking still for a goose is the strange attachment that the barnacles have for the sea. Most wild geese are birds of the boggy grasslands and marshes, but the barnacles rarely stray far from the stinging lash of the ocean's spray. There is always salt rime in their feathers and the thunder of surf in their ears. Even when nesting they cling close to the sea, for they raise their downy young on the rock ledges of northern Greenland's coastal cliffs and fiord walls, where the surging sea is always close below.

The barnacle geese begin arriving back at Barra in the Outer Hebrides early in October. They come in from the north, flying low over the water in ragged wavy lines which look like wisps of gray smoke when they first appear above the horizon. They gabble excitedly, like packs of little dogs barking, when they arch their broad wings and pitch down to the beds of tangle and eelgrass that grow in the sea shallows of Barra's tideflats. Some fly on, to the Inner Hebrides, the Clyde and to the marshes of the Solway, but the main flocks go no farther south than Barra. They spend the winter there, feeding at night on the eelgrass beds inshore, then flying out to sea each morning to rest for the day. The flocks wing seaward until Barra's Heaval Hill is a thin gray-blue lump on the horizon, then they come down onto the sea's surface, sitting high and buoyantly on the water, and until dusk and feeding time come again they breast the long Atlantic swells with an easy graceful skill. Much of their lives is spent this way offshore on the open reaches of sea.

In April when the Hebridean crofters begin plowing their sandy *machair* fields, the barnacle geese begin flying northward on the long sea flight to the Greenland fiords. By early May when the Barra *machairs*

are brilliant with primroses and bluebells the last of the barnacles are
usually gone.

But it was mid-May now, and the one lone male remained.

He was a mateless nonbreeder. Geese do not mature sexually until
their second spring, so every May there are flocks of one-year-old nonbreeders loitering on the wintering grounds because in them the springtime migratory urge is slow to develop. This spring a flock of a hundred
or more had lingered behind when the breeding adults left Barra a month
before. Though not ready physically for breeding and nesting, the
nonbreeders nevertheless had begun to feel the initial stirrings of a sexual
awakening. The males courted the females with excited little bobbings
and gesturings, then, after a preliminary sorting, each male fought off
rivals to win and keep the female of his choice. Once paired in their first
spring, they would keep the same mates for life, and even when death
finally broke the bond between them the surviving member of a pair
would rarely remate.

But in the male that now waited alone at Barra, the glandular activity
that incited courtship had built up more slowly than in the others. He
had taken little part in the courtship demonstrations. By early May the
pairing in the flock had been complete, no unmated female remained and
he was a surplus bachelor. He was a large male, a good deal heavier than
an average barnacle gander, and he could have won a mate easily by
driving another male out of the flock. But for him the mating drive was
not yet a pressing urge, and he had felt no desire to fight for a mate.

Once paired, the geese had begun to feel a restless urge to migrate.
They would not nest this year, yet still the ancestral Greenland nesting
grounds beckoned. The restlessness built up like a growing fever and
yesterday when they flew out to sea after feeding they simply kept on
flying northwestward instead of stopping at the customary resting spot
ten miles or so offshore.

The unpaired male had felt little urge to fly on north. The feeding here
was rich and plentiful, and he loved the white and turbulent water off
the isle's rocky headlands where he could pit strength and skill against
the angry backwash of breakers flung back by the gray rock walls. He
followed the flock seaward for many minutes, but the lure of Barra's
eelgrass beds and its lunging surf was stronger than the lure of the flock
and finally he circled back. He watched the flock's twisting flight line fade
into a hazy thread, then as it merged into the sky and disappeared he
dropped down and alighted on the sea, alone.

And almost as soon as the flock passed from sight the ordeal of loneliness began. The barnacle is a flocking species, and the male had never been separated from his own kind before.

That was thirty-six hours ago, and now the loneliness was a sharp and biting torment. The migratory urge, so weak the day before that it was hardly felt, had suddenly become a compelling drive. He knew now what he had to do. He would feed once more, then he would set out on the northward flight, retracing the unmarked route that would take him to the summering flocks of the barnacles.

He had been resting alone on the open ocean since the first yellow flecks of the dawn had stippled the eastern sky sixteen hours before. The sun was low now in the west, and the tide would be creeping back off Barra's beaches again, exposing the eelgrass that grew in the sheltered coves where the water was quiet and the sea's muddy sediments could deposit and mix with the limey sand. And the goose was hungry, for he went ashore to feed only in darkness, and now the mid-May days were long and the feeding periods widely separated.

But he waited for the sun to sink lower, and as he lingered the tremendous swells continued to race in from the west though still there was no wind driving them. Just before sunset, wispy bands of cirrus cloud moved across the reddening sun and radiated eastward like spokes of a giant celestial wheel. These advance forerunners of cloud thickened quickly into a humpy ribbed layer, gray at first, then flaming red as the sun sank lower and illuminated it from below.

The goose watched as the cloud mass moved like an enveloping shroud across the sky. It was moving very rapidly. And the vague gnawing uneasiness within the goose sharpened. He knew that a strong gale far above was sweeping the cloud layer eastward, although there was no wind at all on the surface of the sea. And he sensed dimly that a gale above and dead calm below was a bizarre and ominous contradiction.

He was about ten miles out, a fifteen-minute flight from the Hebridean shore, and he timed the take-off so that he would arrive at the feeding beach just as dusk was changing to night. With no breath of wind to put added lift under his wide wings, the take-off was labored. His wings beat violently at first and his six-pound body lifted slowly off the glassy slope of a swell, but once fully airborne his flight became a symphony of rhythmic movement and effortless power.

His wings were broad for a barnacle goose—more than five feet from tip to tip outspread. They beat the air slowly, arching gracefully on the down-stroke and straightening out with the upbeat, the flight feathers separating like twisted fingers at each wingtip. Normally he would have flown close to the sea where the wind, deflected upward off each sloping wave, would have provided some ready-made lift for his wings. But now the air was lifeless and unmoving, so he climbed for height, testing each new level for a breeze or updraft that might help his wings. He climbed several hundred feet, and the air did not change. So he leveled off on a course toward the distant ragged skyline of the Outer Hebrides which strung out along the eastern rim of his vision more clearly and more boldly now because of his height above the sea.

Near Barra's northern edge a low rocky island shields a one-mile section of shore from the pounding sea. Between it and Barra itself is a shallow sound of protected water where the eelgrass grows in lush profusion and the geese flocks regularly feed. The barnacle flew low now over the sandbar that reached out from the little island's southern corner. Here the great sea rollers exploded into a maelstrom of foaming water and deafening sound. Spray hit him like pellets of shot. He flew on, following the breakers as they scudded in across the foreshore, but although the time was due there was no sign of an ebbing tide. The white fury of water still plunged far up onto the silver sand, even reaching the twisting windrow of seaweed and flotsam that marked the highest tideline.

The life of the barnacle goose was regulated by the comings and goings of the tides, and he knew the times and pattern of those tides as well as other birds knew the times of sunrise and sunset. To him a tide that remained high when the ebb was due was as unaccountable as a sun that stood still in the sky.

He flew behind the island, but even before he reached the shallows where he had often fed he knew that the strange high tide was covering the eelgrass too deeply for feeding. He settled on the water above the eelgrass beds and peered into the shadowy murk below him. Geese do not dive for food as many ducks do; instead they feed in shallow water by "tipping"—reaching underwater to the full extent of their necks, with bodies tipped vertically and tails standing straight up above the surface. The barnacle tried several exploratory tippings but the ribbon-like eelgrass fronds waved tantalizingly in the current well out of reach below.

Cloud now covered all but a narrow eastern strip of sky, the last purple glow of the sun had faded and the night was suddenly very dark. The barnacle waited for the tide to ebb. He waited an hour while hunger and loneliness filled him with a gnawing pain. From beyond the protected water of the sound came a steadily mounting roar of surf and he knew the mysterious Atlantic rollers were growing larger. Yet still the air was dead and without wind.

After an hour the goose could detect another puzzling contradiction. The water over the eelgrass beds was not ebbing as it should, it was rising. It was a foot or two above even the high tide mark now.

The goose had no power of deductive reasoning, but he had a keen capacity for recognizing what was normal and abnormal in the moods and behaviors of air and sea. And he knew that waves without wind and a tide that rose when it should be in its ebb were incongruities that shouldn't be. Yet he barely thought of it now, for the Greenland nesting fiords called with an irresistible power and the sea flight could not be long postponed.

CHAPTER TWO

ALONG the western fringe of the Outer Hebrides an immense blanket of sand has been thrown up by the sea. Beyond the tides' reach it has been piled by gales into a strip of undulating dunes where the white sand is anchored by dense roots and spiky leaves of marram grass, forming a barrier against further invasions of the sea. Inland, behind the dune barrier, the sand has overflowed and mixed with underlying beds of peat to form a broad fertile plain that slopes up slowly to the hills beyond. This is the *machair,* rich in both lime and humus, where sweet grasses, vetch and clover grow in a lush green mat and the crofters tend their little fields of oats, rye and potatoes.

The goose had often fed on the *machair,* for the grazing there was good. But it meant leaving the sea, and he had a deep instinctive distrust of the land, even the *machair* land so close that it was almost a part of the sea. Now that he was deprived of the confidence that came from being associated with a flock, his distrust of the *machair* was more intense than ever. He tipped again over the eelgrass bed, searching with neck extended, but the green fronds were still far below. Tonight he would have to feed on the *machair.*

He took wing and flew back across the dunes and felt a vague uneasiness at being over land instead of sea. In the darkness he could recognize the cultivated fields below by their streaks of white unmixed sand which showed frequently in the brown soil turned up by the crofters' plows. He flew on to where darker *machair* indicated that he was over uncultivated pasture, then he dropped down and immediately commenced grazing. He cropped off grass and clover close to the ground, occasionally probing with his bill into the sandy soil for a root of the buttercup, a favorite food.

After an hour or two he flew back to a sheltered strip of beach in the island's lee to drink and to pick up the sand his gizzard needed for the digestive process. The sand, mixing with the food in his gizzard, would perform the chewing that mammals do with their teeth. His hunger was gone, but he flew back to the *machair* pasture to graze again. Now he fed leisurely, ignoring the grass and clover and selecting only the buttercup roots and their fleshy basal whorls of leaves.

A couple of hours before dawn he became fully satisfied and stopped feeding. Normally he would have waited until after sunrise before flying back out to sea, but tonight he was restless and uneasy, the ocean's strange behavior bewildered him, and he sought the only comfort he knew—the sea. He would rest offshore until dawn, then begin the long flight to the Arctic.

He was barely past the surf line on his flight seaward when a greater shearwater passed in front of him, its languid twisting flight pattern outlined dimly against the gray night sky. The goose knew it only as a bird of the distant reaches of ocean far from land, a bird like the albatrosses and petrels which were much more exclusively birds of the open sea than even the barnacle goose. The geese, though living much at sea, were rooted still to the land, and except during migration they rarely moved more than ten miles offshore from the tidal shallows where they fed each night. But the shearwaters shun the land as desperately as most land birds shun the sea.

The goose flew seaward for a quarter of an hour and during that time he saw two more shearwaters pass phantom-like across the night sky. Suddenly the strange landward wandering of the sea birds gave meaning to the other bewildering events of the night and now he understood the immense ground swell without wind, the cloud mass that moved swiftly across the sky at sunset and the puzzling high tide. Somewhere out at sea an area of violent storm was raging eastward toward European coastal waters and the sea birds were fleeing before it.

The goose arched his powerful wings and glided down. He dropped his broad webbed feet like an aircraft lowering its landing gear and pitched with a small white splash into the sea. The swells were larger now but they were still flat and glassy, for there was yet no stirring of wind.

It wasn't easy to sleep, for the loneliness pressed in on him as though it were a substance in the air itself. His mind seethed with conflict and indecision. The far north breeding territory lured him with a seductive charm, but the decision to begin the long sea flight came hard, for the sea and the air above it were heavy with the threat of impending crisis.

The black night changed slowly to a gray and pallid dawn. When the thin line of the Hebridean hills appeared dimly against the lightening eastern sky the barnacle goose flew. He climbed high until the islands, outlined sharply by their white surf, loomed into lumpy black mounds. Then he turned away from them northwestward where, across six hundred miles of vacant sea, there would be food again along the Iceland fiords and perhaps the nonbreeding flocks of barnacles would be waiting.

Ahead of him now was only a horizonless sea, for all around to north, west and south gray banks of mist made it impossible to tell where sea and sky met.

The Hebrides passed from view. The wall of mist ahead drew closer. A gust of air struck him and twisted him momentarily in flight, then it passed as quickly as it had come. It was the first stirring of air he had detected since the ocean's ground swell started the previous afternoon.

CHAPTER THREE

IN southern Canada the latter half of May is often a hybrid season, no longer spring, or summer either, but a little of both. As Rory Macdonald paused on the zoology building's weather-pitted stone steps and scanned the University of Toronto campus, it seemed that spring and summer were blended in a strange and contradictory scene.

It was summer for the big elms and maples, because their foliage was fully developed. It was summer too for the pair of crows that always nested in the elms at the north edge of the campus, for they were already busily feeding young that had hatched a week before. Yet elsewhere spring lingered. There were still pink splashes of blossom on the apple trees behind St. George Street, and many birds were still in spring migration. From the maple over his head Rory caught the buzzy song of a black-throated green warbler, a bird that would go much farther north before it stopped to nest. He had also seen bay-breasts and black-polls that morning.

Rory sat on the step to watch and listen. There was hardly a person in sight and the campus was strangely quiet. A Baltimore oriole, flashing its brilliant orange belly, plucked caterpillars from a maple branch over-head and between mouthfuls whistled its vibrant springtime song. Rory whistled back in a nearly perfect imitation. The oriole scolded with harsh alarm notes and dropped to the grass, its neck stretched out inquisitively as it looked for the other oriole that wasn't there.

Rory smiled. "Fooled you, didn't I?" The oriole scolded once more and flew back into the tree.

He let his long legs slide down across the stone steps and relaxed luxuriously. Another year was over—another big step toward the goal that had once seemed unattainable. Zoology 29, advanced animal physi-ology, hadn't been as tough an exam as he thought it was going to be and he was confident that he had earned a good mark.

He rose slowly and began walking down toward College Street to look for a newspaper and find out what Alice was doing. Maybe she would be dead by now and her violent career forgotten by the papers. It wouldn't be a new experience. There had been a time when girls were always com-ing into his life abruptly like this, and leaving the same way.

He was tall, narrow in the hips, and his long legs carried him at a fast though somewhat ungainly rolling gait. But he walked with a lithe effortlessness, because boyhood in the Hebrides where even bicycles were luxuries had given him plenty of footwork training. The Vikings, al-though it was a thousand years ago they settled the Hebrides, had left their mark on Rory Macdonald. His hair was fair and he kept it in a short, bristly crew-cut that needed only a minimum of grooming. His eyebrows were bushy and blond, so blond that already they were appearing almost white against the deepening tan of his face. But there the marks of his Nordic ancestry ended, and his eyes were gray, not the deep sea-blue of Viking tradition.

He was good-looking except for one detraction. His nose stood out like a polished door knob, intercepting the sun, and while the rest of his face always took on a smooth tan his nose was perpetually sunburned and peeling.

On the sidewalk ahead a girl with an armload of books had stopped and was waiting for him. She was medium-tall with a childlike chubbiness still in her face, but the figure she carried erect and rather flauntingly under her red sweater was far from that of a child. It was Susan . . . . hell, he had forgotten her last name. He met her in English 4 that winter and Susan, besides having a shape like something out of a bathing suit ad, seemed fairly intelligent and he liked her. But he had never dated her, because Rory Macdonald these days was keeping girls at a safe distance.

"Hello." She smiled as he drew near. "How was Zoology 29?"

"Not as bad as I thought it would be." He took her books, slackened his pace, and she began walking along beside him.

Recently they had seemed to meet frequently like this. The meetings couldn't all be accidental and it was all very fine for his ego, but Rory Macdonald's ego had long since ceased to need such assurances. He had discovered in his mid-teens almost ten years ago that he had more than one man's normal share of attraction for girls, and he accepted it now as casually as he accepted the fact that his nose was too big. There was a time, too, when he had made the most of it. He used to boast with a boyish immodesty, the memory of which now embarrassed him, that he hadn't met the girl from whom he couldn't get everything he wanted before the end of their second night if he felt like really turning the heat on. Actually he didn't prove it often, because he was sailing then and his ship was rarely in port long enough to provide that second night.

But that was another time and another Rory Macdonald. For four years now his determination to overcome the handicaps of an austere boyhood and make something worthwhile out of himself had dictated every phase of his life. It had given him two good reasons for leaving girls alone. First, paying his own way through the university left him with neither time nor money for girls. But the more important reason was that he didn't want to run the risk of any serious girl relationship developing until his career had reached a point that left him free to do something about it. Rory wasn't sure he was capable of seeing a girl regularly, perhaps loving her, and indefinitely postponing the rest of it. With a pub or dockside pick-up this used to be no problem—you took what you could get and forgot her next morning. But several of the girls like Susan whom he was meeting here at university were definitely marriageable material and you didn't go out sleeping with one of them every Saturday night. So Rory had decided at the beginning to leave them alone, for the good of his university career as well as his finances. This he had resolutely done, although it wasn't always easy, because the good looks that had served him admirably during the sailing years were now more handicap than asset.

"Going to play football next term?" Susan asked him. She could be a sensible kid when she wanted to and Rory knew that this was teasing.

"Not a chance," he answered.

"Good football material going to waste whistling at birds."

"It's more interesting than kicking a football all over the place."

"You've got birds on the brain. I suppose that makes you an egghead."

She gave him a taunting smile and moved close so that their arms touched as they walked.

She had walked close to him like this before and he wished she wouldn't. In a way he feared girls like Susan. They were a threat to the bigger, more important things that demanded all the concentration he was capable of for the time being.

At the car stop on College Street Rory returned her books and left her. He bought an afternoon paper at a sidewalk newsstand and scanned the front page quickly. Not a word about Alice. He turned a page and saw the heading he sought near the bottom of page three:

HURRICANE SPAWNS NEW GALES
OVER STORM-LASHED ATLANTIC

Rory leaned against the newsstand and began reading.

Washington, May 23 (AP).—The Weather Bureau reported this morning that Hurricane Alice, on the verge of dying out over the North Atlantic, has collided with a cold front pushing down from the Arctic, producing a new storm almost as vicious as the original hurricane.

Alice, the Bureau said, is technically dead but as a result of her dying struggle with the Arctic air there is now a new easterly gale lashing the Atlantic from the British Isles almost to Newfoundland. Winds of seventy-five miles per hour are being reported by ships. Several ships are having trouble and at least one, a Norwegian freighter with its rudder swept away, is in grave danger.

The Bureau reports that the storm is probably the most severe to hit the North Atlantic in ten years. Storm tides in advance of the storm itself reached record heights in the British Isles and flooded many coastal areas not previously flooded in years.

Hurricane Alice was unusually severe for so early in the season. May hurricanes, Weather Bureau officials pointed out, were almost always mild and short-lived; but Alice. . . .

Rory scanned two more paragraphs, then began reading a Toronto report added to the Washington story.

At one stage, when Hurricane Alice crossed the Carolina coast, it was feared it might hurtle northward as far as Canada. Four days ago there were warnings that Toronto lay in the hurricane's path. However, Alice was deflected when a high-pressure system moved into its path and the hurricane was turned back out to sea.

Rory was sorry in a way that Alice had not come closer to Toronto because compact, violent storms like hurricanes often pick up migrating

birds and carry them long distances before releasing them. Tropical birds
have been carried by hurricanes two thousand miles north of where they
should be, so bird-watching becomes exciting and unpredictable after
such storms. Rory had had high hopes for Hurricane Alice and had followed her violent career closely. But now it was over.

CHAPTER FOUR

RORY folded the newspaper with the hurricane story and tucked
it under his arm. There were still almost two hours before dinner and he
felt like walking the two miles home, so he started back through the
campus toward the zoology building. Maybe P.L. would feel like a walk
too; he would call in and see. P.L. had been attending a convention of
biologists in Chicago for four days and Rory was anxious to tell him of
his final plans.

He went back into the zoology building and turned down the stairway
toward the basement. The stairs creaked eerily and the dim concrete-
floored hallway at the bottom had a musty smell. Along the narrow corridor from far ahead came a faint chorus of bird chirpings. As Rory
walked down the corridor the bird chorus gradually strengthened, and
he began to smell the sharp fetid odor of bird excrement. The bird chirpings mounted to a crescendo where the corridor ended in a door bearing
a red-crayoned sign: "Keep Out, Especially Janitors." Rory knocked
twice, opened the door and stepped in.

It was a big room with three of its walls piled high with tiers of wire
cages containing small birds. In addition to the cages it was cluttered
with filing cabinets, stacks of books, a dirt-smeared wash basin, a table
bearing two microscopes, sacks of baby-chick feed and, in the middle
of the room, an ancient desk buried deeply under a chaos of papers and
scientific journals. The room smelled strongly of ether and bird dung. On
one wall near the ceiling were three narrow windows but they were
covered with thick black paper and the room was illuminated entirely
by electric lights.

Behind the desk, his face barely showing above the stacked papers, sat
a man with tanned leathery cheeks and a small brown bald spot on the
top of his head. The hair that formed a shaggy ring around the bald spot

was something midway between black and gray. His shirt was white and freshly laundered but it was open halfway down his hairy chest. He hunched over the desk without moving, apparently having failed to hear Rory enter because of the chorus of bird noise around him.

Rory stepped closer. The man was bent over a small laboratory scale weighing a sparrow that lay motionless on its back in the instrument's brass pan. A tame robin hopped across the desk and up onto his forearm.

"Turdy, you get the hell out of here." He pushed the robin gently away.

"P.L.," Rory spoke.

The man looked up.

"Hello, Rory. How was 29?"

"Not too bad. Do you feel like walking home?"

"Yes. I'll be ready in ten minutes."

P.L. hastily scribbled a figure on a sheet of paper, then took the seemingly dead bird from the pan of the scale and rose to his feet. He was short, but full-chested, and despite his small stature there was an air of vigorous masculinity about him. He walked across the room and laid the bird carefully on the floor of one of the cages; a couple of seconds later it revived, chirped vigorously and flew to a perch in the cage. P.L. caught another sparrow, dipped a wad of cotton into a small bottle of ether and moved it gently across the bird's bill. The bird ceased struggling and he took it to the scale.

"I want to finish checking the weight of these sparrows. I'm starting something new." P.L. talked rapidly and there was an eager, childlike enthusiasm in his voice. "The effect of differing photo-periods . . . . first, on metabolized energy, second, on gonad development and the sexual cycle. I'm going to keep one group of sparrows under a constant ten-hour photo-period, simulating winter day-length conditions. Another group will live in perpetual summer . . . . fifteen-hour photo-period. Day length . . . . it's all tied up, we're not sure how, with the pituitary and the breeding cycle and the stimulus for migration. Turdy, damn it, get away from these scales! She's getting to be a smart little bitch. She can count to four now. I'm finishing my paper on her and when it's published she'll show those stupid bastards who insist birds are governed entirely by instinct and possess no learning capacity."

P.L. was wiping a white blot of excrement from the paper on which he was recording the sparrow weights.

"You're well named, Turdy," he said. P.L. looked up at Rory then, and several big semicircular wrinkles framed his mouth in a smile. "I really named her that because of her generic name, *Turdus*. But there are other reasons just as good. She's smart, but damned if I can get her to recognize one spot as her bathroom."

P.L.'s head again dropped almost out of sight behind the clutter on his desk. "Twenty-four point one . . . . no, two, grams," he read from the scale. "You're a *little* devil, aren't you? Underweight. You've been chasing the boy sparrows too hard."

Rory sat on a chair by the door to wait. He studied the small suntanned bald spot that barely showed above the desk's papers and periodicals, and he thought, as he had thought many times before, that P.L. was a strange character to have a senior position on the faculty of a large university. In a wrinkled heap on a table near the door lay P.L.'s sport jacket, a vivid creation of brown and green plaid that not one of his students would be seen wearing except to a Hallowe'en masquerade.

Dr. Peter Lawrence Thomas, professor of ornithology, was a bachelor with two passions—loud sport jackets and ornithological research. Every summer he spent somewhere in the bush of northern Ontario with a tent and a canoe, living like an Indian and doing bird population and distributional surveys. Each fall he returned to lecture at the university and carry on laboratory studies in bird physiology and behavior.

It was P.L. who had induced Rory to come to the University of Toronto and they had lived four years in the same North Toronto boarding house. Despite the fact that P.L.'s mind was usually far adrift in a fog of scientific erudition, he was a man in whom Rory placed a great deal of confidence and respect.

P.L. rose from the desk again and returned the anesthetized sparrow to its cage. He had needed a haircut for two weeks and Rory noted that he still needed it. Most of all, Rory thought, P.L. needed a wife to drag him down occasionally out of his scientific clouds. He wondered if the professor had ever had anything to do with a woman. Rory doubted it. Probably P.L. regarded love as a strictly biological condition capable of being measured as he measured sexual development in his sparrows by graphs showing gonad volumes or by the number of spermatozoa per milligram of testes.

As a budding biologist, Rory had ideas on the subject that were not much different, though he suspected he had already had more experience in the matter than P.L. had ever had. During the sailing years, picking up a girl whenever he had a night in port had never been much of a problem. There was usually some little wench eyeing him with a comehither look from a street corner or park bench. But any emotions these one-night affairs produced in Rory were of a superficial easily forgotten variety; in the jargon of the scientist he had now become, it was all just physical response to external stimuli. And he had come to feel that all relationships between men and women were cut from the same thin and meager cloth. Love, he suspected, was largely a creation of the poets.

But still, there came a time in every man's life when his full development as a social being and often his career needed a wife to complete them. P.L.'s time was long past and now he was a lonely, frustrated, aging man living half a life because he had chosen to live it alone. And Rory's time was approaching. He would have his M.A. next year and he hadn't decided yet whether he would go on working for a Ph.D. Whatever he decided, he would be ready in a year or two to settle down in a comfortable zoology professorship somewhere and from there on a wife, the right wife, would be an asset and perhaps a necessity for the climb ahead. The poets could have their love, Rory's needs were more substantial. His wife, and there were several good prospects around, would have to be someone who could fit gracefully and easily into the university-centered social group of professors and scientists that he would have to join. And she would have to be someone who could offset some of the rough edges that Rory still retained from his own crude background.

P.L. was talking again. "I'm using a new adiabatic oxygen bomb calorimeter," he said. "All I have to do is keep a record of the caloric value of food consumed by each bird, run tests on the feces to determine calory loss in the excrement, and the difference is metabolized energy. I'll have Turdy count for you before we go. . . ."

P.L. laid twenty identical pop-bottle caps in a row along the floor, then under every fourth bottle cap he placed a raisin.

"Turdy, come here."

The pet robin flew to P.L.'s side, saw the bottle caps, then hopped along the row quickly, unerringly picking up every fourth cap and snapping up the raisin beneath. The bird ignored all the other bottle caps.

"Turdy, you're a genius!" P.L. exclaimed, stroking the bird's head gently with a finger. "The behavior literature records many birds that have learned to count to three, but she's the first one I know who can count to four."

P.L. was beaming like a father whose son had just headed his class at school. And all, Rory thought, for a pet robin. You *do* need a wife.

P.L. returned Turdy to her cage for the night. He threw the brown and green sport jacket over his arm and they stepped out into the hall. As the professor locked the door he saw its red-crayoned sign. "I'm having janitor troubles again. They've complained to the building superintendent that my birds are lousy and stink up the building. Of course they're lousy. It's their natural state. And for behavior studies I want to keep their lives as natural as possible. Janitors are stupid bastards. I'm my own janitor from now on."

P.L. was lighting his huge curved-stem pipe as they stepped from the gloom of the basement into brilliant outdoor sunlight. They walked across the campus, Rory towering high above his older companion.

"All ready to go north?" P.L. asked.

"I'm going tonight. I took my luggage down to the station before the exam."

"Just going to work on Canadas?"

"Yes, just Canada geese. They want me to cover as much of the west coast of James Bay as I can, checking breeding population and its distribution. But the main job is to start a leg-banding program later in the summer when the geese molt and can't fly and can be trapped. That's what the brass in the wildlife service is most interested in. There are two distinct populations breeding there—one that winters in the Mississippi valley, another from the south Atlantic coast. Nobody knows where the breeding ranges merge and they have to know to control the fall hunting properly. Banding will help sort things out. I'm stopping off for a night at Blackwood to talk to the superintendent of game and fisheries for northern Ontario. He'll tell me where to go, and where I can stay when I reach James Bay."

"That all?"

"Maybe. But if there's time I'm to interview all the Indians I can and look into the effect of the spring goose kill by the Crees. And I'll sex everything I trap and work out a sex ratio. They're finding a sexual differential in the hunting kill. The population may be only forty percent female. And that may mean nesting interference by bachelor males."

P.L. puffed vigorously on his pipe, alternately wrinkling and relaxing the tight brown skin of his forehead so that his hairline bobbed up and down like an excited chipmunk.

"Sounds good," he said. "You might get a Ph.D. thesis out of it."

"Maybe. I like geese. I used to spend hours watching the barnacles back home off Barra. Where are you going to be this summer?"

"With all my janitor troubles I may have to stay in Toronto, unless I can find a student who'll look after my birds. But if I can get away, I might join you for a week or two."

Rory looked at him sharply, surprised. There were certainly worse companions.

P.L. continued: "I've never done any bird work in the muskeg of the Paleozoic plain there. I think I'd like to."

"Fine," Rory said. "Try to make it."

They walked along for a minute without speaking, the rush-hour traffic of Queen's Park Crescent streaming noisily past them. Then P.L. spoke again.

"That hurricane, Alice," he said, "she fizzled out, eh?"

"Not exactly," Rory replied. "She's produced a new storm that's raising hell right now in the North Atlantic."

"Well anyway, she won't be bringing any new birds our way."

Rory handed him the newspaper. "There's a hurricane story on page three," he said. And they walked along more slowly now as P.L. opened the paper and began to read.

They were passing large middle-class homes that stood well back from the street behind meticulously groomed lawns and shrubbery. There had been times when Rory feared he could never become a real part of this environment, that his ambitions and dreams were hopelessly far-fetched. At those times Rory had recognized that his drive to succeed was more than just that alone; it was also a reaching out for security, for a sense of identity and belonging. But he hadn't had those fears for a long time now. His B.A. was behind him, an M.A. and perhaps a Ph.D. were within reach ahead. And now he was sure that he, Rory Macdonald, an immigrant boy who hadn't even owned a necktie until he was seventeen, would some day own a home like one of these they now were passing.

But there *was* a tremendous contrast between all this and the tiny dirt-floored hut in Barra where his ambition, his determination to succeed at any price, had had its source.

PART TWO

Barra

CHAPTER FIVE

O NE-CHILD families were rare on the predominantly Roman Catholic island of Barra and Rory Macdonald was in his fifth year when he realized suddenly that as an only child he was a peculiarity. It was a gray misty day in spring, the primroses rolled in a yellow mat across the Barra hills, and Rory was playing along the rocky edge of the sea with three MacNeill children from the neighboring croft. He was the youngest and as they scrambled over the slippery rocks he was constantly dropping behind.

Peggy MacNeill, two years older, grew tired of moving back to help him, and finally she exclaimed: "Rory Macdonald, I'm no' goin' to help ye no more. Wee ones that dinna have their own brothers and sisters have got tae look after their ownselves."

The realization hit him suddenly then that all his playmates were from large families, whereas he was an only child. It was a perplexing discovery. He pondered it for several minutes, then left the other children to seek out his mother. He walked back hurriedly to the tiny blackhouse of rock and thatch and he could hear the loom clacking rhythmically in his mother's room as he reached the outside door.

"Mother. Why don't I have brothers and sisters, too?"

The loom stopped abruptly. Rory ran through the curtained door into her room. Mary Macdonald's small, plump body was hunched across the big bolt of Harris tweed she was weaving, her face was white and had a hard, taut cast that Rory had never noticed before.

"Some day ye'll know," she told him, "but I canna tell ye now."

Her feet began working the pedals again, the shuttle sprang to life, but the whiteness clung to her face and Rory sensed that somehow he had asked a question that should not have been asked.

The strange absence of brothers and sisters puzzled him more and more as he grew older. But one by one the clues in this childhood mystery fell slowly into place in his maturing mind.

The first clue came about a year later. Six years old by now, Rory remembered it well. His mother, an English teacher in a Glasgow girls' college before her marriage, said suddenly one evening over supper that their crofting community must have a lending library. For several days Rory followed his mother up and down the sandy trail beside the sea as she went from croft to croft explaining the procedure by which they could obtain books on loan from Glasgow and have a community library at little cost.

"There will be a meeting in the church hall next Thursday week to do the arranging. Everyone come."

It was autumn but the meeting night was clear and warm. His father stayed home but Rory was taken along to the church hall by his mother. They didn't talk as they walked rapidly along, but she held his hand and he could feel the tremors in her fingers and he knew she was excited; he was excited too. They arrived early, lit the lamps along the walls, arranged the benches in rows and sat down to wait. Half an hour later the Presbyterian parson came. He sat on a bench for fifteen minutes reading from a small St. John Gospel, then rose stiffly and turned to Rory's mother.

"My wife is ill," he said, "and I promised I'd no' be long. Please excuse me." And he left the hall.

No one else came. Mary Macdonald's face hardened into a grim pallid mask. They waited an hour and a half, then she circled the hall silently blowing out the lamps. "Come, Rory," she said when the hall was darkened, and they started for home.

Above the creaking of the crickets and the endless booming of the Atlantic's surf Rory could hear his mother sobbing softly. She took his hand again, and now her own hand was firm, the tremors gone. The sobbing ceased suddenly and she began talking in a voice that was hoarse and muted.

"They're a tragic people, Rory, but most of all I pity the children, twentieth-century children born into this isolated little island world of nineteenth-century superstition, ignorance and poverty. It shouldna be, it needna be, but now I know that nothing can change it."

She sobbed again quietly, then resumed. "I wish that Barra could follow Atlantis, I wish it could drop out of sight into the sea . . . . and tak me with it."

Perhaps it was then the seed was planted. Perhaps even then Rory knew that some day he would go away and be an important man in one of the cities across the sea.

His father was in bed but still awake when they arrived home. "Anybody at yeer meetin'?" he asked.

"No," Mary Macdonald answered.

"I feart it," he said. "They a' know readin' books can be the ruinin' o' yeer eyes. 'Tis better that the parson do the readin' for a'."

As boyhood passed, Rory began to see that the absence of brothers and sisters was an expression of his mother's rebellion against an unhappy marriage and against an adopted homeland she had come to hate. He was eleven when the full explanation finally came.

His mother had just come home after helping Mrs. MacNeill through her annual confinement. As usual, there had been no doctor in attendance, and Mary Macdonald was very tired. She dropped onto her bed, sighed momentarily, then said to Rory: "A boy, the twelfth MacNeill, another life for Barra to blight and stultify. Ye're alone, Rory, because I decided long ago that one child would be a' that I could shield against an environment like this."

As long as Rory remembered, his mother had always had her own bed. Furnishings were few and simple in the ancient little Macdonald blackhouse and his father slept on the hut's only real bed and mattress. His mother's bed was a crude framework of poles with ropes stretched between them to take the place of springs. He had wondered occasionally about the beds and why they should contrast so strikingly with each other, and now, a precocious eleven-year-old, he realized that this matter of the beds was linked with the decision about childbearing that his mother had just revealed to him.

He was also beginning to recognize that his parents were as different as the beds they slept on, as different as two people could possibly be.

Rory's father, Sammy Macdonald, was born in that same blackhouse sometime around the turn of the century. He never knew the exact year of his birth because all figures belonged to a world with which Sammy Macdonald had little acquaintance. He attended school haphazardly for two or three years, but when the first world war started Sammy was a hulking blond giant somewhere in his middle teens and he went to sea. His first job was in the stokehole of the little mailboat that stopped regularly at Castlebay, Barra's main port and town. A few months later it went to Glasgow for engine overhaul, and Sammy Macdonald's gray eyes stared in wonder at the bustling outside world he barely knew existed before. He liked the looks of it, skipped his ship and found a new berth on a tanker sailing next day with a New York-bound convoy.

That was the beginning of fourteen years of sailing for Big Sammy Macdonald, but he remembered little of where he had been. He saw a map rarely and when he did encounter one he found that reading it was

a slow and laborious job. His mental picture of the world's geography
was sketchy, and most of the seaports he visited quickly became just
names—detached, meaningless and hopelessly mixed up in a brain that
would never get around to sorting them out. He found it easier to remember seaports by the variety of liquor they had to offer, or by the cost and
availability of their prostitutes.

In December, 1928, Sammy was firing on an ancient tramp, the
Swansea, Glasgow-bound across the North Atlantic with a cargo of Canadian wheat. They reached Glasgow the last day of the year. After a drab
and stormy Christmas at sea, the crew of the *Swansea* was primed for a
hell-raising New Year's Eve ashore.

The *Swansea* had not been in port two hours when a pair of portly
matrons struggled up the ladder and came aboard. One of them bustled
aft to the galley where Big Sammy and several others were drinking tea.
She said her piece quickly, as though she had it memorized.

"Hello, gentlemen. We are holding a New Year's Eve entertainment
and dance at the YMCA tonight, eight o'clock. It is for all sailors who
find themselves away from home at this holiday time. There is no charge,
of course. You will be our guests. Will you kindly spread the word among
your crewmates and honor us with your attendance?"

She smiled, obviously embarrassed and uncomfortable, then quickly
went back out the door.

"You know who's doing this?" one of Sammy's shipmates asked. "It's
the police and the storekeepers. They don't want us to celebrate. They
want to get us all in one spot so we can't go round bustin' their store
windows or bustin' their daughters' maidenheads."

"It's the windows they're really scared of," the cook said. "A window
busts and you gotta put in a new one."

It was all too abstract for Big Sammy. All he knew was that he had
been invited to something, and it made him proud. That afternoon he got
a haircut and bought a new shirt. He came back to the ship and waited
excitedly for the night to come.

And that was the night Big Sammy Macdonald met Mary Campbell,
the girl who became his wife.

In one of northern Glasgow's staunch old houses of gray stone, Mary
Campbell that afternoon was waiting nervously and alone for the night
to come, too, and she dreaded its coming. The dress she had selected to
wear to the sailors' dance was the plainest and drabbest she had, a formless thing of navy blue serge that fitted her mood admirably but was a
poor and unbecoming fit for her rotund body. She put it on and looked

at herself in her bedroom mirror. She was short, round-faced, and already plumply stout at age twenty-five. Several years before, she had accepted with calm acquiescence the fact that she was homely and unattractive and could never be anything else. But now she could detect darkening hollows under her blue eyes and she knew the trials and grief of the past two months had left a haggardness on her face that made her more un-attractive than ever.

She started down the stairs. It was a modest middle-class house, modern for its time, with electric lights and a stone fireplace in each principal room. Mary turned into the small room at the foot of the stairs. Originally it had been her mother's sewing room but when her mother died five years ago Mary and her father had turned it into a library. The far wall had numerous shelves of books and placed conspicuously among them was a neatly framed diploma proclaiming that Mary Nancy Campbell had fulfilled the requirements and was hereby granted a Bachelor of Arts de-gree by the University of Glasgow. It was dated 1921; Mary was eighteen then, one of the youngest graduates of the university's history. She walked across to it immediately, took it from the wall and put it in a drawer of a desk that stood in the center of the room. She had intended taking it down for several weeks. Her father had insisted proudly that the di-ploma hang there, but now that he was gone she no longer wanted it so ostentatiously displayed.

She took down a volume of Swinburne poems, sat in the deep chair by the window and tried to read. But the old home's somber silence made her very lonely; thoughts of the evening she must soon face filled her with disgust, and as tears blurred her eyes she closed the book with a little snap and let her chin drop to her chest. Outside in the hall the big grand-father's clock ticked its persistent rhythm and it seemed to Mary that the eloquent ticking was all that remained from an earlier and much happier life.

She was the only daughter of an insurance agent who over the years had built up a profitable marine business, for the procession of new vessels sliding from the ways of the Clydebank shipyards were an insurance bonanza for Glasgow agents. So Mary had had a good education and after her graduation she went back to the university to lecture in English literature.

She was best known in Glasgow, however, as the city's most talented woman violinist, constantly in demand for concerts and social affairs.

She knew she was far from good-looking, and with the same cold matter-of-fact self-appraisal she also knew that she possessed an intellect above the average. She had accepted these personal debits and credits with

neither pride nor regret, until this autumn of 1928 when two cruel blows
came in rapid succession and Mary Campbell was painfully forced to
the conclusion that brains and talent in a young woman were a poor
substitute for beauty.

Her father had died suddenly of a heart attack in mid-October. On the
surface Mary remained composed, but underneath she was numb with
grief, more so than at her mother's death five years before, because in the
interval she and her father had drawn much closer together. She had no
close relatives, but she was not alone. Her strength and the external guise
of composure she managed to maintain had their source in her love for
John Watt.

John stayed close to her during the desolate hours of the funeral and
the evening after. A slight, pallid man, he was for Mary during that
desperate time a bulwark of tremendous strength.

"Come," he told her after the funeral gathering dispersed, "we must
walk."

She followed him meekly, and they walked the narrow streets for a
long time, clinging closely together. It was dusk when she realized they
were walking in The Green, Glasgow's biggest park, where they had
walked so frequently before. They went down to the edge of the Clyde
and sat on a familiar bench. John began reciting in a soft voice.

> As fair art thou, my bonnie lass,
> So deep in luve am I,
> And I will luve thee still, my dear,
> Till a' the seas gang dry.

"That's an easy one," she murmured. "Burns. The second stanza of
Red, Red Rose. It was one of his last poems."

It was a game they often played. John was assistant professor of Greek
and Roman history in the university's classics department, and, like Mary,
a lover of poetry. They had known each other for two years, had been
courting for one year, and Mary was sure that she loved him.

John Watt was more skilled at recalling poetry to express his thoughts
than he was in expressing thoughts in his own words, but now he held
Mary tightly against his side and began to speak in a voice husky with
nervousness.

"Don't think ye are alone," he said. "I love ye, Mary. *Till a' the seas
gang dry, my dear, and the rocks melt wi' the sun.* No ye are not alone,
my darling, ye have me. Ye have me . . . . forever, if ye wish it."

Mary knew that behind his nervousness and rhetoric, John Watt was
proposing. She lay her head on his shoulder, thinking incongruously for a

moment that there were few men short enough to permit her to do this.

"I love ye too, John," she whispered.

That night, back in the old and empty house, Mary Campbell cried herself to sleep with tears that sprang from a curious blending of grief and happiness.

Mary spent two or three evenings a week with John Watt, visiting the art gallery, attending music recitals or just walking. She missed her father greatly, yet she was supremely happy in her new relationship with John.

But John Watt didn't speak of marriage again. Mary, in her happiness, hardly noticed. It was enough for her that the understanding between them now existed; they would marry soon, she took that for granted, and for the present so soon after her father's death she didn't want to rush it.

A month after her father's death John Watt told her he was getting behind in the preparation of lectures and would have to see her less frequently. He called on her only twice in two weeks, and then, late in November, Mary received this letter:

> Dear Mary:
>
> It may be unforgivable, but I hope you will forgive the cold impersonality of this letter. The message I must give is so difficult I cannot possibly muster the courage to tell you personally. It is clear to me now that I have made an error is assessing my own emotions and that in fairness to both of us our association should terminate, for I cannot now see it continuing permanently. I hope and pray you will accept this as I have had to accept it, an intrusion of fate over which our own wishes and feelings can have no control. And I hope that during our professional contacts in the future we shall remain good friends.
>
> Yours,
> John Watt

Mary slumped into the cold leather chair in the library, clutching the letter with trembling fingers. Blinded by her own love, she had failed to detect any change in John Watt, and the letter's message was so unexpected that she insisted to herself for a long time that it must have a different meaning, that what it seemed to say could not be true. She reached out and pulled the window blind until the room was darkened, then slowly the agony of truth forced itself upon her. John Watt, the person who had given her life a meaning and a goal, was now leaving her life as abruptly as an actor walking off stage.

Why or how it happened, she did not know. Looking back she could recognize some signs suggesting that John's interest in her had been cool-

ing. The proposal on the night of her father's funeral was easily explained
—John Watt, kind and sentimental, had merely mistaken sympathy for
love. But they could have drifted apart gradually and it would have been
so much easier for both. Why did he decide to do it so abruptly, with
such dramatic emphasis? Mary didn't know. All she knew was that she
still loved him, and now her life was one of wretched emptiness.

The days dragged painfully on and Mary soon learned the rest of the
story. Three days before Christmas she read in a university news bulletin
that John Watt had married a girl from the university's business office.
Mary knew the girl slightly as a luridly rouged and powdered flapper who
looked as artificial and fragile as a doll and had about the same intelligence. But she had a winsome beauty that the distorting excess of cos-
metics could not destroy, and Mary had to face the fact that a pretty
face had accomplished—in a few weeks, apparently—what Mary had failed
to do in two years.

Suddenly she saw it all in glaring clarity. She was a jilted woman—
jilted, it was obvious now, because of her homeliness. "Ye're ugly!" It
seemed that another voice outside of her was sneering into her ear. For
the first time in her life Mary Campbell began to feel a crushing inferiority
complex over the lack of physical attractiveness she had always accepted
so philosophically before.

She had three invitations to go out for Christmas, one of them from
the woman pianist who had played accompaniment for her at violin recitals for several years. Mary turned them all down because the thought of
facing friends so soon after John Watt's sudden marriage embarrassed
her. Christmas was a gray windy day, and the Campbell house was dark
and cold. Mary roamed aimlessly through the gloomy rooms, wondering
what John Watt was doing. She hoped he was happy.

Early Christmas afternoon she resorted to the one comfort she had left
—her violin. It was a good and expensive instrument that her father had
bought for her two years ago, an Italian handmade violin with a rich
tone that had charmed Mary since the first time she heard it. After a
couple of exploratory scales she began one of Paganini's difficult but lively
Caprices, then after a few minutes she moved spontaneously into the
beautiful opening theme of Mendelssohn's E minor violin concerto. Mary
Campbell turned to the bright and airy themes of this Mendelssohn concerto in times of depression and stress as an alcoholic turns to alcohol.
She loved this moving and spectacular masterpiece of Mendelssohn's
genius and she sped through its difficult trills and arpeggios with unfalter-
ing skill.

When finally she stopped, she had been playing about three-quarters of an hour, but she felt no fatigue. The sorrow and loneliness were still with her, but somehow they seemed less acute, farther away. And she knew that Mendelssohn had worked his magic spell again.

The day after Christmas two ladies from the committee arranging the New Year's Eve sailors' dance called on Mary and asked her to attend. They wanted her to play some violin selections, then remain for the dance afterward. Mary knew she would be in no mood to go out and put on a false front of gaiety for a troop of boorish men she had never met and would never meet again. The ladies pleaded. It was essential, they said, to provide some lassies as dancing partners to lure the sailors off the street. Since it all seemed in some remote way to be a patriotic duty, she agreed reluctantly to attend.

She telephoned her accompanist and asked if she could go. The accompanist could. Mary said it would have to be a very light and popular program—she would play a medley of sea shanties, some ragtime and perhaps one of the new popular tunes.

So Mary Campbell, bitter, depressed, drained of self-confidence and looking very dumpy in her blue serge dress was on hand that night in the YMCA gymnasium when the pipes began to play.

CHAPTER SIX

GLASGOW'S YMCA gymnasium was full of men wearing big boots, unpressed trousers and open-necked shirts; they had big thick-knuckled hands and hoarse voices. Mary sat alone on a chair near the piano, nervous and uncomfortable. She had never had contact with men like these before and she decided at once that she didn't like them.

There were some bagpipe selections, two reels and then Mary was called upon. She stepped up slowly to the piano where she had left her violin, and her accompanist moved up beside her. The room hummed with coarse whispers, laughter and scuffing feet. They were rabble! She hated them. She hated herself for having agreed to come.

The accompanist had opened her briefcase and she was taking out music and arranging it on the piano. There was the medley of sea shanties and *Happy Days Are Here Again*. Then Mary saw the score of the

Mendelssohn concerto; they had played it at their last recital and the music was still there in her accompanist's briefcase.

Mary Campbell's small shoulders stiffened. She turned to the crowd and hesitated nervously. Then in a voice surprisingly loud for her small body she announced: "I shall play Mendelssohn's Concerto in E minor, Opus sixty-four." She hesitated again briefly, then added in the same strong voice: "I shall play it in full, all three movements."

The accompanist turned sharply and stared at Mary, then she recovered quickly, reopened her briefcase and took out the concerto score. Around the big room a restless montage of blank and mystified faces turned toward Mary. She knew that most of them would not have listened to a piece of classical music in their lives before. She knew that even this, the most romantic and beautiful of all violin concertos, would bore them. The three movements would take about half an hour and by the end they would be hating her as much as she hated them, and she didn't care. She *had* to play Mendelssohn tonight. She was playing it strictly for herself.

They listened politely as she began the rich and flowing melody—the concerto's principal theme with which its first movement abruptly begins. Her fingers shifted deftly on the fingerboard, the movement at times becoming too swift to follow by eye as she sped accurately and brilliantly through the difficult double-stops and runs. And she thought bitterly that in this crowded room probably only she herself and her accompanist realized that what she was doing was one of music's supreme tests of technical proficiency on the violin.

By the time she reached the slow and melting second movement, Mary Campbell was completely lost, immersed, in Mendelssohn's lyric melodies. She was living, in those moments, only for the music that flowed from under her bow. She forgot that the audience was there.

She was into the vigorous, accelerating tempo of the third movement's rondo before she realized it. It reminded her of another violin concerto, one of the great Paganini's. His concerto, Paganini explained, depicted a jail scene in which a prisoner is appealing to heaven for release. And then suddenly she saw it. *She* was the prisoner, in a prison of her own making. Her mind came back to the Mendelssohn concerto she was playing. She knew she had never played it better. All the finer shadings of tone color were flowing perfectly and effortlessly from beneath her bow.

Then a boot scuffed and she was reminded rudely of the audience to which she was supposed to be playing. Now she saw them all again, the red coarse faces and the soiled clothing. And what she saw startled her. Every eye was staring, wide and spellbound; every face was an unmistakable mask of awe and fascination.

When she stopped playing there were several seconds of stifled silence, then the room exploded with a din of cheering and applause that lasted a minute. Finally it stopped and Mary sat down. She was happier than she had been any time since John Watt's letter reached her. She was glad she had come.

But her moment of glory was short-lived. The dancing resumed and Mary, as always, became the party's wallflower.

But there were two wallflowers at the Glasgow dance that New Year's Eve and since they were girl and boy they were inevitably drawn together.

Sammy Macdonald had attempted a waltz, failed clumsily and sat alone and self-consciously on one of the wall benches. He eyed the short, pudgy-cheeked girl who had played the violin and was sitting out most of the dances on the other side of the hall. He waited, nervous and uncertain, for several dances, then walked across and sat beside her.

"I liked yeer fiddlin'," he said.

"Thank you," Mary replied.

Words didn't come easily for Sammy Macdonald, but Mary Campbell quickly found herself carrying the brunt of the conversation. Big Sammy, barrel-chested, ruddy-faced, with thick fair hair and a broad mustache, was a striking contrast to the prim John Watt, the only man Mary had ever come to know well. Mary rapidly categorized Big Sammy as a dolt, yet not a bore because he knew how to listen attentively. But if dolt he was, he was at least a good-looking one, and Mary found herself attracted to his rough and crude masculinity.

Big Sammy accompanied Mary Campbell home that night on the tramcar, dutifully carrying the violin for her. At her door, both of them paused, embarrassed.

"A'd like verra mooch tae see ye again," he said, falling from nervousness into his broadest Scotch.

"I should enjoy seeing ye again, Mr. Macdonald," Mary said quickly. "Would ye like to call tomorrow evening?"

They parted without even touching hands. Mary went to sleep that night bewildered and a little alarmed at what she had done; in fact, she wasn't sure what she was doing. She knew only that loneliness for her father, a painful yearning for John Watt and the melodies of Mendelssohn had somehow combined in her sensitive mind with strange emotional effect. Sammy Macdonald had nothing to do with it. He was merely the man whom fate made available at that moment of crisis in Mary Campbell's life.

There wasn't an outbound cargo immediately and the *Swansea* was in port three weeks. During this time Mary saw Big Sammy almost nightly. She neither liked nor disliked him; the emotion he produced in her was more maternal than anything else. They spent hours walking together, talking only occasionally because there was little they could say to each other. But Mary remembered the lonely and harrowing nights she had spent after John Watt's letter had shattered her life, and these nights with Sammy Macdonald were pleasant and refreshing in comparison. When the *Swansea*'s sailing time came close, a panic gripped her. Sammy sensed that something more than silent walking was expected of him. One night near the end, after more than an hour during which neither of them had said a word, Sammy blurted suddenly: "Would ye like tae be marryin' me, Miss Campbell? There isna mooch time left. A'm thinkin' the ship will soon be leavin'."

She had wanted it from the beginning. The day before the *Swansea* sailed, Mary and Sammy were married in a simple presbytery wedding. At the end of the ceremony, Sammy, towering high above his bride, bent down hesitantly and awkwardly. They kissed for the first time.

Next day Mary stood on a grimy wharf and waved as the *Swansea* disappeared down the Clyde into the January fog. She felt no sorrow as her husband of twenty-four hours sailed away for what would at least be months, and perhaps years. She turned, walked slowly back along the pier, and suddenly she was shocked at what she had done. John Watt had won a beautiful bride in a few weeks and now Mary could say she had done as well. With a rush of returning sanity that was as chilling as the Clyde's twisting wraiths of winter fog, Mary knew she had had no other motive in marrying Big Sammy Macdonald.

Yet despite this, she now felt at peace with herself. She could accept again with stoic indifference the fact that she was a homely unattractive woman. But, cursed with a mind too adept at self-appraisal, she recognized too that fundamentally she had made herself a prostitute. She had sold herself to save face and restore her own peace of mind.

Perhaps, too, she thought, there was something else. Both she and John had married physically attractive mates, yet she was sure that both of them would find little happiness in the marriages they had made. Somehow, she liked it this way; somehow, it brought her and John Watt closer together again.

Anyway, it was done, and if it had to be, it was best this way. She had a husband she didn't love, but he would be home at most for only a couple of weeks each year. She would continue teaching; her life would hardly change.

But history did not play the game that Mary asked of it.

In November, 1929, nine months after their marriage, the Great Depression began and a generation went broke. In the seaports of the world, ships began to lay up, rusting and idle, because there were no cargoes to be carried. The *Swansea* was old and costly to run and one of the first to be taken out of service. It tied up in Liverpool in mid-December and its crew was laid off.

Big Sammy Macdonald came back to Glasgow for the first time since his marriage, suddenly homesick now for the Hebrides he hadn't seen in fourteen years. Both his parents had died since he went to sea, but he still owned the now-abandoned Macdonald croft on Barra, and Sammy was obsessed with one idea. He wanted to farm again the rocky impoverished soil that his parents and grandparents had farmed before him.

Mary Macdonald had never thought of such a crisis developing. She argued, pleaded and looked for jobs that would keep her husband in Glasgow. She was well connected and though jobs were scarce Mary found several, but as fast as she found them Sammy lost them. In quick succession he worked as a school janitor, window cleaner, stable boy and water boy at a shipyard. He lasted about a week at each. Finally he insisted on returning to Barra.

Mary Macdonald had a devout respect for the marriage vows she had made but no respect now for the husband with whom she had made them. But her Presbyterian upbringing left her no choice. She knew that she would have to go with Sammy.

Mary hoped to return eventually to Glasgow, but she decided that renting the Glasgow house while living in the Hebrides would be too difficult, so it and the furniture were sold. The clothing, personal possessions, books and music that she would take with her filled two small trunks. They had argued over the books.

"Ye've read them a' surely?" Sammy asked.

Mary nodded.

"Well, be ye readin' them again sometime?"

"Of course."

"They'll be costin' a lot for the shipping," he said.

"And I'll be paying it," she answered.

On a damp gray morning early in May, 1930, Mary Macdonald stepped out onto the deck of the little Hebrides mailboat and got her first glimpse of Barra's bleak bare undulating shoreline. Half an hour later the boat swung into the narrow neck of Castlebay harbor, slid against the weathered dock, and Mary and Sammy Macdonald stepped ashore. After four-

teen years Sammy still knew most of the islanders who crowded the little
wharf, and the greetings were loud and gay. He was home again and glad
to be there; Mary was bewildered and afraid.

The Macdonald croft was six miles away on Barra's Atlantic side and
there was no way of getting there except afoot. They set out, Sammy
carrying all the personal effects he owned in a dirty canvas duffel bag over
his shoulder, Mary carrying a light valise and her violin. The trunks
would come later by horse and cart. They walked in silence, and Sammy,
walking faster, moved ahead. As she followed, Mary curiously appraised
her new homeland.

Barra, turning green now with the Hebridean spring, had a harsh yet
pleasant beauty. It was a barren treeless landscape with protruding knobs
of gnarled granite tracing weird patterns on the springtime mat of green.
In many spots the hillsides were covered with the yellow of blooming
primroses, sometimes so dense that the slopes seemed coated in sulphur.
Mary's aesthetic nature was stirred by the beauty around her, but she
forced herself to see as well the land's real character. The soil was thin
and sandy; the cultivated fields were tiny and spotted erratically wherever the boulders could be cleared away sufficiently to provide working
space for a plow. The only dwellings were the squat little blackhouses,
their stone walls and straw-thatched roofs blending so imperceptibly into
the landscape that at a distance they looked like haystacks. Mary knew
that farming here could offer no luxuries, and few comforts. The struggle
was for bare existence, and the islanders apparently neither asked for nor
expected more.

Far ahead Sammy had stopped and was beckoning for her to hurry.
She walked faster and when she caught up to him he pointed down the
sandy trail.

"Over there," he grunted. "That's it." Sammy's gray eyes were shining
like those of a boy who has just discovered a new bicycle under his Christmas tree. He started to run and Mary dropped behind again.

She looked where he had pointed. The trail twisted down among the
outcrops of rock, then turned and ran along the narrow plain of *machair*
close to the sea. Half a mile away the trail lifted over a rocky hummock
and disappeared beyond. At the base of the hummock, barely discernible,
she could see the little blackhouse that was to be her home. Behind it the
hills rose steeply, in front there was a strip of dunes and beach and
then the sea. There wasn't another human habitation in sight. It looked
like a little stone-encased haystack perched on the very rim of the world.

Mary approached it slowly, wondering if any bride had ever come to
her first home with more distaste and dread. Gradually she began to dis-

tinguish details of its construction. The walls, about six feet high, were of stones crudely cemented together. The thatched roof was a thick blanket of straw and sod with an old fishnet draped over it and weighted with stones so the roof couldn't blow away. Sammy was inside when she arrived.

The plank door was set back in a recess formed by the four-foot thickness of the walls. Mary opened the door and stepped in, her eyes adjusting slowly to the gloom. It was all one room. There were three small windows but they admitted little light because they were set back the thickness of the walls like the door. The floor was packed earth. In the center there was a small fireplace of blackened stones with an iron grill on its top. Sammy already had a fire of peat blocks smoldering and the smoke curled upward clinging in a thick cloud under the pole rafters. The chimney was simply a hole in the peak of the roof with a bottomless galvanized water pail fitted into it so that sparks couldn't set the thatch afire. Now Mary understood why they were called "blackhouses." The rafters and the thatch ceiling were blackened with soot.

Sammy's mother had died three years before and the house had not been lived in since, but its furnishings of three chairs, a table, cupboard and metal bed were still there. Possessions of any kind came hard for the Hebridean crofters; they had a deep respect for personal property and thefts rarely occurred. Not even a window glass was broken.

Sammy looked at the bare bedsprings. "The MacNeills will ha' the mattress and the quilts," he said. "They live over the hill. They'd be takin' them so the rats couldna chaw 'em up. I'll fetch them now and tell Tommy MacNeill we're home."

Sammy stepped out the door, stooping low so that his head wouldn't hit the top of the frame. As soon as he was gone Mary dropped onto one of the chairs, bent over the table and cradled her head in her arms. His words "we're home" thundered despairingly in her ears and she saw now in glaring clarity the enormity of what she had done. She sobbed softly, but for no more than a minute. Then she got to her feet, took out her violin, tuned it quickly and began to play.

The main theme of Mendelssohn's concerto in E minor echoed hollowly in the little low-ceilinged hut, but Mary had never loved it more.

CHAPTER SEVEN

THAT spring Sammy bought a cow, four sheep and half a dozen chickens, largely with Mary's money. He borrowed Tommy MacNeill's horse and plow and got in about four acres of oats and potatoes. Mary tried resignedly to adjust to life in the little blackhouse on the edge of the sea, but it wasn't easy for she was pregnant, tired and frequently sick.

Outwardly, she and Sammy got along relatively well. He was kind and sympathetic but so simple and uninformed that there was no common ground anywhere on which their minds could meet. Early one morning a few days after the cow had stopped giving milk Mary was awakened by weird cries outside. Sammy was running round and round the blackhouse waving his arms and singing a disjointed Gaelic song. He came inside again, flushed and breathing hard.

"What were ye doing?" Mary asked him.

"I put a spell on the rats so they'd quit stealin' the cow's milk," he said.

Mary said nothing in reply. Two days later Sammy announced proudly that the cow was giving milk again.

Sammy built a stone chimney up the outside of one of the blackhouse's end walls and bought Mary a secondhand stove on which to cook. There was no wood for fuel except the odd log of driftwood on the beach, but there were beds of peat at the base of the hillside not far away. When cut from the ground in blocks and dried, the peat burned with a slow hot fire.

Working slowly, a bit each day, Mary lined the inside of the blackhouse with tea boxes and sacking. Sammy agreed reluctantly and bought wallpaper on one of his trips to Castlebay, and Mary put it up with flour paste she mixed herself. She sandpapered and painted the cupboard, table and chairs, although the smell of the paint made her sick each time before she could get much done. She knitted clothing for the baby. When fatigue overcame her she found rest and solace in her violin, or she sat in the light of one of the little windows and read.

Sammy built a baby's cradle, dug his potatoes and cut the oats by hand. Autumn came and the gales swept in constantly off the Atlantic, driving great green combers before them. The surf thundered ceaselessly and sometimes inside the blackhouse Mary and Sammy had to shout to make each other hear. When entering or leaving they had to close the door quickly behind them because the wind would blast in, blowing coals of peat out of the stove and lifting the thatched roof ominously.

One morning late in October Mary felt the pains and when they became stronger and more frequent at midday she sent Sammy to fetch Mrs. MacNeill. Then she went to bed and waited, tense, excited, but not afraid. Mrs. MacNeill arrived and took charge. Everything went normally and early in the evening Rory was born.

That night with the baby crying periodically in his cradle beside the bed, Mary was too excited to sleep. Her small body was stiff and sore, but for the first time since coming to Barra she felt a warm contentment and peace. For now Mary Macdonald had something to love.

And as she lay that night, sleepless but overwhelmingly happy, a new sound kept coming in to her above the booming of the surf outside. It was a rich ringing chorus, a little like the barking of excited terriers, yet much more musical. Sometimes it was faint and mellowing softly in the distance; at other times it was close overhead, shrill and sharp, with a chatter-like quality. It was a wild, exciting sound and Mary liked it. She listened, fascinated and curious. As dawn began to brighten the sky, she lifted herself onto an elbow and peered through one of the small windows that faced the sea.

She saw them immediately. Flocks of wild geese with black necks and prominent white faces were flying up and down the shore in wavering lines, sometimes dipping down close to the breaking surf, sometimes soaring high above. In the bed beside her Sammy awoke and listened for a moment to the musical gabble of the geese.

"Them's the barnacles," he said. "There be thousands o' them and the winter always brings 'em tae Barra. They dinna have nests and eggs like other birds, they hatch outa the barnacle shells that grow on ship hulls. That's why the barnacle goose always loves the sea. They bring good luck tae sailors."

The baby cried. Sammy looked quickly at the cradle.

"Ay now!" he exclaimed. "And it's a good sign surely for the bairn. The barnacles'll like the laddie who was born the night they come tae Barra. The ole women with the evil eye won't hurt our wee Rory 'cause the barnacles'll watch over him."

A few minutes later Sammy dropped off to sleep again, but Mary continued to listen for the chattering passage of the goose flocks. She knew the barnacles could have no supernatural influence on Rory's future; but for herself, the wild music was already a symbol inseparably linked with the love that came into an empty life at Rory's birth.

With full daylight the flocks were gone, disappearing as magically as they came. Mary hoped that they would return, and she need not have worried, for they were back again with the dusk. Every dawn and dusk it was the same, the big birds disappearing mysteriously for the day, but they were always back at night filling the darkness again with their musical chatter.

The wintering flocks of barnacle geese stood out prominently in Rory's childhood memories. One of his earliest yet most vivid boyhood recollections was of a walk one autumn evening with his mother to watch the evening flight of barnacles move in from the sea to their feeding grounds. He was under five, yet the experience impressed him deeply and the details stuck in his memory.

Two miles from his home there was a low uninhabited island about a square mile in extent with a shallow sound separating it from Barra proper. It was known as Goose Island and was one of Barra's main barnacle goose feeding grounds, for the eelgrass and tangle grew in thick waving beds in the sandy shallows of its sound.

Rory and his mother set off late in the afternoon with a lunch of oatcakes and a jar of milk. Mary Macdonald, with a curious mind that demanded knowledge and understanding of everything around her, had bought small nature books by mail from Glasgow and was beginning to recognize the commoner birds. As they walked she pointed out to Rory the flocks of skylarks and ringed plovers on the browning *machair,* and where the road came close to the sea she showed him oyster catchers and purple sandpipers daintily dodging the surf. But most of all on that walk, he remembered the barnacles.

They could hear them long before the big birds came in sight, for mist shrouded the sea and Goose Island Sound itself was hidden by a ridge until they were close. They walked cautiously to the crest of the ridge and looked at the sweeping view of the sound beyond. It was a sight Rory was to see countless times in later years, but never again was it as exciting as that first experience. The water was dotted with thousands of geese, most of them with heads and necks submerged as they fed on the eelgrass under the surface; hundreds had spilled over onto the land and were grazing on the meadows that came down close to the sea. There were hundreds more still in the air, long twisting lines of them, and the distant flocks emerging from the mist over the sea looked like gray threads waving in a breeze. Their flight seemed leisurely, but once when a gaggle of the geese passed low across the hill where they stood Rory was surprised at how fast and powerful the flight was. The rush of air past their wings came down to him like the whine of a gale in a ship's rigging.

Just before sunset the mist lifted and the sun shone brilliantly for a few minutes. The white faces and bellies of the flying barnacles turned pink as the sun disappeared and a red afterglow crept across the sky.

Rory heard his mother sigh softly beside him. "They are fine magnificent birds," she said, "but my bird book doesn't say where they come from or where they go. I hope there *is* an Atlantis out there somewhere and I hope it belongs only to them."

Throughout Rory's childhood the barnacles remained great majestic birds of romance and mystery that appeared like magic out of the sea each autumn and disappeared to the sea again each spring. Rory regarded them with an awe and a veneration he could feel for no other bird.

For Mary Macdonald, the return of the barnacle geese each autumn brought a leaven of beauty and cheer into an otherwise drab life. For Rory they brought visions of distant, romantic lands where some day he would work and live.

When his wanderings along the sandy *machair* road began taking him into other children's homes, Rory quickly recognized that the relationship between his mother and father was not like that of other parents he encountered. His parents rarely spoke to each other; each seemed to work and go his or her own way hardly recognizing the presence of the other. When Rory first remembered the blackhouse it had already been partitioned into three rooms—a combination kitchen-living room at the chimney end, a bedroom for his father in the middle, and his mother's bedroom at the other end. Each room opened into the next one through a curtained doorway and the only outside door was in his father's room, so this central room served as hallway as well. His mother's room contained her homemade bed, several shelves of books and a small loom. Rory slept on a cot in a corner of the kitchen.

The loom was Mary Macdonald's answer to Sammy's feeble and unprofitable efforts at farming. She had quickly picked up the technique of weaving the Harris tweed for which the Hebrides had long been famous, using wool from the sheep that Sammy raised, and dyeing it with natural vegetable dyes that she gathered and brewed herself. Some of the wool was knit into clothing for themselves, but most of it she wove into tweed. The final step Mary disliked very much. To set the color and tighten the threads, the tweed had to be soaked in stale urine. Many of the weavers kept the urine barrel handy beside the house; Mary insisted that theirs be in the small barn several rods away. Her big bolts of cloth were picked up by buyers on their periodic circuits and Mary quickly established a reputation for producing a good quality of tweed that soon became the family's principal source of income.

Sammy at times worked for short periods on one of the herring boats out of Castlebay and whenever he did he selected his clothing carefully, eliminating everything that contained wool dyed brown by rock lichens from the sea's edge. Mary watched the strange ritual two or three times, then asked finally why he did it.

"What is taken from the rocks will always return tae the rocks," Sammy pronounced solemnly. "When a man's washed overboard that's the cause. The rockweed always goes back home."

The little school was nearly three miles away so Mary gave Rory daily lessons at home for five years. He was almost ten when she decided it was time for his formal schooling to begin. On the first morning she had Peggy MacNeill call for Rory. Peggy was the eldest of several MacNeill children, two years older than Rory, spindly, with rumpled black hair and an officious manner. Rory disliked all girls, but he especially disliked Peggy MacNeill, and on the second morning he started for school half an hour earlier so that he would be gone when Peggy called.

Rory's education by now however was already well advanced. He was inheriting his father's good looks and physique, and his mother's sharp, gifted brain. Mary was a good teacher and Rory had learned quickly, as much from her example as from the lessons themselves. She spent much time reading and Rory, largely from imitation, discovered early the magic world of books. Mary had the small library she had brought to Barra with her, and from time to time when she received a good tweed check she would order another book or two from a Glasgow bookseller. Glasgow friends periodically sent bundles of the *Spectator* and London *Times;* they were always a month old but they kept her informed on the world beyond Barra and its happenings.

When Rory started school at ten he had read several of Scott's Waverley novels, and with his mother's help he was reading and beginning to understand Darwin's *The Origin of Species*. Rory also acquired from his mother a keen interest in the natural history around them. They walked frequently across the *machair* and into the hills beyond, patiently puzzling out names of flowers and birds from crude little identification books that were the best Mary could afford. But Rory's main interest in the world of nature remained the big romantic barnacles. They came and went so mysteriously. They were always so wary and far away. He longed to see them at close range and one October afternoon in school he had an exciting idea.

He ran home after school, rolled up an old blanket, took milk and oatcakes and set out for Goose Island Sound. He hurried so that he would get there before the evening flight of the barnacles began. The sun had not quite set when he arrived and there was no sign yet of the geese. He walked up and down the *machair* looking for areas where droppings indicated the barnacles were feeding on shore. He selected a spot where buttercup and clover grew densely and where broad-webbed tracks in the sand showed that the geese had been recently feeding, then he stretched the blanket out and weighted its edges with stones. He pulled up several armloads of clover and spread them over the blanket until it was almost hidden. Then he sat down, ate his lunch and waited.

The wait was short. From far out at sea came a soft melodious gabble that swelled and muted rhythmically as the goose flocks, still invisible, stirred to life. After a few minutes he began to see their thin gray flock lines twisting faintly against the pink sunset. The lines grew sharper, their calling grew louder, and Rory's heart thumped in answer. Now, it was time! Their vision was keen and they would see him if he waited longer. He squirmed quickly under the camouflaged blanket and propped up one edge of it with a stick so that he had a small peephole facing the sound and the sea. He began trembling and he was sure that the clover and blanket that covered him were shaking so violently that the birds would be certain to spot him.

The flocks began pitching down on arched and stiffened wings into the shallow waters of the sound a quarter of a mile from where Rory lay. They began feeding on the underwater plants as soon as they arrived, but there was always a number of them with heads up, resting, refilling lungs with air and watching for danger. As each new flock came in, it was greeted by those already on the water with loud cackling cries. They poured in across the sea in a constant noisy stream and spread out over the sound, first in hundreds, and then, Rory was sure, in thousands.

He managed shortly to control his trembling but after fifteen minutes or so of lying on the damp ground his body grew cramped and cold. The sun set and the evening grew cooler, his feet and then his hands became numb. Out on the water the geese were moving shoreward slowly as they fed and Rory forced himself to remain rigid and motionless. Within him a strange compulsion demanded that he see the barnacles closely, that he know them better.

The pink afterglow of sunset retreated slowly into the sea until it was only a thin bright line on the horizon. Several geese had walked out onto the beach a hundred yards or so below Rory, but none showed signs of coming nearer. He was sure he had selected a spot where they had been feeding during recent nights. They must have spotted his hideout and were keeping away. Rory began to feel discouraged.

The thin line of pink on the horizon disappeared but a gray twilight lingered. Suddenly there was a roar close above that sounded like the surge of a heavy sea about to engulf him. Rory ducked his head instinctively. Then, almost instantaneously, he recognized it as the sound of many great wings beating the air violently in the braking action that takes place just before a flock of geese comes down on land. He peered out from beneath the covering. The big birds were plunging by just ten feet above, their tremendous wings flapping vigorously and broad feet extended. They dropped heavily to the ground about twenty feet in front of him and Rory stared unbelieving, the cold and cramped discomfort of his body suddenly forgotten.

There were about twenty of them and for several seconds they stood stiffly erect, their heads twisting from side to side as they checked the surroundings for danger. Rory waited, his body rigid. They would surely be alarmed by his crude little hideout. But one by one the long black necks bent down gracefully and the barnacles began to graze, their sharp bills cutting off the clover and ragwort stems with a fast nibbling action. At a distance only the broad pattern of their plumage could be seen, but now at close range Rory could see it all in sharp detail. Their backs were not the somber gray he had previously believed; they were a bright silver-gray barred strikingly with black and white, and the face patches on many of them were not a flat white but a rich creamy-white. They were handsome birds and Rory stared spellbound.

As they fed, the barnacles talked constantly to themselves in a soft throaty whisper. More flocks followed and in a few minutes Rory was surrounded by hundreds. Occasionally one of them came within six feet of his face and he could even see the brown irises of their eyes.

He did not know how long he watched them, but he realized after a time that it was dark and only the white faces and bellies of the barnacles were visible. His mother would be worrying. But how could he get away without alarming them and making them much warier for another time? The geese stayed close. He was very cold. He decided he must remain until there was an opportunity to creep away without the geese seeing him.

He dozed and lost all track of time. Then faintly he heard someone calling his name. "Rory . . . . Rory." It came from far away. The geese heard it too and stopped feeding; he could see their silhouettes against the gray sky, their heads high, listening. For a couple of minutes there were no more calls and the barnacles resumed feeding, but much more nervously now, lifting their heads frequently to scan the *machair* around them.

The call came again, much closer and stronger. It was followed instantly by a tremendous thunder of beating wings and shrill alarm cries as hundreds of geese flung themselves into the air. Rory pushed the blanket back and looked up. The air above was a turmoil of furious sound and clashing wings but the geese themselves were only faintly visible against the sky. It lasted only a few seconds. Suddenly the big birds were gone, the air was still and there was only a chorus of excited alarm notes retreating now across the sound.

The call came again, this time unmistakably his mother's voice. "I'm here, mother," he called back.

He rose stiffly onto aching legs and began to fold up the blanket. Now that it was over he was trembling again with excitement. He had been right among the barnacles, almost one of them himself, without their knowing. He felt he had witnessed something forbidden, that he had lived for a brief time in a world that humans were not supposed to know.

He walked uneasily along the road to where his mother waited. She had come two miles to find him and he knew she would be cross.

"I was *very* worried and angry," she said sternly, then her voice softened. "Ye were right down among them, weren't ye?"

"I couldn't leave them," Rory said, "because they'd have seen the blanket and been afraid another time."

"Ay, I know," his mother said. She took his hand and they began walking back. "I wish I had been there too."

CHAPTER EIGHT

THE war brought blackouts, ration coupons and shortages to the Hebrides, but on the stony little Macdonald croft on the Atlantic shore of Barra life went on much as before. For two or three hours each day Mary's loom clacked monotonously in her gloomy bedroom, turning out its bolts of colored tweeds.

Rory grew rapidly. By fifteen he was six feet tall, but thin and shapeless with arms and legs that looked too long for the rest of him. The fires of puberty were beginning to enkindle his big body, but Rory feared and disliked girls, and avoided them whenever he could, because he was embarrassed by his tall ungainly figure. Girls were always whispering and laughing, and he thought they were laughing at him. It wasn't difficult to avoid girls for the little Barra crofts were widely separated. Peggy MacNeill was the only girl he saw regularly and usually he saw her only at a distance. Often, when he saw Peggy coming down the road toward him, he would find an excuse to leave the road and circle across the moor so that they didn't pass closely.

At this time, too, Rory's reading began making him increasingly aware of the meanness and backwardness of his Barra homeland. For a long time he had had vague ideas of going away and becoming an important man in the world of cities and industry that he knew only from books, and the ideas were sharpening now and growing more insistent.

After his fifteenth birthday he stopped growing taller. His shoulders broadened rapidly, his chest thickened and his arms lost their too-long appearance. Like his father, he was becoming a husky, handsome man, but Rory didn't recognize it and the embarrassment and inferiority feeling stayed with him.

That following summer Sammy had three beef steers he was fattening and he decided to herd them and the one Macdonald cow across to Goose Island and let them graze there, saving for winter the limited pasturage he had at home while making use of the rich natural pastures going to waste on the island. It was a traditional Hebrides crofting practice and the summer pastures of the hills and islands used in this manner have been known for generations as the "shielings." It was the summer duty of the older children to live on the shielings in huts of stone and turf, watch the cattle and do the milking.

One morning when the tide was low and the cattle could wade most of the way across Goose Island Sound, Sammy and Rory borrowed the MacNeill rowboat and herded the animals over to the island. They took a blanket, cooking utensils and food because Rory would be staying.

"I'll come over for the milk tomorrow," his mother said, "and I'll bring more bedding and food."

Sammy remained on the island a couple of hours helping Rory repair the shieling hut, then he returned across the sound. Rory began gathering bracken and heather to spread on the ground within the hut for a bed.

He could see a herd of MacNeill cattle a mile away at the other end of the island, and one of the MacNeills, Rory couldn't distinguish whom, was busily working around a hut there. The afternoon light waned, Rory got water from a stream a quarter of a mile away, he milked the cow, started a fire, put on tea water and began peeling potatoes. Then, along the low ridge that bisected the island, he saw the MacNeill coming toward him carrying a small package. A couple of minutes later he recognized her. It was Peggy.

"I chust baked bannocks," she called as she came close, holding out the package wrapped in a tea towel.

Peggy wasn't a spindly awkward child any longer, she was rounding out in the hips and bust, and it struck Rory suddenly that she was now a shapely, pretty young woman. The discovery startled him. He didn't know what to say in greeting.

She came on, walking with a lithe grace. "'Tis lonely out here," she said, "and I thought we'd ha' tea and bannocks together."

Rory was embarrassed at his silence. Finally he managed to say: "I'll make tea."

He saw that her black hair was neat and she was wearing a clean fresh blouse. She was smiling, a little impishly Rory thought, as she sat on a rock across the peat fire from him.

Peggy took over at the fire and indicated quickly that she had come for more than tea and bannocks. She boiled potatoes and fried eggs, they had supper, then began washing dishes together. Peggy's arm touched Rory's repeatedly as she knelt close to him over the dish pan and handed him dishes for drying. Afterward they sat and watched the sun dip slowly into the sparkling Atlantic. It turned cool with dusk and Peggy showed no indication of leaving. Rory noticed she was shivering.

"I'll get a blanket," he said, and stepped into the hut. He came out and put the blanket over her shoulders, then sat down again a few paces away.

"Don't ye ha' one?" she asked.

"It's all I have until mother comes tomorrow," he replied.

"Then we'll have to share this one," she said. Peggy moved over and threw the blanket around both of them, her body pressed closely against his.

"Ye've grown up fast, Rory. Ye're no' a boy now, ye're a man."

"And ye're not a wee girl. I used to hate you."

She laughed softly and turned her face up toward his.

"Ye're good-looking, but there's one thing wrong wi' ye," she said.

"What's that?"

"Yeer nose is too big."

"It's too late to change it now."

It was warm and cozy beneath the blanket. Through her light clothing Peggy's body felt smooth and soft and rounded, Rory thought, so different from the hard, rough, muscular body of a man. The peat fire blazed up fitfully whenever there was a breeze. The night came, and far away a short-eared owl *"keered"* as it hunted. A long time later Peggy and Rory moved inside.

He was awake shortly after dawn, but Peggy had already gone. He stepped outside into the damp morning mist, blew the smoldering peat into flame and put on water for tea and porridge. Then he went back into the hut to ruffle up the bracken of his bed so that his mother, when she came, would not see that two had slept there.

Several weeks later Big Sammy Macdonald asked Tommy MacNeill: "How are yeer cattle on the island?"

"Verra guid," Tommy answered. "Ay, verra guid. And Peggy, there's a graund lass too. She's oldest and says the shielin's her job. She'll havna other children there to help her. Insists on doin' it alone."

On the shieling the summer passed pleasantly for Rory. Peggy visited him almost nightly and after that first night she never again bothered with the pretense of bringing bannocks to share. She wanted only to share Rory's bed.

There are many steps between the boy and the man, and for Rory the first one came that summer on Goose Island. Peggy's visits gave him an exciting new sense of confidence and strength; the old feelings of embarrassment and inferiority drained away. Instead of being gawky and repulsive, as he had thought, he discovered in Peggy that girls could find him attractive. For the first time Rory was seeing himself through another's eyes, and he was not merely satisfied, he was a little proud of what he saw.

And Peggy did more than that for him. She was a simple naïve girl who seemed to have gotten practically nothing from the years she had spent in school. To Rory she became symbolic of Barra's trivialness, impressing upon him more vividly than ever that somewhere in the world outside there must be a bigger, more important role for him to play. The shieling events did not even come close to being a love affair that would tie him to Barra. In fact, it was during this time that Rory's yearning to escape became a goading determination.

He was thinking of it a great deal during that autumn and winter. He had obtained all the formal education he could from the little Barra school and his mother's tutorship, and he began to see now that if he was going to go far in that world outside he must somehow get more education. As a first step he would have to go to sea and save money. And now the sea, always so close, so taken for granted, took on a new and alluring guise that warmed Rory's Viking blood and beckoned tantalizingly. But he didn't mention it yet to his mother because he was sure she would say he was too young to leave home.

He spent much time that winter watching the barnacles. Spring came and the tinkling song of the skylark and the piping twitter of ringed plovers came back again to Barra's *machairs*. The barnacles grew restless and noisier and now the feeding periods were interspersed with noisy sessions of gesturing and displays which Rory recognized as part of the springtime courtship. Sometimes they fought, rising erect in the water and pummeling each other with stiffened wings.

Rory went alone to Goose Island one warm evening in mid-April to watch them again. The flocks came in as usual at dusk but their feeding seemed hasty and impatient. A nearly full moon rose and from Rory's distance the thousands of barnacles feeding on the sound's sparkling water looked like pepper spilled across a silver-sequined tablecloth. They had been feeding less than two hours when a large flock rose into the air and flew back and forth noisily over the others. Then gabbling loudly to the thousands still on the water below, the flock circled and gained altitude until Rory could see it only as a fuzzy shadow high above him in the moonlight. The birds leveled off and flew northward high above the sound and the sea, and for minutes after they were gone from sight the ringing rhythm of their sonorous flight calls kept floating back to him.

The receding calls of the first flock were hardly out of hearing before another flock rose from the water and did the same. Flock after flock followed, each one ignoring the habitual flight route that went south of Goose Island and turning northward instead. Rory watched the spectacle for several hours and he knew he was witnessing a mass departure of the barnacles for distant nesting grounds. When he left the sound finally, late at night, there were only a few hundred of the geese remaining where there had been thousands before.

He envied their freedom, the power of their great wings, and now his own decision was firmly made. He too would go from Barra. He walked back through shimmering moonlight and listened sadly as the musical gabbling of the remaining geese faded behind. Now he knew he wouldn't see the big flocks again; he would be gone before another autumn brought the barnacles back to Barra.

Rory was over sixteen now and a lanky six-foot-two. Without his mother knowing, he wrote to a Glasgow shipping company whose vessels stopped occasionally at Castlebay and asked for a job on one of their ships. Hebridean youth have always taken to the sea and are known the world over as good sailors, and two weeks later Rory received instructions to report to the mate of a ship due to stop at Castlebay in ten days.

His mother was at the loom weaving when he showed her the letter. She read it quickly and handed it back to Rory. For many seconds she looked blankly out the little bedroom window that faced the sea and Rory waited anxiously for her reply. But finally when she spoke she said only: "In ten days." Then she bent silently again over her loom and its clacking resumed.

Sammy was proud that Rory was going to sea, but for the next ten days Mary went silently about her work giving no indication of what she was thinking. The last day came and Rory was packing clothing into the old canvas duffel bag that his father had used years before. Mary was alone in her bedroom and she called him. When Rory stepped in she was sitting on her crude bed of ropes and poles. Her shoulders were hunched forward and she looked very small; her face was lined, her hair was beginning to dust prematurely with gray. He faced her, fearing that now the scene he dreaded would come.

Mary looked up and her eyes sparkled with tears. She passed a hand across her eyes, then the words came in a fast violent outburst.

"Ye are so young, Rory. So young. But I'm glad ye are going. I'm glad ye are getting away from it all. Come back when ye can. . . . I'll miss ye so . . . . ye're all I have in Barra, in the world. . . ."

She passed a trembling hand before her eyes again.

"But don't ever come back to stay. Barra's no place for ye, ye're better than Barra. It'll kill you, I mean your spirit and your mind . . . . as it has killed me. And don't stay at sea, because ye're better than that, too. Don't let your mind stop developing . . . . good brains are rare and the world needs them. Lord, it does need them! Get more education . . . . it'll be hard, but ye can. Rory, ye must! I'll miss ye so. . . ."

Mary stopped then, looking not at Rory but out the little window toward the sea. Rory shuffled self-consciously and didn't know what to say in reply. His mother, sitting there on her strange little bed, had never looked so small and pathetic before.

"I'll send ye money to buy a new bed," he mumbled, and he knew it was an absurd and irrelevant statement.

"Don't!" she exclaimed. "I like my old bed. I had to make it myself. Your father wouldna help me."

Rory had never seen his mother with a hammer or saw in her hands, but now he pictured her working clumsily and defiantly while his father stood idly by. Not until that instant did he see fully the gulf that separated his parents. Suddenly he saw the bed in its real significance—the symbol of a marriage that existed in law but had never existed in fact.

In an hour Rory was ready to go. At the door he shook hands with his father and kissed his mother. Then he said quickly: "Goodbye, I'll be back." He couldn't trust his voice to say more. He threw the duffel bag onto his shoulder and walked rapidly down the sandy trail toward Castlebay. He walked perhaps thirty paces, then turned to wave.

His parents stood silently at the blackhouse door—a big and powerful man, good-looking, with a tangled shock of blond hair and a proud smile beaming; and a small dumpy woman with drooping shoulders and a round, wrinkled and expressionless face. How misleading, Rory thought, were those contrasting exteriors. How different the personalities they hid. Rory felt a sharp twinge of sorrow for his mother.

Then, just before he turned his back, the hazy edge of his vision caught another movement. His eyes shifted toward it. Where the roadway twisted across the ridge behind the blackhouse, he saw a slim figure with long black hair flying in the wind and one arm waving vigorously. Rory waved back gaily. He wouldn't miss her, he was sure of that, for the lesson in self-knowledge that she had left with him on the summer shieling had been well taught. He was handsome and attractive to girls. Wherever he went he knew that, for him, there would always be other Peggys.

He waved to Peggy again, then he turned and did not look back. A minute later he heard his mother's violin whispering softly across the springtime *machair*. It was muffled by the blackhouse walls, faint and already distant, and only snatches of it reached him, but Rory knew the tune well and his memory filled in what his straining ears failed to catch. In another minute the music was lost behind him and the only sounds were the whisper of the wind stirring the clover and the pulsing murmur of the sea.

But for a long time the haunting melody of Mendelssohn's concerto in E minor kept running through his mind.

CHAPTER NINE

Rory's ship turned out to be a cramped and creaking little tub that looked like an oversized oil drum with a point at one end. Someone in a past now long forgotten had indulgently named it the *Clydespride* and according to shipboard scuttlebutt it survived the war because no Nazi U-boat commander could convince himself that it was worth using a torpedo on. The *Clydespride* wheezed back and forth dutifully on various North Atlantic cargo runs between Britain, the United States and Canada. Because of its shallow draft and small size it could pass through the St. Lawrence River canal system and it made several summer runs into the Great Lakes. Stops in the lake ports were short but Rory came to know well the waterfronts of Montreal, Toronto, Milwaukee and Chicago.

In New York a month after he left home Rory bought a bird book and a pair of eight-power binoculars. He began spending much of his spare time, at sea and ashore, studying whatever birds happened to be in the vicinity. To the bewilderment of his crewmates, he spent hours on deck at sea watching the shearwaters and fulmars soaring effortlessly astern.

But after a few months Rory discovered that the Peggy MacNeill experience had a habit of repeating itself. The first few times it happened he thought he was picking up the girl, but after a few times it began to look very much as if the girl was picking up him. Whatever way, he liked it, and it began leaving him less time for bird watching. He continued spending a good deal of time studying birds at sea, but in port the jukebox joints and taverns and the pick-ups they always provided became a greater lure. The ambitious dreams he had had for his future began to dim. He wasn't saving money and the additional education he had planned to get was as remote now as it had been back home in Barra. Rory was finding the present too exciting to give much thought to the future.

On Rory's second trip into the Lakes that first summer, the *Clydespride* suffered one of the engine breakdowns to which it was addicted and it lay in Toronto awaiting repairs. Usually the *Clydespride* was in and out of port so fast there was little time for hell-raising ashore, so the opportunity provided by the engine breakdown was eagerly anticipated by the crew. The boys were discussing it excitedly that first evening at dinner in the galley.

"The chief says we'll be here six or seven days."

"I know Toronto," an aging and balding stoker said. "The street ye young laddies want is called 'Jarvis.' The beer is fair. The prosties are under ten bucks unless ye insist on a young and cute one and she might be more."

Someone spoke to Rory. "How about it, Rory? Going to give it a try?"

"Not me," Rory answered. "I'll find a jukebox joint and a dance floor. They're young there, and free."

The stoker squinted at him. "I was young once," he said, "and picked it up free, too. It was more fun those days because the girls wore more clothes and ye never knew what ye'd discover underneath. Sometimes ye'd think ye were getting a plump one but by the time ye worked yeer way down through all the petticoats ye'd find she was thin as a telegraph pole."

But despite his original decision to avoid it, Rory followed the boys that night to have a look at Jarvis Street and its wares.

Next morning the hangover wasn't so bad, but the disgust and remorse over the night before remained with him. Late that afternoon most of the boys headed for Jarvis Street again. Rory picked up a sandwich at the galley, put it in his pocket, got his binoculars and went out alone to look for birds.

He left the dock area and walked for a mile or more along a broad white beach facing Lake Ontario. Rory identified herring and Bonaparte gulls, common and black terns, but the flocks of little sandpipers that scurried along at the water's edge were too nondescript and confusing for him to make much out of them. But they were a fascinating challenge, and Rory began to feel that this was far more interesting than last night's costly escapade had been.

He came to a spot where a large marshy area lay inland from the beach. The shore birds were more numerous here, wheeling about in large flocks as they moved from mudflat to mudflat, glistening like clusters of silver pendants whenever they twisted in flight so that the sun touched their white bellies. Rory sat down and watched the flocks come and go as he ate his sandwich.

A short time later he saw a small man coming along the beach toward him. The man appeared to be wearing only khaki shorts and a pair of binoculars, and he was stopping frequently to scan the shore birds. Rory had never known another person except his mother who was even remotely interested in birds and the prospect now of meeting a fellow bird watcher excited him. He pretended to be concentrating on the sandpipers, but with stealthy side glances he was watching with much more interest the approaching man. He was a queer-looking character to encounter in what was practically the middle of a big city. As he came nearer Rory could see with certainty that he *was* shirtless and barefoot and dressed only in shorts. He was tanned deeply, had long dark hair that formed a shaggy ring around a central bald spot polished brown by the sun. In addition to the binoculars he had a soiled and much-used khaki haversack hanging from one shoulder.

"Find it yet?" he asked as he approached Rory.

Rory didn't know what to say and flustered a little. "No, sir," he said, then added: "Or . . . . what do you mean, sir?"

"The phalarope! It was here this morning. *Fulicarius.* First *fulicarius* for Toronto in more than ten years." The man looked like a hobo but he had the precise enunciation of an Oxford professor.

"I saw phalaropes this spring at sea," Rory said, "but they were still in winter plumage and I couldn't tell whether they were red or northern."

"At sea?" the man said and looked sideways for a moment at Rory. "What were you doing at sea?"

"Sailing. I'm on a ship over in the harbor."

"Where did you see phalaropes?"

"In the Minch, and once coming into New York."

"Do you spend much time watching pelagic birds at sea?"

"A good deal. Whenever I'm off watch."

"We don't know much about the distribution of pelagic birds. Ornithologists don't spend much time at sea, and sailors who do are never ornithologists. You're a rare combination; you could do some important work."

"What can I do?" Rory asked.

"Keep records of what you see and send them to me." He went on to describe in detail what Rory should do. He told him to keep a daily diary recording the ship's noon position and to make regular two-hour checks, listing the species and numbers of sea birds visible from the ship at the time of each check. He wrote his name and address on the back of an envelope and handed it to Rory.

Rory read: "Dr. P. L. Thomas, Department of Zoology, University of Toronto." Then he introduced himself. "I'm Rory Macdonald of . . . . I guess you'd say Barra."

They walked on, repeatedly scanning the shore bird flocks with their binoculars.

Suddenly Dr. Thomas asked: "How old are you?"

"Seventeen this October."

"Why don't you save your money and get into a university somewhere?"

"I'd like to do that."

"There aren't enough students going into biology. We need all the good ones we can find."

They parted a few minutes later. Before returning to the street the professor took a rumpled T-shirt and sandals from his haversack and put them on. "The police make me wear these things," he said, "before I can get on a street car. Stupid bastards, aren't they?"

They did not find the *fulicarius,* but the meeting with Dr. Thomas became a turning point in Rory's life. Or perhaps, more accurately, the turning point came the night before when too much Canadian beer and a frowzy prostitute he barely remembered had filled him with disgust and made a bird watcher out of him again.

CHAPTER TEN

THE *Clydespride* went back down the St. Lawrence to the sea and Rory began sending his bird records once or twice a month to Dr. Thomas at the University of Toronto. The professor seemed delighted with them and periodically he sent Rory reprints of articles from the ornithological journals dealing with sea birds and migration. In a small way Rory became a part of the big fascinating world of scientific research and it made him feel proud.

The new contact with Dr. Thomas had revived Rory's original plan to leave the sea and return to school somewhere. And now its vagueness was gone and the plan had a specific goal. He would enter a university and become a biologist. It would be costly and he began saving money carefully.

Rory stayed with the *Clydespride* for more than two years, then late in the third summer he left her in Glasgow and went back to school. Now he had little time or money to spend dating girls, although the opportunities were as plentiful as ever. For the first few weeks the ambition that had driven him back to school and the natural inclinations of a sailor in port had conflicted, but his ambition prevailed and for all of the following winter and spring he didn't go out on a single date. He worked hard and in that one year of study in Glasgow he tied up the loose ends left by his haphazard Hebrides schooling and obtained everything he needed for university entrance.

There was never any doubt about where he would attend university. The blunt and forceful Dr. Thomas had assumed from the beginning that Rory would come to Toronto, and Rory had assumed it too although he had never analyzed why. One obvious reason was that Canada and the United States between them offered great opportunities. But he suspected that another less practical consideration might be a stronger though unconscious motivation. During his trips up the Great Lakes Rory had been fascinated by the northern forests of spruce and balsam that crowded down to the shorelines and filled the air with the heady odor of their pungent resins. These dense forests contrasted strangely with the almost-treeless Barra he had known before. They lured him. Rory felt a strong desire to know them better.

When Rory notified Dr. Thomas that the Glasgow results were released and favorable, Dr. Thomas wrote back and told him to consider himself enrolled at University of Toronto. But Rory then had to tell him that immigration department red tape would prevent him from reaching Toronto in time for that year's term. He received a scribbled note in reply that said simply: "Too bad. The stupid bastards." It was signed "P.L." and Rory never addressed or thought of him as "Dr. Thomas" again.

Rory got a job bellhopping at a Glasgow hotel and waited. It was spring again before everything was initialed, witnessed, signed, sealed and sworn and Rory was authorized to enter Canada as an immigrant. He returned to his old shipping company and made arrangements to work his way to Canada on a sister ship of the *Clydespride* making one of the first trips into the Great Lakes after the freeze-up. On an evening early in May, Rory reached Toronto and, still carrying his dad's ancient canvas duffel bag, he climbed down to the wharf and found a public telephone booth. He called P.L.

"I'm here."

"It took you long enough!"

P.L. told him there was a room available in the boarding house where he had lived many years. "Want to look at it?"

"Okay." And Rory wound up living in a third-floor room in the same North Toronto boarding house with P.L.

The north still lured him and he got a summer job with the provincial government's lands and forests department as a fire ranger in northern Ontario. Early in June a bush plane dropped him off alone with supplies, a canoe and a pile of textbooks at a little log cabin on an isolated wilderness lake. The books were principally P.L.'s choices. There were few forest fires and Rory had ample opportunity to study, to familiarize himself with the forest's trees, plants and animals and to practice handling a canoe. He had three months of it and when he came out in September he had enough money owing him to pay his university fees and a good chunk of the winter's living expenses. P.L. assured him it wouldn't be difficult to find week-end and evening jobs that would pay the rest.

On his first night back in Toronto he wrote proudly to his mother: "Tomorrow I start university. . . ."

Rory worked three more summers in the bush as a fire ranger, attending the university each winter. During university terms he worked at a variety of evening and week-end jobs and he managed, by frugally shunning frills and luxuries, to keep his living expenses paid as they became due. There were times after long sessions of studying and writing examinations that Rory felt like having a night on the town. He would think of the Jarvis Street bars and of the girls who would put on a front of indignant offense when a strange man sat beside them, and he wondered if the old talent for handling such situations was still in him. But the desire was never strong enough to goad him into finding out. Rory Macdonald, the sailor-boy Lothario, seemed to have vanished somewhere in his past; and Rory Macdonald, the student, had more essential things to do with his time and money.

As for the university girls, they were different and in their way they were more dangerous, and Rory didn't even consider doing any dating in that field. A tavern pick-up could be used for a night and then ditched and she couldn't come chasing after you again, because if you were smart and didn't tell her too much she wouldn't know where to find you. But university girls were always here in the same crowd with him. Any relationship started with one of them would be harder to terminate. Besides, they were well rounded girls, attractive intellectually as well as physically, and this was a danger too. It made them marriageable material and Rory wanted no temptations of that sort dogging him until his future was firmly in hand.

There were always summer jobs for advance biology students, most of them field research projects for the government, army, air force or the pulp and paper companies. In March of his fourth year at the university Rory received a letter from the federal government wildlife service asking if he would be interested in doing a study that summer of the Canada goose population around James Bay. His mind responded instantly with vivid memories of the barnacle geese of Barra. The Canadas of James Bay were a different species, but he could think of nothing more pleasant and exciting than spending a season with the geese again. Rory accepted the job eagerly.

He received his expense money late in May just as Hurricane Alice began lunging up the Atlantic coast and across the Carolinas. Rory waited two days before deciding when to go to James Bay, because if Alice came near Toronto he wanted to be on hand afterward in case it brought a few tropical birds with it. But Alice had swung back to sea and began racing up the North Atlantic.

On the day before Zoology 29 Rory went downtown to check train times and buy his ticket. He would have to spend a night at Blackwood on the way north to talk with the provincial superintendent of game and fisheries there about his James Bay plans.

Now Zoology 29 was over and his luggage was already at the station. He and P.L. had almost completed their two-mile walk home from the university and the rush-hour traffic streaming past them was beginning to wane. Barra and the barnacles seemed so far away, like another life in another world.

But no part of a man's life stands alone, isolated from its other parts. Usually the links between are simple and obvious, but sometimes they are subtle and unseeable like the strange new link with Barra that Hurricane Alice was forging now for Rory Macdonald.

CHAPTER ELEVEN

HURRICANE ALICE had become a giant whirlpool of wind and rain three hundred miles in diameter with a central eye of calm about twenty miles across. Originally the winds revolving around this eye had reached a maximum of a hundred and twenty miles an hour but now they had dropped to seventy-five. The whole great doughnut-like structure was plunging northeastward up the Atlantic at forty miles an hour, the way a top spinning at high speed travels slowly across the floor while it spins.

The tremendous power that had given Alice her birth and still kept her alive was the hot vapor-saturated air she had sucked up from the surface of the tropical seas where her violent life had begun. This vapor was actually a latent and potent fuel, for the heat energy it had absorbed in the process of evaporation remained locked within it to be released again when it condensed into cloud and rain.

But now, over the cold waters of the North Atlantic, her fuel supply was waning and Alice weakened. Off Newfoundland she turned eastward and her winds dropped to fifty miles an hour. Senile and tiring, she was near death when her charmed life won another respite.

A mass of cold air was pouring ponderously down the Atlantic from Greenland. Hurricane Alice, spawn of a steaming tropic sea, met this frigid Arctic air midway between Newfoundland and Ireland and the two air masses were much too different in character and composition to mix without violence and struggle. The Arctic air, heavy and dry, pushed underneath and Alice's moist warm winds began riding up its sloping unyielding wall. As she lifted into higher altitudes the remnants of tropical vapor she still carried could condense more rapidly and for her last brief dying hours Alice's old vigor and violence returned. Her winds rose to seventy-five miles an hour and the Arctic air was dragged into the wind system with them.

In the turbulent blending of Arctic and tropic airs, Hurricane Alice lost her identity. But in the act of dying she had spawned another Frankenstein, for the new storm she had triggered was a seventy-five-mile-an-hour gale lashing a million square miles of North Atlantic into battering waves and shreds of foam that extended from Scotland halfway across to Newfoundland.

Aboard U.S. Coast Guard cutter *Erie,* patrolling at weather station Bumblebee eight hundred miles due west of Ireland, Chief Weather Observer Chuck Lane had been eagerly following the radio reports on Hurricane Alice for several days. It had looked fairly certain that Alice, groggy perhaps but still packing plenty of punch, would be reaching Bumblebee.

The big smooth swells racing out ahead of the storm came first, and for ten hours the *Erie* rolled violently in a sea that continued to grow rougher while the air remained calm. Then the barometer began dropping and Alice's first gusty winds began whining intermittently through the weather ship's maze of radar and radio antennas. The gusts became stronger, then merged into a steady gale. It was a dark, hot mid-afternoon when this happened and Lane left his weather shack at the *Erie*'s stern and went forward to the bridge, pulling himself cautiously along a lifeline while knee-deep water from a boarding wave churned around his rubber boots.

Commander Gunn stood beside the helmsman. He turned when Lane stepped in.

"Is this the worst your hurricane can do?" the captain asked.

"It might do worse. What's the wind velocity?"

"Not forty knots yet."

Lane waited on the bridge for more than an hour but the gale didn't increase. Alice, definitely, was now dying out.

But early the following morning it became apparent that Alice wasn't going to die the way an aging hurricane should die. Instead of the winds easing gradually, they stopped abruptly with a rapid drop in temperature and a rising barometer. Lane recognized what was happening. A cold front was pushing in underneath the remnants of the hurricane. Radio-sonde balloons released that morning and traced by radar verified it, for there were seventy-mile-an-hour gusts again aloft. Lane left his midday weather report at the radio room for transmission to Washington and went again to the bridge.

"Bad news," he told Commander Gunn. "Hurricane Alice is heading for heaven, but she's going to leave behind a blow that'll be worse than if she had stayed around herself."

For about an hour after leaving Barra's coastal waters the barnacle goose flew northwestward through gusty, turbulent air. Sudden up-drafts and down-drafts clutched at his wings and the barnacle knew there was threat and menace in this restless air, but the loneliness, the desire to be again with birds of his own kind drove him on. Then the rain squalls began and the air temperature suddenly dropped and there were no more gusty erratic winds but a firm, freshening gale instead that blew steadily out of the northeast.

The gale mounted quickly. In half an hour it was a wild, frantic, screaming fury, a storm unlike anything the barnacle goose had experienced before in his ten months of life. The waves became steep and jagged with boiling white tops that looked like snow; the long smooth rollers had disappeared.

The barnacle had three choices of action—to turn back toward the Hebrides, to struggle on toward Iceland, or to conserve energy by turning and flying downwind with the gale. Return to the Hebrides would mean the stark and wretched loneliness that he felt an overpowering desire to escape. Flying with the gale would mean being carried out into the Atlantic. The barnacle had never flown far in that direction, but he knew without having been there that it must be an almost limitless reach of empty sea where no coastal feeder could long survive. He knew this from long experience with waves that reached the Hebrides, because to a bird like the barnacle with senses sharply tuned to the changing rhythm of the sea every wave by its spacing, speed and contour told the story of how far it had come. Not only would there be no food in that direction, there would be no rest either, for already the sea was too rough to alight upon. He might alight briefly and endure the frothing, battering wavecrests for a short time but in the end it would prove more fatiguing than staying on the wing.

So he pressed on toward Iceland where the nonbreeding barnacle flocks would be waiting. It meant flying with the wind buffeting him fiercely on the right wing and shoulder, and despite the raging pressure of the storm he thought he was making slow headway against it. But Iceland, even in favorable flying weather, was a fifteen-hour flight away.

He had been flying about three hours when he began to fear he had made a choice he could not carry out. The gale had continued to grow in fury. Far below him now the sea was lost in a great white shroud of mist, boiling and racing before the wind, and it puzzled him because this wasn't mist-producing weather. Above was a leaden overcast through which only an eerie twilight penetrated. In the detached and nebulous world between, the goose and the gale continued their struggle. His great wings beat with dogged perseverance. Frequently a stronger gust would twist him violently, sometimes almost rolling him over before he could regain flight control. Driving sheets of rain pelted him like showers of pebbles.

Normally he could fly twenty-four hours without rest, yet now after only three hours there was an aching fatigue in the big breast muscles that powered his wings. Iceland was far beyond his reach; so now were the Hebrides behind him. His pain-racked body demanded rest, any rest no matter how brief. He stiffened his aching wings and glided down toward the surface of the sea.

The white layer of mist leaped up toward him and he leveled off just above it. Here close to the sea was a chaotic world of violent movement and sound not apparent at the level above where he had been flying. Through gaps in the mist he caught glimpses of gray mountainous waves, ragged, white-streaked, writhing and tossing as they plunged madly before the gale. Then a swirling eddy of the mist lashed up around him and he tasted the salt in it and knew immediately the puzzling mist's origin. The wind was tearing the tops off the waves. It wasn't mist, it was spray, flung up so densely into the air that it was difficult to tell where the sea ended and atmosphere began.

It left no doubt. To alight on this sea for rest, even for a moment, was impossible. The barnacle had to continue flying.

For another few minutes he struggled against the gale, fighting desperately against being carried westward out to sea. His wings and breast muscles stabbed with the pain of the tremendous exertion he was demanding from them. Then he knew it was futile and surrendered. He turned until the blast of the wind was on his tail and he flew helplessly before it, putting himself completely at its mercy.

Flight was easy now that he was no longer trying to struggle against the storm. Strength came back again to his wings, the throbbing pain of fatigue drained out of them. He could fly this way, carefully conserving energy, for another night and day if he had to, but even this would bring exhaustion in its time. He knew the sea before him was vast and empty. And he knew that another night and day would be little time to let a storm with the fury of this one abate, yet somewhere, somehow, before that time he must find an opportunity for rest if he was going to survive.

PART THREE

Kanina

CHAPTER TWELVE

RORY MACDONALD'S train rumbled noisily through the moonlit night. He was heading for the goose flocks again and he lay in his lower berth too excited to sleep. The train left farming country behind and plunged on into the forested transition zone which separates Canada's settled and industrialized south from its vast subarctic wilderness of the north. Here, instead of flat fields, there were hills of riven rock lifting like gigantic gnarled knuckles and little lakes sparkling like silver in the forested hollows between.

Finally he slept, but he was awake again as the dawn light crept like a wan and pallid vapor over the forest rushing endlessly past his coach window. Now the big southern hardwoods like oaks and maples were gone and only conifers like spruce and balsam remained. This was the ridgepole of the continent, the great divide where the country no longer slopes southward to the Great Lakes and the Mississippi but northward to Hudson Bay and the Arctic. It is here where the rivers flow north and where only spruce and balsam can survive to form the principal forest that the great subarctic begins.

Rory felt a glowing thrill of adventure. And he had yet another full day's train travel north before his journey would finally end at James Bay, the inland sea that draws its icy salt water from the Arctic Ocean itself.

He left the train at Blackwood shortly after noon and checked into a hotel. It was a small prosperous-looking city, the only urban center in a huge region of northern Ontario hinterland, but its sawmills, lumber piles and stacks of pulpwood gave it a characteristic frontier-town appearance. After lunch he telephoned the superintendent of game and fisheries. He had learned before leaving Toronto that the man's name was Alex Murray.

A man's voice came on the phone with a brisk: "Murray here."

Rory introduced himself.

"Yes siree!" Murray interrupted quickly. "I knew you were coming. I want to meet you. Give you a hand to get started. Got to go out this afternoon but I'll be back at five. See me then, eh? Anybody you meet'll tell you where my office is. And I'll phone the wife and tell her you'll be coming home with me for dinner."

At five o'clock Rory was sitting across a desk from Murray in a small, crowded, second-floor office. Alex Murray was a big man with flushed cheeks, graying hair and a bluff cordiality. He wore a neat khaki uniform.

"Call me Alex, eh?" he said. He walked to a large map of the region that hung on the wall behind his desk.

"This'll refresh your geography," he continued. "You'll get a train out of here early tomorrow morning that'll take you to Cochrane. When you get there you'll be about two hundred miles from the south end of James Bay. You'll get another train out of Cochrane that'll take you down to the bay. It goes down north two days a week and tomorrow's a train day. Here it is, see." He ran a stubby finger up the map. "And here's Moosonee, the rail terminal on the bay. That's your jumping off place. Moosonee's a sort of jumping off place for the whole eastern Arctic. Planes, mission boats . . . . they all base at Moosonee and work out from there. Now . . . . you got any plans?"

Rory shook his head.

"Well look," he went on, his voice so loud that Rory feared people on the street below would be listening, "we don't very often have a plane at Moosonee, but there's a plane there now. The ice just went out of the rivers a week or two ago so's float planes can land and we've got a wild-life management officer down there checking beaver populations and set-ting trapping quotas for the Indians for next winter. The plane'll be there about two weeks and you can fly with them. Why don't you hop up and down the coast for two weeks, have a general look. You can spot your geese from the air, then pick an area where geese are numerous and stay there for the summer to do your main work."

"They told me you'd do all you could to help," Rory said, "but I didn't expect you to toss in a plane."

"You'd like to do that, eh?" Murray boomed. "Thought you would. So I talked to our man at Moosonee on the radio this afternoon and it's all fixed. He'll meet you at the train tomorrow night. Look for a uniform like mine and that'll be him. I'll tell him to watch for a great big blond bruiser with a sunburned nose and that'll be you. He'll be meeting the train anyway. Everybody meets the train at Moosonee, a big event. Want to know what the population of Moosonee is? Count the people at the station when the train pulls in, the whole damn population'll be there."

"Where will I eat and sleep?" Rory asked.

"We have an office there with a kitchen and a few bunks in a room behind it. You better hole up with our fellows there to start with. When you get down the coast away from Moosonee there's only Hudson's Bay Company posts and Indian camps, but the post managers and their wives are always delighted to see someone with a white skin. You can board with one of them. They'll be so happy to have company they'll treat you like a king. Say, we better move along home and get something to eat. Hungry? I am."

It was a pleasant evening despite the fact that Alex Murray spent most of it talking. Murray's wife, Jean, a small, plain-looking woman, was as silent and retiring as her husband was brash. She had an excellent steak dinner waiting for them and when it was over Rory and Murray retired to the living room with a bottle of Scotch whisky.

"Rory, you're going to get a kick out of that train tomorrow," Murray told him. "The one from Cochrane to Moosonee. We call it the Polar Bear Express. Doesn't have any schedule, but it always gets you there sometime. It's supposed to leave at ten-thirty, but all that means is it'll leave sometime before noon. Handles a lot of freight, down to the pulpwood camps and so on, and usually runs two passenger coaches, one old coach up ahead and a better one, but not much better, behind. The front one's for the Indians, the back one's for whites, not officially now, because we don't have Jim Crow laws up in this country. . . ."

He poured himself another drink without pausing.

"We don't need Jim Crow laws in this country. The Indians know their place. We could teach them southerners in the States something, you know. You have to handle inferior races firmly but quietly, that's the thing, quietly. Do it quietly and then you don't have a lot of do-gooders in other parts of the country shouting at you about race discrimination. You have to have race discrimination. Our Indians now, they're good trappers, but they're lazy and stupid as hell and no good for anything else. . . ."

"Maybe they just appear lazy because they're undernourished," Rory interrupted. "And are they really stupid, Mr. Murray, or do they just need better opportunities for education?"

"I tell you they're lazy and they're stupid! And call me Alex, eh? And they're dirty and lousy, that's why you got to keep them by themselves in trains and restaurants. You'll start seeing them tomorrow when you catch the train at Cochrane. And remember, the Indians you'll see there are civilized and dressed up—wait till you see the real bush Cree at places like Cape Cree down the bay from Moosonee. Down there they're cut off from white influence and they're another hundred years behind the Indians you see out along the railway. Not much better than animals. . . .

"Oh, you get one once in a while who's got some brains," Murray continued, "but they're real exceptions. We just had a case the other day. A Cree girl, she came from one of the posts down on the bay, pretty smart, good-looking too, there were lots of pictures of her in the papers. She went to teachers college here in Blackwood, got her teaching permit and got a job in a country school near Cochrane when the regular teacher got sick and had to quit. Well, the school trustees should have known better. The parents didn't want an Indian teaching their kids and I don't blame them. They had to make an issue of it and have her fired and then the papers found out and started to raise hell about race prejudice and all that. That's what I mean about keeping them in their place and doing it quietly. There shouldn't have been all the trouble. The trustees should have left the school closed in the first place instead of hiring an Indian. I hear the Indian girl's going back down to Cape Cree on the bay to live with her own people again. That's where she belongs. If they want to come out and get an education to go back and work with their own people, that's fine, we should encourage it. But nobody wants Indian teachers teaching *our* kids."

Alex Murray stopped and took a long drink.

"How long are you going to stay down there?" he asked, quickly changing the subject.

"Probably until September."

"Well, when the Indian squaws start looking pretty enough to sleep with, brother, it's time to head back for civilization because when that happens you're going off your rocker." Murray laughed heartily. "But that teacher, she was a good looker. Not bad at all. You'll probably get to Cape Cree. You might get a look at her."

"Do you remember her name?"

"Jean!" Murray shouted. "What was the name of that Indian teacher?"

His wife came to the living room door, a dishcloth in her hand. "Her name?" she said. "I've forgotten. But I think it was very unjust, firing her."

"There you are, see!" Murray exclaimed loudly to Rory, dramatically gesturing toward his wife with one arm. "The papers even got her aroused. See what I mean about doing it quietly?" Then he turned to his wife. "My dear," he went on, "we just *can't* have Indians teaching our kids. Now can't you remember her name?"

"It was a beautiful name," she said softly, "and she was a beautiful girl." She paused, her head bent forward. "I think I remember. It was Kanina . . . . Kanina Beaverskin."

CHAPTER THIRTEEN

THE U.S. Coast Guard cutter *Erie* hung poised on the crest of a wave, trembled for a moment like a living creature, and then plunged into the trough. In his bunk, Chief Weather Observer Chuck Lane clutched the sideboard and braced himself for the impact of the next sea. The *Erie*'s bow hit with a rumbling boom. The ship shuddered and Lane could hear tons of water thundering back along the deck over his head. He waited, unable to breathe, as he had waited hundreds of times during that interminable, sleepless night. "Lift, my God, girl, lift!" One of these times, he thought, she was going to hit the bottom of a sea like that and keep right on going down. She lifted sluggishly, as though it were a tremendous effort, climbed slowly to the next crest, and began the terrifying process all over again.

The storm had been raging now for a day and a night. It had been daylight for two hours, a gray, drab, oppressive daylight, and Lane lay in his bunk wondering if there was any point in getting up. It would be impossible to cross the deck and reach the weather shack on the stern, so there wasn't much work he could do. While he contemplated this, the violent pitching of the *Erie* changed. The thundering of the seas against her bow softened and then stopped, and she began to roll viciously in the troughs. The ship came around slowly and resumed pitching but it was a different pitching for now the seas were striking her from astern. They had been heading into the gale but now they were moving downwind with the gale astern.

Lane jumped out of his bunk and began to dress, clinging to a stanchion with one hand to keep his balance. Something strange was going on. He went out into the companionway and started up toward the bridge. To reach the bridge he had to step outside briefly and it gave him an opportunity for a quick look around. Flying spray filled the air and the great gray waves faded into a nothingness of mist a few ship-lengths away on all sides. For a fleeting second before another wave hit he stared dumbfounded at the bizarre apparition crouching on the deck in the lee of the funnel, and then he was inside, slamming the door behind him against the shower of spray.

Commander Gunn spoke to Lane as soon as the weatherman was inside.

"I was going to notify you, Mr. Lane," he said. "We are leaving station. There's a Norwegian over here having a nasty time of it, lost his rudder. About three hundred miles from our present position."

Lane nodded. And then suddenly his startled senses began to function and he realized what that apparition beside the funnel was.

"We have a stowaway aboard, sir," he said. "A goose. That's right, by God, a goose! Strangest looking goose I ever saw. He's got a big white face."

It wasn't an island because it was free-moving and it pitched and drifted with the sea. It wasn't an iceberg or an ice floe either, although it was more like one of these. Whatever it was, it terrified the barnacle goose and he wanted to leave it, but his wings were limp with exhaustion and he knew he couldn't leave it, he knew it represented his only chance to survive.

He had found it in the darkness and he knew it was there long before its lights appeared through the blinding spray in front of him. He was passing downwind of it when his wings detected the faint turbulence that indicated an obstruction altering the air-flow somewhere upwind. He turned then into the wind, hovering painfully on wings that were numb with the strain and fatigue of long hours of flying. He felt for it again, all his senses concentrated on this one delicate task, and once more he detected it, a slightly different surge of turbulence amid the chaos of the gale.

He struggled upwind, bucking the full force of it with wings that had little reserve of stamina left. The wind speed now was greater than the flight speed that the barnacle was capable of, but he found he could still make slow progress into the gale by utilizing the broad deep troughs between the seas into which the wind didn't reach. He flew low, only a few feet above the water, sprinting forward when he was in the quiet of the troughs, lifting as quickly as possible over each wind-torn wavecrest and then dropping into the sheltered trough again beyond.

The turbulence he was tracing came and went. He lost it each time he dropped into a trough and usually picked it up again when he lifted into the wind zone to clear a crest. At each return it was slightly stronger than before. Then he could hear it, a screeching whine very different from the roar of wind and waves alone. Yet there was nothing visible but the same white misty wall of driving spray.

When the strange lights appeared and he saw that it was unlike any rock or island he had ever seen before, the barnacle hesitated. But the struggle against the wind had sapped the last dregs of strength from wings now almost paralyzed by exhaustion. With one final desperate effort he fought the blast of the gale for a few moments longer, then he dropped, utterly helpless to do anything else. He landed on a surface that was strangely cold and unyielding, like smooth ice but not that cold, a little like rock but slick and flat in a way that rock could never be.

Its strangeness terrified him, but there was luxurious relief simply in letting his wings droop lifelessly and relaxed at his aching sides. But rest was brief. Whatever it was he had found, it lurched and rolled wildly and the seas were breaking over it constantly. He had been on it only a few seconds when a roaring wall of white water raced down toward him and he had to take wing again to get out of its path. As soon as he was in the air the gale swept him away so rapidly that the strange floating island was almost lost in the white mists before the barnacle could turn and start struggling back. Again the pain of fatigue clutched at his breast muscles; again he reached it and alighted as the last of his strength melted away.

It happened repeatedly during the rest of that dark wild night. Each time the barnacle goose settled on the ship he could snatch only a few moments of rest before another wave would hurtle him into the air again.

The darkness changed to a gray pallor as dawn crept down through the writhing blanket of spray which obscured the sea. Then the barnacle discovered the protected lee of the funnel where the wind and water couldn't reach him and where at last his exhausted wings found genuine rest. It was here, about two hours later, that Chief Weather Observer Chuck Lane saw him.

The gale blew with little relaxation that day and the following night. As the pain of the barnacle's exhaustion eased, gnawing pangs of hunger replaced it, so that in effect the pain merely moved from one part of his harassed body to another. On the next day the wind dropped gradually, the white spray left the sea and the horizon appeared under a dark low overcast sky. The ship continued to toss violently but the waves lost some of their steepness and by afternoon few of them were coming aboard. Now the ship came to life; men appeared and began moving busily about the decks.

The barnacle goose had never seen men closely before. Instinctively he feared and distrusted them. He flew to a platform high up on one of the masts and clung there precariously, frightened by the shouting men below and by the wild erratic arcs that the mast was tracing against the sky.

The day wore tediously on, the pain of his hunger eased and in its place came a wearying weakness. As normal visibility returned, other birds began to appear around the ship. They were big long-winged fulmars and shearwaters, birds for whom the gale would have posed no threat, for they were birds fitted admirably to spend their lives on the open sea far from the protective lees of the land. They gleaned their food from the masses of minute marine life that made up the plankton pastures of the sea's surface waters. They flew effortlessly, gliding on rigid wings, using the deflected up-drafts on the wave slopes instead of their own muscles to keep themselves airborne, and when the sea was too rough to alight upon they could even doze on the wing, flying for days without stop and without real sleep.

The barnacle watched them and he knew that compared with them he was a bird of the sea in only a clumsy inept way. He was a strong flier and a fast flier, but he was dependent on energy-consuming powered flight and totally incapable of their effortless gliding. And to feed he needed the shallow tideflats where the eelgrass grew or the grassy pastures at the edge of the sea. He was a bird of the sea, yet tied inexorably to the land. And where land lay now he had no idea. Meanwhile the effect of three strenuous days without food was beginning its assault on the barnacle's big body.

But that evening of the third day of the storm the barnacle ate again. He had watched two men carry the container to the rail and empty its contents into the sea and had paid them little heed until he saw the fulmars and shearwaters swooping down on the refuse which floated astern, and then he knew it must be food. The barnacle left his swaying perch near the top of the mast and pitched fearlessly into the quarreling knot of sea birds, lunging out at them, beating them with blows of his big wings, driving them away, and he ate greedily. He did not know what he was eating. He knew only that it was vegetable food of some sort that filled the gnawing void within him, yet it was strange, alien, unsatisfying food and he did not like it.

Like many species of sea birds, the barnacle had now learned that the strange moving islands that floated across the sea with men aboard periodically spewed food behind them. It was a lesson that would strangely influence the barnacle's life. And since all living things are linked by the invisible threads of a natural world that knows no boundaries except the boundaries of life itself, this isolated and trivial event in mid-Atlantic would inevitably influence other lives too. One of them would be the life of a boy speeding northward that night on a Canadian train two thousand miles away. Another life it would touch with searing effect would be that of a girl whom the boy had not yet met. For no life is an island "intire of itselfe," the great Donne said. No life can change without changing other lives with it.

The sea was smoothing out and the barnacle did not return to the ship. But he could not bring himself to leave the ship entirely for it was the only familiar landmark now in a world that was foreign and strange, so he stayed close astern that night, flying periodically after the ship's retreating lights as it sailed steadily westward. With dawn came the urge again to seek the summering grounds where there would be companions of his own species. But his normally acute skill for orientation, with its keen sense of time, direction and space had been hopelessly muddled by the storm. Now he was bewildered and lost. The urge to fly was strong, but he had no knowledge of where to go.

He began watching the other sea birds for clues to the direction of the nearest land. He knew he was still far at sea, still outside the hundred-fathom line of the continental shelf, for over the shelf ocean species like fulmars and shearwaters disappear and land-based species like the gannets and gulls take their place. The absence of continental-shelf birds told him he was at least five or six hours of flight from land, and he had no idea how much farther.

He also knew that any fulmars and shearwaters here at sea at this time would be nonbreeders, and having no ties with the land their movements could tell him nothing. But shortly after dawn smaller black white-rumped sea birds began to appear. These were the petrels and the goose knew that many of them would have nests and eggs somewhere ashore. He was familiar with the nesting ways of the petrels because their nesting had begun in the Hebrides before he left. They nested in burrows in the turf and one bird would remain several days on the nest eating nothing while its mate foraged for food hundreds of miles away on the open sea. Every four or five days the bird at sea would return to the nest, fat and well fed, and take over the nesting duties so that its starving mate could go to sea and feed.

Many of the petrels were nonbreeders too, but it was easy to recognize them for they flew aimlessly, constantly circling and wheeling, obviously with nowhere to go. The breeders, dispersed by the storm and heading back now for land, stood out because they flew fast and direct, holding to one course. And the course they flew was west, away from the pink and red mosaic of the rising sun.

The barnacle watched them for an hour until he was certain of it, then he took off and flew westward too. The island that had moved on the sea and given him his chance for survival disappeared slowly beneath the red-flecked horizon behind him.

The goose flew steadily without rest until late in the day. Then hunger again began sapping his energy and he began dropping periodically onto the sea for rest, letting the energy build up anew in his weary wing muscles before he could push on. He continued to fly at intervals during the night, holding his westward course first by the lingering afterglow of the sunset and then, when that was gone, by faint streaks of aurora borealis on the northern horizon. Dawn came, bathing the sea in a shimmering sheen of red, and the barnacle saw that he was still over open oceanic waters, still outside the continental shelf, still perhaps a day's flight from land. And his fatigue and his hunger were a torturing pain, no longer confined to his wing and breast muscles but stabbing through his whole body.

Now he was spending as much time resting as he spent flying, but late that morning he began to detect the changes he had been seeking. First he noticed a minute decrease in the seawater's saltiness, the effect of melting coastal ice and inflow from fresh-water rivers. The water turned slightly greener, indicating an increase in microscopic plankton animals. He must be passing over the continental shelf, and he became sure of it within another hour when he ceased to encounter fulmars and shearwaters and began encountering gulls instead. Then he could see the "ice-blink," the thin yellow haze hugging the horizon ahead, caused by the reflection of sunlight from ice fields beyond his vision. All these were signs of coastal waters. The landfall could still be two hundred miles away—five hours of flying, but in these promises of approaching land the barnacle goose found a revival of strength and he flew on strongly now.

He began passing over small slushy pancakes of floating ice that clicked and swished as they rose and fell on the swells. The ice thickened gradually until it was a solid jagged mat of white that hid the sea. It was old sea ice that had floated down on the Arctic's currents. Repeated freezing and thawing would have flushed the salt out of the ice, and the barnacle knew that melt-water puddles on its surface would be fresh water. After five days with only salt water to drink, the barnacle craved fresh water. He landed at the first shimmering sheet of surface water and drank hastily. The cool, cleansing freshness of it soothed his parched and salty throat. He flew on, refreshed and eager and hopeful.

But landfall, when it came in the dusk of that evening, was singularly lacking in hope and promise. He had left a Hebrides five days before that was green and luxuriant with burgeoning spring. Now he had reached a shore that was barren and lifeless, a low rocky shore still blanketed with snow through which stunted spindly bushes protruded like grotesque

ghosts of another time when life had been possible. There were no swaying beds of eelgrass here, no rich *machair* grazing grounds, not a trace of
green growth of any kind. There were only small knobby buds on the
bushes that reached above the snow and the barnacle ate them greedily.
They filled his stomach, but in a deficient, unsatisfying way that left the
hunger still there.

There were no nesting birds yet on this bleak and wintry coast. During
darkness he had apparently veered northward from the westerly course
that the petrels were flying. Now he was probably several hundred miles
north of the petrel breeding grounds that had been his original goal.

When darkness came again he flew back out to sea and settled for the
night on the ice because there was no open water. Now the loneliness
pressed in on him again, a loneliness accentuated by the alien hostility of
the land to which he had come. And then he recognized that it was a
different loneliness from what he had felt before, a loneliness not just for
others of his own kind but for a particular one who must be waiting
somewhere to join him and be his mate. Because, while his body had
wasted and weakened during the long struggle against the Atlantic, the
mating drive had continued to mount and grow within him. In the
Hebrides it had been weak, its onset delayed. Now it was a rabid passion,
filling him, demanding fulfillment.

CHAPTER FOURTEEN

RORY left Blackwood early on the morning following his evening
with Alex Murray and he reached Cochrane about 10 A.M. The Blackwood train went on and Rory looked for the train that would take him
to Moosonee. Two faded wooden passenger coaches stood on a track
beside the station platform, but there was no other promise of a train.
Both coaches were old, their paint peeling, the front one noticeably older
than the other.

The little platform was crowded with people, about half whites and half
Indians. The crowd was divided sharply into two groups, Indians at
one end, whites at the other. The whites were mostly bush workers and
prospectors wearing big leather boots, plaid jackets and jeans tucked into
their boot tops.

The Indians at their end were silent or conversing in low voices. They were much more shabbily dressed than the whites, many of them wearing soiled hand-me-down fedoras and rubber boots instead of costlier leather ones. The Indian women, practically every one, wore bright bandannas around their heads, the only color in an otherwise drab and shabby crowd.

At ten-thirty, the scheduled time for departure, there were still only the two coaches in sight, but the people on the platform began trickling hopefully onto the cars. Then a small Diesel locomotive that looked inappropriately modern for the rest of the train appeared and began busily rumbling around the yard. Periodically it sorted out a boxcar or an empty flatcar and attached it to the passenger coaches. The first car to join the growing train was a baggage coach. Rory waited to see his luggage safely loaded, then picked up the overnight bag he was carrying and climbed onto the rear coach.

The front third of the car was partitioned off as a restaurant section with a long counter and stools, and the seating section behind it was already filling with passengers. The seats were hard with leather upholstery and wooden arms, and the floor was gouged by many years of conflict with lumbermen's hobnailed boots. Ancient gaslights with frosted globes hung from the ceiling.

Rory sat in an empty seat. From time to time the coach jolted violently as the growling Diesel added another boxcar ahead. Then he dozed. Some time later he was awakened by a tremendous jolt that almost shook the gaslights from the ceiling. The Polar Bear Express was under way. He looked at his watch; they were one hour and twenty minutes late.

An hour later Rory decided to have a look at the passenger coach ahead. He walked up past the lunch counter and stopped a pace or two inside the other car. His own car had only whites in it; this one had mainly Indians with a white lumberjack or pulpwood cutter here and there. There was quiet talk, most of it in a language Rory didn't know but that he supposed was Cree, and most of it came from the front half of the coach where the Indian men were gathered. The Indian women were crowded to the rear of the coach where Rory was standing. The women were silent, staring sullenly out the windows; many were very fat with round, stooped shoulders, finely wrinkled faces and unkempt hair. The younger women, even three or four who were still girls, were as unattractive as the older ones, for all of them had round, vacant, listless faces with narrow eyes and broad noses.

Several of the men were drinking beer and eating cold beans or salmon straight out of the cans with spoons. An old woman near him was placidly smoking a pipe.

Rory was standing slightly sideways and now he turned and moved his eyes back toward two seats hidden from view behind him. In the first one a young mother rocked a baby gently in her arms and crooned softly in Cree. In the other seat, the last seat of the coach, a girl sat alone. Her head was bent forward and he couldn't see much of her face because her black hair had fallen loosely around it. It was very long hair, held primly in place over her ears with silver barrettes but hanging freely around her cheeks and reaching well below her shoulders behind. It had a soft luster, the ends were modestly curled, and it looked attractive in a natural, carefree way that showed no evidence of fussing. Her skin was very brown, browner than that of many of the other Indian women, but it was smoother too, and fine textured. Instead of a drab, formless sweater-coat, as all the others seemed to be wearing, she wore a snug blue high-necked pullover. Rory couldn't see a book in her lap but he knew by the quick movement of her eyes that she was reading.

For a moment he was startled. She was an Indian like the others, yet strikingly different; she seemed more Indian-like in some respects—the very brown skin and the coal-black hair—yet she was extremely attractive.

The seat across the aisle from her was empty and Rory stepped back and sat down in it. She didn't lift her eyes from the book. Now he saw her in profile and began to wonder if she was as attractive as he had first thought. Perhaps the way she contrasted with the other women in the coach had misled him. Then she turned and looked squarely at him for two or three seconds. Her hair fell loosely back into place as she lifted her head. Her eyes were large, their darkness and the long black lashes accentuated by big areas of white. The oriental slant was hardly detectable, but her eyes did narrow sharply and lifted a little at the outside corners. And now, after seeing her eyes and her full face, Rory had no doubt. She *was* beautiful, and very much so.

It was an exotic, nonconforming beauty, the type that results when racial features normally regarded as unattractive by other races are somehow balanced and modified so that they combine into an individualistic pattern of beauty unique and all its own. She obviously did not strive for it, the beauty was simply there in a form that neither grooming nor neglect could do much to alter.

Rory could see now that she was reading a small pocket book. It looked like a lurid drugstore love novel but he couldn't be sure because she held it on her lap so that its cover was hidden in the folds of her blue plaid skirt. She lifted her eyes from the book and gazed out the window, shifting slightly in the seat as she did so. Her movement raised the book and revealed the cover for a moment, and Rory stared, unbelieving. He had had only a glimpse, but it was enough to recognize the familiar cover design of a book he had in his own library of paperbacks. She was reading Julian Huxley's *Man in the Modern World,* a book of scientific essays, interesting and stimulating yet not easy reading.

Now he was baffled. Here, in a shabby train coach crowded with uncouth natives and smelling of unbathed bodies, sat a lone and beautiful girl, an Indian obviously like the rest, reading essays of Julian Huxley! Suddenly he was filled with a torturing curiosity. He was reminded immediately of his mother playing Mendelssohn and reading the *Spectator* in the crude little blackhouse on Barra. Would he try to talk to her? He knew that he must.

He looked at her again, hesitating. She continued reading her book. There had been a time when he could have handled a situation like this easily and surely, but he was out of practice now and the boldness and bravura of youth were gone. He seemed bereft of ideas and didn't know how to approach her. The big upper muscle of each thigh began to tremble nervously.

Then suddenly, inexplicably, he realized who she was, and wondered why he hadn't thought of it sooner. She couldn't be anyone else. This was Kanina Beaverskin, the controversial school teacher who had been fired because she was an Indian.

Waiting wasn't going to make it any easier. Rory rose impetuously, stepped across the aisle and sat beside her. She looked up quickly, startled, her shining hair trembling with the sudden movement of her head. She did not smile.

"I've never been to Moosonee before," he began, suddenly calm and confident now that he had the job started. "Is there a hotel there where I can stay?" He had a place to stay, but this seemed a natural question to ask.

"Not exactly a hotel," she replied, "but a boarding house or two." Her English was perfect with no trace of an accent. She offered no more information. For a few seconds her face remained a flat expressionless inscrutable mask, then it stiffened, frowned a little, and Rory could almost hear the words: "Okay, if that's all, go back to your own seat."

"Will there be a taxi at the station?" he asked. "I have a lot of luggage."

For an instant she smiled. The whites of her eyes, accentuated by the black lashes and dark skin, flashed momentarily. "There are no taxis at Moosonee," she said patiently. "There are no cars. Just a pickup truck or two shipped in by train." Her face hardened again and she said nothing more. She stared at him briefly, then bent her head and resumed reading.

Rory wasn't accustomed to having a girl so pointedly ignore him. He tried again.

"Huxley does a good job of popularizing science, but it's heavy reading in some places, isn't it?"

She looked up quickly. "It's heavy reading in *all* places, but it's giving me plenty to think about."

"Don't miss the last one, a biologist's interpretation of war. I think he calls it 'War as a Biological Phenomenon.' "

Now she looked him up and down carefully and coldly, making no effort to hide it. Rory squirmed. She asked him bluntly: "Who are you?"

"I'm not in Julian Huxley's class," he said, "but I *am* a biologist. My original home was Barra in the Outer Hebrides. I sailed a few years, mostly the North Atlantic, picked up some more schooling in Glasgow, then I came to the University of Toronto and I'm in honor biology. Right now I'm heading for James Bay where I'll be doing research for the federal government on Canada geese. My name is Rory Macdonald. Now, who are you?"

He thought her face brightened imperceptibly and for a moment two very attractive dimples flashed in the brown skin at her mouth corners. Then the cold impassive mask returned.

"I'm worse than nobody," she replied. "I'm a teacher. But some of your people decided it was better to close my school and have nobody in it than leave me there."

"I know," Rory said quietly, "and I'm sorry."

"You know?"

"I've guessed. You are Kanina Beaverskin?"

"That's right. I'm famous . . . . notorious, aren't I? But do I look poisonous?"

"You look as if you could be Miss Canada or Miss America," he said. "I don't blame you for being bitter. But I hope you don't think your experience typifies the attitude of all whites to the Indian."

"It's a lot more typical than you probably think."

"What are you going to do now?" he asked her.

"I'm going back."

Rory waited for her to enlarge on her reply, but she remained silent.

"Going back where? And what are you going to do?"

"Going back home, to Cape Cree. And I don't know what I'll do, except become a respectable Cree again. I might set up a little school

and teach the children. There's no government school there and few of
them even learn to read English."

Rory nodded. "I'm sure you'll be able to do a lot to help change and
improve your people."

She looked at him sharply. "Their way of life needs improving . . . .
urgently," she said, "if you mean things like diet and health services. But
if you mean change to your way of life, they would only suffer and
lose. They are a proud people, with a culture and traditions that are as
old as anything your people have. I'm not sure they *should* change. . . ."

Rory studied her carefully. She was opening up now. She talked softly,
but quickly and jerkily.

"I made that mistake," she went on. "I tried to change. I tried to cross
to your side. And now look—I'm going back. Your people are driving
me back."

"Don't you want to go back?"

She stared out the window and didn't answer.

"You *don't* want to go back, do you?" he repeated.

"No, I don't want to go back, because I'm not suited for their life
now. I was brought up, mostly, in your world. Now I'm stranded between two worlds—yours and theirs, and I'll never be a real part of either.
I'm a nobody. It would be the same with them if they tried to change."

Rory was fascinated by her. She was still staring out the window, the
back of her head with its ebony hair toward him. He looked at the book,
now closed on her lap, and he was embarrassed by the questions that
kept coming to him, demanding to be asked, demanding answers.

"How were you brought up? How does a Cree girl from a trapping
camp on James Bay wind up reading essays by Julian Huxley on eugenics
and Darwinism and . . . . ?"

"It's all behind me, and I'm going to forget it. Talking about it won't
help me forget." The softness had gone from her voice and now it was
crisp and hard.

"Aren't you afraid you'll be lonely when you get cut off in the bush
with a people who probably just read comic books?"

"They don't read comic books. They *can't* read. And I've been lonely
all my life anyway."

Rory shrugged and smiled. She was facing him again now, but she
didn't smile in return. "Okay," he said. "Let's go back and have something to eat. Will you let me buy your lunch?"

"No thanks. I'm not hungry."

"It's two hours past lunch time, you know."

"No! I don't wish to!" She said it loudly and there was a sharp, almost hysterical note in her voice. Her eyes narrowed and flashed angrily, then she opened her book and began to read again. And Rory knew that was the signal for the end.

"I am sorry . . . . Miss Beaverskin," he said. He rose slowly. "Perhaps we'll meet again."

She glanced up briefly, nodded and said: "Perhaps." Rory hoped she would smile. But she didn't.

He walked back to the restaurant section and ordered a glass of milk and a fried-egg sandwich. Was it such a social *faux pas* in this country to invite a girl to lunch? She couldn't have been much angrier if he had invited her to sleep with him when they reached Moosonee tonight. He doubted if all her bitterness was justified. And he doubted if he had ever met anyone he wanted to know more about.

The train lurched along, across flat muskeg country now, because they were traveling over the coastal plain that slopes down imperceptibly to James Bay. This was the beginning of the vast sodden muskeg that stretches across a hundred thousand square miles of northern Ontario, and it was the reason for Rory's coming, because its tremendous network of lakes and moss-filled bogs provides a nesting territory for unknown thousands of the big Canada geese. It is so flat that surface water drains away slowly and large tracts are so saturated with stagnant acid water that trees cannot grow. There was still spruce forest wherever the ground lifted a little to give the soil drainage, but across vast tracts of low-lying ground there were only scattered clumps of stunted tamarack with twisting swathes of spongy sphagnum bog between them.

The day was warm, but here, as the train rolled northward, spring and winter were still in conflict for possession of the awakening land. The bogs were showing only the first faint tracings of green. The ice was gone from the rivers, but in the lakes and ponds where there was no current to break it up, the ice remained, gray and cracked but still stubbornly defying the springtime sun.

Rory ate his sandwich and went back to his seat. He wouldn't rush the matter now, but when they reached Moosonee he would join Kanina Beaverskin again and help carry her luggage wherever she was going.

CHAPTER FIFTEEN

KANINA BEAVERSKIN stared at the book on her lap but she couldn't see the words. She was hungry, but she couldn't go back for a sandwich now after telling the young biologist that she didn't want to eat. She didn't want to meet him again. He had asked too many questions and she had told him too much.

It had been a heartbreaking decision, this decision to go back to James Bay and seek a new life there. It had come hard and painfully. And now there could be no turning back, the road she must follow lay clearly ahead, but this biologist Rory Macdonald—too handsome, too logical and comprehending—had suddenly loomed as an unanticipated roadblock. His story, she judged from the little he had told her, seemed uncomfortably similar to her own—the story of a mind denied development by an intellectually sterile environment and its struggle to escape. But in the one fact that really mattered their stories were glaringly opposite, for Rory Macdonald had won his struggle and she had failed.

Most of all she feared meeting him this summer at Cape Cree, for they would be difficult and trying months while she adapted again to the primitive life of her people. And Rory Macdonald would contrast too sharply with the men of her own race at Cape Cree where a man's worth was measured solely by the number of beaver he could trap each winter. He would be too eloquent an emissary of the world she must now forget.

She looked again at the book on her lap. If she was retreating from that world, why was she bothering herself with its problems by reading this? She didn't know why. Her mind was split and confused. She tossed the book impulsively to the empty seat across from her. There, she thought, that was the final gesture, from now on she would be a *Mooskek-owak*, a Swampy Cree, and nothing more. It meant "The Ones of the Muskeg," and she hadn't thought of herself as a *Mooskek-owak* for a long time.

Kanina Beaverskin had come full circle and she was back now to where it all had started seventeen years ago. She had come out on this same train and though only four then, Kanina could remember it all in frightening detail. There was the kind woman with the white cap, white dress and white skin who talked in words that Kanina couldn't understand. There was *Payuksis,* her little dirty-brown teddy bear with only one arm. And there was the frail frightened Cree girl crouching in terror under her blanket on the train seat and coughing blood from a wizened chest that stabbed with pain. After seventeen years the little girl whose lungs were riddled by tuberculosis seemed a total stranger; Kanina found it hard to believe now that that girl had been herself.

She had only two memories that went back beyond the train trip. The first one was of the gathering in the little church at Cape Cree when the missionary distributed toys which he said had been sent by white children because they loved their little *Mooskek-owak* brothers. Kanina was under four then, but she remembered the missionary, tall, slender and white-haired, standing at the front of the church calling the children forward one by one and giving each a toy that he took from the big wooden box beside him. Kanina was one of the last to be called and for a long time she feared she was going to be forgotten. When finally her name *was* called, there were only a few toys left. She went tremblingly up the aisle. The missionary stooped and seemed to spend a long time fishing around in the toy box, but finally he straightened up and handed Kanina the teddy bear. She clutched it tightly to her breast and felt a thrilling excitement, for it was the first toy she had ever had.

White children must be very kind, she thought, to send their toys to the *Mooskek-owak* children. She didn't notice for a long time that her teddy bear was soiled, that its white stuffing protruded through many tears, that it had only one arm. When she did get around to noticing these things she didn't care, for she loved it by then as she loved her mother. She named it *Payukmispitoonsis,* which was Cree for "Little One-Arm," then quickly abbreviated it to *Payuksis,* or "The Little One."

Kanina could remember faintly that she had the painful cough even then.

Her next recollection was of the white boat that brought the doctor and the nurse to Cape Cree on a chilly July morning when Kanina was four.

"Boat coming!" The cry went up when the boat was only a silver speck on the horizon and the children raced excitedly along the shore to meet it. Kanina ran too, despite the biting pain that the exertion produced in her chest. It came closer, chugged up through the mouth of the Kistawanee River and moored at the Cape Cree wharf while the entire Indian population of around four hundred crowded silently and curiously on the shore. The missionary, his long black cassock whipping in the wind, went on board, then reappeared at the little cabin door a few minutes later with the doctor and the nurse beside him. He began speaking to the Indians in Cree.

The government, he told them, had sent the doctor and the nurse to examine them all and make the sick ones better. Many of them with the cough and the chest pains had a very bad sickness, he said, a white man's sickness against which the *Mooskek-owak* had no resistance, because their bodies were not accustomed to the white man's diseases. Already the sickness had killed many, and the white doctor and nurse had come so that no more of them would die. Some who had the sickness badly and were coughing blood would have to go out to a government hospital far to the south because there were stronger medicines there. When the sickness was gone the government would bring them back to their families again.

The missionary turned and spoke briefly to the doctor, then he resumed again in Cree: "The doctor will be putting up a hospital tent and he will begin examining you there this afternoon. The doctor wants to see the sickest children first—the children who have blood when they cough."

Kanina's parents took her back to the tattered tent of canvas and moosehide that was their home. She had no brothers or sisters, but it was many years later before she learned the reason—that nine out of ten Cree babies were dying of malnutrition or the coughing sickness. She didn't know then that she was her mother's sixth child, that at the age of four she had survived longer than any of the others.

Kanina was one of the first to be examined. She went timidly into the doctor's tent, clinging tightly to her mother's hand and trying desperately to hide herself behind folds of her mother's big black skirt. The doctor spent only a few minutes examining her, then he spoke briefly to the missionary.

"The doctor says Kanina must go to the hospital," the missionary told her mother. "If she goes immediately she will get well again and return. If she waits it will be too late. She will go on the plane that is coming tomorrow."

The next day Kanina cowered in a rear corner of her tent home as the shout went up outside: "Airplane coming!" She heard the other children running, heard the plane as it landed on the river opposite the wharf, and she clung frantically to *Payuksis,* her only possession except the clothes she wore. Then there was a solemn and silent procession to the plane, her father carrying her because the doctor wouldn't let her walk. The nurse with the white dress was waiting at the wharf where the plane was moored, and three of Kanina's playmates who were to go out to the hospital too were already in the plane's cabin. Her mother's eyes were dry but when she kissed Kanina's cheek Kanina could feel the trembling in her lips. Her father lifted her into the plane and the nurse came in behind her and closed the door.

The plane's engine roared and through the window she could see the green water streaking past beneath them. She cried and the crying started another painful spasm of coughing. The nurse held her hand and it was comforting, and Kanina knew she was going to like this woman who always wore a white dress. She looked out the window again and now the spruce trees were little pointed cones below. She held *Payuksis* tightly against her. He was all that she had now.

They landed at Moosonee and there was a truck waiting at the dock to take them to the train. Kanina knew it was a truck because she had seen toys like it in the missionary's big box and he had told the Cape Cree children what trucks, cars and trains were and how they worked. The truck made two trips to the station and Kanina, wrapped in a blanket, went on the first trip. She was surprised at the size of the train coaches that sat in front of the station. Each coach was almost as big as the Hudson's Bay Company store at Cape Cree where her father and the other Indian men traded their furs. She wondered how the engine at the front could ever make them move.

At the station there was an Indian who spoke to them in Cree. He told them that white people when they wished to urinate or have a bowel movement didn't go back into the woods but had a special room for the purpose, and the nurse was going to take them to that room in the station now. She took Kanina first and closed the door behind them. Kanina had a terrifying sensation of imprisonment because the room was so small, but she forgot it immediately when the nurse turned on a tap and the water gushed out. Kanina tried it and the water gushed out for her too. Then the nurse pointed to the big white bowl on the floor with water in it and Kanina understood. The nurse showed her how to tear off a piece of paper and clean herself afterward, then she flushed the toilet and the water roared through like the rapids on a river and Kanina was sure that the nurse had done something wrong and broken it. They washed their hands and went out, then the nurse took another child in. It couldn't have been broken after all.

Kanina thought how strange the white people were. It would be nice, she thought, to have a place like that in winter when the snow was deep or in the spring when you had to hurry to keep the mosquitoes from swarming onto your uncovered legs. But why use it now in summer when it was so warm and there were few mosquitoes?

She remembered her first white people's meal. It was on the train and

they sat at a white table and most of the foods were strange and dis-
tasteful, for in the past she had eaten only bannock, the unleavened
Indian substitute for bread, and fish, meat, berries and tea. The table was
covered with a bewildering array of curious things. She recognized the
knives immediately, although they were very shiny, rounded and blunt.
Her mother had a big fork for lifting meat out of the stew pot but
Kanina had never seen small forks like these or spoons before. The nurse
cut her meat into little pieces and made her understand that she must
put the food in her mouth with the fork. It was hard to do and the fork
struck her teeth and gave her cold chills. When the nurse wasn't looking
Kanina took a handful of the meat and pushed it quickly into her mouth
with her fingers, then after that she ate nothing more.

Kanina traveled on a train for a long time and she remembered sleeping one night on a coach that had beds instead of seats. She passed
through towns where the buildings were as tall as many spruce trees end
on end and the cars and trucks more numerous than canoes at Cape Cree.
When she reached the sanatorium there were many more nurses and they
gave her the first bath she had ever had. The big white tub was terrifying
until she discovered the water in it was warm and soothing, and then
she liked it. They dressed her in a long white gown, led her to another
room and lifted her into a bed. It was a soft bed with white sheets and a
big pillow for her head. It thrilled her because she had never had a bed
of her own before, she had always slept between two rabbitskin robes on
balsam boughs on the tent floor. She lay *Payuksis* beside her and pulled
the sheet and blanket up carefully around his neck, then she looked
stealthily around her. The room had big windows and there were two
other beds with Indian children in them.

The sanatorium days passed quickly. She learned to like the salads and
vegetables and the other strange hospital foods. But there were times when
she tossed in an anguish of homesickness for her mother and father and
the ragged tent snapping in the wind at Cape Cree. Sometimes at night
when she lay on the brink of sleep she thought she was back there and
thought she could hear the whipping of the canvas over her head, but
then she would come fully awake and realize the snapping sound was
only the wind blowing through the venetian blinds on the big sanatorium
windows.

The weeks became months. Kanina's homesickness for Cape Cree
diminished and in time she came to think of the "san" as her home. The
separation from her parents was complete for they could not read or
write and Kanina received no letters. She thought of them less and less

and began having difficulty recalling what they looked like. Eventually she found it impossible to picture them in her mind.

The coughing stopped and the pains left her chest. A librarian came each day to read to her and to the other children in the room; Kanina picked up English quickly and was soon understanding everything read to her. She grew impatient with waiting for the librarian to come and longed to be able to read the books herself. And then a teacher began coming in each morning to give her school lessons. Kanina soon learned to read and write.

Sometime near the end of that first year she was able to leave her bed, but a vestige of the tuberculosis infection persisted in one lung and she had to remain at the hospital. The seasons slipped by, the vivid greens of summer and the whites and grays of winter came and went and came again, and Kanina stayed on at the san, no longer sick yet still not well enough to leave.

She loved reading and frequently helped in the sanatorium library. She grew rapidly, her thin body filled out, her face rounded and sometimes a nurse would take time to braid her long black hair and tell her that she was growing into a very pretty girl.

At first there had been many Cree patients but the number dwindled gradually until eventually Kanina was the last one. The nurses told her that the government had built other hospitals closer to James Bay, and the Crees were being treated there. Kanina had no opportunity now to use her native Cree language. Slowly she forgot it. Even little *Payuksis,* worn and tattered now but still devotedly loved, had his name Anglicized to "Little One-Arm," and sometimes Kanina had to think hard before she could remember what his Cree name had been.

Her tenth birthday came. She had been in the sanatorium for six years and was starting fifth-grade school work. Her education, habits, tastes, attitudes and outlook were those of a white child. Only her skin remained different.

Early in that sixth sanatorium spring, a week or so after one of her periodic X-rays, Kanina was called in to the doctor's office.

"We have good news for you," he said, smiling. "The last small scar has disappeared from that one bad lung and it's safe now for you to go home. We've been in touch with your parents. They have been inland trapping all winter, but according to word we have, they are out now at Cape Cree for the summer. The ice hasn't broken up yet and planes with ski landing gear are still getting in."

Kanina stared at the floor. She wouldn't recognize her parents or be able to speak to them in their language. She thought of the sanatorium library, her schoolwork here, and the soft bed that was always so clean. She had only vague memories of Cape Cree, but she knew there would be none of those things there.

"A nurse will be here in three or four days to take you north on the train," the doctor was saying. "Will you be glad to get back home?"

Kanina continued staring at the floor and did not answer.

CHAPTER SIXTEEN

THE plane's engine had been droning thunderously in her ears for a long time. There were five others on the plane, two of them Indians, two of them crew, and the fifth a Royal Canadian Mounted Police constable. Somewhere, far behind now, was Moosonee where the nurse had placed Kanina on the plane and left her to make the last leg of her trip alone. And somewhere ahead, it couldn't be far now, was Cape Cree. Kanina gazed at the shoreline of James Bay twisting erratically below them. It was April, and in the south, where the sanatorium was, spring had arrived; but here the land was still white and rigid with winter.

Suddenly the engine's roar softened and the plane tilted, throwing Kanina against the side of the cabin. Below them a broad river, its ice unbroken and still bearing a white cloak of snow, twisted with looping bends through the forest and muskeg and emptied into the ice-locked bay. The southern shore of the river's mouth formed a rounded cape that protruded like a swollen lower lip into James Bay and in a ragged clearing about a mile upstream Kanina could see a cluster of tents and buildings.

Inland beyond the clearing as far as she could see the country was pocked with a myriad of ponds and small lakes, their white ice outlining them sharply amid the darker strands of spruce forest. Many of the lakes were clustered so closely together that only narrow necks of land separated them.

The plane came closer to the disordered huddle of tents and buildings on the river bank. At one end were three frame buildings, gleaming white with red roofs showing through the snow, which Kanina knew would be the Hudson's Bay Company store, warehouse, and the post manager's

residence. Another red-roofed building with a small square spire Kanina
recognized as the church, and the small white cottage beside it would be
the missionary's home. There were a few other buildings, gray and nondescript, but most of the remainder were tents yellowing with age and
smudged with smoke from the black stovepipes that protruded through
every roof.

Kanina did not have to ask. She knew the river was the Kistawanee.
The vast interior lakeland through which it flowed was the ancestral
hunting territory of her people, and the settlement was Cape Cree. She
was as frightened now, coming back, as she had been on that other
faintly remembered day of six years ago when she left this same spot.

The plane came in low across the Indian encampment. She could see
the untidy heaps of firewood beside each tent, the blackened cooking
pots and water pails lying outside, the chained dogs and the dogsleds.
And one of those tents was her home.

Everyone was running to meet the plane, scurrying like ants along
paths trodden in the snow. The plane's ski landing gear dropped onto
the river ice with a crisp rumble of sound and they taxied in toward the
shore. The narrow beach and the low sand bank behind it were crowded
with Indians waving and gesturing excitedly. The pilot cut the engine
and the plane came to a stop in front of the crowd.

Someone opened the door and the passengers began climbing out. No
one paid any attention to Kanina. When all were out Kanina, clutching
"Little One-Arm" against her chest, looked timidly through the door.
The Mountie was standing below. He helped her down the ladder and
she stood on the ice silent and trembling, tears dimming her eyes. The
Mountie spoke to her in slow, faltering Cree.

"I speak only English," she said.

He switched to English. "Are you staying here?" he asked. "Or going
on with the plane?"

"This is Cape Cree, isn't it?" she asked.

He nodded.

"Then I have to stay here," she said.

A big woman with a black shawl around her head ran across the snowy
beach from the crowd of Indians. She was wearing rubber boots and
smoked a pipe. She snatched the pipe from her mouth and began talking
rapidly. Kanina heard her own name mentioned, but she understood
none of the rest of it, and she stood stiffly, bewildered and silent. When
Kanina didn't answer, the woman stopped abruptly a few paces away and
stared. She put the pipe back in her mouth.

"Is your name Kanina Beaverskin?" the Mountie asked.

"Yes."

"Well the lady says she's your mother."

He spoke to the woman then in his slow uncertain Cree. For a few seconds she didn't understand, then she looked back at Kanina and her brown furrowed face gleamed with a smile of recognition. The pipe dropped from her mouth into the snow and she leaped forward. She dropped onto her knees and hugged Kanina tightly against her, talking again very fast.

Her mother picked up the pipe she had dropped and then took Kanina in her arms and carried her up the bank. She put Kanina down, took her hand and led her toward the cluster of tents. A short stout man with a flattened nose and wide flaring nostrils walked silently beside them. Kanina wondered if he were her father, but she didn't know how to ask. A troop of children followed noisily. Kanina felt conspicuous and embarrassed.

The tents were scattered about, facing this way and that, with twisting paths in the snow between them. They were not actually tents but crude hybrid products of lumber, logs, sheets of metal, flattened gasoline drums, canvas and an occasional moosehide. The crudest of them were simply frameworks of poles covered with canvas, some cone-shaped like tepees, others dome-shaped like Eskimo igloos. But most of them were square or rectangular, about the size of the garages that Kanina had seen beside city homes but with lower roofs; they had sides formed of boards or sheets of tin, and peaked canvas roofs supported by pole rafters. Each one had a rusted stovepipe sticking out the roof. Kanina studied the dwellings curiously, for she had no memory of them and this was like seeing them for the first time.

Her mother led her toward one that was a chaotic jumble of wood, canvas and tin like most of the others. Kanina noticed that it had only a flap of canvas for a door. They went inside and the man with the wide nostrils followed them; Kanina was sure now that he must be her father. The tent had a board floor and in a rear corner was a steel bed that Kanina remembered instantly, for several quilts and plaited rabbitskin robes lay on it in an untidy heap revealing a platform of boards underneath instead of a spring and mattress. But she remembered nothing else of the tent's meager furnishings. Near the door there was a big rusted steel gasoline drum and the stovepipe running up from it through the canvas roof meant that this was the stove. The drum lay on its side, raised off the floor by several flat stones, and a square of metal cut crudely from its front was hinged to form a door. The upper surface, originally part of the drum's rounded side, was pounded flat to form a cooking surface and it had two round jagged holes cut from it over which small sheets of tin fitted as stove lids. The stove had two smoke-blackened pots and a frying pan sitting on it and there was a pile of firewood on the floor beside it.

Kanina's eyes moved on curiously around the tent's single room. There was an old cupboard painted a vivid blue with open shelves above it cluttered with tin containers, bottles, metal cups, matches, boxes of shotgun shells, candles and a glass coal-oil lamp. There were two crude handmade chairs and an old wooden trunk filled with fish nets and steel traps. Two pairs of snowshoes hung from a pole rafter and a big shotgun leaned against the foot of the bed. There was little else. Kanina saw no table for eating, nor was there any bed for herself.

Kanina sat on one of the chairs, her mother and the man sat on the bed, and a long, embarrassed silence followed. Kanina studied them with quick stealthy glances. Her mother had a kind and pleasant face despite its toil-worn haggardness. The fine wrinkles that fanned out from her eyes and mouth corners seemed to give her a permanent smile, and under the rough and hardened exterior there were still remnants showing through of the beauty now beginning to reappear in Kanina.

The doorway of the tent was crowded with giggling children who stared in curiously. Finally her mother spoke to them and one girl, larger and older than the rest, pushed through the group and came inside. The girl turned shyly to Kanina.

"I am Helen Cheechekan," the girl said in English. "I remember when you went away. It was long ago. I went three years to the residential school at Moose Factory and I have learned there to speak English. Your mother asks why you speak only English. Why do you no longer speak our *Mooskek-owak* tongue?"

"I haven't had any *Mooskek-owak* people to talk to for a long time," Kanina replied. "I have forgotten it, but I will soon remember it again."

Helen translated it for Kanina's mother and the woman nodded vigorously. Then Kanina asked: "Is the man my father?" Helen nodded. "Yes," she said, "he is Joe Beaverskin. He is a good hunter. And your mother's name is Daisy. They are here at Cape Cree early this spring and so also are many other *Mooskek-owak* families because it was a hard winter in the inland country. There were few beaver, there was no game, the people were hungry. Now there are only rabbits to eat and the people wait for *niskuk,* the geese, to come back."

Kanina looked at her father more closely. He had broad shoulders and a thick chest, but he wasn't a big man because he was short, a good deal shorter than her mother. His trousers were held up by a frayed and dirty rope around his waist instead of a belt. He had a large round face and Kanina had never seen so wide and flattened a nose. His small, dark, deep-set eyes stared lifelessly ahead. Kanina hadn't heard him speak a word and she began to wonder if he was displeased over her return to Cape Cree.

Her mother began asking questions about the hospital and Kanina's life there. Each question and answer was relayed through Helen and the Cree words began to sound familiar again. In a few minutes her father rose, still not speaking, and walked outside. The Indian children gradually drifted away from the door.

Some time later Daisy Beaverskin went out and Kanina saw her go into the neighboring bush with an axe. Kanina stayed behind and talked shyly with Helen Cheechekan. Her mother returned in a few minutes with freshly cut poles and a big bundle of balsam boughs. She laid four poles on the floor in a corner to form a rectangle about five feet long and two feet wide, then she filled the space with balsam twigs until they formed a soft springy fragrant mattress. She took a quilt and a rabbitskin robe from her own bed and tossed them onto the balsam boughs. Kanina knew that this was to be her bed.

Helen Cheechekan left, saying she would come back later to help Kanina relearn her Cree. Kanina's mother threw several pieces of wood on the hot coals in the stove and began preparing a bannock. Her hands were smeared with black gum from the balsam boughs but she didn't wash them. She opened a large bag of flour that stood by the tent wall and in the surface of the flour at the top of the bag she scooped out a hole about twice the size of her fist. Into this she poured a cupful of water and began stirring it with a finger. The water absorbed flour, grew pasty and she added a sprinkling of baking powder, pouring it straight from the can. She continued mixing it within the flour bag until she could lift out a round lump of dough that was ready now for the stove without a utensil having been used. She greased the frying pan heavily, patted the dough into it and placed it on the stove to fry slowly.

She smoked her little curved-stem pipe constantly and her rubber boots scuffed on the floor as she shuffled about. A large black pot on the stove began bubbling vigorously, its tin lid bouncing and releasing little puffs of steam. Kanina got a peek into the pot once when her mother lifted the lid. The liquid inside was yellowish and protruding through the thick film of grease on the surface was the carcass, apparently in one piece, of a small animal which Kanina took to be a rabbit. Water in another pail on the stove came to a boil and Kanina's mother threw in a large handful of tea leaves. There was no table in sight and Kanina wondered where they were going to eat.

Her father came back, grunted a few words to his wife and sat on the floor near the gasoline drum stove. Kanina's mother lifted the tea pail and the stew pot from the stove and put them on the floor. She took the lid from the pot and turned it upside down on the floor to form a plate, then with a large fork she transferred the rabbit onto the lid. Next she removed the bannock, now a crisp brown, from the stove and put it beside the stewed rabbit. She took down metal cups and a large knife from a shelf above the blue cupboard and filled one cup with flour, then sat on the floor herself. The meal was ready and Kanina sat hesitantly beside them.

Joe Beaverskin sliced a chunk of meat from the rabbit's haunch, took it in his fingers and waved it back and forth to cool. A few seconds later he stuffed it into his mouth in one piece and began chewing rapidly. He filled his cup by dipping it into the tea pail, then took the cup of flour and sprinkled flour into his tea until it was whitish and pasty. He put the cup on the floor beside him to cool.

The woman sliced off a piece of meat and handed it to Kanina. It was hot and greasy and she had to move it back and forth from one hand to the other while it cooled. Her father turned the frying pan upside down and dumped the bannock onto the floor. He tore a piece off with his fingers, dunked it in the broth that the rabbit had been stewed in and moved it to his mouth, dripping the liquid in a thin yellow trail across his trousers as he did so.

There were no plates, knives or forks, no butter for the bannock, no milk or sugar for the tea. Kanina nibbled on the meat but it was tough and strong-tasting and she didn't like it. Whenever she lifted it to her mouth the juice ran down her arm and under the sleeve of her sweater. The bannock tasted good, much like bread, but after seeing it dumped on the floor Kanina could eat only a mouthful or two. Her mother and father ate heartily, dipping their cups repeatedly into the tea pail and bolting slice after slice of meat. Kanina tried another couple of nibbles at the meat and bannock, then she felt a dizzying attack of nausea and couldn't eat any more.

Later that day Kanina and her new friend Helen Cheechekan walked around the Cape Cree settlement. The midday sun was warm and the footpaths were wet and slushy. Helen told her that practically all of the Cape Cree families had spent the winter inland trapping beaver, each family on its own ancestral trapping territory handed down from generation to generation. Some of them went two hundred miles inland, which meant a two-week trip on snowshoes to get out, but about half of the families had already made the long trip out with their furs to their summer camps here on the coast. Now, Helen said, they were waiting for the spring goose hunt that would take them inland again as soon as the first flocks of *niskuk,* the big gray Canada geese, returned from the south. But the goose hunt, she explained, wouldn't take them as far inland as the winter trapping did, because the lake and muskeg country ten to fifty miles in from the post was one of the finest goose regions in the whole James Bay country. Kanina listened attentively, for this annual routine of *Mooskek-owak* life she had long since forgotten.

The church and missionary's house were in the center of the Indian village but Kanina noticed that the Hudson's Bay Company buildings were removed so that the space of about a city block separated them from the ragged Indian hovels. They walked that way and Helen showed Kanina the store where the furs were traded. Then Helen took Kanina past the residence where the post manager and his wife lived; Kanina gazed at it and she felt a wistful yearning.

It was a big house, its white paint new and clean. It had a picturesque white fence around it and leading up to the front door a board walk from which the snow was carefully shoveled. It had a wide veranda across its entire front and numerous windows with clean white curtains. Beside it on a wooden tower was a large windmill whirring in the breeze; the nurse had pointed out windmills like it when Kanina was in Moosonee and had explained that they produced electricity for lighting and pumping water in places where the electric wires of the big southern cities didn't reach.

"They are the Rumseys," Helen said. "Nice people. He's Bert Rumsey and she's Joan, but everyone calls them Mr. and Mrs. Rumsey. The inside of their house is supposed to be fixed up wonderful, full of all kinds of things, but Indian children must never go inside the fence, it's a real strict law, so the inside of the house is really a big mystery."

The inside was no mystery to Kanina. She knew what it would be like. There would be thick colored rugs on the floors, deep soft chairs, a sofa, and electric lamps that turned off and on with switches. There would be a bathroom with water taps and a big white tub, beds with white sheets, pictures on the walls. And there would be books. If the Rumseys had ever had children there might be easy books that Kanina herself could read. Life in the tent where they sat on the floor to eat wouldn't be so bad, Kanina thought, if she had books to read.

She knew that behind those white-curtained windows lay a tiny outpost of that other world, the world she had liked and had come to regard as her own, the world that now seemed irretrievably cut off behind her. As she gazed at the Rumsey house, tears filled her eyes and a choking ache gripped her throat. They walked back toward the Indian encampment and Kanina could pick out her own home near the river bank. There was gray wood smoke lifting from its stovepipe and its tattered ends of canvas were snapping in the cold breeze that blew in off James Bay.

CHAPTER SEVENTEEN

WINTER lingered and while it remained game was scarce for the cooking pots in the *Mooskek-owak* tents at Cape Cree. Three times a day in the Beaverskin tent Kanina and her parents sat on the floor to eat, but the meal was never more than bannock, meat and tea, and often not that. Sometimes for two or three days at a time there was no meat and they ate only bannock and the pasty, flour-thickened tea that Kanina came to dislike strongly.

Beaver that winter had been scarce and the pelts that Joe Beaverskin traded at the Hudson's Bay Company store did little more than pay for the winter supply of food that had been advanced the autumn before. The small credit that remained would buy only the essentials—flour, lard, tea, and powder and shot. Meat, normally the staple of their diet, had to come by Joe Beaverskin's gun or from the fish nets and rabbit snares tended by his wife.

Game was harder to obtain now than at any other time of the year. Every evening Joe Beaverskin would sit in the tent painstakingly refilling his shotgun shells to use again, and every morning he would walk away silently to hunt, his snowshoes crunching through the crust on the snow that had frozen overnight after the previous day's thaw. Each day Daisy Beaverskin would pull her nets through the hole she kept cut in the river ice and sometimes there would be a whitefish or two, though usually nothing. Every day she visited her rabbit snares, often to find that a fox had been ahead of her and eaten what the snares had caught, because this was a time of hunger not only for the *Mooskek-owak* but for all the meat-eaters of the muskeg lands.

Once they ate an owl and several times her father brought in squirrels. Whatever the meat, it was always stewed in the same big black kettle, and the pot was never cleaned for nothing could be wasted and each new item of game was boiled in the greasy broth that remained from whatever had been there before. Kanina longed for a glass of milk, a salad or cooked vegetables. Her parents' meals disgusted and at times nauseated her, but hunger finally forced her to eat them.

The faces of the *Mooskek-owak* people grew thin, eyes became glassy, the usual laughter and gaiety were gone.

Spring, when it finally came to Cape Cree, came with an explosive rush. One afternoon early in May a warm pelting rain began. It rained steadily all that night and most of the next day and then it ended suddenly with a hot sun swiftly routing the gray overcast of cloud. The river ice turned dark and rubbery, patches of ground began showing through the snow and the warm air tinkled with the sound of running water.

On the second day after the rain, the ice of the Kistawanee River began to murmur and bulge while the Indians watched eagerly from shore. Two hours later the river ice suddenly shattered with a rumbling roar that shook the ground like an earthquake. Black cracks shot through it, big chunks were thrown into the air by the pressure of rising floodwaters beneath, then the grinding mass of ice began plunging downstream. Break-up, most dramatic and meaningful event in the north's violent march of seasons, had come. It was the signal that winter's famine and perils had ended, a guarantee that spring and the goose flocks would quickly follow.

Next day the Kistawanee was clear of ice, and overnight the willow twigs along its banks had turned a brilliant yellow. Now the *Mooskek-owak* wandered tensely among their canvas huts and wigwams, every ear straining, every eye scanning the sky. Kanina found herself waiting and watching too. Then near midday it came, floating down faintly from high above, the rich resonant melody of honking geese. This first flock was so high that its thin wavering V looked like a tiny thread floating across the sky. Instantly a hundred *Mooskek-owak* throats answered, mimicking so perfectly the honking call of the geese that for a moment Kanina thought it was another flock down almost at tent-top level. Kanina had never heard it done, but she knew that this mimicking call, practiced from boyhood, was the method that *Mooskek-owak* hunters used to lure the curious *niskuk* within shooting range. This time it was only an expression of the hunters' excitement, a venting of the eager joy that filled every heart, for this first flock was far beyond calling range and it flew on, quickly passing from view.

Kanina felt the excitement herself. She knew that of all the wild sounds, this, the springtime call of returning geese, was the most stirring and cheering for the *Mooskek-owak* people. It meant good food and full bellies again after months of near-starvation.

The Indian camp suddenly seethed with activity. Men and children scurried about and there was laughter and shouting once more. Tents came down so that only bare pole skeletons remained and canoes that had lain all winter under shelters of branches and canvas were dragged out and pushed into the water. Everyone was running between the camp and river carrying loads to the canoes.

Kanina watched as her parents put their canoe in the river among the others. Her father quickly pulled the canvas roof from their tent, rolled the blankets inside it and threw the bundle into the center of the canoe. Daisy Beaverskin pushed the axe and cooking pot into Kanina's hands and motioned quickly that they were to be carried to the canoe. Helen Cheechekan, carrying a big blanket roll, came up and walked beside Kanina to the river.

"This is the goose hunt," Helen said eagerly. "The lakes where the *niskuk* nest will have ice for two or three weeks yet. The *niskuk* flocks will be hungry and they will fly around a lot while they wait for the ice to melt. It is easy then for the hunters to call them down and shoot them. There will be meat to eat tonight."

The flotilla of canoes pushed off and turned upstream. Kanina sat among the rolls of canvas in the middle of the Beaverskin canoe, facing her father who paddled silently in the stern. They were only a few feet apart, but Joe Beaverskin never looked at her nor gave a sign that he knew she was there. Frequently now the honking of geese came down to them from high above and each time the riders in the canoes babbled excitedly to each other in Cree that Kanina didn't understand.

It was late afternoon when they reached a clearing on the Kistawanee's bank and beached the canoes. Kanina noticed that the clearing was dotted with tepee-shaped skeletons of poles left from previous years. Here the goose flocks were more numerous and often they flew low and near. The men took their guns immediately and disappeared along the twisting trails that led inland. The women and children began setting up camp, tying canvas to the pole frameworks, lighting fires and cutting balsam boughs.

Kanina heard the guns booming frequently. At dusk the men returned and many of them were carrying geese—big gray long-necked birds with white cheek patches. Joe Beaverskin had one and he dropped it with a triumphant smile in front of his wife, giving her a playful hug as he did so. Kanina watched curiously for she had never before seen him smile or make any emotional advances like this toward her mother.

The women plucked and cleaned the geese hastily and Kanina shrank back with distaste as the children began gleefully throwing entrails at each other. The children's game brought loud scoldings from the parents and any entrails the children had taken were quickly retrieved and saved. Each woman who had a goose carved it up and shared it with any neighboring family whose hunter had failed to shoot a bird of his own. Daisy Beaverskin gave a good deal of theirs away. That night every *Mooskek-owak* tent had goose meat in its cooking pot.

Kanina's mother stewed theirs over an open blaze outdoors and put the intestines in a pan to fry slowly at the edge of the fire. They ate that night in the light of the flames, squatting on the wet ground. The fried intestines were greasy and Kanina couldn't eat any, but the boiled meat was tasty and tender and Kanina liked it. Afterward her stomach felt full for the first time in nearly a month.

That night in the yellow moonlight that filtered into the little tent she saw her mother and father lying close under their blanket and whispering softly to each other. They were a transformed couple, the sullen moodiness of the past weeks now suddenly gone. Kanina could feel within her own small body some of the emotional stirrings that the beginning of the spring goose hunt set free, for the time brought relief and tranquility to harassed minds as well as abundant food for their bellies. The return of the geese rekindled once more the primal fires of life and for the *Mooskek-owak* it was a joy again to be alive. Kanina didn't know then the adult implications of all this, but she saw it years later vividly portrayed in the birth records of her people. Far more *Mooskek-owak* babies are born in February than in any other month of the year—nine months after the joyous return of the *niskuk* flocks to the muskeg lands of the James Bay shore.

That night on her small bed of balsam boughs Kanina knew only that she was too excited to sleep. And her parents on their bed lay in each other's arms and stirred restlessly and seemed to stay awake a long time too.

The days that followed were full and active ones. The men hunted constantly and the women were kept busy preparing the *niskuk* that the hunters' guns brought down. The birds had to be plucked and cleaned and the feathers saved in bags for quilt-making. The pellets of shot had to be picked out of the flesh or viscera with a knife point and saved in a tin can for the hunters to reload and use again. Much of the meat had to be dried so that it would keep to be eaten later. Kanina watched with fascination as the women cut the thick breast meat from the skeletons with a few deft strokes of their knives, procuring from each goose a single neat slice that they hung on racks of green willow over the small drying fires.

There was food but otherwise life was harder here at the hunting camp than it had been at Cape Cree. Here there was no floor in the tent and Kanina slept rolled in a rabbitskin blanket fully clothed with only a thin mat of boughs separating her from the ground. Often it rained and their crude tent leaked and she was usually wet and cold.

The women were too busy to make bannock and for days at a time there was only boiled goose to eat and flour-thickened tea or the greasy broth to drink. Kanina enjoyed the first few meals of it, but each fresh batch grew greasier as the fat accumulated in the pot and after a week one meal a day of it was all she could stand.

Then the ice in the ponds and lakes broke up and melted. The goose flocks disappeared as the birds split up into mated pairs and went into hiding for the nesting. Three weeks after it started, the hunt ended and the *Mooskek-owak* took down their tents and returned to Cape Cree.

The June days grew longer and now there was plenty of food. Every morning Daisy Beaverskin would paddle the canoe down to the river mouth and lift her gill nets and now there were usually several fish each day. Periodically she would boil up a batch of their dried goose meat. But the meals were always meat and bannock, and Kanina's craving for vegetables and fruit grew stronger.

Every morning after breakfast her father would wander off to spend the rest of the day with the other men, playing cards on the ground outdoors or simply lying on his back on the grass and staring at the big white cumulus clouds that marched majestically across the sky. While he loafed in the sun, Kanina's mother worked steadily. She carried water from the river, gathered and split firewood. She made beaded moosehide moccasins and slippers which she traded at the Hudson's Bay store for her tobacco.

Kanina's mind was sharp and quick and the Cree language came back to her easily. Soon she was conversing with her mother, far from fluently, but by going slowly they could understand each other. Daisy Beaverskin was dirty and Kanina hated the pipe she was always smoking, but her mother was kind and made it plain that she loved Kanina, and Kanina loved her mother in return. Kanina wondered if the white people would bathe any oftener than her mother did if they had to carry all their water up a steep bank from the river, had to split wood for the fire to heat it, and then had to take their baths in a metal wash tub so small that even Kanina couldn't sit down in it.

But Kanina never talked to her father. For a brief time during the goose hunt he had been gay and amiable, but now he was morose and silent again and rarely took any notice of her. When they were eating and her father had the knife and Kanina wanted to cut herself a piece of meat, she asked her mother to pass the knife to her because if she asked her father he would ignore her. She began to fear him and avoided him whenever it was possible. She began coming in late for meals so that he would be finished and gone before she ate, and her mother understood and without mentioning it she too began waiting to eat with Kanina. Kanina dreaded the coming of autumn, for then they would have to travel by canoe far inland to their trapping camp and the family would be alone for the winter. Her father would be much closer then and it would be impossible to avoid him.

Kanina had been back from the san about four months when one morning she was walking again past the Rumsey house. She came here frequently, usually alone, and usually in the mornings because then the sun shone through the windows and it was possible to catch glimpses of the inside. Today she was alone, and this time Joan Rumsey was sitting on a chair on the veranda sewing. Mrs. Rumsey was a tall woman with a thin face that was always smiling and she had black hair that was turning gray on the sides. She wore pretty frocks of flowered print, not the dark somber flannels that the *Mooskek-owak* women used for their plain homemade dresses.

Kanina walked past slowly, stealthily eyeing the house and Mrs. Rumsey through the slats of the white fence. She turned and walked back. She paused at the gate. Her mother had told her never to go inside the fence where the lawn and the brilliant flower gardens were. Helen Cheechekan had said it was "a real strict law." But Kanina felt an overwhelming desire to talk to Mrs. Rumsey as she had once been able to talk to the nurses. White women were always kind and nice; you didn't have to be afraid of them. And maybe . . . . no, Kanina felt *sure* that Joan Rumsey would have books she could borrow to read.

She opened the gate slowly. The hinges creaked and Mrs. Rumsey looked up from her sewing. Kanina strode quickly up the board sidewalk.

"How do you do," Kanina said, striving to be as polite as possible.

"Hello," Mrs. Rumsey answered and her smile was warm and tender. "You're Kanina, aren't you? The Beaverskin girl who came back from the san?"

"Yes," Kanina replied. She stopped at the veranda step and looked curiously through the open door in front of her. She could see a polished table inside with magazines and a vase of flowers on it.

"Come up and sit down," Joan Rumsey said.

"Thank you, I should like to," Kanina said and sat on a chair.

"You learned to speak English well. Did you like it at the san? Or were you glad to come back home?"

"I liked it better at the san," Kanina said. "I had a big bed all my own. And every meal I had a knife and a fork and a plate. It was clean there. Our tent isn't very clean. And I learned to read at the san, but now I don't have any books and I'm afraid I'll forget how to read."

She paused and looked sideways at Mrs. Rumsey. "Do you have any books?" she asked. "Easy books that I can read?"

"Yes, I have," Mrs. Rumsey said quickly. She seemed excited. "I had a little girl like you, Kanina. She's a big girl now and she works in one of the cities down south. I'm sure she would like you to have her books."

Joan Rumsey jumped to her feet. "You wait," she said. "I'll get some."

"If you don't mind," Kanina interjected quickly, "could I come inside with you? I don't see inside houses now."

As soon as she had said it, Kanina knew it must be very wrong. But Mrs. Rumsey took her hand and smiled and said: "Yes, dear, you come right in."

She took Kanina into the living room and told her to wait on the sofa while she went upstairs to look for the books. Kanina studied the room, fascinated, almost breathless. It was beautiful. The paper on the wall was yellow with small red roses, and the drapes at the windows were yellowish too. There were electric lamps, a radio, and bookshelves with many books on each side of the big stone fireplace. Kanina's eyes moved hungrily around the room.

Mrs. Rumsey came into the living room again and sat down on the sofa and Kanina noted with happy relief that she had found some books. They began looking over them together. There were five and the largest was one called *Black Beauty,* which Kanina remembered from the sanatorium library.

"This big one is about a horse," Mrs. Rumsey said. "But it's too big and hard for you, isn't it, Kanina?"

"Oh no!" Kanina exclaimed. "I have read it, and I want to read it again."

Joan Rumsey told her when she had read them to come back and there would be more. Then she began asking Kanina about her life in the tent. She asked her where she slept and Kanina said she had a bed of boughs on the floor. She asked about the meals and when Kanina described them the smile left Mrs. Rumsey's face.

"Do you know how much you weighed when you left the hospital?" Joan Rumsey asked.

"I weighed seventy-six pounds at the last."

"Let's see what you weigh now, shall we?" Mrs. Rumsey stood up. "I have scales upstairs in the bathroom. Come."

Kanina was delighted at the opportunity to see the Rumsey's bathroom and went up eagerly. She stepped onto the scales. She weighed sixty-eight pounds.

"I was afraid of that," Mrs. Rumsey told her. "It's not a good sign. You should be growing and gaining weight."

They went back downstairs and Joan Rumsey gave her a big glass of milk. It was sweet and cool, the first she had had since leaving the hospital, and Kanina drank it quickly. Mrs. Rumsey poured her another. Kanina knew it wasn't milk from a bottle like they had at the hospital, for there wasn't a cow within several hundred miles of Cape Cree; it was made from powdered milk which tasted just as good. Then Kanina took the books and thanked Mrs. Rumsey and started for home. She ran excitedly down through the Indian tents, clutching the books tightly against her. She loved them. And she loved Joan Rumsey.

Her father was eating when she stepped into the tent and his small dark eyes focused immediately on the books.

"Where did you get them?" he asked in quick guttural Cree.

"From Mrs. Rumsey."

"You must take them back."

Tears came in Kanina's eyes. She asked: "Why?"

"You must take them back," her father repeated, "because they are no good for *Mooskek-owak* children. You must learn to paddle, to tan skins, to snare rabbits, for they are the things by which we *Mooskek-owak* live. The hospital taught you none of these things, they taught you to read books, they taught you how to be a white person, but you aren't a white person, you are a *Mooskek-owak*. Soon we will have to start for the trapping camp. There will be heavy loads to carry on the portages. You are too weak now. You must start carrying water and chopping wood so that you will become strong and there is little time left."

Her father's wide nose was twitching angrily and his black eyebrows were lowered in a frown that almost obscured his eyes. In those few seconds he had said more to Kanina than during the four months she had been back at Cape Cree. Then he concluded with a statement that suddenly explained everything.

"It is hard for a *Mooskek-owak* hunter to lose all his sons and have only a daughter," he said. "It is worse when the daughter is taken away and comes back not a *Mooskek-owak* any longer, but a white person with brown skin."

Kanina sat silently on the bed. Her father left the tent shortly afterward and her mother came and sat beside her. She put her arm around Kanina and for a long time neither of them spoke.

But Kanina did not return the books. That afternoon when she and her mother were alone in the tent, the canvas flap opened and her father came in with Mrs. Rumsey and a tall sharp-nosed Indian whom Kanina recognized as Jock, Bert Rumsey's store assistant. Jock was one of the few Cape Cree Indians with a knowledge of English and he was employed most of the time as interpreter at the Hudson's Bay store. Kanina was startled to see them.

"Mrs. Rumsey wants to talk," Joe Beaverskin said briefly to his wife. They all sat down, Joan Rumsey and Jock on the chairs, the three Beaverskins on the bed.

Mrs. Rumsey turned to Kanina and smiled pleasantly. "You go out and play, dear," she said.

Kanina stepped outside. They were going to talk about her! She slipped around to the rear of the tent and sat down quietly. Inside she could hear Mrs. Rumsey talking, with periodic pauses for Jock to translate her English into Cree.

"Kanina is no longer sick," she was saying, "but she isn't strong yet like other children. I have come to tell you I don't think she should go into the bush for the winter trapping. It will be too hard for her. She needs better food than the beaver meat and bannock you will eat all winter. She needs milk and cod-liver oil and fruit and vegetables. If you agree she could go this winter to the Indian residential school at Moose Factory. She did so well at the hospital school, I think you should let her go. . . ."

"*Numwach!*" It was the Cree word for "no." It was her mother's voice and it came clearly and loudly to Kanina crouching outside.

There was a pause, then Joan Rumsey was talking quietly again.

"She has lost weight. She has lost eight pounds. It is a bad sign. You wouldn't want the cough to come back and the doctors to send her to the hospital again?"

Then her father spoke in Cree. "Yes, she will go to the school," he said. "She will be only a big trouble in the bush. She is no good for the *Mooskek-owak* life."

"*Numwach!*" her mother said again.

"Mrs. Beaverskin . . . . five times you had the great pains of child-birth and five times the cough came or there was no food and each baby died. Then the sixth one came, and the cough came again too, but that time the doctor came to Cape Cree before it was too late, and Kanina went to the white people's hospital and she didn't die. Will you let her die now? Will you come out of the bush in the spring, just you and your husband alone again, as you did five times before? There will not be another time for you. Your childbearing time has ended, I know, because no longer do I see the soft rolls of sphagnum moss drying in front of the Beaverskin tent every month. Kanina is your last. You must let her go to the school."

Kanina could hear her mother crying softly now, and Daisy Beaverskin did not say *numwach* again. No one spoke for a long time, then Kanina heard the one word that changed her life: *"Aha."*

Jock interpreted it for Joan Rumsey: "Mrs. Beaverskin says 'yes'."

CHAPTER EIGHTEEN

KANINA spent four years attending the Indian residential school at Moose Factory, the trading post and Indian settlement at the southern tip of James Bay, a few miles from the end of steel at Moosonee. The school drew Indian children from Cree bands scattered along four hundred miles of James Bay coastline but the enrollment was small because most *Mooskek-owak* parents insisted on keeping their children with them. During those four years Kanina spent only a few weeks each summer with her parents in the tent at Cape Cree and she was never there long enough to become accustomed to either her parents or Indian camp life. She had no other contact with them because they couldn't write letters and Joan Rumsey became a substitute parent. The white woman was very interested in Kanina's progress at school and she wrote to Kanina regularly. At the end of the fourth year Kanina passed the high school entrance examinations with an average mark of eighty-six. But this high mark had come easily, Kanina had not worked hard.

Now it was June, Kanina was fourteen, and she was again flying back to Cape Cree. There was a teen-age lankiness in her slender body but her face had already acquired the beauty and the delicate balance of features it would carry with little alteration into maturity. She looked out at the tiny scuds of cloud that whipped like pellets of shot past the wing-tips of the little bush plane; the cloud puffs were gray and somber, a fitting reflection of her mood, for Kanina wasn't happy to be coming home.

She had gone as far now as the residential school could take her; she had gone much further than most *Mooskek-owak* children, because few of them attended school at all and of those who did only a small percentage stayed long enough to reach grade eight. Kanina had stayed at school to the end because Joan Rumsey had objected strongly whenever her parents talked of taking her out. But now it was ended. The nearest high schools were in the towns far to the south, and no *Mooskek-owak* had ever attended one because the cost of sending a child out to school and paying his board while there was more than a Cree trapper could earn in a year. Kanina's appetite for knowledge was merely whetted, and she wished for some miracle that would permit her to go on, as white children did, for several more years of schooling. But she had already faced too many grim and hard realities in her fourteen years of life, and she was no longer capable of the slightest self-delusion. She was sure there was no chance whatever of going on to high school.

In her last letter Mrs. Rumsey had said there was a heavy run of sturgeon in some of the estuaries down the coast and fish dealers flying in by plane were paying a good price for them. The letter said many Indian families had moved down to the estuaries to fish and Kanina's parents were among those who had gone from Cape Cree. As the plane glided in over the Kistawanee River for its landing, Kanina wondered if her parents had returned. She looked from the cabin window as they taxied in toward the beach and she couldn't see her parents in the crowd, but she could see Mrs. Rumsey waiting at the water's edge. The plane floats crunched onto the gravel and Kanina climbed down and jumped ashore. Joan Rumsey ran up and kissed Kanina's cheek.

"You are growing so fast, Kanina!" she exclaimed. She took Kanina's hand and they walked up the river bank. "The sturgeon are still running," she said. "Your parents have not come back and you'll have to stay with us."

So Kanina moved into the big white house and had an upstairs room all her own. A boat or plane was leaving every few days for the fishing camps down the coast, but Joan Rumsey never suggested that Kanina rejoin her parents there. And neither did Kanina. She hadn't seen her parents for almost ten months, but she felt little desire to see them now for it would mean leaving the big house where she was very happy with the Rumseys. Four years at the residential school had widened much more the cultural and intellectual gulf that separated Kanina from her parents. Kanina's life was oriented now to a world her parents had never seen and did not know.

She liked working and living in the house. Mrs. Rumsey taught her to bake and to sew on the sewing machine, and Kanina made herself a pretty yellow dress from material Joan Rumsey gave her. At times Mr. Rumsey let her clerk in the Hudson's Bay Company store, and Kanina liked this most of all. Bert Rumsey received newspapers in bundles of a week or so at a time and when each new supply arrived he and Kanina would have a long session together working out the crossword puzzles.

By late July Kanina had almost come to regard the Rumseys as her real parents. She didn't want to go back to the squalid little tent where they squatted crosslegged on the floor to eat and where she had to sleep on the balsam-bough mattress fully clothed because she didn't like undressing in front of her father. Then late one day there was an outburst of shouting from the Indian village which meant that the fishing camp families were arriving. Kanina and Mrs. Rumsey walked together to the shore where a crowd had already gathered. Six canoes were coming up through the river mouth.

"Do you see your mother and father?" Joan Rumsey asked.

Kanina, possessing the keen eyesight of her race, said: "Yes, the second canoe."

As the canoes came nearer, her mother waved vigorously to Kanina, then began paddling rapidly. The canoe shot up onto the beach and she jumped out quickly and ran to Kanina, her big round body bouncing lithely like a rubber ball.

"Kanina, Kanina, I have waited so long to see you!" she exclaimed in Cree. She bent forward and they embraced. Her mother held her for a long time and Kanina could feel the woman's arms trembling. Over her mother's shoulder Kanina saw her father give a brief nod of recognition, then he ignored Kanina and started silently to unload the canoe. Her mother released her and Kanina turned to look for Mrs. Rumsey. But the white woman had left them, she was far along the beach walking quickly back toward the Hudson's Bay Company house. Kanina took a step to follow her, then stopped as she realized suddenly that she didn't belong in the big white house with the Rumseys any longer. She turned back slowly to her parents.

The Beaverskins unloaded the canoe and began carrying the canvas tarpaulins, blanket rolls and the bulging packsacks up the bank to their old homesite. The walls and the framework of poles for the roof were still standing and the gasoline drum stove, the bed and familiar blue cupboard stood in their usual places on the exposed floor. All they had to do was tie the canvas roof back on and their Cape Cree home was ready to be lived in again.

"I've been living with the Rumseys," Kanina said hesitantly to her mother in Cree as Joe Beaverskin finished tying down the canvas roof. "My clothes are there."

Daisy Beaverskin turned sharply. "Why did you go there?" she asked, staring hard at Kanina. "You should have stayed with one of the *Mooskek-owak* families."

"Mrs. Rumsey asked me to go there," Kanina answered, "and I stayed because I liked it."

"They didn't want you," Kanina's mother said. "White people never want *Mooskek-owak* children. They only had you because they didn't know that the *Mooskek-owak* can always look after their own."

"They *did* want me. I helped Mrs. Rumsey with the housework and I worked in the store. They want me to stay there and I want to stay too."

"The Rumseys are kind," Daisy Beaverskin added noncommittally and she said nothing more.

The tent roof was on and they went inside. Kanina couldn't figure out whether her mother expected her to move into the tent with them or remain with the Rumseys. At least her mother hadn't sent her back to the house for her clothes; that was an encouraging sign. Daisy Beaverskin lit a fire in the stove and put the stew pot on. Then she went out. Kanina waited, wondering what she was expected to do. The fire burned low and she put fresh wood into the stove. The stew pot began to simmer, it smelled like boiling fish and Kanina hated it. Her mother must have gone visiting. Kanina got back on to her feet to go out herself when the canvas door swung open and Daisy Beaverskin stepped sideways through the doorway carrying a big bundle of balsam boughs. The woman waddled to the rectangular frame of poles on the floor and began methodically laying a new bough mattress for Kanina.

The evening meal was fish and tea, for Daisy Beaverskin had not had time to make bannock. Joe Beaverskin came in and the three of them ate in silence except for the swishing sound her parents made as they sucked the fish broth from their fingers. When the meal was finished Kanina's mother tossed some leftover scraps of fish back into the pot and then rose to her feet.

"Come," she said to Kanina. "We will get your clothes."

They walked through the Indian village, Daisy Beaverskin leading and Kanina following silently a few paces behind. The summer evening was hot but Kanina's mother was wearing, as always, the big rubber boots, the gray long-sleeved sweater and the black shawl knotted snugly around her head. Tonight when she went to bed she would remove only the boots and shawl; next winter when the temperature would be below zero for weeks at a time she would wear the same clothes with only mittens and perhaps another sweater added, but she would rarely be cold. Kanina had seen *Mooskek-owak* women like her come into the hospital with the heavy underwear caked to their bodies and she had helped the nurses rip the underclothing away in shreds before the women could be bathed. Her mother would probably be like that, for Kanina had never known her to undress.

Chained dogs snarled at them whenever they passed too near, because in summer the dogs were always starved and vicious with raw sores where the collars chafed their necks. The Indian philosophy of dog care was a simple one. Feed them well in winter when there are sleds to be hauled, but in summer it is a waste of meat to feed dogs more than the minimum required to keep them alive. The circle of packed earth around each dog's chain stake was surprisingly clean. A dog living on two or three fish a week leaves few droppings.

The big bulldog flies droned around their heads in buzzing swarms. Several times they had to step across little streams, green and slimy and sluggish, that oozed like open sewers out of the screen of spruce forest that formed the big communal outdoor latrine behind the village.

From now on, Kanina thought, this would be home.

They reached the white fence and Kanina stepped forward and opened the gate. Her mother stopped suddenly, staring wide-eyed and frightened at the Rumsey house. Kanina waited. Her mother's lips trembled and she didn't move.

"You go," she said. "Say I thank her."

Kanina went up the boardwalk alone and rapped lightly on the screen door. Mrs. Rumsey appeared in the hall.

"I came for my clothes," Kanina said.

Joan Rumsey looked out at Kanina's mother standing by the gate.

"Mother is afraid to come in," Kanina told her. "She wants to thank you for having me."

"She must come in!" Joan Rumsey declared. "We'll have a cup of tea." She stepped out onto the veranda with Kanina and beckoned. Daisy Beaverskin's round wrinkled face smiled but the Indian woman didn't move.

"Speak to her, Kanina. Tell her I *do* want her in."

Kanina passed the message on to her mother in Cree and Daisy Beaverskin began walking slowly up the walk. When she reached the veranda

Joan Rumsey took the woman's arm and led her in to the living room. Daisy Beaverskin had been in the church and in the store but she had never been inside a house and she looked around her with the terrified gaze of a newly caged animal. She sat stiffly on the edge of the sofa, her eyes shifting rapidly.

"I'll put the kettle on," Joan Rumsey said and went out into the kitchen. Then Mrs. Rumsey called: "Kanina, Jock is working at the store tonight, go over and tell him I want him at once, please."

Kanina stepped out into the hall. "I interpret better than Jock," she said.

"I know you do," Joan Rumsey agreed. "But tonight I think we'd better have Jock."

Kanina came back with the tall, sharp-nosed Indian interpreter. There were cookies, sugar and cream, a teapot and four cups and saucers on the coffee table in front of the sofa. Kanina saw the four cups instantly. It meant that this time she wasn't going to be asked to leave.

"You pour the tea, Kanina," Joan Rumsey said. "Pour your mother's first."

Kanina sat on the sofa and began pouring. She saw that her mother was relaxed now and sitting back comfortably. There was a glint of pride in Daisy Beaverskin's dark eyes as she watched the manner in which Kanina handled the dainty china cups and saucers. The Indian woman had never drunk tea out of anything but a metal mug before and Kanina knew that for her mother this was a new and foreign experience, yet one over which her own daughter was presiding. And Kanina realized then that Joan Rumsey had planned it this way to give her mother a glimpse of the other life that had claimed Kanina.

With Jock interpreting, Mrs. Rumsey and Kanina's mother talked for a couple of minutes about the sturgeon fishing and the prospects for next winter's beaver trapping. At first the Indian woman gave short timid answers, but she gained confidence and soon began talking freely. Then Joan Rumsey began discussing Kanina.

"Kanina did better at the residential school than any *Mooskek-owak* child has ever done before. Did you know that?"

Jock repeated it in Cree. Kanina's mother didn't know it, but she smiled proudly and nodded.

"Kanina wrote the same examinations that all the white children write, but only a few of the cleverest white children ever earn marks as high as Kanina did."

Jock had to explain what examinations and marks were before he could translate the statement into Cree. Daisy Beaverskin smiled and nodded again.

"Kanina has gone to school much longer than most *Mooskek-owak* children, but there is still much that she could learn in the big schools in the white people's towns in the south. She learns quickly and easily. It would be a mistake for her to stop learning now."

This time Kanina's mother did not nod or smile. She just stared searchingly into Joan Rumsey's thin face.

"She should go on to what the white people call 'high school'," Joan Rumsey continued. "She would have to live in a town down south and go to school with white children. It wouldn't be free like the residential school, but Mr. Rumsey and I would pay for it and Kanina could work in the house here with me each summer to earn it. She could live with my sister in Blackwood and go to school there."

Kanina listened, hardly believing, and she watched her mother eagerly as Jock repeated it all in Cree. The woman's brown wrinkled face gathered into a frown. "It is no good," she snapped, "learning to be a white person. She must learn now to be a *Mooskek-owak,* she must learn to paddle, to frost-dry the beaver pelts, to snare rabbits, or no *Mooskek-owak* man will marry her."

"Kanina can learn those things quickly any time she has to," Mrs. Rumsey argued. "But if she is going on to school she must do that now. She might become a nurse or a teacher and the government might pay her to come back to Cape Cree and nurse or teach her own people. What would it matter then if she didn't know how to snare rabbits? She would be very important in Cape Cree. And Daisy and Joe Beaverskin would be important because they are her parents."

Kanina's mother stared at the floor for a long time after Jock had translated it. Then, without lifting her eyes, she began to talk. Her voice was soft, like the murmur of wind in the spruce tops, and her Cree was flowing and musical, for it is a rhythmic language of soft vowels and few harsh consonants. Periodically she paused while Jock interpreted what she was saying.

"I have waited so long for my time to be a mother," she began slowly, "but my children have always been taken from me. First it was the cough that made them spit blood on the snow. Now it is the white people's school. I thought that this year the schooling time would be ended and my daughter would be coming home. I thought that now at last I would be the mother that my woman's heart has always yearned to be, and I was very happy. I wanted to teach her to tan the moosehide and make moccasins, how to smoke the fish so that it will keep for winter but not taste too strong . . . . how to be a *Mooskek-owak* woman."

She paused then for several seconds. When she resumed she was looking straight at Joan Rumsey but the white woman's face was blank because she didn't know yet what the Indian woman was saying.

"I know it is good for the child to go to school," Kanina's mother continued. "So I will let her work here with you and you will send her to the white people's school. Now *you* will be Kanina Beaverskin's mother. It will be better that way for Kanina, but it will be more painful than the frostbites of winter for this old woman who bore her and nursed her but could never be her mother for long."

Daisy Beaverskin jumped nimbly to her feet despite the bulk of her big body and her eyes were glassy with tears. Jock was still translating her words for Joan Rumsey when the Indian woman strode through the front door into the dusk outside and scuffed across the veranda and down the boardwalk toward the gate. Kanina followed her mother outside but her throat was too choked for her to call goodbye. The Indian woman shuffled quickly down the slope toward the *Mooskek-owak* tents and she did not look back.

CHAPTER NINETEEN

JOAN RUMSEY said she hadn't seen her sister in Blackwood for several years and she decided to make the trip outside with Kanina. They left in mid-August so that Mrs. Rumsey could have a visit with her sister and so that Kanina would have a week or two for shopping and acclimatizing herself to the city before school started. As usual, practically the entire Cape Cree population was strung out in twisting lines along the river bank to see the plane off, the women and girls in one section, the men and boys in another. Kanina could see her father standing stiffly and stolid-faced among the men. She searched through the women several times, but her mother was not there.

Early next morning Kanina and Joan Rumsey boarded the train at Moosonee and headed south. Twice before Kanina had traveled on this train—the trip out to the hospital and the return to Cape Cree six years later—and both times she had dreaded the destination to which the train was speeding her. This time she was happy and looking forward excitedly to the new life ahead of her. Late that night they arrived at Blackwood.

Mrs. Rumsey's sister was on the platform waiting for them; she was like Joan Rumsey, but even taller. Mrs. Rumsey introduced them; her sister's name was Baxter. Mrs. Baxter just nodded and said "Hello, dear"; then she looked at Kanina for a long time. Finally she turned away saying: "The car is over here."

Mrs. Baxter drove them home, chatting animatedly with her sister but saying nothing more to Kanina. It was a large brick house and Kanina liked it. This, she thought, was to be her home—probably for several years. Joan Rumsey took her immediately to one of the bedrooms upstairs and Kanina began undressing. Then Mrs. Rumsey went back downstairs to her sister.

Kanina was tired but she was too thrilled to sleep and her throat was dry with excitement. She could hear the two women talking in the living room below, but they were only voices, she could not distinguish words. Some time later she got out of bed to go to the bathroom for a drink of water. She opened her door quietly and tiptoed into the hall. The women were still talking but they were turning out lights and getting ready to come upstairs.

"I know, Joan," Mrs. Baxter was saying, "but you didn't say in your letter that she was an *Indian* girl."

Joan Rumsey answered in a low voice and Kanina couldn't distinguish what she said.

"Well, I hope she doesn't leave lice in that bed. . . ." It was Mrs. Baxter's voice again.

Now they were at the foot of the stairs and coming up. Kanina slipped back into her room and closed the door. She heard no more of the conversation.

She sat on the bed, bewildered and frightened and trembling a little. It had sounded as if Mrs. Baxter didn't like her because she was an Indian, but there were good Indians and bad Indians, just as there were good and bad white people, so no one could dislike her for that reason alone. Kanina thought about it for a long time. She had never encountered anything like it during the six years she spent with white people at the hospital. Finally she decided that Mrs. Baxter *did* dislike her simply because she was an Indian. But why? She got back into bed, as bewildered as ever.

Early next morning there was a light rap on her door and Joan Rumsey came in, already fully dressed.

"My sister doesn't have a room she can spare for you," Mrs. Rumsey said in a low voice. "You won't be able to stay here after all. Get dressed and pack your bag quietly. I'll call a taxi and we'll leave right now."

She went downstairs and Kanina heard her telephoning. Kanina carried her bag down a few minutes later and noticed that Mrs. Rumsey's bag was also packed and standing beside the front door. The taxi came and they went out. Joan Rumsey closed the door softly behind her. Mrs. Baxter hadn't wakened.

They went to a restaurant downtown for breakfast and Kanina was too embarrassed to tell Mrs. Rumsey that she knew the real reason for their hasty departure from the Baxter home. As they ate, Joan Rumsey told Kanina that she had lived in Blackwood and knew many people here and would have no difficulty finding a boarding house for her. There was a public telephone near their table and Joan Rumsey made a call while Kanina finished eating. Kanina heard Mrs. Rumsey say she was looking for room and board for an Indian girl who would be attending high school. She heard her repeat at least three times that she was an Indian girl; Joan Rumsey was going to have no more misunderstandings.

"Her name is Sadie Thomas," Mrs. Rumsey said when she sat down again with Kanina. "She has a small boarding house near Park Collegiate, the school you'll be attending. She often has students boarding with her. She has a room empty now that you can have. We'll go right out there."

Sadie Thomas was very different from Mrs. Baxter. She was a short plump motherly woman with white hair and a round, childlike, cherubic face. She came to the door wiping her hands vigorously on her apron.

"Joan Bell!" she exclaimed. "I haven't seen you for years!" Kanina had never heard Mrs. Rumsey's maiden name before. Sadie Thomas turned immediately to Kanina. "And this is Kanina? You are a beautiful girl, Kanina. I hope you'll like the room."

It was a small rear room, not nearly as large or as well furnished as the room at Mrs. Baxter's. It had a double bed, a chest of drawers and a small table; the table, Kanina thought eagerly, would be her desk for doing school homework. Kanina knew she would like living there.

Joan Rumsey stayed two weeks, sharing the room with Kanina. She took Kanina shopping several times for school clothes and Kanina was frightened by the size and bustle of the big stores and she stayed close to Mrs. Rumsey. They never saw Mrs. Baxter again and so far as Kanina knew Joan Rumsey didn't even telephone her sister to tell her where they had gone. Kanina thought frequently of Mrs. Baxter's strange dislike for her, but the more she thought about it, the more puzzled it left her.

The night before school opened another student boarder moved in, a tall blonde named Trudy Brown. Trudy shook Kanina's hand vigorously when Sadie Thomas introduced them. "Gee, it'll be fun having another girl in the house," Trudy said eagerly. "There wasn't last year. It was like a graveyard."

Trudy had a vacant, drowsy-looking face and big dreamy eyes. She boarded here because her home was in a village, too far out for daily commuting to school. Later when Trudy had gone to her room Sadie added in a whisper: "Trudy's not too smart. She's starting her second year in grade ten."

Next morning Kanina put on one of her new dresses, a blue printed cotton with a flared skirt. She was very proud of it. Mrs. Rumsey arranged her long black hair neatly with a silver band across the top of her head and they went down for breakfast. Sadie Thomas grasped Kanina impetuously by the shoulder exclaiming: "The boys will surely whistle at you!"

White people were hard to understand, Kanina thought. They were so different . . . . like Sadie and Mrs. Baxter.

Trudy and Kanina started for the school together. Joan Rumsey went to the front door with them; her face was white and tiny wrinkles tugged at the corners of her eyes. She looked more nervous and excited than Kanina.

The school was huge, with long halls and numerous rooms. It was full of students, some talking quietly in small groups but most of them moving about noisily. Trudy wended her way through a crowded hall to the principal's office, towing Kanina behind her.

"You'll have to register here," Trudy said. "I gotta leave now. I'll see you later."

A secretary took Kanina's name and told her she would be in Room 12. Kanina found the room and waited shyly in the hall outside while students streamed back and forth past her. She didn't see a single Indian and she began to feel lonely and conspicuous. A girl with long red hair ran past, bumping Kanina roughly. "Sorry," the girl said, turning. She had brown eyes and a small upturned nose, and she looked at Kanina for several seconds, a grimace moving slowly across her face. "An Indian, eh?" she added. "In that case I'm not sorry." Then she laughed and walked away and two other girls standing near who had heard it laughed too.

A bell rang and students began filing into the classrooms. Kanina joined the jam at the Room 12 door and she saw the redhead ahead of her going into the same room. A tall boy jostled against her and his hand moved firmly across her stomach. She couldn't tell whether it was an accident or deliberate. He bent down and whispered: "Hi. Park Collegiate needs a few more good-looking dishes like you."

Kanina slipped into one of the rear desks. A woman teacher came in. "Many of us may not know each other," she said, "so I'd like each pupil to stand and introduce himself or herself."

The redhead sat near the front and was one of the first to rise. "Marjorie Ball," she said, giving each syllable an exaggerated emphasis. Many laughed and Kanina gathered it was because Marjorie was well known and her introduction unnecessary.

When Kanina's turn came she was trembling violently. She rose. "Kanina Beaverskin," she said softly. Marjorie Ball grimaced and held her nose. Several girls giggled. The tall boy who was sitting at a desk across the aisle from Kanina clucked his tongue and gave a brief muted whistle.

They were in the classroom for about an hour. The teacher told them the subjects they would be studying and the books they were to buy. Then they filed out.

Trudy Brown was waiting at the girls' door for Kanina. "Hi," she said, her big eyes smiling as she took Kanina's hand.

"Hey, squaw," another girl called. "Why don't ya go back to your wigwam?"

Trudy looked at the other girl, her face blank and embarrassed for a moment, then she laughed—a brief throaty artificial laugh.

There were four girls around them now. One of them was Marjorie, the redhead. "Kanina," Trudy began an introduction, "this is my friend, Marjorie Ball. She lives near us. . . ."

"We've met," Marjorie interjected, staring coldly. Then she turned to Trudy. "Is she your friend, Trudy? Does she live with you at Sadie's?"

Trudy was frowning now, obviously puzzled by the turn that events were taking. "Well . . . ." she said, looking self-consciously at her feet, "I just met her last night, so she's not a *real* friend."

"I wouldn't have an Indian for a friend," Marjorie declared. "They have lice and fleas and stuff. They let the boys take them to motels all night."

Everyone, including Trudy, laughed. Kanina broke away from them and ran across the schoolyard and up the street. When she went into the boarding house she could hear Mrs. Rumsey and Sadie talking in the kitchen. She slipped upstairs quietly and lay sobbing on the bed. Then Trudy came in.

"I'm going to move!" Trudy declared loudly. "I'm going to move in with Marjorie Ball. Marjorie says I can."

They were in the dining room and Kanina heard Sadie ask: "But Trudy, why?"

"I didn't know about Indians," Trudy went on. "I guess I was dumb. Indians have lice and fleas and stuff. Indian girls go out with boys all night. I can't live with an Indian. I just have to move or I won't have a friend in the whole school!"

"Where's Kanina?" Joan Rumsey asked in a cold, crisp voice.

"I don't know," Trudy answered. "I don't care. She's here somewhere. I'm leaving this place!"

Trudy ran up the stairs and into her room. Joan Rumsey followed her and came into the room where Kanina lay face down on the bed. Mrs. Rumsey closed the door and sat on the bed beside Kanina, patting her lightly on the shoulder.

"What happened, dear?" she asked.

"No one likes me because I'm an Indian. I'm going home to Cape Cree."

"It is my fault, Kanina," Joan Rumsey said. "I knew it would happen. But I didn't know how to talk to you about it. I wanted to warn you . . . . so you'd be prepared, but I was embarrassed and ashamed so I told you nothing. I left you to find it out by yourself. It was unkind and I'm sorry."

Kanina sat up and wiped her eyes with a handkerchief.

"It looks worse at the first than it really is," Joan Rumsey continued. "It will die down when people get to know you as an individual, but it will never disappear. You will have to face it all your life. The weak ones can't face it and all over the world they are retreating back to the protection of their own little Cape Crees."

Joan Rumsey stopped. She was breathing hard and rubbing one thumb in the sweat-filled palm of the other hand.

"Do you want to stay, Kanina? Or do you want to go back to Cape Cree?"

Kanina's eyes were dry now and only a thin red line remained on their lower lids to indicate that she had been crying.

"I will stay."

"You have a list of the books you need?"

"Yes."

Joan Rumsey took her purse from the dresser and handed Kanina a ten-dollar bill.

"Here," she said. "There will be a crowd at the bookstore and they will tease you again. But I won't go with you. I can't help you. You must start now to face it alone."

The following months were cruel and humiliating. Except for Joan Rumsey's weekly letters and an occasional word of encouragement from Sadie, Kanina faced the daily school ordeal alone. But she liked the work and learned easily, and the prospect of abandoning it was a greater pain than the taunts she had to endure to stay.

Joan Rumsey's prediction that the hostility would ease but not disappear made itself gradually apparent. Kanina's presence at Park Collegiate became accepted; there was no more teasing and mockery, she was simply ignored. She was always lonely; even in a crowd she was isolated and alone. The effect, so far as school work was concerned, was beneficial. She spent hours in the public library dipping into everything from detective thrillers to Kant's *Critique of Pure Reason,* which she didn't understand but read just the same. She developed a keen fondness for verse, sometimes spending all of a Saturday afternoon reading poetry anthologies, frequently reading a poem she liked over and over again. She had plenty of time for study and her marks were always among the top three or four in her class.

For five years there was no appreciable change in the pattern of her high school life. Each summer she went back to Cape Cree, worked for two months in the big white house with Joan Rumsey and saw little of her parents. Each September she came back to Sadie Thomas' boarding house and Park Collegiate for the familiar round of snubs and social ostracism. She could have been popular with the boys if she had wanted to, but the dates they sought always involved taking her out alone. She was never asked by a boy to be his date at a mixed party where there would be other couples. Kanina wanted companionship but she turned down the dates and after a month or two of this each autumn the boys would give up and join the girls in ignoring her.

Trudy Brown never came back to Sadie's to live. She reached grade thirteen one year ahead of Marjorie Ball and Kanina, but failed in several subjects and returned for a second year. This put Trudy, Marjorie and Kanina together during their fifth and final year at Park Collegiate.

Kanina began thinking a good deal now about what she might do next. She did not know whether the Rumseys were prepared to invest anything more in her education and she knew this year might be the last. Whatever happened, she didn't want to go back to Cape Cree to stay, for she was no longer a part of the life there; yet she knew it was going to be difficult to fit herself into a white community, whatever the work she chose or the qualifications she had for it. Sometimes she wondered if the education she was getting would be worth what it was costing the Rumseys. But even in her most depressed periods she had no thoughts of stopping school, for she was driven on by a burning intellectual curiosity, the lure of learning for its own sake regardless of the use she might later be able to make of it.

The last year passed quickly, the final exam was written late in June and Kanina's high school life had reached its wretched end. When she walked from Park Collegiate for the last time she felt neither happiness nor sorrow, only a vague and gnawing uncertainty. What would happen to her now?

She went back to Cape Cree for the summer. Early in August she received by mail her graduation diploma and a report giving marks attained in each subject. Her lowest mark was a seventy-four in trig, her highest ninety-one in modern history. Joan Rumsey studied the report proudly.

"I'm not surprised, Kanina," she said. "I knew you would do very well. . . ." She paused, seeking words. "I can only say I am very proud of you. You should have the opportunity to go to university. But we could never afford it, and being an Indian and a girl you would never find summer jobs that would pay enough to be much help."

Joan Rumsey paused again, hiding her hesitancy by picking up the report and studying it carefully once more.

"I'm afraid," she went on, "that it will have to be nursing or teaching. Would you like to go into a hospital for nursing training, or go to teachers college?"

Kanina had thought it all over well, in case the opportunity came. Teaching, she had decided, would keep her closer to the books and the intellectual world that interested her.

"I would prefer teachers college," she replied, "and I hope someday I'll be able to repay you for it all."

Joan Rumsey put her arm around Kanina's shoulders. "That report," the woman said, "has paid for everything to date."

Kanina applied for enrollment in the Blackwood teachers college, was accepted, and in September she was back again in the little rear room at Sadie Thomas' boarding house.

CHAPTER TWENTY

IT would be easier at teachers college, Kanina thought, because students there would be more mature and serious than the high school crowd. Kanina was confident that for this one last year at least she would be able to join the social life of her class.

On opening morning they gathered in the auditorium and Kanina took a seat near the back and looked about her. She could see several students who had been with her in Park Collegiate and among them, sitting beside each other six or seven rows ahead, were Marjorie Ball and Trudy Brown, the Park Collegiate inseparables who had made Kanina's life miserable from her first day at high school. Dr. Karr, the principal, stepped onto the platform and the hum of voices suddenly stilled. He was a tall man with a stern unsmiling face and thick bulbous lips that rolled back over his teeth like red half-moons when he talked. Dr. Karr outlined the subjects they would cover during the year and introduced the teachers. Then he announced that they would be divided alphabetically into ten classes.

"The first class," he said, "will be those whose surnames start with A, B or C. This group may leave now and gather in Room 1 on the first floor."

Kanina Beaverskin rose and walked from the auditorium. About thirty-five others followed her, among them Trudy Brown and Marjorie Ball. As she walked down the hall she could hear Trudy and Marjorie talking to each other not far behind her. Then their conversation suddenly stopped.

"Oh no! Surely not here. Do you see what I see?" It was Marjorie's voice.

They drew up beside her and Kanina smiled, trying to make it look as if she hadn't heard. Marjorie took Trudy's hand and barged on past, pulling Trudy behind her. She looked back quickly at Kanina. "I thought we saw the last of you last June," she said.

During the first few weeks Kanina kept to herself, for she had decided to go slow at the beginning while mentally sorting out the flippant and puerile like Marjorie so that she would know whom to avoid. Periodically Marjorie Ball would refer to her as "the James Bay squaw," usually picking a time when there was a good audience, but no one except Trudy seemed to pay much attention. There were no snubs from other classmates, no references to her race, and Kanina was sure that college was working out the way she had hoped. After a month she decided it was safe to seek a more active part in the school's extracurricular activities. She joined the drama club and was given a part in a play they would be staging for Christmas. The cast began rehearsing two nights a week. It was a small part but the rehearsals with coffee afterward were an exciting introduction to that other side of school life always barred to her before. She had never been happier.

One morning late in October Kanina walked into the room a few minutes before nine o'clock and left her briefcase on her desk. Marjorie, standing beside her desk opposite, glanced up but did not speak. Kanina hurried back out to check with one of the drama club girls about the time for that evening's rehearsal and the nine o'clock bell rang as she re-entered the room. Students began going back to their desks. Dr. Karr came in and strode rapidly to the front of the room, his face stern and solemn as usual.

"Dr. Karr," Marjorie said very loudly, "someone has stolen my pen and pencil set!"

Dr. Karr questioned her, at first disbelieving, but Marjorie insisted the set was on her desk a couple of minutes previously and no one had left the room since. The principal stared sullenly at the class, the big lips pulling back now over his teeth.

"If anyone has the set he may speak up and we'll forget the incident," he said.

Students looked self-consciously at each other, but no one spoke.

"All right," Dr. Karr resumed, "every desk will be searched." He instructed the first student in each row to search the desks.

The pen and pencil were found among the books in Kanina's briefcase.

He was very tall when he stopped beside her desk. "Miss Beaverskin," Dr. Karr said quietly, "please come with me to the office."

She faced him there a minute later, trembling, her head swimming dizzily.

"Why did you do it?" he asked.

"I didn't do it," Kanina replied.

"How did it get with your books?"

"I was out of the room. There was plenty of opportunity for someone to put it there."

"I expected you to deny it." He paused, lowered his eyes and began absently screwing and unscrewing the cap of a pen that lay on his desk.

"It is true, isn't it," he resumed, "that your race doesn't have the traditional respect for personal property that we have?"

"In a way that's true. Among Indians who are still relatively uninfluenced by whites, private ownership is always subject to the higher overriding law that no one may retain something, for his own use only, when another person has greater need for it."

Kanina had not thought of herself as an Indian for a long time, but now, suddenly confronted by a crisis into which her race was going to be dragged, she felt a warm and defiant pride for her *Mooskek-owak* blood.

"We are a united, casteless people," she went on, "socialistic, if you want to call it that. When one has, all have. My people's life and environment demand this. In good times the law is rarely applied, but in bad times it is the only system under which my people could survive. If there is no meat in your pot, you eat out of your neighbor's pot. If your neighbor has a gun and yours is broken, you take his gun when you need it, but it isn't stealing because then it is your gun too. It wouldn't work in your society. Your people would abuse it, but among my people the law is never abused."

Dr. Karr leaned forward and his lips rolled back over his teeth. "I see," he said. "So you decided you needed Marjorie Ball's pen and you took it because you regarded it as your pen too? It may be your law, but you can't live by that law here."

"I did *not* take it," Kanina said coolly. "The customs of my people have nothing to do with it, because I chose several years ago to abandon their life and ways and seek another life in your society. . . ."

But Dr. Karr interrupted and went on talking slowly. "It is difficult for races and cultures as different as ours to mix successfully. Our values and moral standards are too different. Every Indian comes into white society on probation. Distrust and suspicion remain until you have proven yourself capable of living our way. To do this you must forget that you are an Indian. . . ."

Kanina's slender body suddenly tensed. Composed before, she was now trembling with anger.

"But you won't let us forget!" she exclaimed. "I have tried to forget. But when I fail to act the way some of your people think an Indian should act I find that someone has planted a stolen article in my possession. You know there is no proof I stole it. But you *want* to believe that I am a thief, because you think that Indians have to be thieves."

The swarthy skin of Kanina's cheeks and neck was flushed with red. Her mouth was dry and her lips trembled.

"Miss Beaverskin," Dr. Karr said curtly. "It is my duty to expel you from the school. I am very unhappy because your acceptance here for teacher training was an experiment and many people in the educational field have been watching anxiously to see how it would turn out. It has turned out the way many of them feared."

Dr. Karr's fingers were nervously screwing and unscrewing the pen cap again.

"But I don't intend to expel you," he resumed. "You came with an excellent report from your high school and you will still be given the opportunity to qualify as a teacher if you wish. But I shall have to ask that you drop out of any extracurricular activities you are now taking part in. If I didn't demand this, the students would."

He looked up. "Do you wish to stay under those restrictions?"

"I can't stay if it means that I am admitting a theft I didn't commit."

Dr. Karr shrugged and tossed his hands in a palms-up gesture of finality. "Well, there it is," he said. "You must make your own decision."

Kanina stared at him through eyes misted with tears. The tears thickened and Dr. Karr's narrow face with the big repulsive lips faded away. In its place she saw the large round face and the wide flattened nose of Joe Beaverskin, her father. He was squatting on the tent floor at Cape Cree with the black stew pot beside him and he was pushing big chunks of meat into his mouth while the greasy broth dribbled from his chin. Kanina shuddered and she knew she could never go back. The tears thinned and her eyes focused again on the solemn immobile face of Dr. Karr.

"Is that all you wish to say?" he asked.

"No," she answered slowly. "I will change my decision. If I may, I will stay."

CHAPTER TWENTY-ONE

KANINA returned to the social seclusion she had known before, attending classes and keeping up her studies but taking no part in the school's other activities. The pen and pencil were not mentioned again, by Dr. Karr or anyone else. She decided resignedly that it was futile to attempt to defend herself before the other students and she knew her silence was accepted by all as an admission of guilt.

She wrote examinations in June and she stayed on afterwards at Sadie Thomas' boarding house because she was sure she would soon be able to start looking for a teaching position. Every two weeks Joan Rumsey sent her the usual check from Cape Cree for board and clothing money, and Mrs. Rumsey said she would continue to do this until September when Kanina commenced teaching. Kanina's teaching certificate arrived in July and she began studying the newspaper ads for teaching positions. She selected one from a village not far outside the city, applied by letter, and received a phone call the following evening from one of the school trustees.

"Miss Beaverskin, you have an unusual name," he said immediately. "Do you have some Indian ancestry?"

"I am a Cree from the Bay," she replied. "A full-blooded Cree."

"And you are twenty years old?"

"Yes, sir."

"I would like to meet you. Could I call at your home in town?"

"Yes." Kanina gave him the address.

She met him at the door early the following afternoon. He was fortyish, short, but dark and virile-looking. Sadie Thomas was out shopping and Kanina led him into the living room. He stood in the center of the floor, his eyes roving restlessly up and down Kanina's slender body, and for many seconds he didn't speak. The silence was embarrassing her. Finally he sat down.

"I must say, I didn't expect to find an Indian teacher as attractive as you," he said. "First I should explain that the other trustees are busy and I am selecting our new teacher alone . . . . myself."

Kanina nodded, studying the man uneasily.

"Now," he continued, "if you would like to . . . . I would like to discuss the details in private . . . . in my hotel room . . . . I will drive you downtown."

"We can discuss everything that is necessary here," Kanina answered.

"Miss Beaverskin," he resumed, "you realize, I'm sure, that school boards will be reluctant to hire an Indian girl. But you are probably willing to offer more . . . . in the way of qualifications . . . . than white girls, for example, are customarily willing to."

Kanina stared at him, alarmed. There was a smile on his face and she hated it.

"Come now, you're no child," he said. "If I am satisfied you will have the job."

"If you can't be satisfied sitting where you are, I don't want your job!" she declared. "I'm a teacher, not a prostitute."

He jumped to his feet. "Thank you very much, Miss Beaverskin," he said, all suaveness and gentleman again. "I'll be making my decision shortly and will let you know."

He left, and Kanina didn't rise from her chair to see him to the door. She remained seated, trembling violently for several minutes, her mind a hurly-burly of distress and bewilderment. Were Indian girls the sluts that white men seemed to think? Or was this just another falsehood fabricated to bolster the theory of racial inferiority? Kanina had not had enough contact with members of her race to know the answer.

She replied to many ads that summer but September came and she had not obtained a teaching position. She knew the Rumseys would guess the truth yet she was too embarrassed to refer to it in her letters. She considered applying to the Indian residential school at Moose Factory, but discarded the idea. In the Indian mind there were white man skills and Indian skills, and the two, they thought, could never mix. They would have no confidence in a school teacher of their own race. It was hard enough now to induce them to send their children to the residential school; Kanina was sure her presence there would undermine still more their confidence in the school.

She had no friends in Blackwood except Sadie Thomas. She could have had boyfriends but the opinions they all seemed to have of her as an Indian girl frightened her, and she avoided them. She did not consider going back to Cape Cree because she was still confident that she would find a teaching job. But in the meantime she knew she could not remain a ward of the Rumseys. She must support herself.

The best she could find was a $15-a-week job as a waitress in a small restaurant about two blocks from Sadie Thomas' house. It would pay for her board and not much more, but she wrote to Joan Rumsey and told her she was working and would no longer need money. She didn't tell Joan Rumsey what the job was.

She disliked it intensely from the beginning. The restaurant had a crowd of youths who sat drinking cokes and reading comics by the hour. They began ogling her as soon as she appeared the first evening, whispering to each other. Three of them in quick succession asked for dates. She quit work at eleven o'clock that night, walked hastily from the restaurant and ran home before anyone could follow her. She entered her room breathlessly and her eyes shifted to the teacher's certificate that had been pinned up proudly for two months on the wall. She snatched it down angrily and crumpled it into a bureau drawer. It was a worthless scrap of paper.

She worked at the restaurant all winter and into the following spring. The job's one blessing was that it was close to Sadie's and, although boys often walked from the restaurant with her, she could always be home before her self-appointed escort could get very far into his seduction routine.

She continued to check the newspaper ads but there were no teachers being sought now in mid-term. Early in May, however, she saw an ad seeking a teacher for a one-room rural school near Cochrane. She wrote a letter of application the same afternoon before beginning her evening shift at the restaurant. For several days she waited impatiently for each mail.

The acceptance letter came eight days later and Kanina read it excitedly. There were fifteen pupils spanning all eight grades, the letter said, and the salary was $120 a month. The previous teacher had retired because of poor health and the school was now closed. The letter was signed by the trustee board chairman, a man named Ralph Bick, who offered to meet Kanina's train at Cochrane if she wired and told him when she would be arriving.

Kanina quit the restaurant job that evening. Next morning she wrote a letter to Joan Rumsey telling her about the school, bought her train ticket and wired Mr. Bick that she would be arriving the following afternoon. Then she bought herself a new two-piece set of Irish linen luggage because her old suitcase, owned originally by the Rumseys, was too battered now to stay closed. The two bags of plastic-coated linen with cowhide bindings cost her almost twenty-five dollars. She couldn't afford them, and after train fare it took most of her savings. That afternoon she packed. The new bags took all of her clothing and personal things and she had two cardboard cartons of books.

Mr. Bick met her train the next afternoon. A small quick-moving man with gray, wiry hair showing under his peaked tweed cap, he walked briskly across the station platform as soon as Kanina stepped down from her coach.

"Miss Beaverskin?" he asked.

"Yes. You are Mr. Bick?"

He nodded and they shook hands. He wore overalls and rubber boots and appeared to be a farmer. They waited for her luggage and then he led her to a small truck; he loaded her luggage into the back, they climbed into the cab and drove away.

The region around Cochrane levels out into a flat clay plain that forms an island of tillable soil in the thousands of square miles of forest and muskeg around it. But many of the farms they passed were rundown and impoverished. They seemed to have been driving a long time when Mr. Bick stopped the truck suddenly.

"There it is," he said.

It was a small school, very old looking, its exterior covered with faded and cracked gray tarpaper. Kanina had never seen a school look quite as shabby, but it was *her* school, and she gazed at it now with a tingling thrill of pride and joy.

"It's late," Mr. Bick said. "You better wait till tomorrow to see inside. Now," he went on, "that's my place over there." He nodded to a farmhouse a couple of hundred yards up the road. It was small but had been painted red sometime in recent years and looked more prosperous than most of the farm homes she had seen on the drive out. "The other teacher boarded with us, but you can look around and board somewhere else if you like."

"I think I would like to board with you."

He started the truck again and it ground in low gear up the muddy lane to the Bick house. He honked the horn and a small woman and two boys in their early teens came out onto the veranda as Kanina stepped down from the truck. Mr. Bick introduced his wife and sons, then he and the boys carried her luggage and books to an upstairs front room that had a window looking out toward the school.

"Will you be ready to start tomorrow morning?" Mr. Bick asked her. "Yes."

He turned to the boys. "Come on," he said. "We'll tell everyone school is starting again at nine tomorrow."

They left her and a minute later she heard the truck back out to the road and rattle away.

Mr. Bick took her across and unlocked the school next morning. She followed him inside carrying an armload of books and looked around quickly, anxiously; it was dark and cold and smelled musty. The only lights were three gasoline lanterns that hung on wires from the ceiling. The desks were old and carved with initials; there was a table at the front for the teacher and a small blackboard. A big iron stove squatted in the center aisle. She saw no books, no maps, no pictures on the walls.

"It ain't much," Mr. Bick said, "but it's all we can afford in this country."

She arranged her books on the teacher's desk while Mr. Bick brought in wood and started a fire in the stove to dry out the building. He left her a few minutes later and Kanina waited nervously for her pupils to arrive.

She heard a group of them coming down the road and she went to the door to meet them. They filed in shyly, each one carrying a lunch bucket; the school, drab and tomblike before, was suddenly filled with color and noisy activity. She had feared from the rundown appearance of the district that the children might be rowdy and troublesome, but it became apparent quickly that all were well-disciplined and cooperative. She read them animal stories, and at recess she went out into the schoolyard and turned a skipping rope for the girls.

Mrs. Bick had given her a lunch and Kanina stayed at school with the children during the noon hour. By now she had learned their names, and they chatted with her eagerly about pets at home and about younger brothers and sisters who would be coming to school next year. Kanina liked them, and she was sure that they liked her. Not one even seemed to have noticed that she was an Indian.

The afternoon class had just begun when there was a firm knock on the door. Kanina walked down the aisle and opened it. Two women stood outside.

"You the new teacher?" one of them asked.

"Yes." Kanina tried to smile cordially.

"Well, I'm Mrs. Carter, Betty and Jack's ma, and I've come to get my kids." She stood very erect and stared defiantly at Kanina.

"Is there anything wrong?" Kanina asked.

"Yes," Mrs. Carter said quickly. "Ralph Bick didn't have any business hiring an Indian. I don't want ya teachin' my kids. I don't trust ya. I don't trust no Indian."

"I'm gettin' my kids too," the other woman said. "The King kids. There's two of them. Ralph Bick didn't tell anybody you're an Indian. We just found out."

Kanina could only stare at them, speechless and trembling. Here it was again, the same haunting, plaguing bogy that had entered her life that night long ago when she met Joan Rumsey's sister. She turned back falteringly into the gloomy classroom.

"Betty and Jack Carter, the King children," she said slowly, "you may leave. Your mothers are waiting outside."

Events moved quickly after that. Three more pupils were absent from school next day. On the third day only four out of the original fifteen showed up—the Bick boys and two others—and Kanina went through the motions of teaching like a wooden puppet, animated but bereft of real life. That afternoon at four o'clock when the pupils left, a young man walked into the school carrying a big camera.

"Miss Beaverskin?"

"Yes."

"I'm a reporter from town. We heard they are dismissing you and closing the school because the parents won't have an Indian teacher. Have you heard about it?"

"I haven't heard," Kanina answered coolly, "but it's probably true."

"Something like this happens every once in a while," the reporter said. "The papers will be on your side, you know. How long have you been here?"

Kanina saw no reason why she shouldn't talk freely. She answered his questions for half an hour and before it was finished she had summarized her whole life. Then he asked if he could take pictures of her. Kanina agreed.

He left and Kanina walked slowly to her room at the Bicks. At supper Ralph Bick sat stiffly at the head of the table and hardly a word was spoken by anyone. Kanina could feel the impending crisis. She went up to her room. Shortly before eight o'clock cars and pickup trucks began gathering outside the school. She sat by her window and watched. The door downstairs closed and in the faint light she saw Ralph Bick walk out the drive and down the road toward the school. Kanina knew what was happening. And she knew without waiting for the parents' meeting to end what the outcome would be.

Around ten the cars and trucks began to pull away. The school lights went out. The door downstairs opened and she heard Ralph Bick come in.

He knocked on her door a few minutes later and Kanina opened it. He stood outside in the hall, a small nervous man in overalls, his face white and solemn.

"I'm sorry," he began. "I guess you know, eh?"

"Yes. I know."

"I argued with them, but they were furious. Wouldn't even consider lettin' you stay till school closin' time in June. It ain't right. But what can you do?" He paused, and continued a moment later. "There were reporters there. It'll give us a bad name when it gets in the papers."

He handed her a check. "I told 'em we'd have to give you a month's pay."

Kanina remained at the Bicks for three more days while her mind wrestled with the problem of what to do with the life and plans that had collapsed around her. The Bicks subscribed to no newspaper but several came by mail from relatives and Kanina read a number of news stories and editorials bitterly condemning the racial prejudice that had taken her job. The arguments were eloquent and high-sounding in abstract type, she thought, but she wondered if the editors would hold as firmly to their opinions if she were standing in front of their desks applying for a job and not safely isolated from them in the northern Ontario bush.

Kanina saw herself now with a clarity she had never known before. She knew she could live in the white man's world, but only as a waitress or a domestic; his professional world, the world that would use her mind instead of her hands, was barred from her. It left her two choices. She could be the white man's hand servant or she could go back to Cape Cree and take up the *Mooskek-owak* life where she had left it at the age of four. The seventeen years since then had molded her into a person who could only shudder at either prospect. She thought of her mother and father sitting on the tent floor eating slabs of meat with their fingers. And she thought of the boys lounging in the restaurant at Blackwood and running their hands stealthily around her hips when she brought the coffee to their tables. She had to choose one or the other.

It had all been a tragic seventeen-year mistake. It would have been better if she had not gone out to the hospital when she was four, because they had merely cured her body of one trouble and planted another in her mind. They had saved her life but in doing so had set in motion a process that had now turned it into a life not worth living. She knew what she had to do. She was a *Mooskek-owak* by blood if not by training, and she could never be anything else because blood was the real determiner.

On the third day after her dismissal her mind was made up. At supper she spoke to Ralph Bick. "There's a train to Moosonee in the morning," she said. "Will you drive me in to catch it?"

He nodded silently.

In town next morning she cashed her check. In a drugstore she saw a paperback edition of Julian Huxley's *Man in the Modern World* and bought it to read on the train. Then Mr. Bick drove her to the station and saw her luggage safely onto the baggage car while Kanina bought her ticket to Moosonee.

"One-way or return?" the ticket clerk asked her.

"One-way," she answered quietly.

Ralph Bick left her after a quick embarrassed goodbye and Kanina stood alone on the platform. She looked hesitantly at the two faded coaches. On her trips to and from high school she had always ridden in the cleaner rear coach used by the whites, because she had felt that going to a white school gave her white status. But now at last she knew where she belonged. Kanina climbed slowly into the Indian coach ahead.

CHAPTER TWENTY-TWO

NOW it was dusk, the last thin red sliver of sun had faded behind the jagged spruces in the west and the Polar Bear Express was reeling madly down the last sloping miles to Moosonee. Kanina watched listlessly as the stunted spruces and the flat greening fingers of sphagnum bog flashed by her window. She had not eaten since breakfast and she was very hungry. But she had been afraid to go back to the restaurant car because she knew that Rory Macdonald, the tall blond biologist with the sunburned nose, was in that coach. Ever since she had met him soon after the train left Cochrane she had felt a vague and unsettling anxiety.

She was aware now of the attraction she had for men. She was fairly sure, if she wanted to encourage the acquaintanceship, that this young and good-looking scientist could provide the serious and intelligent sort of companionship she had sought for so long. But now it was too late. The lesson of the past seven years had finally driven itself firmly into her consciousness. There was no place in either the Indian's or the white man's society for an Indian intellectual and the sooner she could revert to the simple *Mooskek-owak* life, the happier she would be in the end. Discussing Huxley and such, with a university student who seemed as well read as she, would only postpone and make more difficult the final break that had to come. She had to avoid this Rory Macdonald.

The siren on the Diesel locomotive ahead burst into a growling wail. They were pulling in to Moosonee and the passengers began lifting packsacks and parcels down from the luggage racks. Kanina stood up and saw the book of Huxley essays on the opposite seat where she had thrown it several hours before. She would have to stay in Moosonee at least tonight, perhaps a couple of days, and it would be lonely. She would want to read and she looked again at the book. Then she turned away quickly and left it lying on the seat as she stepped out into the vestibule between the coaches. She was done with that world of books and ideas.

The train ground to a stop and she looked out at the crowded, dimly lit platform. A trainman opened the coach door and she was the first one down. The white passengers were detraining from the far end of their coach and she got a glimpse of the tall young biologist striding along the platform toward her. Kanina elbowed her way quickly through the crowd and walked rapidly down Moosonee's one street toward a small boarding house where she had spent nights before. She looked back. The crowd, most of them Indians, milled noisily around the train. Rory Macdonald wasn't in sight.

She went to bed that night wearing her nylon slip because her pajamas were still in her luggage at the station. It would be the last slip she would ever own, she thought bitterly, because she would have no use for nylon lingerie in the tattered tent at Cape Cree.

After breakfast next morning Kanina noticed that two men were fueling a government plane moored at the river dock. She walked down. One of the men wore a khaki uniform and was obviously the pilot.

"I've been out to school and I'm looking for a ride home to Cape Cree," she told him. "If you're stopping there will you have room for me?"

He looked her over, his eyebrows lifting approvingly.

"Sure will, miss. And you sure don't look like a Cape Cree gal."

"I have some luggage at the station."

"How much?"

Kanina thought of the two cartons of books and wondered if there was any point in taking them. If she started a school for the children she would need some of them, and there was no time now to sort school books from the others. She would have to take them all.

"Four pieces," she told the pilot.

"We'll have a truck down here in a minute. The driver'll pick them up. We're leaving in half an hour."

She left her baggage stubs with the pilot, then walked back to pay for her room. When she returned to the plane her luggage was aboard and the engine was idling slowly, warming up. The pilot motioned her in and she climbed into the rear seat while he waited on the dock.

"Where in hell's that goose guy?" she heard the pilot ask.

"That's him coming," the other man said.

The plane was moored so that it faced the river and Kanina couldn't see the shore behind. A few moments later she heard running footsteps on the wharf. The pilot said: "Get in the back." Rory Macdonald appeared at the door, climbed in and sat on the double seat with Kanina. A large pair of binoculars hung on a strap around his neck and a small haversack hung from one shoulder.

He smiled a big beaming smile. "What! You again so soon!" he declared. "My luck *is* running well!"

Kanina nodded and said: "Hello."

"You disappeared so fast last night I thought you must have gone back on the train for something," he said. "I went on to look for you and here. . . ." He was reaching into the haversack. "You forgot this."

He held out her copy of Huxley's *Man in the Modern World*.

"I don't want it, thanks," Kanina said. "You keep it. Huxley's modern world is too far removed from my world now."

Rory stared at her. "You're being childish," he said. "You don't have to become an exile just because some stupid backwoodsers won't accept you for their school. You're trained to do an important job. You're needed. I refuse to believe my people are so stupid they won't accept you. You're exaggerating a few petty snubs."

"Tell it to your people who hire school teachers," she said. "Don't tell it to me."

The pilot and his companion had climbed in and the motor roared. There was too much noise now for conversation and Kanina settled back into the seat, relieved that the discussion was over. The water streaked by beneath the plane's pontoons and they took off. Looking sideways stealthily, she saw Rory Macdonald putting the Huxley book back in his haversack, then he turned his back toward her and began scanning the ground below through his window. His shoulders were broad and powerful, she noticed, despite the tall lanky appearance he had when he was standing. A minute later he looked back at her and smiled. Kanina realized with embarrassment that she had been staring at his back steadily since the plane took off and she turned quickly away.

The plane bumped lightly on the thermals of warm air lifting off the James Bay shore beneath them. It was almost June but the inland lakes were still icebound and only the rivers, where there was a current, had open water. She saw that Rory Macdonald was studying the ground below with his binoculars and she knew he was looking for geese.

Half an hour later they landed on the mouth of a river that had six Indian tents on its shore and they taxied in to the beach. A band of thirty or forty Indians met them.

"We're going to interview these families about their beaver trapping," the pilot said. "It'll take half an hour so you might as well walk around." Then to Kanina: "If we need an interpreter I'll call you."

The four of them climbed out of the plane. Kanina saw Rory Macdonald studying the Indians curiously.

"Do all these people sleep and live in those six tents or wigwams or whatever they are?" he asked Kanina.

"Quite likely," she answered. She walked away along the narrow beach, hoping Rory would stay with the pilot. But he followed and out of the corner of one eye she saw him move up beside her.

"I haven't seen a goose yet," he said.

"You will," she told him and walked on.

They walked slowly, and he was much taller than she. Kanina looked up, then had to turn her eyes away quickly because he was looking down intently at her. The silence, with him so close, made her self-conscious and uncomfortable.

"Where do geese go for the winter?" she asked, feeling that she had to say something.

"There are at least two distinct populations of Canada geese nesting around James Bay," he told her. "They're all the same species, but each population is a distinct unit with its own ancestral breeding range and its own wintering range. They never mix. One is the Mississippi flyway population. They winter down the Mississippi valley, and nest here on the west side of James Bay, but well north toward Hudson Bay. The other population we're sure of is a South Atlantic population. They winter in the South Atlantic states and their breeding range here on the bay is south of the breeding range used by the Mississippi population. They never encroach on each other's territory, winter or summer. Hunting regulations have to be tailored for each population. You could wipe out one without affecting the other."

"How do you know all this?" she asked.

"From leg-banding. You've seen banded geese shot up here?"

"No," she said, "but I've heard of Indian hunters shooting banded geese. They hand the bands in at the Hudson's Bay posts. Some of them think the banded geese are sent by God from heaven. And I've known some missionaries who encourage the idea. God isn't as helpful as he used to be. And sometimes the Indians want to know why. If he sent manna to the Israelites, they ask, why doesn't he send us some when our old people and children are starving in the winter. It's a tough one to answer, so some missionaries are glad to get a little help, such as geese from heaven bearing silver bands."

Rory laughed at her quietly. "They're aluminum," he said. "And whoever's doing it—God or the biologists—it hasn't given us a very complete picture yet of the breeding ranges here around the bay. That's why I'm here—to fill in the picture of nesting distribution. If I can band a few and some of the banded geese get themselves shot next fall in the south, it'll help figure the business out."

"What population would the geese around Cape Cree belong to?" she asked him.

"Cape Cree is far enough north to have Mississippi flyway geese. We *do* know that."

She had asked the first question merely to fill in the silence that embarrassed her, but now she found herself listening intently.

"Geese are remarkable birds, all of them," he was saying now, "but two species especially—the Canada you have here and the barnacle goose we have in the Old World. They have all the qualities that man admires in his fellow men—industry, strength, intelligence and, most pronounced of all, the capacity to fall in love."

He laughed softly as he went on.

"Most biologists would be horrified to hear it expressed in those words, yet the bond that develops between a pair of mated geese cannot be very different from what we call love. Geese mate for life and once pairing has occurred only death can separate them. They have a family life too. Young birds as a rule leave their parents as soon as they can fly, but not geese. A goose family remains together almost a year. Not till it's time for the parents to start nesting again do they kick the youngsters out and say 'Okay, children, you're old enough to look after yourselves.' "

He stopped, but Kanina wished he would go on. She didn't know whether it was Rory Macdonald himself or what he was saying about the geese that fascinated her.

"Where are all your geese now?" Rory asked her.

"We haven't reached good goose country yet," Kanina answered. "They need pothole muskeg . . . . muskeg that's full of small lakes and ponds with little islands in them. They nest on the islands to keep away from the foxes. We'll start seeing pothole muskeg five or ten minutes from here and we'll be flying over it for forty or fifty minutes the rest of the way to Cape Cree."

"How early do you see the first geese?" he asked her.

"Late in April. There's always ice on the lakes for two or three weeks after they get back. They stay in small flocks, flying around to feed or sitting on the ice . . . . they're family groups, I suppose. As soon as the lakes open up, the flocks disappear. I suppose that's when the old birds start nesting."

Why was she telling him all this? She didn't really want to talk, yet a vague impelling urge kept her talking.

"My people hunt the geese while they are in the spring flocks," she continued. "They'll be out at the goose camps hunting them now, because this spring is a week or two later than usual. There's still ice on the lakes, I noticed from the plane. After beaver meat all winter, and sometimes not much of that, it's a happy time when the first geese get back in the spring."

She paused and looked at him sharply.

"Have you ever been hungry? I don't mean hungry because one of your meals is late, I mean the slow hunger that comes when you live for weeks and weeks on a couple of mouthfuls of food each day."

Rory Macdonald was slowly shaking his head.

"It happens here many winters. You should try it as part of your goose research. Until you've felt that hunger kneading your stomach like a lump of bannock dough week after week you can never understand how that first flock of spring geese looks to my people."

Now she was angry with herself for talking too much.

"And that's the life," Rory said, "that you have decided to return to?"

"Yes," she said firmly. And when their eyes met now she stared at him openly with no trace of the shyness she had felt before.

They were in the air again a few minutes later and soon they were flying over the pothole muskeg she had described. The country was very flat to the horizon and interlaced with a labyrinth of lakes and ponds, all of the water areas gray and somber with sheets of ice still intact. Twisting among the lakes were black fingers of spruce forest on the gravel ridges and hummocks where root systems could circulate above the water which underlay all of this land. Filling in the spaces between lakes and forest was the soft brown of the boglands beginning to show edgings of green now with the first faint touches of the northern spring.

She had heard Rory making arrangements with the pilot before they took off and now they were flying low while Rory studied the frozen lakes and bogs slipping past beneath them. Kanina kept a watch out her side of the plane. Suddenly Rory grasped her arm and pulled her toward him. "Geese, eleven of them!" he shouted in her ear above the engine roar, pointing excitedly through his window. "Look at them, quick!" He was still tugging on her arm. He pulled her until she was leaning far across in front of him and looking out the window on his side. She was pressed against his chest and the hand on her arm held her so firmly she couldn't move away. She could feel the rapid movement of his breathing and his face was so close that for a moment their cheeks brushed.

Kanina didn't see the geese because her head spun dizzily and she was conscious only of his closeness. It was only a couple of seconds before she pushed away from him and moved back to her own side of the plane but her heart was pounding like gunfire in her ears. She realized with a shock that for the first time in her life she had felt pleasure in being close to a boy.

Rory leaned toward her. "Sorry," he shouted. "I missed the geese this spring in Toronto. I always get excited when I see them again for the first time."

Kanina saw many flocks of geese after that, but she did not attempt to tell Rory because she knew from his rapid note-taking that he was seeing them from his side of the aircraft too. Then the plane banked and she saw the big Kistawanee River below. She saw the familiar cluster of buildings and Indian tents, but a number of them were only roofless frames and she knew that the lateness of the spring was holding many of the families at the goose-hunting camps up the Kistawanee.

The plane's aluminum pontoons hit the water with a roar like the beating of many drums at once and Kanina was home—this time to stay.

The crowd on the beach was smaller than usual. She could see Mrs. Rumsey walking down from the big white house to meet the plane, her light dress snapping about her legs in the breeze. She would be surprised to see Kanina; she would be more than surprised, she would be shocked, when Kanina told her she was not returning to her room in the Rumseys' house but was going back with her parents.

The plane touched the beach. Rory Macdonald opened the door on his side, climbed down onto the pontoon and turned to help Kanina. Then Joan Rumsey saw her.

"Kanina!"

Kanina waved but couldn't smile. Joan Rumsey's hair was now almost totally gray, but except for that she was the same tall, smiling, thin-faced woman Kanina had first met ten years before. Kanina looked quickly over the crowd of Indians on the bank above but couldn't see her parents. She walked across the beach toward Mrs. Rumsey, dreading the meeting that now must come.

"I had to come back," she said, looking firmly at Joan Rumsey. "There is no place for me there. It took a long time but I see it now. I am a *Mooskek-owak*. I should never have tried to be anything else. I am sorry, because you tried so hard to help me. . . ."

Joan Rumsey took her hand. "Never mind now," she said quietly. "It is nice to see you again."

Rory Macdonald moved close to them and Kanina was glad of the diversion. She introduced Joan Rumsey to Rory, then Rory went back to the plane for her luggage.

"May I store two boxes of books in the house?" Kanina asked.

"Of course," Mrs. Rumsey said. "You can have them in your room."

"I won't be wanting the room again. I am going back with my parents."

"You can't," Joan Rumsey said quietly, with firm and obvious self-assurance. "Your parents are away. They are hunting geese."

Kanina had feared it. Everything possible that could make things more difficult seemed to be happening. First there had been the unexpected meeting with Rory Macdonald on the plane, and now this, her parents' absence, would force her back again into the Rumsey house.

It was nearly noon and Joan Rumsey invited them all to the house for lunch. They walked up slowly, the men carrying Kanina's bags and books. Bert Rumsey met them in front of the store and shook Kanina's hand vigorously. "A new batch of crossword puzzles just came in on a plane yesterday," he told her. Mrs. Rumsey had the pilot and Rory take the luggage directly to Kanina's old room. During lunch Rory described the goose research he hoped to do.

"Later on," he said, "I'll be leaving Moosonee and moving down this way. Where . . . . it'll depend on where I find geese, but from what we saw on the flight this morning Cape Cree looks promising. Would you be able to board me?"

"We would like to very much," Joan Rumsey told him.

"I'd like to travel out on trips, into the goose country, maybe a week at a time," Rory continued. "Can I rent a canoe, an outboard, tent and so on? And hire an Indian guide who speaks English?"

Bert Rumsey nodded. "There's a good guide here," he said, "our interpreter at the store. I could let you have him. His name's Jock."

Kanina said little during the meal. Afterward they all walked back to the plane. There were the usual thanks and goodbyes, then at the last Rory Macdonald stepped close to Kanina and whispered: "I'll be bringing back your Huxley essays in a week or two. You'll be wanting them again by then."

"I won't," she answered and stepped away from him to thank the pilot. Out of the corner of her eye she saw Rory climbing into the plane but she didn't look at him again. Kanina and Joan Rumsey waited on the beach as the plane taxied to midstream, turned into the wind and took off. When it was gone Joan Rumsey turned quickly.

"Now let's go back to the house and talk," she said.

While they washed dishes Kanina told her about the pen incident at teachers college, about the restaurant job, the long search for a teaching position and the dismissal that came after just three days in her first school.

"There was a plane in yesterday with mail," Joan Rumsey said. "We read about it in the papers. Now . . . . . what's all this nonsense about going back to your old life?"

"It has to be that or a life as the white man's servant. If I'm not good enough to teach his children, I refuse to wash his dishes in a restaurant or make his beds in a hotel. Or be his prostitute, the profession they seem to think I should follow. I have *some* pride left. I'm not ashamed of being a *Mooskek-owak,* but I am ashamed at being such a poor one, at having let myself grow up without learning any of the *Mooskek-owak* skills. The only life that's open to me now is the one I'm not trained to lead.

"You tried to help me," Kanina went on rapidly. "You didn't know and neither did I that professional training for an Indian is wasted. I'm grateful, but it was all a mistake. I know your people now better than you know them yourself. You've been isolated here, I've been outside living with them. . . ."

"Kanina," Joan Rumsey interrupted softly, "don't decide anything in a hurry. . . ."

"I'm not! I have taken seven years to decide. I have been trying to persuade myself all those seven years . . . . ever since that first day at high school, that what was happening to me wasn't really true."

"You are not used to the Indian life," Joan Rumsey argued. "You haven't lived it since you were four. You can never go back now. A winter in the bush, the way they live, will kill you."

Mrs. Rumsey put a hand on Kanina's shoulder and spun her roughly until they faced each other. Kanina stared at her, stunned and frightened, for she had never seen this glassy savage look in Joan Rumsey's eyes before.

"Kanina Beaverskin," the white woman said with slow emphasis, "maybe it *was* a mistake, but it would be a much bigger mistake to try to go back now to your Indian life. I have been your mother for eleven years and I don't intend to let it end this way. You are going to stay here with us until something turns up. If I have to, I will lock you in your room!"

The shock and surprise at Joan Rumsey's anger passed quickly and Kanina stared back at her calmly.

"Making threats you can't carry out won't help either of us," Kanina said. "You have been a good mother. It isn't your fault it has turned out this way . . . . and I don't think it is mine. I can't remain dependent on you any longer. It is unjust to you, it would be still more unjust to me. What would happen to me if you were transferred to another post? Would I have to tag along like a helpless puppy, tied forever to your apron strings? I am starting all over to create a new life. I must prepare myself to be a *Mooskek-owak* wife. I have waited too long . . . . and if it kills me next winter and they bury me out there with all my brothers and sisters, it might be the best way out."

The hard glint had gone from Joan Rumsey's eyes and now they were moist with tears. Neither of them spoke for several seconds.

Then Kanina asked: "Where are my parents? On the Kistawanee?"

Joan Rumsey nodded meekly.

"Will there be a canoe going up tomorrow?"

Joan Rumsey nodded again. "There's usually someone going back and forth every day," she said. "You'll find your parents at the first camp ten miles up."

CHAPTER TWENTY-THREE

THE following morning Kanina went across to the Hudson's Bay store to buy new clothes. Bert Rumsey served her silently as she bought rubber boots, thick woolen socks, mittens and heavy, horrid-looking, long-legged underwear. Then she bought what was most essential of all— a black flannel shawl. This, more than anything else, was the badge of a *Mooskek-owak* woman. She hated it, but she knew she must wear it.

Kanina already had a parka and several sweaters she could continue wearing, but much of her city clothing would be of no use to her now. She would like to have bought jeans or slacks for they would be very practical for the life she was now going to lead, but at Cape Cree skirts were still the only acceptable wear for women and Kanina knew she must conform. Nothing would harm her more than to come back to them flaunting white man's ways.

Back in her room Kanina changed into the new clothing. The long underwear and woolen socks made her legs look like stovepipes. The shawl was hot and uncomfortable and it made her look much older. She wore the same blue sweater and blue plaid skirt that she had been wearing since she left the Bicks at Cochrane.

Kanina slipped out without Joan Rumsey seeing her and walked down to the Indian camp. All but about ten families were away hunting. Kanina saw a woman carrying water from the river and recognized her a moment later as Helen Cheechekan, the girl who had talked to Kanina in English and become her friend that first day she was back at Cape Cree from the

sanatorium eleven years before. It was almost two years since Kanina had
seen her last and now she noticed with a shock that her friend during
that time had lost all traces of her youth and had suddenly become a
typical Indian squaw, fat and dowdy from poor food and handmade
clothes. She was stooped now under a shoulder yoke that bore two large
lard pails of water and there was a baby strapped in its cradlelike
tikinagun on her back.

"*Wacheyu,* it is Kanina," Kanina said as she approached. "Do you
know if anyone is going up to the goose camps today?"

"Yes, my husband and I go this morning."

"Will there be room for me?"

"There will be room," Helen said, looking curiously at Kanina. "The
white people's schools are not closed yet for summer. Why do you go?"

"I am going back to my parents." Kanina paused there and didn't
know how to go on. Suddenly she realized that the rest of the story
would be difficult to explain to any of the *Mooskek-owak* here at Cape
Cree, even to someone like Helen whose outlook had at least been
broadened a little by a few years at residential school. The theory that
some people were born inferior or somehow less deserving than others
would be an idea so foreign to their thinking, so incompatible with their
cooperative way of life, that their minds would probably fail to grasp it.

Kanina left Helen, went back to her room and began hurriedly sorting
clothes. Most of her dresses, underclothing and shoes she placed in the
bigger bag to leave with the books here at the Rumseys'. She would never
want them again. The small bag would hold everything that was worth
taking with her. She picked up her purse containing lipstick and compact
and unhesitatingly tossed it into the bigger bag to be left behind. She
looked at a hairbrush and comb for a moment and decided to take them.
The toothbrush? Some *Mooskek-owak* children had been taught in recent
years by visiting government doctors to brush their teeth, so Kanina could
take her toothbrush without appearing eccentric. She came to her teaching certificate, tore it into small pieces and let the scraps of paper flutter
into the waste basket beside the bed.

She closed up the two pieces of luggage and pushed the bigger one
and the two cartons of books into a back corner of the clothes closet.
Then she picked up the small bag and with her new boots scuffing
clumsily at each step she went quickly down the stairs. Joan Rumsey met
her at the bottom.

"I must do it! I must!" Kanina cried. "Surely you can see it. Please
don't make it harder for me now!"

Joan Rumsey embraced her silently. With her lips close to Kanina's ear she murmured: "I am only going to say goodbye and . . . . come back whenever you want to."

Then they parted and Kanina walked rapidly outside. She went into the store to say goodbye to Bert Rumsey and remembered that she had to make one more purchase.

"I would like a metal plate and a stainless steel knife, fork and spoon," she told him. Her parents, her father especially, would probably disapprove, but Kanina had determined that she would take at least this one civilized refinement back into the darkness with her.

Her gleaming linen-covered wardrobe bag with the rich cowhide bindings looked strangely out of place among the soiled packsacks, canvas bundles and blackened pots that filled the center of the big twenty-foot canoe. Kanina sat near the middle on a roll of blankets. Helen Cheechekan with her baby was in the bow and Helen's husband—Kanina hadn't learned his name—sat at the rear beside the outboard motor clamped to the canoe's square stern. Under the powerful thrust of the motor, the canoe was swiftly breasting the Kistawanee's current. Occasionally a wisp of cold spray would whip back from the bow and hit Kanina's cheeks like tiny shattered pellets of ice.

She looked at the motor and thought of how conditions had changed since her first goose hunt up the Kistawanee eleven years ago. Then there were few outboards and the *Mooskek-owak* paddled their canoes by hand against the surging springtime current. Since then beaver had become more numerous although it still took a good trapper and a good trapping territory to produce $500 worth of fur a year. But this to the *Mooskek-owak* was prosperity and one of the things it had done was put an outboard motor on every family's canoe. Now, in the *Mooskek-owak* hunter's scale of values, an outboard was almost as essential as a wife, and he saw nothing incongruous in skimping on food so that he could buy gasoline for his motor. There was logic to it. Gasoline or food, it was all fuel, and what went into his motor certainly reduced what would otherwise be consumed by the muscles of his shoulders and arms on the end of a paddle.

They could be dispassionately practical about food supplies, Kanina knew. On a long trip a *Mooskek-owak* family rarely attempted to ration food so it would last to the trip's end. They would start out carrying all the food they conveniently could, and then eat it as fast as they felt inclined, reasoning that the faster they ate it the shorter the distance they would have to carry it, and the less they had to carry, the less food their bodies would require. It was typical of them, anyway, to live the present to the fullest and make little provision for the future.

As she thought of these things, Kanina realized she was coming back to the *Mooskek-owak* life with a serious handicap. She knew she would never be capable now of achieving that stoical, carefree attitude of her people which helped minimize the harshness of the present by blotting out all thought and fears of the future.

The lean agile Indian in the stern guided the canoe skillfully around hidden rocks and across sandy shallows. At the shallowest spots, Helen would jump to the bow and point out the twisting channel for her husband, frequently thrusting a paddle into the water to test its depth, knowing exactly and shouting a warning when there was not enough depth for the motor's propeller to clear. Kanina watched her closely. This, she thought, was one little example of the scores of skills she must master—skills that most *Mooskek-owak* girls had learned before they reached their teens. Helen and her husband, she thought, were a team dependent on each other in a close and practical way that white couples never knew. A white man with an incapable wife might be miserable but he could always carry on his job, for it rarely required a wife's help. But a *Mooskek-owak* hunter had to have a capable wife to complete himself, to make possible the full application of his own skills. Kanina thought guiltily of herself. She must lose no more time now in training herself for the role she was born to fill.

After an hour or two they rounded a bend and Kanina saw the camp on a point ahead. It was a clearing about the size of a football field with spruce forest crowding close behind and a gravelly beach strewn with canoes in front. Tents were scattered over it, fires flickered. Several women and children came down to the beach to meet them. Helen called to them as the canoe drew close.

"Kanina has come home. Are the Beaverskins here?"

Before anyone could answer there was an excited cry from one of the nearer tents. The flap flung open, a big woman darted out and Daisy Beaverskin was running nimbly down the slope toward the beach.

"Kanina! It *is* Kanina. I knew that someday you'd be coming back to me."

The canoe touched the beach and Kanina jumped out. Her mother and the other women gathered excitedly around her, talking rapidly, grasping her hands. The fears and uncertainties of the past several years were over and she was back now among people who loved her.

She was sitting in the tent alone with her mother a few minutes later.

"I have not come back for a visit," Kanina told her, and it seemed strange to be speaking Cree again. "I have come home to stay."

"I am glad," the woman said. She asked for no explanations and Kanina made no attempt to give her any.

"I will work with you and learn the things a *Mooskek-owak* woman should know," Kanina continued. "I will go with you for the winter trapping. Someday I will marry a *Mooskek-owak* man but there is much for me to learn first."

Daisy Beaverskin puffed slowly on her pipe and her dark eyes gleamed with joy.

The hunters came back late in the afternoon and Kanina was sitting by the fire at the front of the tent when her father came up carrying two geese by their long necks. He glanced casually at her as though she had never been away. His small dark expressionless eyes showed neither surprise nor pleasure.

"*Wacheyu.*" He spoke the Cree greeting quietly, dropped the geese beside the fire and went into the tent. His wife called and he returned to the doorway.

"Kanina has come home. She will not be going away again," Daisy Beaverskin said. "She will learn now to be a *Mooskek-owak* wife."

Kanina watched her father closely for some expression to break through the stolid mask of his face and indicate what he was thinking. His thick eyebrows lifted and for a moment Kanina didn't know whether it meant approval or disapproval. Then he smiled and his head nodded.

"I am glad you have come back to your people," he said in Cree. Then he added: "*Netanis.*" It was one of the Cree words for "daughter," but an intimate form that meant "my daughter" and stressed the family relationship. Joe Beaverskin would now have another stomach to hunt for, but his use of the word *netanis* meant that Kanina was being welcomed with a warmth he had never accorded her before.

Later when they ate their meal of stewed goose Kanina took out her plate and put her own portion of meat on it. She began cutting the meat with her knife and fork and she saw her father watching. After several seconds Joe Beaverskin pointed at her plate and laughed heartily. Kanina relaxed and laughed with him. He was taking it as a big joke. If that was to be his only reaction Kanina would have no worries.

Kanina began immediately learning her job as a *Mooskek-owak* woman. She started that evening by taking the axe and walking up the river to chop firewood; the axe was clumsy in her hands and she was reminded forcibly that she had never used an axe before. Next morning she began helping her mother pluck and clean the geese, noting carefully what parts of the birds provided the soft downy feathers that were saved for quilt-making.

That day the wind shifted to the northeast, bringing cold weather and a thick overcast of cloud in off James and Hudson Bays. Then day followed day, the cold lingered, the ice remained on the lakes and the goose hunt continued well past the time it normally ended.

Daisy Beaverskin enthusiastically assumed the task of teaching Kanina the *Mooskek-owak* way of life. She taught Kanina how to mix a batch of bannock dough in the flour bag without using a dish, how to fry it in deep fat and how to bake it by tilting the pan against a rock in front of the fire. They set traps along the river for muskrat and went each morning to check them. At first Kanina found skinning the rats and cleaning the geese a loathsome job, but she forced herself to do it and slowly she grew accustomed to the nauseous smell of the goose entrails and the slimy smear of blood on her hands. She learned how to cut the thick breast meat from the geese in one large slice for drying, and how to sever the legs and wings and remaining flesh to be used immediately in the stewing pot. She tended the drying fire and learned to control it so that little smoke touched the meat, because the *Mooskek-owak* dislike their meat strongly smoked.

Three times in six days she saw the government plane fly over and each time she watched it disappear with a twinge of sadness that she knew she should not feel. Rory Macdonald would be up there gazing down at the *Mooskek-owak* camp as he scanned the muskeg for his geese. And while her reasoning argued that she should do everything possible to avoid seeing him again, another part of her, hidden somewhere in the shrouded undiscernible depths of her consciousness, was looking forward eagerly to their next meeting.

Joe Beaverskin was as friendly now as he had been cool and unfriendly before. Kanina had been in the goose camp a week when she was sitting one evening beside the fire helping him reload shells for the next day's shoot.

"Calling and shooting the geese is man's work," he told her, "but it is good for a woman to know how it is done. You will come with me tomorrow to the goose blind and see the hunt."

Kanina knew he meant it as a question.

"I would like to go very much," she answered.

CHAPTER TWENTY-FOUR

AFTER abandoning the ship and reaching the bleak ice-imprisoned shores of southern Labrador, the barnacle goose had rested for just one night and then flown on. He flew on pressed by two violent cravings. One of them was hunger, expressing the instinct of self-preservation. The other was the call to the mating, the instinct of species-preservation, the need for linking of like with like which characterizes all living things.

There had been no indecision as to which of his two urges was the stronger. He must escape this desolation of rock and ice and snow by following the coastline either south or north. To the south he would find more abundant food. To the north, somewhere in the vastnesses of the Arctic, lay a warmer, more temperate shore, the nesting ground of his species where a mate would be waiting. So the choice was automatic, instinctive. The dawn was still only a misty gray infiltrating the night when he rose from the ice where he had rested since the previous evening and spread his wings and flew—toward the north.

He flew that day as though a madness goaded him and the urge to find a mate of his own kind mounted and quickened until by the second day it *was* a madness and he flew then with a strength and a desperation he had not possessed before. At first the coastline was low and flat, and the snow of the land and the white ice of the sea seemed to melt together with no perceptible line between. Early on the second day, hills and then mountains appeared. They were steep jagged peaks, many of them springing abruptly in sheer cliffs from out of the sea. It was a gigantic world of immense scale against which the barnacle goose was an infinitesimal speck, winging his lonely way deeper and deeper into the Arctic's lingering winter.

Periodically the harrowing pangs of his hunger would let him fly no more and he would stop then to pluck buds from the stunted bushes that reached above the snow. On that second day he reached Cape Chidley, Labrador's northern tip six hundred miles from where he had first touched land. Here the coastline turned sharply back southward again and he followed it with blind abandon because ahead to the north there was only a bleak white nothingness of rafted ice floes.

The days were long. The sun hung suspended in the southern sky for eighteen hours at a time. He followed the coastline wherever it led because here in this strange land it was the only thing he could recognize as a guide. It led him south and then north again around the ice-encrusted shores of Ungava Bay. By his fourth day of flying the coast had once more turned south. The barnacle didn't know that this eastern shore of Hudson Bay would lead him eight hundred miles southward into the heart of the continent, into the flat muskeg lands of the James Bay plain a thousand miles from the surf and the fiords of the sea. In his bewilderment he was just flying and searching.

The ice grew thin and spotty and sometimes for miles it disappeared entirely. Gaunt and stunted trees appeared. The buds on them were greening, there were soft catkins on the willows, and occasionally there were ponds where the ice was melted and juicy root stems formed a network on the bottom. The barnacle ate, not well, but better than he had before. On the sixth day he was on a coast where the water was shallow and muddy, there was a salt tang to it still and weak tides ebbed and flowed along the shore, but in no other way was it like the sea. Now the barnacle for the first time had a feeling of imprisonment, a vague fear that this was not the sea, that land was closing in relentlessly around him. And it was a strange land again, not high and rolling with cliffs to shatter the surf, but flat and low and marshy, sloping back gently to a smooth and featureless horizon.

Early on that sixth day of his coastal flight the barnacle saw a thin faint line far out over the water that he recognized instantly as a flock of geese. Emotions pent up for the twelve days that he had now been separated from his kind were suddenly released and a hysterical frenzy seized him. He flew after them, calling shrilly, but the flock was far away. Fatigue and the hunger-weakness still dragged on his wings and he knew he could never overtake them. He dropped back to the water and his heart was heavy and desolate. In a few seconds the goose flock had disappeared.

The barnacle goose flew on. The next flock he encountered was on the ground. He heard the soft gabble of their voices first, and then he saw them, a flock of about thirty, clustered like big brown clods of dirt on a turfy point that thrust like a hooked finger out from shore. A tense excitement filled him. He arched his big wings and glided down toward them.

But he saw before he landed that they were not barnacle geese like himself. They were bigger, and they were brown where he was silver and gray. His coloring was richer and showed sharper contrasts of blacks and whites, and his white face patch was much larger and more striking than theirs. The barnacle was first startled and then bewildered, and he sliced the air violently with rapidly beating wings and climbed up and away. He circled the flock about a hundred feet up, peering down at them, curious and wary.

They were geese, but unlike any geese he had ever seen before. He called to them, a soft bark-like *"ark-ark"* of greeting. They called back lustily from the ground, necks stretched up, their heads waving, and their voices were different from his. He circled twice more, then he saw some of the birds on the ground performing their courtship display, running toward each other with necks bent low and twisting from side to side, their heads almost touching the ground. It was the courtship display of his own kind too and the sight of it filled him with a feverish excitement. All fear gone from him now, he stiffened his wings again and pitched down among them.

They greeted him with low nasal grunt-like notes and bobbing heads and the barnacle responded by bobbing his own head and neck in the same way, because it was the instinctive greeting of his kind too. And then he knew that, though different, they were close kin. Their plumage and even their voices were different from his, but their principal language—the language of posturing and display—was the same.

The barnacle didn't know that these were Canada geese and that he belonged to another species very closely related. He did not know that the biological relationship was so close that mating and hybridization between them was possible. He merely knew that, though they were different superficially, these geese were potential mates. He knew his search had ended and here he would stay.

He was far to the south now of where he had been, but even here remnants of winter lingered. He had seen while flying above the coast that the inland lakes were still covered with ice. Here on the shore a few buds were swelling but there was still practically no green growth. The geese were eating hard dry cranberries that had clung on the creeping bushes since the summer before, and the barnacle goose began eating them too. His loneliness was gone. The berries filled his stomach with an invigorating, satisfying comfort.

The barnacle quickly sized up the flock he had joined. Some of them were old birds already mated from previous years but most of them were yearlings like himself in the process now of sorting themselves out in the pairing that would last for the rest of their lives. The old ones were quiet, sedate, each pair keeping to themselves at the edge of the flock and ignor-

ing the fighting and the courtship antics of the younger birds. Among
the yearlings, most were tentatively paired but this pairing had not yet
been firmly cemented and there was still much mate-snatching and fighting. The sexes were identical in plumage but distinguishable by behavior,
for the males were aggressive and belligerent whereas the females were
staid and demure, joining only occasionally in the courtship displays.

Seeing the other young ganders displaying before the females aroused
his own mating urge to a fervent pitch, but the barnacle stemmed the
desire that filled him and waited. His wasted body was in no condition
yet to challenge one of the other males, even the smallest of whom were
bigger than he. Yet he knew that a newcomer entering the flock at this
stage could win a mate only by conquest. And in the first hour, he
selected her. She was a small female, but still a little larger than he, with
the dusky feathers of her immature plumage still showing in her white
cheek patch. Her voice was softer and mellower and slightly higher in
pitch than that of the other females. He watched her, rapt and eager.
She had a suitor, a male much bigger who displayed before her at frequent intervals, but she hadn't acknowledged the other's advances with
courtship gestures of her own. The barnacle knew that her own mating
urge had not yet been fully aroused by the male's courting. She had not
yet accepted him.

The barnacle had been with them about two hours when finally, their
hunger appeased, they flew. He sprang into the air with them, for now
he was one of them, and they formed quickly into V-formation with one
of the old mated ganders leading at the V's point.

There were two reasons for the V-ing. First, it put each bird in a position where it avoided the slipstream of rough air that swirled back from
the bird ahead. Secondly, it permitted each flier to salvage some of the
energy expended by the bird in front of it. Horizontal vortexes of spinning air whirled back from the wingtips of each bird and the V-formation
put each goose in a position where one wing—the inside wing in the V—
could ride on the vortex produced by the outside wing of the bird in
front. Thus the inside wing did not have to work as hard because it was
re-using some of the flight power spilled back by a forward companion.
On long flights they could rest each wing in turn by shifting from one
arm of the V to the other.

Mated geese flew together within the flock, the male usually ahead of
his mate, helping her with his wingtip vortex in a manner not very different from the way a man might help a woman by taking her arm. As
they sorted themselves out into their V-formation, the barnacle had
crowded unobtrusively into the spot directly ahead of the small female he

had chosen, between her and the male who was her suitor. Already he was developing a possessive feeling toward her. Immediately ahead of him the other male responded with a quick brief series of guttural notes that indicated more surprise than anger. The barnacle knew that this act of forcing himself between them had become unwittingly a declaration of purpose.

That day, the next and then another, the barnacle flew and fed with them, keeping close to her but never openly defying the other male. He could feel the strength, the old stamina, slowly returning. He waited, because he knew it would be an uneven battle and he would need all the weight and strength his body was capable of producing.

They had circled this inland sea and now they were on its western coast. Periodically they made short flights inland into boggy forested country where lakes were numerous and still covered with ice. The barnacle feared these inland sorties and he followed the flock reluctantly, always feeling a bracing relief when they returned to the coast. He wondered why the adult pairs had not already begun nesting and he wondered where the nesting cliffs were located, because everywhere here the shore was flat and marshy. The barnacle could judge these birds only against the habits of his own species that he knew. Because the barnacle goose was a cliffside nester at the edge of the sea, he thought all geese must be cliff nesters. He did not know that the Canada goose, like most geese, was a nester of the fresh-water bogs and land-locked lakes; he did not know that the inland flights he feared were to inspect the ice of the lakes, nor that most of the James Bay geese had already moved inland onto their summer territories and that his flock would also be doing it soon.

Meanwhile the pairing of the yearlings was becoming more firmly established and the flock was becoming smaller because some, as they paired, flew off inland by themselves. He had been with the flock three days now; his mating drive was a fierce internal fire, his strength was returning and he knew he must not wait. It was low tide and they were on a mudflat fringed on three sides by willows. The males were displaying boisterously before any females still unclaimed. Fights over the same female frequently broke out. In fact, a pairing rarely became final until a fight had cemented it, because sexual development in the females lagged behind that of the males and a female usually needed the stimulation of being fought for before her own emotions reached the point at which she would accept a male.

The barnacle suddenly ran toward the female and then, four or five feet away, he stopped abruptly, stretched his neck to its full length upward and gave a loud challenging call. It was entirely spontaneous, he hadn't

planned it, and the instinct passed down to him by thousands of generations of barnacle geese was now taking full charge of his actions. He
watched the female and the other male suitor standing a few feet beyond
her. She was ignoring it all but the other male was moving slowly toward
him.

Now the barnacle arched his wings over his back and dashed at the
female with neck stretched downward and his head and bill skimming
the mud. He gave the wild strident cry again. It was more like a threat
display than a prelude to love-making, and indeed it was both—an expression of love to the chosen female and a challenge to other males.

The other male joined in and for several minutes they performed
fanatically before her, each male pretending to ignore the other. They
advanced on her repeatedly, necks weaving sinuously from side to side;
then they would stand back from her, as erect and tall as they could make
themselves, feathers puffed out, their harsh calls filling the air. As the
intensity of it grew, the other geese of the flock abandoned their feeding
and gathered around.

The female, who had been oblivious at first, now started to take notice
as the excitement of the males began to spill over into herself. Finally she
lowered her neck, twisted her head from side to side, and answered their
frantic calling with a soft tremulous hesitant note of her own. She was
almost ready to take a mate, and the effect on the two males was dramatic
and instantaneous. They lost interest immediately in the female and they
turned now and faced each other.

Each stood stiffly, plumage ruffled out to make them look much larger
than they really were. The loud excited notes of the courting display
changed now to angry hissing. The other geese moved back, making
room.

The Canada, several inches taller than the barnacle, lunged at his opponent, hissing defiance, his big wings outspread. He jabbed rapidly at
the barnacle's head and neck with his bill and hammered him with the
big bones of the under surface of each wing. The barnacle goose reeled
backward, his lighter weight no match for the fierceness of the Canada's
first attack. The Canada came at him again. This time the barnacle dodged
and caught the Canada with a stiff wing blow as the bigger bird lunged
past him. They came at each other repeatedly. Feathers flew from the
necks and heads of both birds under the vicious jabbing of their bills.
Sometimes, when a blow of the Canada's wings caught him squarely, the
barnacle would almost turn over backward under the tremendous impact.
His chest was quickly bruised and paining under the hammering.

But the barnacle's stubbornness and the agility of his smaller size made up for what he lacked in weight and strength. Several times as the Canada hurtled at him in a new attack, the barnacle was able to dodge sideways and when the Canada plunged past the barnacle would attack from behind, jabbing the back of the other's head and neck until the feathers were matted with blood.

It happened again and this time the barnacle's bill got a hold on the other's neck that the Canada couldn't shake off. The barnacle clung there like a bulldog and he could taste the hot salty blood of his opponent in his mouth. The barnacle was behind and above now and the Canada's lashing wings couldn't reach him, but the barnacle's wings were free to pound unimpeded.

The battle was over right then. It didn't end then, because the barnacle held on grimly, hammering wing blows on the other's quivering body for many minutes more. He released the Canada finally when the bigger gander had surrendered and all his struggling had ceased. The defeated one rose slowly, then, when he realized he was free, dashed madly away through the surrounding ranks of geese to the outer rim of the flock. There he stood, swaying weakly, his bill open and gasping.

Every inch of the barnacle ached, but he turned with a proud exaggerated erectness and ran to the female who had inspired it all. With neck stiff and head high he advanced until his puffed-out breast touched hers, then he poured out toward the sky a shrill high-pitched cry that was almost a shriek. It echoed eerily among the willows. It was his "triumph-note," the victory song, unlike anything else in the varied goose vocabulary. Most ganders use it only once in their lifetime because it is reserved for that one ecstatic moment when a gander takes a mate. The echoes of it were still rippling back and forth faintly when the female answered with a weaker and more musical note of her own. She accepted him. The pairing was final now until death.

He reached his neck past hers and softly preened the feathers of her wings. And that was all, for despite the intensity of his desire for a mate they were still yearlings and there would be no sexual union until another spring came to complete their physical development. But the mating was definite and irrevocable, lacking nothing in finality because the physical consummation was still a year away.

The barnacle was tired and sore, but a-tingle too with a warm zestful contentment. The days of loneliness, the terrors and rigors of the ocean flight, they were forgotten now, swept clean from his mind as a foreshore is swept clean and fresh after a high tide. His mind was too full with the delights and ecstasies of the present to dwell now upon the past.

He stayed close to her and they talked constantly in soft muted undertones. The defeated Canada male did not come near again. Then the barnacle saw that she was growing restless. Frequently she looked up and honked loudly at the sky. After an hour of this she sprang into the air, calling back to him urgently, and he flew too, following close behind her. The rest of the flock stayed behind on the tideflat; the barnacle and his mate were flying alone.

She led him inland. They passed the coastal tangles of willow and then flew on over the tamarack bogs and the black clumps of spruce forest. At first he thought it would be a brief overland flight and then a circling back to the tideflats and the edge of the sea, so he followed her silently while his old fear of flying over land built up within him. But her flight was direct and purposeful and he realized soon that there was to be no turning back. He lagged behind her then, calling her back to him, but she didn't understand and she flew on. For a moment he thought of leaving her and flying back to the coast alone but the thought was fleeting for she called to him then and her call had the seductive lure of a siren's song. He flew on, bewildered and afraid.

She flew for about a quarter of an hour and they passed over numerous small lakes and ponds. They came to a much larger lake that had a broad expanse of brown marshland at its one end, and the marsh was separated from the lake by a narrow neck of beach overgrown with willows. The ice of the marsh was melted but the lake, dotted with small islands, still wore its winter dress of white.

He could see flocks of geese resting on the lake ice ahead and these other geese called as he and his mate drew near them. She led him low across the marsh and the beach strip. As they glided down to one of the flocks the barnacle watched with mounting dread as the forest of the lakeshore, black and terrifying, closed in like an imprisoning wall around him.

He longed for the surf and the sea, its limitless space and freedom. His heart was torn now between an old love and a new love, but he knew what the choice must be. He stood close to her on the ice and reached gently across her back with his neck. Softly, caressingly, his bill preened the feathers of her opposite wing.

CHAPTER TWENTY-FIVE

IT was June, but the day on which Kanina accompanied her father on the goose hunt was crisp and cold. The breath of the *Mooskek-owak* hunters hung in small white clouds in the frosty air when Kanina, her father and three other hunters left the camp soon after dawn. They walked in single file along a portage trail that led back into the gloomy corridors of spruce forest behind. The trail was narrow and twisting and trodden deeply into the soft moss by the moccasins of many generations of Cree hunters.

Kanina had never followed the trail very far inland from the river but she knew it went in to Kishamooskek Lake, a shallow lake about ten miles long, averaging two miles in width, and one of the largest of the hundreds of lakes in the muskeg country around Cape Cree. *Kishamooskek* was Cree for "big swamp," and she knew the lake was named for a large area of marshland at its one end. The marsh consisted of thousands of acres of shallow water growing with shoulder-high cattails and sedges instead of the usual smothering muskeg growth of sphagnum moss. Because of its shallowness the marsh ice thawed early and the geese could reach and feed on the roots in the bottom ooze before there were any green shoots appearing elsewhere. Kishamooskek Marsh was thus a favorite feeding ground for the springtime geese flocks and a popular shooting spot for the *Mooskek-owak* hunters.

The marsh was about a mile inland from the hunting camp on the Kistawanee River but the trail leading in to it was perhaps twice that distance because it twisted erratically around deadfalls and ponds. It took more than half an hour of rapid walking before Kanina and the hunters emerged suddenly from the dark forest into the dull daylight of the open lakeshore. Kanina stopped to survey the scene in front of her. They had been coming north. Now to the west stretched Kishamooskek Lake still somber and dirty-white with its lingering ice and flecked here and there with lifting windrows of morning fog. The lake was dotted with islands. To the east, her right, was a great flat region covered with a bronze mat of dry swaying cattail leaves and looking almost as large as the lake itself. This, she knew, would be Kishamooskek Marsh. In front of her, directly opposite the spot where the portage trail emerged from the forest, was a narrow neck of sandy beach overgrown with willows separating the lake on the west from the marsh on the east. The beach strip was a hundred feet or so wide and curved off northward for a mile or more where it merged into the spruce forest of the opposite shore.

They began walking out along the beach. There were no geese in sight but Kanina could hear faintly all around her the gabble of their voices muffled by the morning fog. She knew from hearing the hunters talk that the geese flocks rested each night and midday far out on the lake, on the ice or in open patches of water, and each morning and evening they flew across the beach strip to feed in the marsh. The hunters had their shooting blinds here on the beach and it was during the flights back and forth between feeding and resting grounds that the big birds could often be decoyed down close enough to be shot.

They reached Joe Beaverskin's blind first. It was a small open-topped corral of willow branches, dry grass and cattail leaves, barely large enough for two persons to crouch in and be hidden. Kanina and her father stopped here, the other hunters went on. The blind was located in an open spot that had an unobstructed view of the surrounding sky. Joe Beaverskin took six wooden decoys from the blind and carried them out onto a strip of ice that still lingered along the edge of the marsh. The decoys, crudely resembling crouching geese, had been hewn by hand from blocks of wood and then charred in a fire to turn them black. The diagnostic cheek patch was added by slicing off a piece of the charred wood to let the white wood beneath show through. Kanina's father arranged the decoys to look like a small flock of geese resting on the ice, then he came back to the blind. He and Kanina sat on a small log inside and waited.

Geese began passing over, so high they looked like strands of black beads strung across the leaden sky. Joe Beaverskin ignored them for they were too far away to be called down. The day brightened, the morning mists disappeared and occasionally Kanina heard shots from other parts of the marsh.

They had been in the blind about half an hour when two geese approached low across the lake. The birds were flying a course that would take them across the beach strip well out of gunshot to the north. Joe Beaverskin crouched lower and nodded quickly toward the pair of geese.

"*Man-tay-o!*" he whispered sharply. It was the Cree word meaning "a stranger," or "someone far from home." Kanina looked quickly at her father. He was hunched under his heavy canvas parka, obviously tense and excited. Then she looked at the flying geese and saw that one of them was smaller and lighter colored than the other. The larger one was a typical *niska* or Canada goose but its mate had a lighter, more buoyant flight and a whiter belly. But the most striking difference between them was in the plumage of their heads—the Canada goose had the characteristic small white cheek patch, but in the smaller goose the whole side of the face was white and even at this distance the white face stood out sharply.

"Man-tay-o!" her father whispered again. "I have hunted the *niskuk* for thirty springs but never have I seen a *niska* that looked like him. The white-faced one is a stranger, he has flown to the *Mooskek-owak* country from far away."

She saw her father nervously fingering his big double-barreled shotgun and Kanina began to feel some of his excitement too. She crouched until only her eyes were peering above the willow sides of the blind. The pair of geese came nearer, flying fast with deep rapid wing-beats, but they were going to pass far out from the beach.

Then from her father beside her came a deep throaty double-syllabled *"Ka-ronk!"* It was a perfect imitation of the call-note of a lone *niska*. It wasn't loud but it had a resonant carrying quality and the two geese, still several hundred yards away, hesitated in their flight and Kanina could see their heads and necks turn curiously toward the blind.

"Ka-ronk, ka-ronk!" her father called again, louder and more insistent.

Now the geese turned, swinging in a wide circle but still keeping at a safe distance. They flew across the beach strip and were over the marsh. Then they saw the decoys on the ice and turned sharply again, heading in straight toward the blind.

"Ka-ronk, ka-ronk, unk-unk-unk," her father's voice coaxed them down.

Kanina saw the Canada goose set its wings and begin gliding in on a long slanting descent toward the decoys. But the white-faced one held back, its wings beat strongly and it climbed sharply away, calling excitedly to its mate with a strange and entirely different note that sounded like the yelping of a small dog. The Canada goose looked back momentarily, then it too turned and climbed upward again. Joe Beaverskin muttered angrily beside her.

The geese circled away and landed on an open lead of water among the cattails, beyond gunshot but still in clear sight. The big birds were still curious, swimming back and forth restlessly with heads lifted high studying the decoys. Joe Beaverskin kept talking to them and the Canada goose began answering him, note for note, while slowly swimming closer.

Kanina watched her father with pride. Here, she thought, was the Indian in the role in which he fitted and belonged, not a parasite on the white man's society huddled on a shoddy reserve and selling baskets to white tourists, but a proud and primitive hunter using ancestral skills practiced from childhood to win the food he needed for his belly. Joe Beaverskin was a simple unlearned man, but he understood intimately one basic principle of life that most white men, shielded behind their artificial civilization, have long ago lost sight of. He saw himself clearly as an integral part of the natural world. In his way of life there was no confusing chain of time clocks, pay envelopes and grocery stores hiding the fact of man's real and ultimate dependence on the land and the food it can produce. His was a simple basic relationship of hunter and hunted. When the land and his own skills were productive, he ate; when not, he went hungry.

The inexorable northward march of civilization would in future years bring changes to the *Mooskek-owak* life, Kanina knew, but she hoped fervently that her people's proud independence, their oneness with the land that supported them, would never have to be replaced by a parasitic life on the white man's dole.

Yet even as she had these thoughts, Kanina was also being sharply reminded of her own unsuitability for this *Mooskek-owak* way of life. While her father kept skillfully talking the geese in closer, Kanina was feeling not a primitive hunter's thrill in the impending kill, but an uncontrollable sympathy for the hunted. She knew it was an absurd and sentimental thought for a member of a race who had to live by hunting, yet she could not overcome it. As the geese swam nearer, Kanina's dread of the killing that must soon occur grew stronger. Most of all she felt a sharp sympathy for *man-tay-o,* the white-faced one. It was staying back well behind the Canada goose, obviously bewildered and alarmed by surroundings it had never encountered before. Kanina had also been a stranger once in a land that bewildered and terrified her. She understood the turmoil that must be raging in the white-faced stranger's mind. She hoped that her father would not be able to shoot it.

Suddenly Joe Beaverskin's calling changed to an imperative high-pitched *"onka-onka-onka,"* the cackling call of a goose that has just made a rich discovery of food. Now the Canada goose began swimming in rapidly to the decoys, all fear erased by the coaxing quality of Joe Beaverskin's last call. Kanina waited, tense and breathless. The goose was close enough now. Why didn't he shoot? Then she realized that her father was ignoring the Canada goose and concentrating on luring the strange one into gun range. The white-faced goose was lagging behind its bolder mate but still following slowly. Another minute would bring it, too, within range.

Kanina trembled violently and felt an overpowering urge to protect it. She raised her head slowly and deliberately above the edge of the blind. For a second or two her father couldn't see what she was doing because his side vision was cut off by the fur-rimmed hood of his parka. Then he and the geese saw her simultaneously. Joe Beaverskin grunted angrily, reached out and pushed her quickly down into the blind again. The geese sprang with loud cackling cries into the air. Joe Beaverskin jumped to his feet with the gun to his shoulder, but it was too late and he didn't fire. The geese, flying low across the water, disappeared behind a screen of cattails. When they came in sight again they were out of gun range.

Her father's face was distorted with rage. He slapped her sharply on the cheek with the palm of his hand, a thing he had never done during her childhood because Indian parents rarely strike their children.

"Go!" he shouted. "Leave me! You are stupid and careless. You will never learn to be a *Mooskek-owak*. Go back to the white people and their books."

Kanina rose slowly and silently. She was embarrassed and ashamed.

"I am sorry," she said softly and walked away.

She went slowly along the trail through the spruce forest back toward the camp on the Kistawanee. She was angry at herself for the weakness that had made her do it. Her father thought it was carelessness. What would he do if he learned that she had done it deliberately? He must never know. But would it matter? They were enemies again now, anyway.

But as the embarrassment and shame passed, Kanina began to doubt if she really was sorry. She tried at first but couldn't ignore the relief that came with the thought that *man-tay-o,* the strange one, was still a wild free living bird out there in the marsh with its Canada goose mate, and not a bloody heap of flesh and feathers at her father's feet in the goose blind.

Kanina waited anxiously in camp that day for the hunters to return. Late in the afternoon she heard them coming and she wandered nervously to the back of the camp where she could unobtrusively scan their goose kills as they emerged from the bush. The hunters appeared, carrying two or three geese each. No one had shot the white-faced stranger.

Kanina returned to the Beaverskin tent happy and relieved. Her father was there, but he didn't look at her or speak. The old gulf of unspoken hostility and contempt had come between them again.

Before the *Mooskek-owak* went to their beds that night the wind shifted into the south, the air grew warmer and they knew the cold spell was breaking. Next day the sun was hot and the hunters came back early to the camp with word that the ice of Kishamooskek Lake was breaking up and the feeding flocks of geese were dwindling. Few geese were shot that day. Kanina scanned the goose kill anxiously once more and the strange one was not among the birds killed. Several hunters had seen *man-tay-o* again that day but it was wild and wary, they said, and refused to be called down to the decoys.

The hunters went back to their blinds for another day but now the hot sun was swiftly swelling the willow buds, green shoots were springing up everywhere throughout the steaming muskeg lands, and almost overnight there was an abundance of food for the *niskuk*. This was the signal for the spring flocks to break up and for the nesting to begin. The hunters came back that day carrying their decoys with them. Not one goose had been killed. The *niska* hunt was over.

Next day the *Mooskek-owak* loaded their canoes and headed down the Kistawanee toward Cape Cree where they would spend the summer. The goose hunt had been good and every canoe had a couple of hundred-pound flour bags filled with dried goose meat. Kanina sat in the middle of the Beaverskin canoe with her back to her father. She couldn't forget the white-faced goose. She felt a strange personal bond linking them. Could it succeed where she had failed and establish a new life among strangers in a strange land? Where had it come from, and why?

Rory Macdonald would know. She found herself hoping eagerly that Rory would come again to Cape Cree.

CHAPTER TWENTY-SIX

RORY MACDONALD lay resting on his cot in the little bunkroom at Moosonee as the long subarctic twilight waned. The other men were out and he was going to have the bunkroom to himself for the evening. It was fortunate, because this was his last night at Moosonee and he had to write some letters.

He had had a busy twelve days, flying almost every day and writing up notes and plotting his goose counts on maps every evening. Now it was over. Tomorrow the plane was making its last flight north and would drop him off at Cape Cree where he would work for the rest of the summer.

The cold spell that had slowed down the melting of the ice had ended abruptly three days ago and since then there had been almost summer heat. The inland lakes and ponds were already free of ice and the muskeg had suddenly become green with burgeoning growth. The effect on the geese had been startling. While the lakes remained icebound, the geese had remained in their flocks, flying restlessly between resting and feeding grounds, and easily spotted from the air. But now the big birds had mysteriously disappeared and that day in six hours of flying he had seen only seven geese. It meant the flocks had broken up and the mated pairs had gone into seclusion for the nesting.

Rory's flights had borne out strongly what the Indian teacher, Kanina Beaverskin, had told him the first day. The Canada geese occurred only in the pothole muskeg. And the biggest and finest region of pothole muskeg along the James Bay shoreline that Rory had covered was in the basin of the Kistawanee River from ten to a hundred miles inland from Cape Cree. So Rory had decided after the first few days of flying that Cape Cree would be the post he would work out of for the summer.

On the floor beside his cot lay two letters where he had dropped them, page by page, as he read them a few minutes ago. Mail came only twice a week to Moosonee and that evening he had received letters from his mother and P.L. He must answer them at once, because when he reached Cape Cree it would be impossible to get mail in or out with much regularity.

P.L.'s letter had rambled through three pages of ornithological news— Hurricane Alice had blown a yellow-billed tropic-bird and some other Caribbean species as far north as the Maine coast; Turdy, his robin "genius," was counting to five now, but still defecated at every opportunity on his *Journal of Avian Research;* the sparrows on the shortened photo-period were already showing gonadal regression; and the head janitor had complained again to the building superintendent that the birds made a racket, stunk, and had fleas. And then P.L. had his most interesting news, added at the end as though it were an afterthought. He had found a student who could care for the birds during July and August; if Rory would write and tell him where he was going to be, P.L. would join him and give him a hand with the Canada goose work. Rory smiled to himself. He'd be glad to see P.L.

His mother's letter was not as pleasant. It had been eight years since Rory last saw her, and during that time they had corresponded regularly, writing on the average two letters a month to each other. For the past year there had been recurring hints in her letters of mounting strife between herself and Big Sammy, his father. Once several months ago she had said that many of her books were accidentally burned in the stove. When Rory asked her in his next letter how such an unusual accident occurred, she didn't answer the question, but said that Sammy was getting tired of digging peat blocks for fuel and she was now doing the peat-digging herself.

In the letter he had just received, Rory's mother was now for the first time talking openly of the rift between herself and her husband. Sammy had sold their one cow, had done no planting of grain or potatoes that spring and had told her that he intended to do no more farming.

"Your father has decided," the letter said, "that we can live easily off my tweed money. He says he sees no point in farming while I spend money on books and papers. Actually very little of my money is spent on books or newspapers, as you know, but your father's knowledge of arithmetic is so inadequate that it is impossible to make him see this. I am beginning to feel now that both of us will be happier separated. I shall do nothing hastily and intend to think it over well. It will not be easy to re-establish myself at my age but I still have friends in Glasgow and I could return to teaching. Actually I have not been very happy since you left eight years ago. I am proud of you, my son, and I regard your fine achievements as proof that I have fulfilled my responsibilities to society well. With this main task of my life completed I am beginning to wonder if any purpose is being served by my remaining here the martyr that I feel I have been. I think I am entitled now to seek some happiness again for the last years of my life."

Rory had read the letter several times, wondering as he had wondered many times before how she had ever come to marry his father. He knew there must be a strange story behind it. It was too personal a matter to mention in a letter but when he saw his mother again in person he must ask her the story. Whatever the explanation, he couldn't blame her now if she decided to live the rest of her life among more congenial friends.

Rory got up from the cot and went to the bunkroom table. He put a stack of paper in front of him and began to write. He told P.L. he would be in and around Cape Cree for the summer and would be glad to see him there. Then he wrote to his mother. It was a difficult letter because he couldn't ignore her problem, yet he was uncertain as to how much he should discuss it. His father would be unable to read the letter, so he was free to write anything he wished, yet he had a feeling that the least said about it the better. Finally he decided to treat the matter in a brief and casual manner.

"If you decide to leave Barra," he wrote, "I shall understand." And he left it at that.

He finished the letters and went to bed, but he didn't get to sleep easily. He began thinking of what Alex Murray, the game and fisheries superintendent, had told him that night in Blackwood. "When the Indian squaws start looking pretty enough to sleep with, it's time to head back for civilization because when that happens you're going off your rocker." Rory smiled as he recalled it. The teacher, Kanina Beaverskin, looked pretty enough to sleep with the first time he saw her, so according to Murray's diagnosis, he was off his rocker already.

Rory had learned a good deal about the Indian girl's history, because she was well known as the Cree girl who had done well in the white man's schools. Since the loss of her teaching position and the publicity that had accompanied it, she had been a frequent topic of conversation at settlements up and down the bay wherever the plane had landed. Rory now knew all about her years in the sanatorium and of how she had been informally adopted by the Rumseys and sent out to school. And now that he knew more about Kanina, Rory was anxious to see her again, but when he tried to figure out why, his thinking became vague and involved. She was interesting and she was pretty, that was obvious enough. And she was a sort of medium-grade intellectual who would be starved now for some intelligent companionship, which he supposed gave him some kind of an advantage—an advantage for what, he wasn't sure.

But the principal thought that kept pushing into his mind seemed a wild and irrelevant one. Something kept reminding him that, come what may, no man who had aspirations of some day joining an austere and learned university faculty could ever marry an Indian. It was an absurd thought and at first it annoyed him. Then he began to see the point that his subconscious mind was trying to reveal to him.

It wasn't an absurd thought at all. It was the basic fact underlying any relationship that might develop between them. If he couldn't marry her, and obviously he couldn't, she could never become a threat to his career. He had been shunning the university girls because they were marriageable and could conceivably tempt him into an early marriage before his career was ready for it. But Kanina Beaverskin, safely isolated here in the northern Ontario bush, could never be anything but a transient passer-by in his life.

If there was no possibility of creating entangling responsibilities for the future, did it leave him free to push things as far as she would let him? If some of the stories he had heard about Indian girls were true, it should be possible to push things fast and far.

Whatever happened between them, it would be over in September and the slate wiped clean again. It would be ended then as unreservedly and irrevocably as the shieling affair with Peggy MacNeill.

CHAPTER TWENTY-SEVEN

RORY could see Kanina among the Indian women on the river bank as the plane touched the beach at Cape Cree early the next afternoon. She was no longer the trim eye-catching girl she had been when he saw her last, for now she wore rubber boots, thick socks and a drab unbecoming shawl that hid most of her hair. Rory stepped out onto the plane float and waved to her. She nodded in reply but didn't smile. Then Bert and Joan Rumsey came through the crowd.

"I hope you are still planning on staying with us," Joan Rumsey said.

"I am, if I may," Rory told her.

He thanked the pilot. The plane taxied to mid-stream and took off. Then Bert Rumsey took one of Rory's bags, Rory took the other, and the three of them started up the sand path from the beach. It wasn't until then that Joan Rumsey saw Kanina. She walked over quickly to the Indian girl and Rory followed her.

"I'm glad you are back, Kanina," Mrs. Rumsey said. "When did you get in from the goose hunt?"

"We came down yesterday," Kanina said.

"You remember Mr. Macdonald?"

"Oh, yes." She smiled at Rory then and the dimples formed fleetingly at her mouth corners.

"Come up and we'll have a cup of tea with Mr. Macdonald," Joan Rumsey invited.

"No thank you."

"Oh yes. You must."

"No! I do not wish to." Rory saw her eyes narrow angrily then, the way they had that first day on the train when he had invited her back to the restaurant car for lunch.

Joan Rumsey's mouth dropped and her face looked suddenly as if it had been slapped. "All right, dear," she said, "but come and visit us soon."

"I'll be starting a school for the children shortly," Kanina answered. "I'll be coming for my books."

They faced each other for a few moments of embarrassed silence, then Kanina turned and followed her people back toward the tent village. Rory and the Rumseys headed again for the big white house. Joan Rumsey was silent until they were inside. Bert Rumsey put down Rory's bag and returned to the store; Mrs. Rumsey led Rory into the living room.

"We feel very sad about Kanina," she said when they were seated. "She is extremely intelligent."

Rory nodded. "It didn't take me long to discover that."

"She would be very successful, as a teacher or anything else she tried." Joan Rumsey's narrow angular face with its thin frame of gray hair stared motionlessly ahead as she talked. "It is a tragedy—throwing herself away here. It is a double tragedy, because it's a tragedy for her people too. Even just one of them like her could be doing so much if she were out there proving by her own example that they are as capable as we are. And she would be winning much more for her people than for herself. Their population is increasing because now we give them medical care and many more survive, but the land won't feed and support any more of them. The time is coming when the surplus *must* go out and be assimilated into the white society and economy. If all of them try to stay, nature will solve the problem in her old way . . . . a bad winter, game will disappear, and then the surplus that the land can't support will starve. That has always been nature's way of keeping the land and the people in balance. And then we will ask: What good are our Indian and Eskimo hospitals? We save the sick only to confine them in a land that can't support them, so they starve instead."

Joan Rumsey was running her fingers nervously through her gray hair.

"The intelligent and adaptable ones like Kanina must go out first," she continued, "and pave the way for others to follow. Her coming back here . . . . it is tragic, not just for Kanina, not just here in Cape Cree, but in every tent and wigwam and igloo from Labrador to Alaska and to the Arctic Sea. I had big hopes for Kanina. It is hard to see it ending . . . . like this. You may be talking to her. If you are, try to change her mind, try to make her see the role she could be filling."

Rory looked up sharply then, puzzled by the last remark. "I expected when I got here I would be seeing her all the time," he said.

"It may not be so easy," Joan Rumsey replied. "She will probably avoid you."

"Well in that case," Rory said quickly, "I'll not waste time. I have to interview hunters. I'll need an interpreter. I'll ask Kanina and get started this afternoon."

Joan Rumsey smiled then. "It's worth trying," she said slowly. "But she'll probably tell you to use Jock, the interpreter at the store. I'll take you down and you can ask her."

They went out the door and turned down toward the clusters of Indian tents, Rory slowing his rolling long-legged gait to keep pace with Joan Rumsey beside him. They passed the first tents and Rory looked around him curiously. The men lay about on the ground, talking, laughing and playing cards; the women seemed to be all busily working—preparing food, sewing clothes, making moccasins, filling quilts with goose down. Rory had noticed on the plane flights that the Indians at these isolated posts were different from those living close to white influence at Moosonee, although all belonged to the same Swampy Cree tribe. The Crees here seemed much more shy and reserved toward whites. As Mrs. Rumsey and Rory approached each group, the talking and laughter stopped and the Indians would nod self-consciously and then remain silent until the two white persons were past. The Moosonee Indians were quick to copy the white man's styles, but here the Crees clung to styles that appeared to have been borrowed from the white man a generation ago and not changed since. The women of Cape Cree still wore dark unpatterned shawls instead of gaily colored bandannas, and the men wore old suit coats and vests and serge trousers and only a few of the younger ones had zippered windbreakers or denim jeans.

"There's the Beaverskin tent and that's Kanina's mother in front."

Rory looked quickly where Joan Rumsey had indicated. The woman, crouching beside a fire, was large with round shoulders and drooping breasts that bulged grotesquely under her torn brown sweater. Her face was haggard and wrinkled like a prune. She was smoking a pipe. Rory stared at her and his thoughts were a chaotic intermingling of fascination and disbelief. Surely this misshapen hag was not Kanina's mother!

They stopped in front of her and the Indian woman looked up and smiled without taking the pipe from her mouth. The wrinkles and the haggardness remained but there was a warmth in her face when she smiled, and an unmistakable vestige of the beauty now reappearing in Kanina.

Joan Rumsey spoke one word: "Kanina."

The Indian woman turned toward the tent and called rapidly in Cree. Kanina appeared in the doorway.

"I'd like to talk to some of the men about their goose kills," Rory said quickly. "Will you interpret for me?"

Kanina didn't answer. Joan Rumsey interjected hastily: "Jock is busy at the store."

"He can't be so busy," Kanina said coolly. "He was down at the plane a little while ago."

Rory studied Kanina. There was a mischievous half-smile lighting her dark eyes and Rory had a feeling that she was enjoying his and Joan Rumsey's discomfort.

Then she said casually, as though there had been no doubt about it from the beginning: "I'd like to help you, Mr. Macdonald. When do you want to start?"

"Right now. And will you call me Rory?"

"Okay." She smiled broadly then and the dimples pierced the dark skin at her mouth corners.

"I must go back," Joan Rumsey interrupted. "Speak to your mother for me, Kanina. Tell her I'm pleased she is looking so well."

Kanina spoke in Cree to her mother and the Indian woman looked up briefly and smiled at Joan Rumsey. Then the white woman turned quickly away, Kanina's mother went into the tent, and Rory and Kanina faced each other alone.

"Let's start with your father," Rory suggested.

"He's not around, and we're not on speaking terms anyway."

"Why?"

"I've been anxious to tell you. I thought I'd let you settle down first, that's why I didn't mention it down by the plane. It's a goose, a very strange goose. . . ."

Rory listened excitedly as Kanina told him about the strange white-faced goose on Kishamooskek Lake. He knew, as soon as she described it, what the goose must be, but he didn't interrupt as she went on describing in detail how her father had tried to call it into gun range and how in the end she had risen in the blind to frighten it away.

"It's very exciting news," he said as soon as she was finished. "I'll show you some pictures to check the identification, but I don't think there's any doubt. It must be a barnacle. They are old and very dear friends of mine."

Rory could feel an excitement sweeping through his big body as he pictured again the barnacle flocks that had thrilled his childhood. And now, with luck, he would be meeting a barnacle again!

"Every once in a while a barnacle strays or gets storm blown to this continent," he continued, hardly aware for a few moments that he was expressing his thoughts in words. "Hurricane Alice hit the North Atlantic very hard . . . . about two weeks ago. There could still have been the odd yearling nonbreeder straggling north then. A big powerful male might have flown with the wind and made it to Labrador. Then he's wandered down here and joined a flock of Canadas. I'll bet he's mated now with that Canada you saw him with. All geese hybridize when they can't find mates of their own species."

Rory was sure he could see some of his own excitement mirrored in Kanina.

"I must see him," he said. "He'll be like a childhood friend from home. Will you show him to me?"

Kanina's eyes dropped until they were hidden by their black lashes. She stared at the ground where the toe of one of her rubber boots kept twisting erratically, pushing a hole in the sandy turf. Rory could sense the conflicting desires against which her mind was struggling. He knew she was striving for the strength to say no, and he pressed his own will upon her before she could say it.

"Come up to the Rumseys' with me," he said. "I'll show you some goose pictures to be sure of the identification. Then I'll ask Bert Rumsey to rent us a canoe and outboard for tomorrow."

Finally she spoke and Rory could detect the wistful note of surrender in her voice. "We'll need a small canoe," she said, "something you can portage in to Kishamooskek. We won't be able to search the lake and marsh unless we take in a canoe. And it's a swampy two-mile portage."

"Okay. Maybe we can take two canoes and leave the small one in on the lake, because we'll be going back there again. And we'll have to start early. Geese are active early in the morning when they're feeding; they're easier to find then. When's sunrise?"

"Three-thirty."

"Okay, we start at three-thirty."

They sat on the veranda with Joan Rumsey and had the tea that Kanina had refused earlier in the afternoon. Kanina looked at pictures in Rory's bird books and identified the goose definitely as a barnacle.

"Call it a barnacle goose if you like," she said, "but I'm going to continue calling it *man-tay-o*. It's Cree for 'the strange one.' It sounds a lot more romantic."

"All right," Rory said, "I'll call it *man-tay-o* too."

He left Kanina on the veranda with Joan Rumsey while he went across to the store and arranged with Bert Rumsey for an outboard and two canoes. While he was away Kanina had gone up to her former room and brought down the large luggage bag of clothes she had left there two weeks before. She rose to leave as soon as Rory returned. He picked up Kanina's bag and walked down to the Indian tents with her.

Joan Rumsey was waiting, her thin face smiling jubilantly, as soon as Rory came back.

"I don't know how you did it, but I'm delighted!" she exclaimed. "She asked, herself, for her bag of good clothes; it wasn't my idea. And when I invited her up for breakfast she accepted immediately. She's going to be here at three."

Rory didn't know exactly how he had done it, either, but it didn't surprise him. For a while he had thought that Kanina was going to be an exception, but when he had turned on the pressure she had responded like all the rest. The old girl-magnetism was still there; four years of disuse at the university while he applied himself to bigger things had not affected it.

CHAPTER TWENTY-EIGHT

IT was still dark when Rory went downstairs a little before 3 A.M. and walked into the kitchen where Joan Rumsey, wearing dressing gown and slippers, was making porridge. A few moments later the front door opened and there were light footsteps coming through the dining room. Kanina appeared in the doorway. Rory looked at her and almost stopped breathing.

She had discarded the shawl, the thick woolen socks and the rubber boots. She wore gray gabardine slacks and the same snug blue high-necked sweater she had been wearing when he met her first on the train. Over the sweater was a bright red corduroy jacket with a belt that pulled it in sharply at the waist and her hair was held with a red ribbon that matched the jacket. On her feet were moosehide moccasins with red beadwork on the toes. There was a faint, almost indiscernible touch of lipstick on her lips.

She looked down demurely and said: "I made them myself."

"What?" Joan Rumsey asked.

"The moccasins. I'm becoming a very good *Mooskek-owak,* you know."

"I've never seen you looking prettier," Joan Rumsey said.

"It's a good thing we're getting away early," Kanina replied. "My people will think I'm wearing a man's pants."

Joan Rumsey began frying bacon, then started making sandwiches for their lunch.

"May we have some tea, sugar and a can of milk?" Rory asked. "We'll have a fire and make tea at lunch."

"Certainly," Joan Rumsey said. "Will you be eating on a beach?"

Rory looked at Kanina. "We might be," she answered.

"I'll give you a blanket to keep the food out of the sand."

Daylight came swiftly as Kanina and Rory ate breakfast. When they were finished Mrs. Rumsey gave Rory the lunch and blanket, and they stepped outside into the wan and eerie light of the approaching day.

The two canoes and outboard were on the shore where Rory had made them ready the evening before. The outboard was on a large square-sterned canoe and a smaller canoe was on a line and bridle for towing. Rory pushed both craft clear of the beach and they climbed into the larger one, Kanina in the bow and Rory by the motor in the stern. He started the motor and turned the canoe upstream. Behind them a red crescent of sun emerged above the eddying fog banks of James Bay and painted the water with twisting streaks that looked like blood.

Kanina sat facing forward and Rory's eyes kept moving back repeatedly to the narrow curving outline of her back. The red collar of her jacket was turned up so that only her black hair showed above it. Below the jacket her gray slacks clung with alluring snugness to the slim roundness of her hips.

For two hours the motor hummed steadily and they did not try to converse above its noise. Then the dense riverbank wall of spruce opened into a clearing ahead, Kanina pointed and Rory turned the canoe toward it. He cut the motor when they were close and the canoe grated onto the beach gravel. They jumped ashore.

"Let's not waste any time," he said. "The earlier we get in there, the more chance we'll have of finding *man-tay-o*."

They hauled the big canoe onto the beach, then he tied the paddles across the thwarts of the small canoe to form shoulder rests for portaging it. Rory took off the sweater he was wearing, rolled it and looped it around his shoulders for padding. He crouched midway along the canoe and lifted it off the ground so that its weight rested on his knees. Then he crooked one arm under it and in one quick movement his body came erect and the eighty-pound canoe rolled upward and over and came to rest upside down on his shoulders.

"You're no greenhorn, I see," Kanina said simply and began leading the way.

They crossed the camp clearing with its tent and wigwam skeletons and entered the bush. There was still an early-morning chill and dampness in the air that was greatly accentuated here under the thick spruce and balsam canopy. With his head under the canoe, Rory couldn't see much except the slim supple form of Kanina moving lithely ahead of him. It was his first portage of the season so he was out of shape and had to stop about every ten minutes to rest. It was almost an hour later when Kanina told him during one of the rests: "I think we're almost there."

A few minutes later they emerged suddenly into brilliant daylight. Rory walked across a strip of beach and put the canoe down at the edge of the lake.

"Kishamooskek?" he asked.

She nodded. "Yes."

It was a pretty spot. The lake was very blue and dotted with small islands. The big marsh behind them was laced with twisting green fingers of cattail and sedge. In front of them, separating lake and marsh, was the glistening white ribbon of beach. It was seven o'clock, but the sun was already well up in the sky and the day was turning warm.

"Okay, *man-tay-o*," Rory said, "where are you?"

They launched the canoe and Kanina took a paddle and climbed into the bow. Rory stepped into the stern and pushed off. The haversack of lunch was at his feet and his binoculars hung from his neck. It was good to be paddling again, to hear the gurgling slap of water caressing the canoe's resonant bottom and to feel the little craft respond like a living creature to the gentlest twist of his sprucewood paddle. Rory had always thought since his first experiences with canoes here in the Canadian north that the canoe was primitive man's most beautiful and most practical creation. What other conveyance can carry its heavy load as far as a waterway goes, yet be so light that it in turn can then be carried on a man's shoulders to where another waterway begins?

This was the land where, unknown centuries ago, the canoe was conceived and born. And sitting ahead of him now was one of the race who had produced it. Kanina had taken off her jacket and she was paddling now in the blue short-sleeved sweater. She paddled smoothly and gracefully, and her body swayed so that the power of her shoulders as well as her arms went into each stroke.

"You would be a very good dancer," Rory said. "I know by the way you paddle."

"My ancestors had invented the birchbark canoe before your ancestors discovered the wheel and made the first cart," she answered. "So I should know something about paddling canoes, shouldn't I?"

"I suppose you should."

"And did you ever think," she went on, "that the story of our canoe and your wheel helps explain why our races are so far apart technically today? My race had very efficient transportation by canoe while the people of your race still had to carry everything they possessed on their own backs. Yet despite our head start, history left us stranded, a primitive race still, here on the edge of the Arctic, while your race has taken possession of the world. All because the luck of history gave you the wheel."

"I don't know what you're trying to say," Rory told her. "But it sounds interesting. Why don't you start all over again?"

"Okay." Kanina laughed a little. "We had the canoe. It was perfect for the land and people who produced it, because we had lakes and rivers leading everywhere. It was a technological blind alley, so useful in its original form that there was no incentive to change or improve it. Have you got that point?"

"Yes."

"Well, while my people were getting along nicely with our canoes here in the Americas, your race was evolving on the flat dry steppes somewhere around the Caspian where you needed land transport. One day a couple of thousand years after we had had the canoe, some smart Sumerian ancestor of yours discovered that he could put two potter's wheels on a shaft and he had a cart. And the superior position of the white race was assured right then. Your cart was a makeshift contraption demanding improvement, and you certainly did improve it. What started as a simple wheel is now a tremendous technological complex of gear ratios, horsepower and kilowatts and Lord knows what. Now you even put wings on it and drive it through the air at the speed of that Sumerian potter's shout. Do you understand me now?"

"Yes. Go on. You're very interesting."

"That's about all there is to it. All over the world people climbed out of their Stone Age beginnings, and some climbed fast, and some climbed slow, and some like my people barely climbed at all. And your race prospered on the top of the heap because the wheel happened to have tremendous technological potentialities that the dug-out, the sled, the kayak, the coracle and the canoe didn't possess. Interesting, isn't it? I wonder what would have happened . . . . I wonder what the world's racial structure would be today if the American Indians of five thousand years ago instead of the Sumerians had discovered the wheel, and then the pulley and the gear and the steam engine and everything else that came in the wheel's wake. Probably I'd be an immigrant in the New World of Europe and you'd come down from your little tent village in the Hebrides and train to be a school teacher and I'd insist on you being fired because I wouldn't want my superior brown-skinned children to be taught by a backward inferior white native."

She stopped talking then and Rory had no reply. There were flaws in her argument, but her basic thesis that the relative position of the world's races was largely a matter of accident was probably true. It was true enough, anyway, that he didn't want to argue otherwise against a mind as incisive and informed as hers.

"What did you call yourself this morning at the Rumseys'?" he asked her. "A moose something or other."

"*Mooskek-owak*. It's our name for ourselves. It means 'the ones of the muskeg.' *Mooskek* is swamp or muskeg. *Owak* or *owyuk* means the ones or the people."

"Can't you see that you would be doing an important service for your people if you got over your silly little huff and went back out to teach school somewhere? You're producing a surplus population. Before long some of you will have to get out and work with white people or starve. I know there's prejudice out there, but it's all based on misunderstanding and it wouldn't take many individuals like you to abolish for all time the old myth that Indians are stupid and no good."

Kanina began talking slowly. "You forget," she said, "that I've been out there fighting your prejudices for seven years. I didn't see any of them breaking down as a result of my example. In fact they seemed to be getting worse. And finally I broke down instead. They aren't based on misunderstanding; it's refusal to understand. It can't be broken down from our side, I know that now. It can only be broken down from the inside by you, all of you. When you clean your house of some of its ignorance, it'll be time then for some of us to move in and prove that Indians can be useful, responsible citizens. I'll be doing my small part here, teaching children, preparing them for the time when your people are prepared to accept them. You go back and do your share of the job. It's really your job, not mine."

They paddled on in silence after that and approached the first island. The islands were small, the largest of them no more than three or four acres, and only the larger ones were high and dry enough to support trees. Some had small fringes of beach or mud, but most were surrounded with floating mats of sphagnum which made it difficult to distinguish where land ended and water began.

"It looks like a good goose lake," Rory said. "If the barnacle is paired with that Canada, they'll have a nesting territory here somewhere. If they're nonbreeding yearlings, they'll be defending a territory to come back to next year."

They moved from island to island, making a circuit of each with the canoe, then passing on to the next. Several times they saw Canada geese, a lone one each time, each one probably a male on watch while the female remained hidden on a nest nearby. They had been searching about three hours when Rory saw a pair of geese flying low over the water a quarter of a mile away and he knew even before he got the binoculars on them that their search had ended. He saw instantly that the leading goose was smaller and whiter. Then, through the binoculars, he saw the round white face patch on the leading bird and for a brief thrilling moment he imagined he could be back in Barra with the Atlantic's surf again pounding in his ears. And there *was* a pounding in his ears, but it was the thumping of his own heart.

"There he is!" Rory said.

The geese were in sight for eight or ten seconds, then they passed from view behind a rather large island that carried a thick growth of spruce and balsam. Rory removed the binoculars from his eyes and shifted his gaze along to the other end of the island, waiting breathlessly. But the geese didn't reappear.

"They're down on the water behind that island," Rory said. "We'll land and sneak through and get a closer look."

They resumed paddling, executing each stroke carefully to avoid splashes and to keep the paddles from striking the sides of the canoe. Neither of them spoke. They came up slowly and Rory turned the canoe in toward a small white sliver of beach. When they reached shallow water he stepped out of the canoe and held it with his hands to keep it from grating on the sand. Kanina slipped off her moccasins, pulled up her slacks and waded ashore. Then, instead of dragging the canoe out of the water, Rory picked it up and put it down noiselessly on the beach.

Kanina put her moccasins on again and they moved stealthily into the gloom of the spruces, stopping frequently to listen. Kanina dropped back and let Rory lead. Suddenly he stopped, his head turned sideways. He had heard a faint guttural gabbling—the voice of a Canada goose feeding. It was followed by a sharp series of richer mellower bark-like notes. Rory hadn't heard that bark-like chatter for eight years, but he recognized instantly the feeding talk of a barnacle goose.

He turned to Kanina and smiled. She smiled too, her lips moving back delicately over her white teeth and the dimples forming at her mouth corners.

They crept forward again, their bodies bent low to keep below the bushy screen of alders and sweet gale that grew along the island's shore. Rory could see the water of the lake now and there was a large area here on the island's westward side where it was shallow, with green spikes of reeds and sedges growing up through it profusely. He felt Kanina tugging on his sleeve and he turned and looked back at her. She was pointing, a little to the right, not straight ahead where he had been searching. He shifted his search now to this area and he saw the geese instantly. They were in plain view about a hundred yards offshore and he wondered how he could have missed them before. Both birds were feeding busily, their bodies tipping up repeatedly, their heads and long necks reaching down into the water. Every few seconds they would raise their heads above the surface with muddy roots and stems draping like grotesque whiskers from their bills.

Rory dropped onto his stomach where he could watch the geese through a thin screen of bushes without being seen by them. Kanina moved up and lay beside him so that their bodies almost touched. Rory studied the geese through his binoculars. After a minute he passed the binoculars to Kanina and she took them eagerly. Periodically the geese paused in their feeding to chatter softly to each other.

Then Rory saw what he had been waiting and hoping to see. The geese raised their heads after another underwater search for food and this time the barnacle had a bill filled with roots but the Canada goose came up with nothing. The barnacle didn't eat it. Instead the bird hunched forward, wings quivering and its long neck curving gracefully so that the bill almost touched the water. With its slender neck pumping up and down rapidly, it offered the food to the Canada. The bigger goose accepted the food, then the barnacle with wings fluttering reached over the Canada's back and daintily preened the wing feathers of the other goose. There was a tenderness and gallantry in it that made Rory feel he was watching something very personal and private that a man shouldn't see. He knew he was witnessing a courtship display that biologists rarely had the opportunity to see in geese in the wild.

"Did you see it?" he whispered quickly to Kanina. "That proves it. It proves they're mated and it proves the barnacle is the male."

Kanina nodded without taking her eyes from the binoculars.

"I told you geese could fall in love. Do you believe me now?"

She nodded again.

They watched for perhaps ten minutes, passing the binoculars back and forth between them. Once more during that period the barnacle performed another courtship feeding, terminating it as before with a dainty preening and caressing of her wing feathers.

"Could anything be more like a kiss?" he asked Kanina.

For Rory it was a moving experience. All his childhood recollections of the barnacles of Barra flashed back now in nostalgic retrospection and for the first time since leaving the little blackhouse by the sea he felt a twinge of homesickness. It seemed incredible. He was in the spruce wilderness of subarctic Canada more than three thousand miles from the Hebrides, yet he was watching a barnacle goose that may have left Barra's Goose Island Sound about the time that Rory left Toronto.

They crept away finally and left the geese undisturbed. Back on the little beach they launched the canoe and paddled silently away. When they were well clear of the island Rory stopped paddling.

"It's hard to believe," he said. "It's harder to believe now, somehow, after seeing him, than it was when you first told me. Because now I can see how misplaced he is here. It's all wrong, a barnacle so far from the rocks and the surf and the sea."

Kanina had turned in her seat and was looking back at him.

"You know," Rory continued, "that old devil has got himself in an awkward spot. I'll bet he's very uncomfortable here in a shallow little land-locked lake like this. But now he's fallen for a lady goose who's as fond of fresh water and muskeg country as he is of the sea. He's entitled to a divorce . . . . on grounds of incompatibility."

Rory resumed paddling slowly. He was still talking.

"And what'll they do next fall at migration time? Every fiber of him then will be yearning for the sea, and every fiber of her will be yearning for the marshes of the Mississippi valley. But she'll be surrounded by geese of her own species, all of them starting south in the normal way, and she'll simply go along with them, doing the instinctive thing. But he'll be all mixed up. His instinct will be urging him to retrace the route that will take him back to the sea. But he'll also have an instinctive urge to stay with her. He'll have to choose between his love for her and his love for the sea."

They paddled on for perhaps a minute, then he added: "Fascinating problem, isn't it? We've got to catch that goose and mark him so that he can be recognized again. There's a chance then of finding out what he does."

"Catch him!" Kanina spoke now for the first time. "How?"

"It might not be so hard. There's a time in mid-summer when they molt their wing feathers and can't fly."

CHAPTER TWENTY-NINE

I T was almost noon when they got back to the beach at the end of the portage and pulled the canoe up on the sand.

"The last time I invited you to have lunch with me you were very emphatic about saying no," Rory said.

"Try me again."

"Miss Beaverskin," he began, "it is almost nine hours since you ate breakfast. Would you care for lunch?"

"Mr. Macdonald. It would be an honor and a pleasure. But no Martinis, please. They make me very irresponsible."

Rory looked at her, half smiling. "I'll bet you are very attractive when you get . . . . irresponsible," he said.

He took the axe and went into the bush for firewood. When he returned, Kanina had Joan Rumsey's blanket spread out on the beach and the food arranged on it. She had taken off her moccasins and her slacks were rolled up over her knees.

"The sand feels nice on your bare feet," she said.

"It looks nice too. Your bare feet, I mean. Do they look as nice all the way up?"

"That's a secret. I didn't know you'd be curious or I'd have left my long underwear on. Do you know anything about Robert Herrick?"

"He was a poet, an Englishman."

"Yes, and he was a preacher too, and he got unfrocked or something because he was more interested in writing poems about girls' legs than he was in preparing his sermons."

"There's a preacher I have great respect for. What did he say about girls' legs?"

"I'm not sure I'll remember." Kanina was looking down at the sand. "It was something like this:

> Her legs were such Diana shows
> When tucked up she a-hunting goes
> With. . . .

Oh I remember now. . . .

> With buskins shortened to descry
> The happy dawning of her thigh."

Rory laughed. He looked again at the gentle curve of her legs where they disappeared beneath her rolled-up slacks. "The happy dawning of her thigh," he repeated. "Very appropriate. My mother would like you. She is very fond of the English poets. Often quoted them like that. How do you remember the stuff?"

"All the time I was at school I didn't have anything to do but read. Your people saw to that. I wasn't what you'd call in demand, you know, socially."

Why did she always get back to this? Rory started chopping wood. She *was* a great deal like his mother.

He lit the fire. Kanina waded out into the lake and filled the billycan where the water was knee-deep and free of the sand that the waves stirred up along the shore. Rory jabbed a stick into the sand so that it slanted over the fire and he hung the billycan on it. Then they sat on the edge of the blanket and began to eat Joan Rumsey's lunch.

The fire crackled and periodically he added wood. Kishamooskek Lake was very blue with gray patches of wind riffle scurrying here and there where vagrant gusts of breeze roughened the surface. Rory was reminded again of the Goose Island shieling with its blue sea and crackling peat fire, but the resemblance ended there for there was little similarity between Kanina and Peggy MacNeill. He watched Kanina furtively. Would he ever again in his life encounter so strange and contradictory and mixed-up a person? She was one of the most cultured persons he would ever meet, yet in the most uncultured setting he would probably ever encounter.

The tea pail started to boil and Kanina lifted it from the fire. She put in tea and set the pail on the sand beside the fire for the tea to brew. In a minute she began pouring it into their metal mugs.

"Milk and sugar?" she asked him.

"Yes, milk and sugar."

They began drinking their tea. She sat with her knees pulled up close against her chest, and the exposed dawning of her thighs was now at least six smooth brown teasing inches. Rory stared at her openly, wondering what to do next. She was gazing at her toes which she kept wiggling childishly in the beach sand. Then she turned her head slowly. She was smiling.

"Why don't you stop worrying about me?" she said to him. "Let's enjoy our picnic. Take those big boots off, the sand on your feet is very pleasant."

He began unlacing his high boots, glancing back frequently at her.

He pulled off the boots and socks and twisted his feet into the warm sand.

"Do you like living that way, in that tent, no bed, no bathroom?" he asked.

"No. But I'll learn to like it."

That, he thought, was surely his cue. If she was going to insist on living like an animal, he could play the game that way too.

He reached out and took one of the hands that were clasped over her knees and began drawing it gently toward him. Suddenly she had a startled, frightened look. She came against him slowly and he could feel the round fullness of her bosom pressing against his side. Then he pushed her backward, down onto the blanket and he held her firmly with a hand on each shoulder as he sat beside her. Her long hair lay in a rumpled disorderly mass on the blanket, like a furbished frame around the dark exotic beauty of her face. Her eyes with their slight oriental narrowing at the outside corners were partially closed.

"You are the most beautiful girl I have ever met," he said softly. "I have said that to girls before, but this is the first time I've ever really meant it."

He bent down quickly and kissed her. Her eyes were closed now. Her lips came apart slightly and pressed firmly against Rory's. Then he dropped onto the blanket and lay beside her and drew her slender body toward him. She pushed away, struggling, but for only a few seconds, then she relaxed and came against him. They lay like this for several minutes and he was conscious of nothing but the soft crushing weight of her body and the rapid staccato rhythm of her breathing.

He began running one hand up slowly under her sweater, giving her plenty of opportunity to resist if she wanted to. She held his wrist and pushed her shoulder firmly against his to impede his hand. He stopped and waited. Then she relaxed once more and lay silent and unresisting, her eyes still closed. He began forcing his hand upward again. Now she let go of his wrist, her shoulder drew back from him slowly, and his hand was free to move at will under her sweater.

Rory knew in that instant that with a bit of gentle force he now could have her. Any resistance she had possessed before was now melting away. And he knew in the same instant that he must not go on with it.

What he felt in those next few moments he never succeeded in analyzing very satisfactorily. It wasn't physical impotence because his loins remained a searing fire of desire, and to call it mental impotence didn't really explain much, although he supposed the term did cover it vaguely. There was a fleeting memory of his mother involved in it and an awareness that she too was a person like this with a refinement and scholarly comprehension that raised her far above the mean and stagnant environment in which she had to live. All he knew for certain was that Kanina was giving herself to him, that he wanted her as he had never wanted a girl before, but a peculiar strength or weakness, he couldn't tell which, was stopping him from going on. It was so puzzlingly different from what he had planned.

He removed his hand and pulled her sweater back down into place. He sat up.

"I am sorry, Kanina."

She sat up and didn't answer. She shook her head vigorously to straighten her rumpled hair and stared silently at the lake. Then she turned back to him slowly. Their eyes met fleetingly but she didn't smile. She put her hand on the side of the tea pail.

"It's still warm," she said. "Shall we have another cup?"

"Yes, please," he told her.

"Milk and sugar? I'm sorry to have to ask again, but I have completely forgotten."

CHAPTER THIRTY

T HEY arrived back at Cape Cree late in the afternoon and Rory made no arrangements to see Kanina again. They had talked little after leaving Kishamooskek Lake. When he beached the big canoe in front of Cape Cree, Kanina stepped out onto the sand and turned to him briefly.

"Thank you," she said. "I have had a very pleasant day." And then she was gone, running quickly up the bank toward the Indian tents.

That evening during dinner Rory told the Rumseys briefly about the trip and their discovery of the barnacle goose and his mate.

"Did you talk to Kanina about her going back outside and finding a school?" Joan Rumsey asked him.

"Yes. But I didn't change her mind. She's determined to stay here."

It had been a long day and Rory was tired. He went to his room right after dinner, wrote up notes about the barnacle, then went to bed.

The following morning at breakfast he asked Bert Rumsey: "Would Jock, your interpreter, be free to help me interview Indian hunters?"

He saw Joan Rumsey turn her head quickly and stare at him. "What's happened?" she asked. "Has Kanina got stubborn again?"

He knew the question would come, and he had an answer ready.

"No. Kanina would do it. But I thought I might get along better interviewing men if I had a man interpreting."

"I don't know why you should," Joan Rumsey commented curtly, but she said nothing more. Her husband replied: "Jock is free in the evenings, you could use him then. Do you want him tonight?"

"Yes."

There was a minute or more of silence. Then Rory spoke again.

"I should write a couple of letters about the barnacle goose. When will there be a plane to take out mail?"

"Not for a few days, maybe," Bert Rumsey replied. "But there will probably be one within a week."

Rory went back to his room. He stood at the window which looked down toward the Indian camp and he could see, sandwiched among many others, the ragged brown tent of the Beaverskins. It was incredible that that filthy hovel was now the home of . . . . had he meant it yesterday? . . . . yes, she *was* the most beautiful girl he had ever met. And she had a hell of a lot more than good looks and sex appeal. She was very irrational and stubborn on the race question, but even allowing for this she still had a brain that intrigued him. Rory had met few girls, at the university or anywhere else, who had the background of reading and the mental acuteness that Kanina seemed to have.

But could anyone possibly sink any lower in the social scheme of things? Yet yesterday when he had tried to exploit her social status in the traditional way, it had suddenly seemed wrong and he couldn't go on with it. Had he turned into a prude?

He wasn't sure, either, why he had decided to use Jock as his interpreter. He knew, and Joan Rumsey knew too, that it wasn't for the reason he had just offered downstairs at breakfast. He was confused, that was all he could say, and somehow it had seemed like a good idea to stay away from Kanina for a few days. To figure out where she fitted in his system of feminine taxonomy. Did she belong to the "available" group, or the "unavailable"?

He walked away from the window, sat down at the little writing table beside the bed and started his first letter.

Dear P.L.:
    Chalk up another very interesting record for Hurricane Alice. . . .

He went on to describe the barnacle goose but he did not mention Kanina in connection with it. He described the bird's Canada goose mate and the courtship display and feeding he had observed. Then he wrote on:

As you know, the question always arises in connection with these wind-blown strays as to whether they ever find their way back home. In this case the question is complicated and made more significant from a behavior aspect by the fact that our stray has mated outside its normal range with another species very different in its way of life. Will he go back to the sea? Maybe back to Barra? Or will he go south and remain inland with her, adopting the migratory pattern of the Mississippi flyway Canadas? This is a very exciting problem—do you agree?—and if we can answer it, it could throw some light on whether migration is entirely instinctive or partly a learned behavior. By trapping and marking the goose, there is a strong chance in this case that we could find out where he goes.

Several men doing migration studies have been using colored plastic neck bands which make a bird identifiable with binoculars for a mile or more. You've seen some of the papers on their work. I think the neck bands are just plastic strips tied with a slip-proof falconer's knot so that a four- or five-inch streamer is left hanging loose, and I would like to try this method of marking the barnacle goose and perhaps his mate up here. We could probably capture them when they are flightless during the summer molt.

If we succeed in marking them, we could then prepare a mimeographed letter describing the project and circulate it widely among bird clubs and U.S. wildlife authorities in the Mississippi valley. This is a heavily populated region and the wintering goose flocks there are under fairly close observation. If the barnacle winters there with his mate, there is a strong possibility they would be observed and reported to us.

The other possibility, of course, is that he might find his way back to the wintering range around the Hebrides. If this occurs, there are circumstances again making it probable that the goose could be observed. First, the winter range is restricted, most of them wintering around Barra, my home. Secondly, my mother is there and she could check the flocks for us.

Would you have time to check on the neck-banding technique and bring with you a small supply of the plastic we shall need? I hope, incidentally, you still plan on coming. Yellow would be the best color, as brilliant as possible, but check first to learn whether anyone else is already using neck bands of this color on barnacles or Canadas, otherwise we'll be risking confusion. I could ask the wildlife service at Ottawa about this, but it is a digression from the work I'm really here to do and I'm afraid some stuffy character down there might regard it as sentimental nonsense and tell me to stick to my original assignment. Hence this letter to you. Regards.

Rory.

Now, what about the letter to his mother? Her presence in Barra next winter was essential to the project. She had the same passionate love for the barnacles that he had, and he knew it wouldn't be difficult to get her enthused over the problem of *man-tay-o*. But how far should he go? Did it justify putting pressure on her to remain in Barra for the winter?

He started to write, describing the barnacle and the challenging problem it posed. "It is a question," he wrote, "of what will turn out to be the stronger motivation—his love for his mate or his love for Barra and the sea." Then he described the plan to mark the barnacle so that it would be recognized again. "I hope you will be able to help us by watching the Barra flocks this winter," he wrote, "but I know you have your own personal problem which. . . ." He stopped there for several minutes and didn't know what to say, then he concluded: ". . . . which may make it impossible for you to remain there for the winter."

He read the letter again. It was too indefinite. He *must* persuade his mother to stay in Barra.

He added this paragraph: "The decision is up to you, of course, but this problem is so fascinating and important biologically that I do feel justified in urging you to stay in Barra. Without a thorough check of the Barra flocks our chances of success will be reduced fifty percent. There is certainly no one else there to do it for us. I don't intend to equivocate or beat around the bush. I am asking you to stay. Will you?"

He put an airmail sticker and stamp on the envelope. If it wasn't delayed too long here at Cape Cree waiting for a plane, and if his mother answered promptly, he should have a reply from her in two to three weeks.

Fate was not kind to Rory's plan to avoid Kanina. He went out for two hours that evening with Jock and interviewed several hunters about their kill of geese that spring, and when he returned to the Rumseys' house at dusk Kanina was there.

"Don't rush upstairs, Rory," Joan Rumsey said. "I just put coffee on."

Rory stepped to the living room door. "Hello, Kanina," he said. She smiled fleetingly, then looked quickly away. He sat in a chair near the door.

"Kanina came for some of her books," Joan Rumsey said. "She's starting a school for the children."

Rory had noticed the cardboard carton of books by the door in the hall.

"That's a good idea," he said. "Where are you going to hold it?"

"In the church," Kanina replied.

"What will you teach them?"

"Not much. The children aren't here long enough to teach them very much. Three or four months. I might be able to teach them English, maybe a bit of arithmetic. If they just get that, it'll help make their lives a little easier, a little fuller."

"Why don't more of them go to the residential school at Moose, as you did?" Rory asked Kanina. "There's time there for the teachers to accomplish something."

"Not many parents will let them go. It's more important anyway for them to stay with their parents and learn the bush, the hunting and trapping, the skills by which they will have to live when they grow up. That has to come first. Too much education will make them dissatisfied with the life they have, and there isn't any other life for them. I should know."

Joan Rumsey stood up. "Let's not get started on that," she said and headed for the kitchen to bring in the coffee.

They talked for an hour, the conversation drifting from beaver conservation to Cree and Eskimo legends, the educational philosophy of John Dewey and Rory forgot what else. He forgot because he repeatedly found his whole attention focused not on the conversation but on the lucid and knowledgeable way that Kanina took part in it. She talked quietly, sometimes tossing her head for emphasis in a way that made her hair shimmer appealingly, never holding the floor for long, but never out of the discussion for long either. When it was over Rory took the carton of books and walked down with her through the Indian village to the Beaverskin tent. At the canvas-flap door she took the books from him.

"Thank you," she said. "I didn't expect it would turn out to be such a pleasant evening."

"I didn't expect . . . . either," he said fumblingly. Then she stepped inside, dropping the canvas flap behind her.

The moment she was gone from him Rory realized he loved her. With a dizzying feeling that started his knees shaking he knew he had discovered the fierceness and absolute finality of genuine love. There had been no physical stimulation tonight to confuse the issue; it had happened, or at least had become apparent to him without even the touching of a hand. Now he realized what had happened to him on the beach at Kishamooskek yesterday when his love-making came to a paralyzed halt; a part of him, a subconscious part of him, had known it then.

He started walking back through a wan moonlight that barely showed the path. A soft night breeze, pungent with the mossy scents of the surrounding muskeg, began stirring the canvas of the dark and silent Indian tents around him. And even in these first chaotic moments of discovery, while his body reeled drunkenly, his mind saw clearly that he could never marry Kanina Beaverskin.

He walked back slowly toward the Rumseys', then decided he didn't want to go inside and turned down toward the river instead. He sat on a boulder. The night was silent except for the faint slapping murmur of tiny waves on the shore and the occasional wail of a dog kept awake by hunger.

He couldn't consider marrying her. It was unthinkable. It would be the end of everything he had planned for and dreamed of since the childhood years in Barra when he had determined to escape and win success in this world outside. He had worked too hard, it had taken too long to jeopardize it all now with an Indian wife. His own background was handicap enough. In small ways he would show the effect of it all his life, for one never quite throws off entirely the habits and standards adopted in childhood. Traces always remain. He needed a wife from a good family, socially suave and polished, who could help him overcome the handicap of his background, not a wife who would bring bigger handicaps into his life, as Kanina surely would.

Kanina Beaverskin had all the essential requirements of a good wife and partner except one—her race. She was intelligent, attractive, and, if she had the opportunity, she could probably become a good and gracious hostess. But his society would never give her that opportunity. Rory knew what the pattern would be if he married her. As a professor's wife, Kanina would be treated very politely, too politely probably, but she would never be really accepted. Rory would be known as the biologist who went north one summer and came back married to a squaw, a beautiful one, but . . . . a squaw. And when opportunities for advancement came, somewhere behind the scenes there would be a board of V.I.P.s weighing Rory Macdonald's assets and liabilities, and his wife, inevitably, would be a major item in the tally of liabilities.

He thought of his mother's marriage, and the unhappiness and frustrations that had dogged her life because she made the mistake of marrying out of her class. He thought with bitterness that he could marry a harebrained slut like Peggy MacNeill without reproach, but Kanina Beaverskin must remain outside the pale of his society because she had a bit more of the pigment *melanin* in the outer layers of her skin. It did not matter whether he approved or disapproved. He belonged to a gregarious species, he had to live and work with others of his kind, and to win their approval and the advancement this could bring he had to respect the attitudes and beliefs of his fellow men as much as his own.

Rory rose and began walking slowly up the slope toward the house.

He was in love, but there was no glad elation in it, there was only defeat and despair. It had been so easy before to condemn the injustices that Kanina had suffered, to decry under a halo of self-righteous indignation the racial bigotry of his countrymen. It had been easy because he had been doing it from the safe immunity of the sidelines—an onlooker, not a participant. But now he was out in the arena, personally involved in the contest himself, and the race question had such a different look from here.

An hour ago he would have argued hotly that he was personally above and incapable of racial bias. Now he was bowing out meekly and letting race determine the major decision of his life. And he wasn't trying to fool himself. He knew exactly what he was doing, and why.

On the other side of the camp a sled dog howled dismally at the pale crescent of the moon. All around, other dogs joined in and the chilled night air shivered with the strident clamor of their baying. Then the moon was smothered in a cloud, the canine chorus died and Rory Macdonald was alone again with the qualms and accusations of his own troubled thoughts.

CHAPTER THIRTY-ONE

THE following morning Rory and Jock began preparing for their first field trip into the goose country inland. About forty miles south of Cape Cree a large river, the Otter, emptied into James Bay and it was somewhere in that area, Rory thought, that the breeding ranges of the Mississippi and South Atlantic goose populations must merge. So Rory decided to investigate the pothole country up the Otter first. It would take two weeks. He rented a big eighteen-foot canoe, an outboard motor and tent from Bert Rumsey. They stowed sleeping bags, cooking gear and

food in packsacks for the portaging. By late afternoon they were finished
and ready for an early start in the morning.

And Rory hadn't seen Kanina all day.

But he saw her that evening just before dark. He was standing at the
window of his room again, looking down over the Indian village, when
Kanina came up the path toward the church carrying an armload of
books. In the dusk he didn't recognize her at first because she was wearing the rubber boots and the big black shawl again and she looked like
any of the other Indian girls. She was almost at the church before he
realized who it was. Kanina went inside the little frame building with its
squat, square spire and Rory waited, his heart thumping, for her to
reappear.

Darkness settled down quickly but Rory waited at the window even
after the light became so dim that he would barely see her when she did
come out. She appeared again finally, a wraith-like shadow in the night.
The darkness swallowed her in a few seconds but Rory's eyes strained
for another glimpse. Then he saw the door of the Beaverskin tent open
and close quickly, revealing briefly the small shawled figure in its faint
yellow square of light.

He walked away from the window, his head swimming as though he
were drunk, and turned on the light. He lay on the bed and stared at
the ceiling. He was in a fine mess now, as big a mess as that barnacle
gander out on Kishamooskek. He loved a girl he couldn't possibly
marry. And for the next three months he might be seeing her frequently.
He hoped he *would* be seeing her frequently, but he doubted that it
would be a good thing for either of them.

Rory and Jock were away from Cape Cree for fifteen days and during that time Kanina Beaverskin was not out of Rory's thoughts for more
than a few minutes at a time. It was a successful trip for its contributions
to the goose research. They found no Canada goose nests—Rory had
hardly expected they would—but they did find several concentrations of
geese which told their own story. More than half of the geese were in
pairs or in small flocks; these would be nonbreeders. Only about one
goose in five were singles—lone birds that flew off honking in alarm when
the canoe approached. Each of these would be a mated male on guard
while the female hid somewhere near on the nest. Rory kept a careful
record of beaches and open beaver meadows where he hoped to be able
to trap and band flightless birds later in the summer.

The last night they camped at the Otter's mouth and that evening at
sunset the sky was braided with white wispy streamers of mare's-tail

cloud. Rory saw Jock anxiously watching the build-up of clouds. Finally the Indian said: "Wind tomorrow. We stay here."

The thought of waiting another day suddenly seemed a chilling, unbearable prospect. "It's going to take one hell of a big blow to keep me from reaching Cape Cree tomorrow," Rory said.

"What your hurry?" Jock asked him. "We still got food."

"Man doth not live by bread alone," Rory said. "Can you figure that one out, Jock? It's in the Bible."

"Sure I know what it means," Jock answered quickly. "It means next time you better bring Joe Beaverskin's girl with you. Then you won't be in damnfool hurry to get back."

Rory laughed, but Jock's remark surprised him, because Rory hadn't mentioned Kanina once during the trip.

"Why bring Kanina Beaverskin into this?"

Jock smiled at him. "Why? I guess you know, eh?"

"Yes. I guess I know," Rory replied. "But I didn't know anyone else knew."

"Lots know. But don't worry. Nobody gives a damn long as it's her. We don't like white men coming up here and monkeying around with *Mooskek-owak* girls. But nobody cares about Joe Beaverskin's girl. She's not real *Mooskek-owak*. She's no good. All she any good for is reading books. No *Mooskek-owak* boy wants to marry her. She couldn't skin a beaver kit. So see . . . . you go right ahead and nobody gives a damn."

So this was what Kanina's people thought of her? Rory remembered how Kanina had defined herself during that first meeting on the Moosonee train. Stranded between two worlds, she had called it, and belonging to neither. Now he saw the full tragedy of it. But it would never change his decision about marriage, of that he was sure, for one ruined life was better than ruining two.

The wind rose in the night and Rory was awakened several times by the snapping of the taut canvas over his head. He awoke again shortly after dawn, wriggled quickly out of his sleeping bag and looked out of the tent at the blue and white James Bay combers tumbling in on the beach.

"Jock!" he shouted. "Time to get started."

The Indian's dark eyes opened drowsily and he lifted himself onto one elbow, listening to the wind and the beat of the surf.

He shook his head. "Too big storm," he said.

"It's not too big for our eighteen-footer. Come on. I've got work to do," Rory declared.

Jock crawled wearily from his sleeping bag.

"Next time, by God, I bring Joe Beaverskin's girl, and then you two do your work right here if the wind blows."

Rory took over the outboard for the return trip because he was more experienced with this kind of water than Jock was. It was a rough trip and the canoe shipped water frequently over the bow. Jock sat pale, and then livid, all the way, expecting to drown any moment. Rory kept the outboard throttled down to half-speed most of the way and it was late afternoon when they reached Cape Cree.

Joan Rumsey came down to the beach when they landed. "You're very brown," she told Rory, "all except your nose. I didn't know a tan could look so handsome with blond hair."

"Have you seen Kanina?" he asked.

"No."

Rory went to his room, walked straight across to the window and looked over the Indian camp anxiously. The Beaverskin tent was in its usual spot so they were not away fishing. He went out and started down toward the Indian tents to look for her.

He went to the church first, paused on the gray wooden steps and listened. There was no sound from within so he opened the door. No one was there. He walked down the narrow middle aisle, glancing from side to side into the seats. He could see no books, paper, pencils, crayons —none of the equipment she would need for even the simplest school. He came out, turned down toward the adjoining tent village and met Jock coming up the sand path in the opposite direction.

"She ain't there," Jock said immediately. "I saw her take a canoe up the river. Probably lifting whitefish nets."

Rory walked back beside him. He launched Bert Rumsey's small canoe and began paddling upstream. Here, shielded from the wind by the trees along the river bank, the air was hot and still. The evening chorus of bird songs was beginning and he could hear white-throats and the spiraling song of olive-backed thrushes. He paddled about half an hour and there was no sign of Kanina or her canoe. Ahead of him now was a large wooded island, although the river channel around one side of it looked so narrow and sand-clogged that the island seemed almost to merge with the mainland shore. He would have stayed in the main channel, but he heard a bird song he did not recognize coming from somewhere on the island's other side, so he turned the canoe into the narrow sandy arm of the river instead. The song came again, a rather loud repetitive *chorry, chorry, chorry,* and the bird seemed to be beyond a screen of willow bushes which cut off most of Rory's view ahead.

He paddled silently around the willows. The channel broadened into a round hidden pool with a glistening semicircle of beach along the island side of it. Rory never did see or identify the bird that had brought him there. First he saw the red canoe pulled up on the beach and a second later he saw Kanina, about ten canoe-lengths ahead of him. She was standing in hip-deep water with a thick white lather of soap clinging to her shoulders. She wasn't wearing a bathing suit. She wasn't wearing anything.

Rory caught a glimpse of brown breasts with black hair draped around them, then Kanina saw him and dropped down to her knees so that the water hid her to her shoulders. He paddled on slowly.

"If you are a gentleman," she called, "you will go back and give me ten minutes to finish my bath and get dressed."

He smiled and paddled on toward her.

"I don't know whether I'm a gentleman or not," he said, close enough now that he need not raise his voice. "But I'm a man, a very weak man, I'm afraid. Far too weak to turn my back on a stroke of luck like this."

He paddled very slowly, teasing her.

"What do you think you're going to do?" she asked him curtly, a husky faltering note of apprehension in her voice.

"Maybe I'll steal your clothes," he told her. "And then, what will you do?"

There was a steely hardness on her face and in her voice when she answered him. "I'll wait until dark and paddle home and say you took them by force. Which would be the truth, anyway."

"I think I could get your clothes or anything else I wanted without resorting to force," Rory answered. "Sometimes it's bought, sometimes it's taken by force, but it can also be won by mutual agreement. It's a matter of the man's technique. . . ."

But he did not finish it. Suddenly he knew it sounded terrible. He was insulting her. And there was no sign of fear on her face now, there was only a grim unmoving contempt.

"I thought you were going to be different from the others," she said coldly. "Why do all you white men think that Indian girls are push-overs? You are a conceited little boy. You turn that canoe around and get out of here or you will regret it. The Mounties don't like white fellows rushing Indian girls. If I say the word tonight it can go out on Bert Rumsey's morning radio schedule and there could be a Mountie flying in from Moose Factory before noon tomorrow. Is that what you want?"

Rory stopped paddling and the canoe coasted forward slowly. He had started it as a joke, but it was certainly a joke no longer. The river was clear and he was close enough now to see the brown curves of her hips and bosom under the water.

"I am sorry, Kanina," he said. "I was joking. . . ."

"I don't care whether you are sorry or not. You have said it now . . . . now I know what you really think of me."

"Kanina! I *didn't* mean that. I don't know why I said it."

"I know why you said it. You said it because you believe it. You believe you are a great big blond Apollo irresistible to all women. You believe I'm a slut. Now get out of here!"

Rory back-paddled and turned the canoe. He took one look back at her.

"Will you mind if I come back in ten minutes?" he asked.

"I'm certainly not inviting you."

He paddled past the willows and out onto the main channel of the river again. He was embarrassed and angry—with himself. He waited fifteen minutes to give her plenty of time, but just as he was starting back Kanina paddled out from behind the island. She was wearing the blue pullover sweater and the black shawl. Their canoes came close together. Even with that horrible shawl, Rory thought, she was still beautiful.

"Please don't hate me for it, Kanina," he said. "I don't know how to apologize any differently, or any better. So will you forget it?"

"No, I won't forget it." She looked at him briefly. "But I'll overlook it if you think you can be a gentleman again."

"I will be."

They paddled slowly side by side back toward Cape Cree. They were silent for perhaps a minute, then he asked her: "How's the school going?"

"It won't work," she said. "The parents aren't interested. I had ten children the first day; by the fourth day it was down to two. I talked to some of the parents but they weren't interested in making the children attend. So I gave up."

Her face was hard and solemn, with lips pressed tightly together, and she stared straight ahead of her.

"It is a sad thing, I think," she continued. "I even wept over it. But it was mostly my fault. The children soon lost interest. I couldn't keep them interested."

"I'm sorry. . . ." Rory began. "No. I don't know. Maybe it's a good thing. Maybe now you're ready to agree that the place for you is out with my people."

"Every time we meet we argue about this," she said impatiently. "You've heard about my dismissal from that school and that's all you know. Just listen while I tell you all the rest of it."

Kanina talked slowly and patiently for at least fifteen minutes. Their canoes glided along silently side by side, their paddles rising and falling in unison, the wet blades glinting in the slanting rays of the sun. She started by telling him about her first night in Blackwood with Joan Rumsey's sister. She described the opening day at Park Collegiate and Trudy Brown's stormy departure from Sadie Thomas' boarding house. She went on, incident by incident—the teachers college, the search for a teaching position and finally her decision to come back to Cape Cree.

"And that's where you came in," she concluded. "Now, do you think I should be going back to all *that?*"

They paddled on silently and Rory didn't know what to say. The whitethroats were singing in a gay and ringing chorus from the spruces along the shore and the evening shadows were pushing dark fingers out across the river.

"Well, what have you got to say?" Kanina asked him. "If you were a school trustee would you hire me?"

"I certainly would."

"If you were a businessman, whose success depended on the goodwill of your community, would you hire me for your school then? Would you be willing to make some personal sacrifices of your own to support the principle of it, to set an example?"

Rory stared straight ahead and did not answer. He paddled mechanically. It sounded almost as if she knew. Kanina waited several seconds and then resumed.

"You keep telling me I should be out there fighting it, suffering, on behalf of my people," she said. "But how about you? Would you be willing to do some suffering too in your own private and business life?"

The question was so personal that Rory wondered if she could be doing it to taunt him. His big body grew taut and there was suddenly a cold strangling dryness grasping his throat.

"Well, if you were a school trustee like that, what would you do?"

He knew what he would do, because he had already faced the question. He had put his own success and future not only before the principle Kanina was talking about, but also before the love that filled his own heart. Furthermore, in spite of all her eloquence, he was as certain as ever that he could do nothing else. He must think with his brains and not his heart.

"I would try to do the right thing," he answered her in a voice that was dry and crackling like autumn leaves that had lain in the sun.

"I think you would," she told him. "You've got some strength of will. But not many of your countrymen have."

And Rory realized then that Kanina did not know. She wasn't taunting him. It had only seemed that way.

"Isn't it about time we went and checked on that barnacle goose again?" he asked, his voice suddenly firm and confident again. "How about tomorrow?"

"No!"

"Why?"

"Do you expect me to go anywhere with you again?"

"Maybe I shouldn't expect it, but I can hope."

They came around the last bend and the dingy huddle of Cape Cree tents and buildings overhung with smoke lay just ahead. There wasn't much time left.

"It was a very crude remark," he said. "You said you would overlook it. You're as interested in that goose . . . . *man*. . . ."

"*Man-tay-o*."

"Yes, *man-tay-o*. You're as interested in him as I am. Aren't you?"

"I guess I probably am."

She began paddling faster and Rory had to exert himself to keep up with her. They beached the canoes together. Kanina pulled hers up on the sand and began walking away.

"Wait, Kanina."

She stopped and turned and stared back at him, her eyes narrow and cold and unmoving, her dark brow furrowed. And then, as she looked at him, her face softened and he thought he heard the beginning of a faint sigh.

"All right," she said, and now the sigh was there, obvious and unmistakable. "But three-thirty is too early. How about seven?"

"Seven will be fine. Shall I tell Mrs. Rumsey you're coming for breakfast?"

"No. I'll meet you down here."

"A lunch?"

"If you want one. All I could bring would be flour and lard and dried goosemeat."

"I'd like to try it," Rory said.

"Okay. Leave the lunch to me then."

She turned then and walked quickly up the river bank.

CHAPTER THIRTY-TWO

THE barnacle and his mate were still there—not in the same spot but on a similar weed-grown shallows bordering another island less than a quarter mile from where Kanina and Rory had seen them on their first trip. They had found the small canoe at the end of the portage where they left it but it had taken them more than an hour after that to find the geese. Now the sun was hot and high in the cumulus-dappled sky and they were lying again on a cushion of moss and spruce needles watching the geese through a screen of willows and alders.

Rory handed the binoculars to Kanina. She took them eagerly and began to study the feeding geese. She had worn the rubber boots and the black shawl that day, and not the gay red jacket and slacks of their first trip to Kishamooskek, and she had been very quiet all morning. Several times Rory had tried to make conversation and each time she had answered him with a nod or a brief comment and then had nothing more to say. Since they left Cape Cree she hadn't once smiled sufficiently to put the dimples in her cheeks. Rory thought ruefully that he would surrender his summer's salary if it could erase from Kanina's memory his crude and tactless remark of the afternoon before.

Seeing the barnacle again, here far from the sea, filled Rory with the same strange emotion he had felt before. And then he saw the barnacle perform another courtship feeding of his mate, to follow it with the soft, caress-like preening of her wing. He turned quickly to Kanina. She had seen it too, much more clearly than he, for she had the binoculars to her eyes. Kanina turned her face to Rory; she sighed very softly, so softly it was barely audible to him a yard away. And now she smiled.

Some time later they crept back to where they had left the canoe and paddled quietly away. When they were a hundred yards or more off the island Kanina stopped paddling and turned.

"That bird . . . . ," she said, "when I think of it all, when I see him looking so much in love, he makes me feel . . . . strange. I hope he won't leave her, I don't care how much he loves his Barra and his sea. He won't, will he?"

"Lord knows."

"Once I had two Martinis on an empty stomach, it was Bert Rumsey's birthday, and seeing those geese again makes me feel a little . . . . I think . . . . like that. Just happy, without knowing what you're feeling happy for."

"Yes," Rory said. "I feel it, too."

With that she quickly removed the dingy shawl, shaking her head to loosen her hair, and a gay transformed Kanina emerged. Rory noticed happily that she was wearing the red hair ribbon under the shawl. She resumed paddling. Ten minutes later they ran the canoe onto the beach strip between the lake and the marsh. Then she removed her boots and stepped out barefooted onto the hot silvery sand, carrying with her a small white flour bag in which she had brought their food.

"This will be strictly a *Mooskek-owak* meal," she said. "You won't like it unless you are very hungry."

"I'm very hungry," he told her.

Rory went into the trees and came out a minute later with a bleached white spruce stub. While he split it for firewood, Kanina arranged a fireplace of rocks and then began mixing bannock in a powdered milk tin.

"How would you like the bannock—baked, or as dumplings with the goosemeat?" Kanina asked.

"Dumplings? Can we have dumplings?"

"We can."

"I'd like them . . . . very much . . . . please."

Kanina quickly lighted the fire while Rory continued splitting wood. She produced two blackened billycans, filled them with water and hung them over the fire to boil.

"Now," she said, "I have a special treat. My mother wasn't very anxious to let me have them."

Rory stopped chopping and watched her. Kanina took a cloth bundle from the flour sack, unrolled it and revealed two large bones from which the meat had recently been removed. Rory recognized them as caribou femurs.

"Are you going to feed me bones?" he asked.

"Yes."

Kanina said nothing more and tossed the bones into the fire. When the billycans boiled she put one, the tea pail, to the side, then she took two large spoonfuls of congealed fat from a tin can and added it to the boiling water of the other pail.

"When you dry meat, you lose the fat," she explained, "and when you cook it, you have to put the fat back."

From another sackcloth package she took a large slab of dry twisted blackish meat, cut it into four pieces and dropped them into the boiling mixture of fat and water. She moved it to the edge of the fire where it simmered slowly, the lid bouncing lightly and releasing small puffs of rich-smelling steam.

"Our goose stew won't be ready for the dumplings for three quarters of an hour," she said. "But the bones will soon be ready."

She rose and walked down along the beach, returning a few moments later with a slab of limestone about a foot square and a round fist-sized stone. She put the stones on the sand, fished the bones from the fire with two sticks and dropped them, smoking and charred, onto the limestone slab.

"You've never eaten bone marrow?" she asked.

Rory shook his head.

"It's a delicacy to all northern people, Indians and Eskimos."

She let the bones cool, then with the smaller stone she cracked each one, picking away the splinters until the round yellowish core of marrow was exposed. Kanina lifted one of the sections of broken bone to her mouth and began sucking out the marrow.

Rory stared at her. He wasn't offended by it, in fact he was anxious to try it himself, yet suddenly in this glimpse of Kanina with the charred bone to her mouth he saw how close she was still to her Stone Age past. Here before him now was the primitive Kanina, he thought, that the education and sophistication of the white man's world would never erase. He saw her now as a spirit still of this northern wilderness and its ancient mystery, a mere four or five generations removed from the Stone Age period of her culture, whereas Rory was perhaps four hundred generations removed from the corresponding period of his ancestry.

It was a new and fascinating revelation and now, under its influence, his mind began to wander. His people too had once squatted like that sucking marrowbones beside their fires in the caves of southern Europe and western Asia. But the time was at least ten thousand years ago. Man was still an insignificant member of the earth's animal kingdom then, fighting to survive against other species far better equipped for survival than he. Yet many of those other species, brutes like the mammoth and saber-toothed tiger far stronger and hardier than man, had long since been swept from the earth into the lost limbo of extinction, while man had not merely survived but had spread throughout the world to become its dominant species. How? There were several reasons for it, but one of the important reasons came vividly to Rory's mind now as he stared admiringly at the swarthy beauty of the Indian girl beside him.

Primitive man, he thought, must have been tremendously aided in his uneven struggle for survival by the fact that the male of the species never lost the capacity to feel the emotion that Rory was feeling now. Man's reproductive drive was a constant thing, not limited as it was in other mammals to a brief and passing mating period once each year. Whatever the season, the human female could always arouse the human male, and out of this came a vital contribution to his species' survival. Man, the male, the hunter, could be killed off in legions as he fought his stronger animal foes to bring back food for his women. But no matter how many males were killed on the hunt, the reproductive potential of his species remained little affected. With no long seasons of sexual indifference or impotence to limit his reproductive vigor, one male could keep twenty females pregnant. So man, the species, survived and prospered because that febrile passion of the loins that another age was to euphemistically name "love" knew no restrictions of time or season.

What did it all add up to?

First, it reaffirmed his decision that Kanina was part of another world and another life and could never be a part of his. And second, he supposed, it meant that man was designed to keep twenty women pregnant at one time; without it the human race could never have survived, so he need feel no apologies over the passionate desire for Kanina that filled him now.

"Aren't you going to try some?" Kanina asked him.

"I certainly am. I was day-dreaming."

Rory picked up a piece of bone, scraped away with his knife the charred bits of meat that clung to it and put the broken surface to his lips. He gave it a short hesitant suck and the soft jelly-like marrow flowed into his mouth. It was sweet, slightly granular, fatty but not oily and it possessed only a trace of the characteristic fat taste. He liked it and sucked on the bone again.

The marrow was quickly gone and then they sat silently watching the white steam that spurted in feathery puffs from the goosemeat stew. Rory wondered if now she had forgotten his tactless lapse of the afternoon before. He moved close to her. She didn't move away. He put his arm around her shoulders, cradled her chin in his other hand and tilted her head back gently. Then he moved down slowly and kissed her.

"I used to say that I never kissed the same girl twice."

"Why?"

"Once I've kissed a girl she's never the same again."

Kanina moved away from him quickly. She stared at him.

"There are things about you," she said coldly, "that a girl should despise. . . ."

"I'm joking."

"You may think you are joking, but you're not. You believe it. Sometimes you are so sensible and mature . . . . sometimes you are a spoiled conceited. . . ."

Rory didn't let her finish. He drew her over against him and kissed her again. Her head lay motionless on his shoulder.

"I was still angry at you this morning," she said, "and I *should* be angry now. It must be *man-tay-o.* . . ."

She lay in his arms for a long time and he knew, as he had known that first day here on Kishamooskek, that Kanina could be his for the taking. But after their talk on the river yesterday in which she had described incident by incident the discrimination she had faced, Rory believed he understood more clearly now what was really happening to her on these occasions. It wasn't his love-making or his good looks either that brought her quickly like this to the point of yielding. In his arms this way she was finding a form of acceptance, an attestation of being wanted, the thing denied her in most previous relationships with the people of his race.

But he knew from the outset—from the moment of their first kiss—that once more the same undefinable, restraining barrier lay between them. What the barrier was, he did not know. He did realize clearly, though, that the decision not to go on—if it were a decision—the psychological barrier, whatever it was that stopped him, was a part of him, not her.

The fire burned low and the meat stopped boiling and neither of them noticed. Finally she spoke.

"The dumplings," she said. "We're forgetting the dumplings."

She pushed herself away from him and threw fresh wood on the fire. When the goose stew was boiling again, she dropped four lumps of bannock dough into the broth.

Rory did not like Kanina's goose stew and dumplings. It was greasy, the meat was tough and flavorless, the dumplings hard and heavy. Kanina began laughing as soon as Rory had tried his first mouthful.

"I told you you wouldn't like it," she said. "But I thought you should try it as part of your goose research. And you should also know that compared with other *Mooskek-owak* foods this dried goose, we call it *na-mestik,* is a delicacy. You should try eating skunk or owl."

She was a gay, smiling Kanina again. On the portage across to the river they chatted steadily. At one point Rory said to her: "You seem to have got over feeling bad about the school . . . . about its failing."

"It isn't worth worrying about," she answered. "I have come back to live their life, not to change it."

When they reached the canoe on the river and started the outboard and could talk no longer over its noise, she sat in the bow, smiling back at him frequently, her dark eyes sparkling, her black hair flowing around her face in the breeze.

On the beach at Cape Cree they parted and Rory went straight to the store. Jock was there.

"Can you be ready to start out again tomorrow?" Rory asked him. "Up the Kistawanee this time. Two weeks again."

Jock looked at Bert Rumsey and then nodded approval to Rory.

Rory left the store and walked down through the native village toward the Beaverskin tent. Kanina was outside plaiting a fur robe out of strips of rabbitskin. She was wearing the shawl and rubber boots again. In this clothing and this setting, he thought, she looked so different, so typically Indian.

She nodded at the rabbitskin robe. "It'll be a cold winter," she said. "It's not too early to start getting ready."

"I just arranged another trip with Jock," he told her. "Two weeks again. I wanted to let you know. I'll miss you. You'll be here when I come back?"

"I'll be here." She was staring intently at the rabbitskin robe on her lap and did not look up at him. "And I'll miss you," she added, so softly that Rory barely heard.

CHAPTER THIRTY-THREE

RORY and Jock were away sixteen days. They found several breeding concentrations of geese and signs that the gosling hatch was beginning. Goslings leave the nest and begin wandering around with their parents within an hour or so of hatching. Rory and Jock did not find any broods, because when the goslings are small they and the parents remain closely hidden, but they did find faint trails in the moss and mud where adult geese had led broods from one pond to another. Rory knew they would soon be able to start rounding up birds for banding.

The final day out was the fourteenth of July and before going downstream to Cape Cree they crossed the portage to Kishamooskek Lake to look for the barnacle. Using the smaller canoe cached on the lake, they set out toward the island where Kanina and Rory had found the barnacle on their last trip. As they approached, Jock took his paddle from the water and Rory, in the stern, paddled on slowly and silently. The gurgle of water under the canoe dropped to an inaudible whisper. A finger of mud thickly grown with willows stretched ahead of them, and the shallow bay where the barnacle and his mate had been feeding lay just around it. Rory let the canoe drift noiselessly past the end of the willow point. Then he and Jock saw the two geese about two hundred feet away.

The geese saw them instantly, cackled in alarm, but did not fly. With necks held down close to the water they began swimming rapidly, and *toward the island,* not away. When they reached shallow water, the geese ran frantically ashore and disappeared in the dense jungle of alder and willow.

"They're flightless now!" Rory exclaimed. "Flightless geese run ashore and hide." He was studying the spot where the geese had disappeared. "We'll put the trap there," he said, "and drive them into it. We'll catch them, don't you think?"

Jock nodded. "Eskimos catch geese . . . . hundreds . . . . thousands . . . . that way. *Mooskek-owak* don't. It's harder here in bush country. And soon the fall geese, the waveys, are here from the Arctic, thousands, millions. So driving *niskuk* when they can't fly . . . . hard work . . . . few geese . . . . ain't worth it."

As they paddled back toward the portage, Rory's heart thumped violently. He wasn't sure what excited him more—the approaching showdown with the barnacle or the return to Kanina.

It was late afternoon when they came around the last of the Kistawanee's snaking bends and Cape Cree lay a quarter mile or so ahead.

"A stranger," Jock shouted immediately, above the roar of the motor, nodding ahead toward the settlement.

Rory could see two figures down by the river bank, but they were too far away to identify. He brought the binoculars to his eyes and could see then that one of them was Joan Rumsey but the man beside her was not her husband. He was a short, thick man wearing only khaki shorts. Rory got a glimpse of the small round bald spot on the man's head and recognized P.L.

The canoe moved in rapidly, Jock throttled it down and turned it toward the beach. P.L. waded out and guided the bow in, oblivious to the rough stones under his bare feet.

"You made it!" Rory exclaimed. "I'm glad to see you."

"Made it! Good God, I made it a week ago. Where in hell have you been?"

Rory reached across the gunwale of the canoe and they shook hands.

P.L.'s bare legs and hairy chest were as brown as the Indians. Then Rory nodded back toward Jock. "Meet my guide, Jock," he said. "Jock, this is Dr. Thomas, from Toronto. Dr. Thomas will be helping us with the trapping and leg-banding . . . . if he's brought some clothes to keep the mosquitoes from devouring him."

For a moment Rory thought that P.L. couldn't have heard the introduction, then the professor acknowledged it with a quick "How do you do," but without turning his head to look at the Indian.

Joan Rumsey, P.L., and Rory started walking up toward the Hudson's Bay Company residence. Joan Rumsey left them at the front door and Rory and P.L. went upstairs where P.L. had the room adjoining Rory's.

"Come in," Rory said. "What's the news? Did you get some of that colored plastic for the barnacle?"

They stepped into Rory's room and there were two letters on the table beside the door.

"Yes," P.L. said. "I found some yellow, too. No one else is using yellow neck bands on Canada or barnacle geese, so there's no danger of confusion." Then he saw the letters and added: "Better check your mail before we start talking."

"The barnacle is still there," Rory said. "Molted too, already. We just saw him this afternoon." Rory picked up the letters as he spoke. One was an airmail letter from his mother, the other his university results.

"You don't have to open that last one now," P.L. told him. "I'll tell you what it says. You had a very good year. Firsts and seconds in everything, including Zoology 29."

"I wasn't worrying," Rory said. He held up the overseas airmail letter. "This one's from my mother," he added. "Excuse me while I read it."

P.L. pattered across the room in his bare feet and sat in a chair. Rory sat on the bed, opened the envelope and began hurriedly reading.

"Your letter was a very exciting one indeed," his mother's letter began. "Imagine, finding one of *our* barnacles there, so far from Barra. You will say I am being very unscientific, calling it one of *our* barnacles, but until there is some evidence to the contrary I must believe that that big wonderful bird has gone to you from right here in Barra. As soon as I read your letter the distance between us seemed to shrink suddenly. Now I feel linked with you in a way more real and tangible than our letters have ever done before. Did I ever tell you—surely I have—that my first acquaintance with barnacle geese came on the night that you were born? I kept hearing the strange music of their calls rising above the wind outside. I wondered what they were but I had to wait until dawn. . . ."

Rory skipped a couple of paragraphs, impatiently seeking the news he wanted most to learn. So far, the situation looked promising, for his mother obviously was excited over the barnacle too.

On the next page a paragraph started: "I had decided to write to Glasgow. . . ." It caught Rory's eye and he resumed reading: "to learn if there would be a teaching position there for me when the autumn term begins. But now, after hearing about your barnacle, I have decided to stay. It was a hard decision, but the thought of that goose kept coming back to me. The more I thought of him, the more curious I became. I'm as anxious as you are to learn what he will do next winter." There were a few sentences more, but no mention of his father. Rory looked up at P.L.

"My mother is going to stay in Barra to watch for the barnacle," he said.

"Was she going somewhere else?"

Rory hesitated. He didn't have to go into that with P.L. "Oh no. . . ." He shrugged his big shoulders. "Well, what's the news from U of T?"

Rory knew that, for P.L., the only news worth passing on would be the news of his own research work.

"It's good and bad," P.L. said gravely, his forehead tightening and relaxing in that peculiar mannerism that started his hair line bobbing comically. "Shall I tell you the bad first?"

"Okay."

"Well Turdy had a mental replace, a mental block . . . . a very unfortunate development." He looked up solemnly at Rory. "It's my fault. I expected too much from her. No bird ever counted to four before that I know of. But I wasn't satisfied. I was sure she could reach five. So I began to break down the four-pattern that I had implanted in her, intending to start a new training pattern that would have her counting to five. I thought for a while she was going to adjust okay. Then she went to pieces. A mental breakdown, I suppose."

He gazed out the window for a moment then turned back to Rory and added slowly: "Turdy can't count at all now, not even to two."

Then P.L. threw his shoulders back and brightened dramatically.

"But the other news is excellent, exciting. The work with the sparrows, using artificially controlled photo-periods, you remember. I have a big, unexpected discovery beginning to appear there. It'll shake the ornithological world to its roots. There's been a lot of work done on the effect of photic stimulation on reproductive cycles and bioenergetics in birds, energy balance . . . . you know, it's been going on for years. What induces gonad recrudescence? The evidence has all pointed to an increase in photic stimulation on the pituitary, and then an increase in the flow of gonadotropins to the testes or ovaries. You follow?"

Rory nodded. He was familiar with the main developments.

"Well by God that's not the whole story," P.L. went on excitedly, his brow and hair line bobbing again. "There's an *innate* rhythmic tendency for recrudescence involved too, at least there's something more than photic stimulation involved. I have male sparrows there that have been living under ten-hour days since last summer, but they have testes right now in stage five development, that's with primary spermatocytes in synapsis. . . ."

P.L. slowed down, then stopped, and Rory got in the question he had been waiting to ask.

"How are you getting along with your janitors?"

"Not too bad," P.L. replied heartily. "Not too bad. That's why I'm here. Couldn't have left the birds while the janitors were carrying on the way they were. They kept howling I wasn't keeping the birds clean enough. Stupid bastards. I had to let the excrement accumulate for calorimeter tests. Then next thing they wanted to fumigate the place. Jesus! But I threw them out a couple of times and now they're being sensible. I left a student looking after things."

Now P.L. looked squarely at Rory and went on talking.

"You'd better be prepared for it, Rory," he said slowly. "Research scientists are always going to have this problem. The general public will always be a horde of sniggering morons. You can't tell them what you're doing, they won't understand and won't try. Science . . . . technology has moved so far ahead of the common mind that the common mind will never catch up. Every fool sweeping floors thinks it's his responsibility to criticize what a scientist is doing because some laboratory birds have fleas or because the scientist is doing something that might contradict the Bible or some fool thing like that. Jesus, it's a crazy world!"

From somewhere in his scanty clothing P.L. produced his big curved-stem pipe and a pouch of tobacco. He began filling the pipe.

"Okay, I've said enough," he stated. "How's your work going?"

"It's going well." Rory described the trips and the country he had covered. "I'm surprised," he said, "at the number of nonbreeders. The average hunter who sees a flock of a hundred geese going north in the spring thinks like this: fifty pairs, four young to a pair, that's three hundred geese to come back next fall. He doesn't know that sixty percent or more aren't breeding, that a hundred geese at best mean only twenty adult females and therefore only twenty breeding pairs."

P.L. had lit his pipe and was sitting with his bare legs crossed, puffing thoughtfully.

"What about the spring kill by these gooks up here?" P.L. asked.

Rory moistened his lips. This, the spring hunt of geese by the Indians, was a sore point to the hunting associations and even to some biologists in the south.

"I've checked it carefully," Rory said. "It's not a serious factor. The Indians are responsible for only about a fifth of the total annual hunting kill. And most of the Indian kill consists of yearlings that won't nest that year anyway."

"Oh bull!" P.L. interjected. "They'll nest the next year. There shouldn't be spring hunting up here."

"There certainly should! Those poor devils are eating nothing but bannock for weeks before their spring goose hunt starts. Goose hunting, to a white hunter, is his idea of having fun; to an Indian it's sometimes the difference between living and starving. The Indian takes a very small share. I'm going to say in my report the Indian kill must be the last thing to be interfered with."

P.L. removed the pipe from his mouth and the shaggy fringe of his hair was bobbing again.

"You're talking like a sentimental old woman," he said. "If they can't earn a living doing something worthwhile I'd let the bastards starve."

Rory had thought that the blunt and unconforming P.L. would be the last of all the people he knew who would be capable of racial bias. He had been puzzled by P.L.'s coolness toward Jock down by the canoe a short time ago, but had refused then to believe what it seemed to indicate. Now it was plain. P.L. had no use for them either. Rory smarted angrily for a moment, then the anger passed and he felt a confusion of surprise and sorrow and bewilderment instead.

There were several seconds of taut embarrassing silence, then Rory spoke.

"The hatch is just starting," he said. "Everything will be flightless in a couple more days. Are you ready for some banding trips?"

"Ready? I've been ready a week!"

"We'll try for the barnacle first. We'll go up tomorrow, set up a trap, camp overnight, and I'll arrange for some helpers to join us the next day."

"Does that wild-looking guide of yours have to come along?" P.L. asked. "Those gooks make me uncomfortable."

"We'll need all the help we can get. Jock's a good man. We might have an Indian girl helping us too."

"A girl! A squaw? Oh, Jesus, no! I suppose you're madly in love with some little slant-eyed bitch up here already."

"As a matter of fact," Rory said, raising his gray eyes until they were staring directly into those of P.L., "I am. Now, let's have a look at that yellow plastic."

CHAPTER THIRTY-FOUR

RORY left P.L. sitting alone at the breakfast table next morning and paddled down toward the Kistawanee's mouth where he could see Kanina and her mother in the Beaverskin canoe lifting gill nets. Daisy Beaverskin sat in the stern steadying the canoe with her paddle while Kanina, in the bow, pulled the white soggy net across the gunwales in front of her. Rory came alongside and smiled a quick greeting at the old woman. Her face with its network of fine wrinkles looked like a withered apple. He had thought she was ugly the first time he saw her but now as she smiled back at him there was a warm simple charm in her puckered face that attracted him.

He turned to Kanina. She didn't stop pulling the net. A silvery white-fish came over the gunwale, flapping violently in the linen meshes, and Kanina flipped it into the bottom of the canoe with a quick twist of one wrist and hand.

She let go of the net then and left it resting across the canoe, shook the water from her hands and removed the shawl she was wearing. She ran her hands under her hair at the back, shaking loose the bunchy tangle that had formed under the shawl. She was always removing that shawl, he thought, whenever he appeared on the scene. He liked watching her do it. It made her hair tremble alluringly and when she lifted her hands to her head it pulled her sweater snugly and provocatively around her breasts.

"Why do you do that?" he asked. "Why don't you wear that thing, or not wear it?"

"I don't know why I do it," she said. "I don't like it either. But when I'm with them, I wear it, because I'm trying to be one of them. But when you're around I get confused and don't know what I'm supposed to be. And sometimes I have it off before I realize I'm doing it."

Rory recalled their last trip to Kishamooskek when she was angry at
him and had left the shawl on all morning; then, when she saw the
barnacle, her anger dissolved and she had promptly removed the shawl.
It was a sort of unconscious barometer apparently that revealed how she
felt about him at any specific time. And the impulsive way she kept putting
it on and taking it off was a symbol, Rory thought, of the confused and
divided nature of her personality, a schizophrenic personality trying to
be an Indian one moment, a white the next, and in the confusion being
neither.

"I've seen your friend around for several days," Kanina said. "Are
professors too poor to buy clothes?"

"They're poor," Rory said, "but not that poor. He just doesn't believe
in clothes, that's all, and he likes to be a nonconformist. Maybe he
thinks he's dressing like an Indian, or the way the white man thinks a
well-dressed Indian should dress."

"Well tell him the Indians are all talking and they think it's very im-
proper and immoral," Kanina replied. "The *Mooskek-owak* don't even
undress to go to bed."

"I came out here to tell you the barnacle is in the molt and can't fly,"
Rory said. "Jock and I took a look at him yesterday. I want to be sure
of catching him, so will you help? With four of us driving we shouldn't
miss."

Kanina nodded eagerly. "I'd like to," she said, "but I could never be
seen leaving Cape Cree with that practically naked man. They'd never
let me come back. They don't care very much what I do, but they would
object to *that*."

"You won't have to leave camp with him. Dr. Thomas and I will go
up today, set up a trap and stay overnight. You and Jock could come up
for the drive tomorrow."

"I'll have to come back the same day," she said. "I could never stay
away overnight with a questionable character like your professor friend
involved in the scheme somewhere. Indians have their gossips too."

"You can come back the same day. But if we get too busy, could you
come back alone?"

She nodded and resumed pulling in the net. A minute later she reached
the end of it, dropped it free of the canoe and they started paddling back,
the two canoes side by side.

"I'll tell Jock you'll meet him down by the river at six tomorrow
morning."

"Okay."

They separated as they approached the settlement and Rory paddled on upstream toward the store. When he looked back a few seconds later Kanina had stopped paddling and was tying the black woolen shawl around her head once more. As quickly as that, he thought, she had left his world and was back again in the drab and fetid world of her own people.

P.L. was in the store when Rory walked in. Rory ordered two hundred feet of four-foot gill netting from Bert Rumsey for their goose trap and then walked back to Jock who was in the rear. He described the plans to Jock.

"You and Kanina use a small canoe tomorrow and portage it in to Kishamooskek when you come. We'll need a second canoe for driving the geese. Kanina will be coming back, but the rest of us may stay and try to trap more of the geese there. Dr. Thomas and I will go up in the big canoe today."

Rory and P.L. went across to the house. P.L., as usual, was wearing only a pair of shorts.

"There's a two-mile portage through thick bush," Rory told him as they went upstairs, "and mosquitoes are bad, so cover up your hide. And don't forget the yellow plastic."

Rory went into his own room and quickly gathered up extra clothing and the canvas folder that held his banding kit. P.L. came in a few minutes later wearing a khaki shirt and high boots with blue jeans tucked into their tops.

Hunched under their heavy packsacks they came out of the portage onto Kishamooskek Lake about three hours later. They dragged the canoe from the willows where it was hidden, put in an axe and the roll of fish net and paddled out onto the lake, leaving their camping equipment on the beach behind them. Rory described the shape of the island—the willow point and the small sedge-grown bay beyond it where the geese seemed to spend much time feeding. They paddled slowly around it. The geese were there again. The big birds acted as they had previously, cackling in alarm and swimming toward the island. They went ashore and disappeared at just about the same spot they had the day before. P.L. turned, his brown face flushed and beaming.

"That's the most exciting thing I've seen in thirty-five years of hunting birds!" P.L. exclaimed. "What do you think he'll do this fall?"

"I think we've just seen a good clue," Rory said. "Running ashore like that is typical behavior for Canadas, but it certainly isn't for barnacles. That barnacle goose probably never saw a tree until he came here. Going into a forested shore like that must be a pretty terrifying thing for a bird accustomed to having an unobstructed view to the horizon all the time. He's learning fast to live her kind of life. I'll bet he stays with her this winter."

They paddled to a neighboring island where they could cut stakes for the trap without disturbing the geese, then they brought the stakes back to the barnacle goose bay. Working rapidly in case the geese were still near and might be frightened by a prolonged commotion, they staked the net up so that it formed a four-foot-high, V-shaped fence. The wings of the V came down to the water's edge and formed an entrance about fifty feet wide spanning the spot where twice Rory had seen the geese go ashore. At the point of the V they left an entrance two feet wide opening into a circular corral about six feet across. The job took half an hour and when they were finished they paddled out and surveyed the shore where they had been working. They had disturbed the vegetation as little as possible and only a few feet of net at the outer ends of the V showed. The rest of it was hidden in the thick screen of bushes that cloaked the island's shore.

They paddled back to the beach, had lunch and set up camp at the spot where Rory and Kanina had eaten their lunches. He had told P.L. on the way in that an Indian girl would be coming with Jock tomorrow. Now, the work done, they were sitting on the sand and Rory noticed that P.L.'s brow had begun bobbing up and down in the mannerism that he had learned to recognize as a signal of trouble.

"Now," P.L. said bluffly, "what in hell is all this nonsense about being in love with an Indian girl?"

Rory stared at the sand. There were the ashes of their fire, and there, just to the right, the spot where they had lain on the blanket that first day.

"Wait . . . . ," he said quietly. "Wait until you've met her, and then. . . ."

"I don't have to meet her. I don't know what you're thinking. I don't know what you're planning." P.L. talked rapidly. "But I do know if you don't get some sense and start using it you'll be ruining a good career. You stupid bastard."

That characteristic profanity of P.L.'s had always sounded amusing and peculiarly expressive before. But now, directed at himself, it was cutting, painful, offensive. P.L. was right—he *could* ruin his career, but he had no intention of letting that happen. And he was not going to start discussing it with him now, because, after four years of living with him, respecting and at times admiring him, Rory was beginning to dislike P.L.

"Wait," Rory repeated. "You'll be meeting her tomorrow. And then, I think, you might understand."

CHAPTER THIRTY-FIVE

RORY and P.L. had finished breakfast and were waiting when Kanina emerged from the portage about nine o'clock next morning. Jock, carrying the canoe, was about a hundred feet behind her. Kanina walked along the beach toward the tent where Rory and P.L. were sitting. She was wearing the same clothes she had worn that first day here with Rory —the red corduroy jacket, gray slacks, high-necked sweater, beaded moosehide moccasins and the red ribbon in her hair.

Rory rose to his feet, looking quickly at P.L. to note the professor's reaction. P.L., wearing only the khaki shorts again, was on his feet gazing stolidly at Kanina. She came up to them, dimples at her mouth corners. Rory introduced them. P.L. nodded and said a quick "How do you do."

"Trap up and everything ready?" Kanina asked.

"Everything is ready," Rory said, "except working out our attack strategy."

He smoothed off a spot in the sand with his hand and drew a map of the island. The others gathered around.

"Here's the little bay where the geese spend a lot of time feeding," he said, pointing. "The trap's here where they've been running ashore. Dr. Thomas and I will go in one canoe around the left side of the island; Kanina and Jock, you'll take the right side. One person from each canoe will land on the island and move in toward the trap along the shore— this will prevent the geese from bypassing the trap. Jock and P.L., will you two take the shore? All you'll have to do is step out where the geese can see you and if Kanina and I get behind them with the canoes they should head for the shore midway between you. Don't move fast or wave your arms. If they get too alarmed there's no telling what they'll do. Has everyone got that?"

Rory looked from one to the other. P.L. and Jock nodded. He looked at Kanina. She nodded too and he winked at her quickly. Then he saw that P.L. was staring at him.

"We'll have to time this perfectly," Rory resumed, "and show ourselves to the geese simultaneously. I'll leave time for everyone to get into position and then I'll shout. Just one word. I'll say *Now,* because too much noise might panic them. When I shout everyone move out into view. Kanina and I in the canoes will have to move quickly to cut them off if they decide to swim for the lake."

Rory went into the tent and picked up the plastic ribbon and his canvas banding kit. He came out and they set off immediately in the canoes.

No one spoke. This was it—barnacle day, the day he had been awaiting more than five weeks. It seemed much longer. So much had happened since that first day here when Kanina had shown him the barnacle. A host of small and trivial happenings, and one big one. He had discovered the fierce intensity of real love. And underlying it all, molding it perhaps more than he knew, was the presence of this barnacle goose. Would he have fallen in love with Kanina if the barnacle hadn't brought them together under rather emotional circumstances? Yes, of course he would have. But the barnacle had certainly brought it along much sooner, much faster. He had had vague ideas of making her his mistress for the summer; he hadn't planned it but he was prepared to let it happen if things had developed that way. And maybe if the barnacle hadn't moved events along so fast, she would have become his mistress first, and then when he fell in love it would have been different. Loving a mistress was a much more manageable situation. The ultimate male-female relationship would already have been attained and a man could be much more realistic about a woman then. But he *was* being realistic about it all. He didn't intend to get trapped into marrying her. But this way he didn't have a mistress or a potential marriage partner either. And if she couldn't be one, why shouldn't she be the other?

There was no time now to pursue the thought further. They *had* to catch that barnacle. There was a gaunt feeling in his stomach. He looked at Kanina in the other canoe and for a moment she looked at him. But no smile passed between them. Her eyes had a frightened look and her mouth was pressed firm and thin. She was feeling the suspense too.

As they approached the island the canoes separated, one heading for each side, and the island came between them. Rory turned his canoe in to the beach well back from the tip of the point. P.L. stepped out and waded ashore, lifting his feet carefully to avoid splashing He moved silently into the bushes and in a few seconds disappeared.

Rory resumed paddling. There was just enough breeze stirring the willow leaves to cover the muted gurgle that the paddle made in the water. About three canoe-lengths back from the tip of the sand point, he let the canoe glide to a stop. He would wait two minutes to give the others plenty of time. A white-throat sang, near yet undisturbed, so they were undetected. He kept his eye on his watch. The white-throat sang again. He had his paddle poised.

"Now!" he shouted. It exploded like thunder and came echoing back to him from the neighboring islands.

He dug the paddle into the water and felt it bend under the sudden pressure of his arms and shoulders. For God's sake, don't break it! The water boiled around the paddle blade and the canoe shot ahead. He was clear of the point, out in the open now. He began to turn the canoe. Where in hell was Kanina? He caught a glimpse of red through the willows on the other side, then her canoe shot out into the open too. A watery meadow of reeds and sedges lay between them, every green stem bending before the breeze in the same direction like a perfectly coordinated ballet troupe. Rory's eyes ran around swiftly. There was Jock, among the alders on the far side. But the bay was empty. The geese were not there.

Rory's paddling stopped, his paddle poised in mid-air. Suddenly the squeezing sensation in his stomach ceased and he was relaxed. It was over, and they had failed. He motioned for Kanina to go in and pick up Jock and he paddled in to get P.L. The canoes came together two or three minutes later.

"Well it was a good practice," Kanina said blithely.

"They'll be back," Rory said, "but not while we're sitting here, so let's get out."

They paddled away. And Rory began to be tormented by the thought that perhaps the geese would not be back. Had the repeated visits and then the disturbance of setting up the trap frightened the geese away— permanently? The thought was an appalling one.

They paddled four or five minutes to put them well away from the island and then stopped. Rory began a search of the lake and neighboring islands through his binoculars, moving them in a wide circle until finally he was looking back at the beach strip and the big marsh beyond it.

"No sign of the barnacle," he said, "but there's a flock of Canadas. In the marsh, feeding. Half a mile up the beach from camp. It looks like two families—four adults, eight or nine goslings. If we put the trap on the beach it wouldn't be hard to catch them. That's the next project. After the barnacle."

Most of the islands were low and swampy, but Rory had noticed one half a mile away that had a high sand bank rising prominently at one end of it.

"There's a high spot on an island over there, facing this way," Rory said. "We could watch from there. And if the barnacle came back we'd see him."

They began paddling again.

"Go ahead," Rory told Kanina and Jock. "We'll come along slowly. I want to keep looking."

After a few strokes Rory began another search with the binoculars. Kanina and Jock moved on. But Rory wasn't looking for the barnacle, he was waiting to talk alone with P.L.

"Well?" Rory said when the other canoe was out of hearing. "Now you've met her, what have you got to say?"

"The same as I said before. You're a stupid bastard."

"I haven't done anything stupid yet, and I don't intend to."

"I'm not surprised the girl attracts you," P.L. resumed. "She's a hell of a good-looker. She's probably smart too. But looks and brains . . . . that doesn't matter a damn, she's still a squaw."

P.L. turned suddenly in the canoe's bow seat and stared at Rory. "Did you say you *loved* her? Don't forget that at your age it's easy to fall in love with a pretty face or a pretty ass and think you're in love with the whole girl. You're not going to *marry* her?"

Rory decided quickly to keep P.L. guessing and give him a chance to talk. "I haven't made up my mind yet," Rory said.

"Well, you'd better make up your mind fast. God, man, it's impossible! She couldn't make a go of it alone, so what makes you think she'd fit in any better if she went back as your wife? Remember," P.L. went on, "these people aren't like the Indians we know down south. The Indians we see down there have lived on reserves among us for a couple of hundred years. But these people up here are still primitive as all hell. And you can't move people from a primitive society like this to an industrial, highly organized society like ours in one jump. It has to be done gradually, over a couple of generations."

"That may be true of them generally," Rory said, "but it doesn't apply to Kanina. She adjusted to our society, but our society didn't adjust to her."

P.L.'s brow was bobbing angrily.

"You just don't like them," Rory continued.

"I *don't* like them! They're lazy, they lie around all summer half starving when they could be up at Moosonee working on the railroad. There's work there. Why don't some of the lazy bastards go up and earn some money in the summer?"

"Because they're hunters," Rory told him. "They've always been hunters as long as their race has existed. The respected Indian has always been the good hunter, the man who can go out and kill food when others have failed. Earning a living to these people is all tied up with the hunt and the kill. There's no psychological satisfaction in working for wages and then trading their wages at a store for food. That way the food-getting process becomes incomplete, there hasn't been the traditional pitting of the hunter's skill against the survival skill of the animal hunted. The wage-earning Indian has missed the psychological lift that comes with the kill, and he needs it. To go out and work for the white man is belittling, it's an admission that he's not capable of supporting his family the traditional, respected way. When an Indian works at one of our jobs, we admire him and call him a 'good' Indian, but by the standards of his own people he's a 'poor' Indian, probably a failure as a hunter."

"We're off the track," P.L. declared. "We started to talk about that cute little bitch and you. You could marry her. Sure you could marry her. And you'll graduate, and biologists are scarce so you'll get a job, as a zoology department lecturer somewhere, and then your woes and tribulations will start. There's a lot of politics going on behind the scenes in every university. I know, I've come up through it all. I've been handicapped too, not having a wife, because a wife can help a hell of a lot, but the wrong kind of a wife can hold you back. It doesn't matter how smart or good-looking or adaptable that girl is, she could never become part of a university group. It doesn't matter whether this is right or wrong, it's a fact, that's all that matters. You'd always be the zoology lecturer married to a squaw. A lecturer all your life, frozen at that level, because it would be embarrassing for a university to move a squaw-man into a position of prominence. Meanwhile the students who came up through your classes would become the professors and associate professors over your head."

P.L.'s brow wasn't bobbing angrily now, he was talking quietly, like a father. And now Rory couldn't argue with him.

"What does she do when she gets in a jam and can't face it any longer?" the professor asked. "There's only one thing she knows to do. She comes running back here to live like an animal in the bush. She's done it once, she'd do it again."

Rory knew it wouldn't be as bad as that. He was sure that Kanina could be a good, proficient and stimulating wife *inside their own home,* but she would never be a part of his life outside it. In that regard, P.L. hadn't told him anything that Rory hadn't already decided for himself weeks ago.

Rory began paddling again. Far ahead, Kanina and Jock had landed on the sandy point of the island. P.L. began paddling too.

"Keep your pants buttoned up tight and stay away from her," P.L. was saying. "Send her back to Cape Cree tonight and don't ever talk to her again. After this, if you see her coming turn around and run—run like hell."

Rory paddled on automatically. P.L. hadn't told him anything new, but the professor's blunt talk had brought it all into sharper focus. Now Rory thought he knew why he had never quite got around to making Kanina his mistress. During all the time he had been telling himself he could never marry her, there must have been seeds of doubt in his mind, a vague hope that love would somehow find a way to bring their lives together. But now, after P.L.'s angry tirade, certainly neither doubt nor hope remained.

P.L. was right. He should stay away from her. But even as Rory made the decision he wondered if he would be capable of carrying it out. Had it already passed the point of no return? At the end of the summer he would leave her, he was determined to do that. He *would* do that. But while he remained here, near her, seeing her, could he ignore her then?

He must try. But perhaps it was more than any man was built to do.

CHAPTER THIRTY-SIX

THEY paddled to the island where Kanina and Jock waited. Rory climbed the sand bank hurriedly and turned his binoculars back toward the island and the bay where the trap was set. The view was unobstructed; a bird as big as a goose would not be missed if they watched carefully, especially a barnacle goose whose face patch would stand out like a white flag against the shadows of the island.

"Very good," Rory said. "We'll be seeing them soon." But he couldn't produce in himself the confidence he hoped he was producing in the others.

They settled down to watch. Kanina was lying near and as yet Rory had hardly looked at her. Jock came up the bank and lay on the grass too, silently chewing a grass stem, but P.L. remained below on the beach. Rory was carefully scanning the lake all around through his binoculars.

"I'll bet there isn't another book," Rory began casually, "that has given the English language as many popular quotations as *Don Quixote*."

"Why do you lead me a wild goose chase?" Kanina quoted quickly. "It's in *Don Quixote* somewhere. I'll bet Dr. Thomas knows where . . . . a good ornithological quote like that."

P.L. strode rapidly along the beach without replying and sat down again thirty paces or so away. Uncivil old coot, Rory thought. He turned to Kanina.

"Don't apologize for him," Kanina whispered. "I'm used to it."

Kanina had taken off her red jacket and was lying on her side facing Rory, the jacket spread on the ground under her head and shoulders. She was barefooted again as she had been those other times on the beach across the lake from here, and now he noticed for the first time that her slacks were rolled up over her knees, revealing again that smooth brown "happy dawning of her thigh." With great effort he pulled his eyes away.

The day grew hot, there was a lazy languor in the humid air, the breeze softened and died until even the thin-stemmed aspen leaves gave up their restless stirring and stood sharp and still and strangely serene against the distant empty blueness of the sky. Jock slept, P.L. crouched like an immobile Buddha with his chin in his hands and Rory every few minutes made another hopeless search of the surrounding lake with his binoculars. His eyes were drawn back repeatedly to Kanina's reclining form and each time he forced himself to look away before their eyes could meet. They didn't speak. Sometimes on the hazy edge of his vision he saw her studying him. She would be wondering what had come between them.

Two hours . . . . three hours . . . . Rory didn't know, but his stomach was hungry, his buttocks were sore from sitting, and the jagged spruce shadows that had once pointed north across the lake were now swinging eastward, tracing like needles on a graph the sluggish, westward arcing of the sun.

Many times Rory saw families of ducks swimming along the shaded shores of islands, the birds themselves invisible in the shadows but their positions always betrayed by the silvery V-shaped wakes they left in the dark waters behind them. He was watching a family of them now, listlessly, only half-seeing, more like a dream than reality. They were over beside the barnacle's island, coming slowly around the point that Kanina had come around with her canoe hours before. Rory's head nodded sleepily and he removed the binoculars from his eyes.

"Do you see them?" Kanina asked softly.

"Yes."

"Shall I waken Jock and get ready to start?"

"Start?"

"Yes. It's *man-tay-o*."

Rory came instantaneously alert, the binoculars at his eyes again. Now he saw him, the long neck and erect head, the gleaming white face patch and silvery sides. And the Canada goose mate a length or two behind. He had been watching them without realizing it for at least two minutes, thinking they were just another family of ducks. And Kanina, with unaided eyes, had recognized them before he had with the eight-power binoculars. Even now with the excitement pulsing through him Rory could marvel at the sharpness of her vision, and he could see its tacit and indelible message—that heredity at least had fashioned her for a life very different from his own.

"Jock! P.L.!" Rory called. "It's them. They're back!"

Jock sat up sleepily. P.L. ran up the slope and joined them. Rory watched the geese for several seconds, his hands trembling so that it was hard to hold the binoculars still. Then he rose quickly and the others followed him down to the canoes.

"No noise," he whispered.

They launched the canoes and paddled around their lookout island until it lay between them and the geese. Then they began a wide circle, paddling away from the geese at first to remain hidden behind the island until there was close to a mile between them, then veering toward the lake's shaded southern shore. In the shore's shadow they started back, following it until they had practically returned to their camp, then veering again so that now they were approaching the barnacle island from behind as they had done that morning. They had been paddling half an hour before they were finally in position behind the island. They stopped, the canoes side by side.

"I'll wait two or three minutes," Rory said, "then I'll give the same signal as before."

The canoes separated. Kanina's face was taut and grim. She was more excited than Jock or P.L. He put P.L. ashore and the professor disappeared silently into the bushes. He paddled on slowly to the end of the point and let the canoe come to a stop. Kanina had farther to paddle so he must wait. He began counting the seconds. It was more than half an hour since they had seen the geese. Maybe they were gone again by now.

"Now!" he shouted.

Rory dug his paddle into the water and the canoe shot out past the willows. Kanina was out already, a couple of seconds ahead of him. He saw the geese at once and a great surge of relief and elation filled him because both birds had necks and heads underwater reaching for roots in the mud. He and Kanina paddled fast to cut off the geese from the open lake. The barnacle's head came up first and he saw Rory and turned away with a startled guttural *"wuk, wuk."* Then the female, the Canada goose, was up and she too saw Rory first and started swimming frantically away from him. In that direction they would miss the net entirely, miss it by two hundred feet or more! A quivering spasm seized Rory's stomach. Kanina had turned her canoe and was paddling madly to get in front of them and head them off, but the geese, with their paddles and flightless wings churning the water into a white froth, were moving much too fast for her. They would reach her side of the bay before she could turn them back. She was hunched low, her paddle flashing in the sun like the blades of a rapidly revolving windmill, her canoe skimming the water. But the geese were almost on the beach.

And then—there was Jock. How he got there Rory had no idea, for he was at least a hundred feet from where he should have been, but there he was, emerging casually from the willows, right in their path. The geese veered back into the bay. Jock moved slowly along the beach opposite them, keeping them off the shore, and Kanina and Rory moved in behind them. The birds, hemmed in now on three sides, had abandoned their first wild dash for escape and were reconnoitering carefully. Jock stopped and the geese headed for shore again. Still they were going to miss the net. Slowly, calmly, Jock moved up another four or five paces, not enough to alarm the birds, just enough to steer them a little deeper into the bay. Rory found himself as interested in Jock's performance as he was in the geese themselves. The geese were offside so that he and Kanina in the canoes could do nothing but sit still and prevent them from turning back toward the lake. The real contest was between Jock and the geese, because Jock alone was in a position to steer them into the trap. He moved with a sure superb skill, the hunting instincts of uncounted generations directing every movement he made. Two or three steps at a time, quiet pauses between, he kept edging the geese nearer and nearer the trap. The wait seemed interminable. Rory trembled. Did he have to do it this slowly? At any moment the birds might turn and dash back past the canoes.

And then they were in front of the trap. Jock nodded quickly to Rory, signaling him to close in now with the canoe. The geese saw what appeared to be unobstructed shore before them. The Canada goose recognized it first and dashed from the water and disappeared in the willows enclosed by the hidden V of the trap. At least, they had her. But the barnacle held back, suspicious, afraid, zigzagging erratically back and forth in the shallow water near shore. Rory felt a sudden sympathy for him. Big majestic bird, bewildered exile, you should never be in a plight like this, cornered like a stupid barnyard duck here in a muddy, tepid forest-walled bay a thousand miles from the limitless horizons of the sea.

Now Rory pushed in slowly with the canoe. The barnacle waded ashore, stopped momentarily to look back at the open lake and then dashed into the willow and alder tangle to follow his mate. Kanina and Rory jumped from their canoes, Jock and P.L. came in around the wings of the trap and the four of them moved in abreast. In the dense foliage Rory did not see the geese again until he was close to the point of the trap's V. Then he saw the birds in the net cage beyond and ran up swiftly before they could find their way back through the funnel-like opening by which they had entered.

Rory stood in the trap entrance, breathing hard, the two geese pushing futilely against the fence of netting just six feet before him. Only once before had he been close to a barnacle like this—that evening on Barra years ago when he had hidden under the blanket and the barnacle flock had pitched down to feed on the *machair* just in front of him. And again, as on that other occasion, Rory was struck by the rich silver-gray barring on the back and flanks which gave the bird at close range a regal and delicate beauty.

Rory laid out his banding kit on the ground, stepped into the trap and quickly caught the barnacle goose. P.L. came into the enclosure with him and helped hold the goose while Rory closed the aluminum band around the bird's left leg with the long-nosed banding pliers. Then P.L. took a foot-long strip of the brilliant yellow plastic from the banding kit and tied it around the barnacle's neck, tightening it carefully until it was snug enough so that it would not snag on twigs or weeds, yet loose enough not to affect the bird. Then he secured it with a slip-proof falconer's knot that left a four-inch streamer hanging like a necktie down the front of the bird's neck. Rory began examining the cloaca.

"Make the entry for me—the last page," Rory said, and P.L. took Rory's notebook and pencil from their pocket in the banding kit. Rory dictated: "Species, barnacle goose, *Branta leucopsis*. Sex, male. Age, one year. Penis, juvenile, unsheathed. Cloacal bursa still present. Leg band, 508—03723. Neck band, yellow."

Kanina held the barnacle while Rory and P.L. repeated it all for the Canada goose. The cloacal examination was merely a formality, because there was no doubt now about sex although it did provide needed verification of age. Rory began dictating again: "Species, Canada goose, *Branta canadensis interior*. Sex, female. Age, one year. Oviduct opening still closed by membrane. Cloacal bursa still present. Leg band, 508–03724. Neck band, yellow. Paired with *B. leucopsis* No. 508–03723."

They carried them back to the shore, released them side by side, and the geese swam rapidly out into the open lake, their yellow neck streamers showing vividly against Kishamooskek's blue water. Rory gazed at the retreating geese and said quietly: "Now, you old Barra devil, where are you going to turn up next?"

Jock was wading down the shore to retrieve Kanina's canoe that had floated away in the excitement. P.L. nodded toward him. "That stupid Indian," he said, "he almost lost them for us, standing there like a post, staring at them when he could have been running them into the trap."

"That stupid Indian," Rory answered, "did everything perfectly and practically trapped them single-handed. I'm glad the geese went to his side instead of yours."

P.L. said nothing more. Kanina was smiling saucily and making no effort to hide it.

They dismantled the trap and rolled the net on its stakes and put it in Rory's canoe. It was late afternoon and they had not eaten since breakfast. They paddled away and when they were clear of the island Rory searched the lake and saw two faint specks shimmering in the heat haze among the islands far to the west. He put the binoculars on them quickly and even before he could recognize them as geese he saw the yellow flashes at their throats.

"A mile, a mile anyway," Rory said, "and the neck bands show clearly. Someone should find those geese next winter."

Rory turned the binoculars back toward the marsh.

"The Canadas are still there," he said. "We'll eat and see Kanina on her way back, and then after dark we'll put the trap over there on the beach for a drive tomorrow."

And then suddenly the thought of Kanina returning to Cape Cree alone became a goading irrepressible temptation. The pledge he had made with himself to stay away from her was already tottering. P.L. hated the Indians, unreasonably, it was obvious now, so should Rory let himself be influenced by anything the crotchety professor had said? This was his problem, to work out his own way.

They landed on the beach where Rory and P.L. had camped. Jock and Kanina lighted a fire and Rory got out some cans of food. P.L. sat moodily on the sand. And now, again, Rory was wavering. Leave her alone. Stay away from her. You're going to have to leave her eventually. The longer you wait, the harder it will be.

Kanina was crouched near the fire baking a bannock. He had kept his eyes off her for most of the afternoon but now suddenly he yielded and let his gaze linger admiringly. Then he rose impulsively and went into the tent. He looked back through the door quickly. P.L. was still sitting down by the lake. Rory picked up the banding kit where he had laid it, pulled the banding pliers from their pocket, wrapped them in a sweater and pushed them into the bottom of his packsack. Then he stepped out, holding the open banding kit in front of him.

"I've lost my banding pliers," he said. He pointed to the empty pocket in the kit. "Back where we trapped the barnacle probably. And in that jungle it would take a day to find them again."

"Don't you have a spare pair?" P.L. asked.

"Yes, but back in the room at Cape Cree."

"You'll have to go back for them."

"Yes, I'll have to go back for them. But those geese might move out any time. The trap will have to be set up tonight. You and Jock do it and I'll come back in the morning for the drive."

P.L. didn't comment and Rory saw his graying hair in front start bobbing rapidly. Then the short chunky professor rose quickly, disappeared in the tent, and reappeared a minute later wearing jeans, boots and his khaki shirt. Little was said while they ate.

When the meal was ended Rory looked at Kanina. "Ready?" he asked. She nodded. He went into the tent to get his packsack and P.L. came in right behind him. Rory began buckling up the straps on the pack and noticed that P.L. was doing the same. He stopped and stared at him. The professor's deeply tanned brow was wrinkling spasmodically again.

"You don't think I'm going to stay here alone all night with that wild savage, do you?" P.L. said in a taut, low voice. "I'm going back to Cape Cree with you."

CHAPTER THIRTY-SEVEN

IT was dark when they reached the landing at Cape Cree, dark except for a wan and vaporous light from a retreating sliver of moon.

Even Kanina's swarthy face was pale and unreal-looking when she stepped from the canoe and turned and waited for Rory on the sand. He stepped ashore and stood close to her, and P.L., his self-appointed chaperon, was right beside them.

"Thanks for helping," Rory said to her. "We couldn't have managed without you."

"It was fun. I held *man-tay-o* in my arms. He left something with me. He will be a part of me now."

"We'll be on Kishamooskek again for at least tomorrow trapping Canadas, if you want to go back."

"No. The *niskuk* are yours, but *man-tay-o,* he was mine. I went for him. There is no need to go again."

But Rory wondered if that was really her whole answer. She paused a few seconds longer and she was so close he could hear the soft trembling murmur of her breathing. Her face was turned sideways, looking at P.L. *Damn him.* "Goodnight, Rory," she whispered, but she did not speak to P.L. Rory had no time to reply for suddenly she had gone. There was a ghost-like shadow floating up the riverbank path for a moment and then there was nothing but the night, the night and P.L.

They took their packsacks and walked silently through the darkness toward the house. Bert Rumsey was still up, reading, and he jumped to his feet when they came in.

"Welcome home, travelers," he said. "You must have heard the news and come in for mail. They radioed us this afternoon. There'll be a plane tomorrow."

"When?" P.L. asked.

"Early. Probably around nine. One of my bosses on an inspection tour, he'll stay a few days. The plane goes straight back."

Rory and P.L. went upstairs. At his door P.L. turned.

"We don't have to hurry in the morning, do we?" he asked Rory. "I'd like to wait for the mail."

"Okay, we'll wait." Rory went into his room and closed the door quickly behind him. He left the room dark and walked straight to the window, but the Indian camp was in darkness and there was nothing to be seen except the faint triangular outlines of a few tent roofs against the gray night sky. He knew where the Beaverskin tent should be, but there was no light there. She was going to bed in the dark.

Breakfast was over, the canoe was packed and ready before eight-thirty and there was nothing to do but wait for the plane. Rory was still bitter. How was he going to get two incompatibles like P.L. and Jock to

work together for a month? And when would there be another chance
for a private meeting with Kanina?

They had bought more food and Rory had put the packsack containing it in the canoe. He turned to go back to his room and P.L. was following him. P.L. came into the room behind him.

"I don't believe you love that girl as much as you think you do, or
you wouldn't be treating her this way."

Oh, Lord, he was going to start all that again! Rory sat on the bed and
took a deep breath.

"I love the girl, I'm sure of it, and I don't know why it matters a damn
to you," Rory said. "But if it'll make you any happier, you might as
well know I have no intention of marrying her, never have had. I knew
from the beginning it was impossible."

"That's what I mean. That's what I was beginning to suspect. You're
a selfish bastard, thinking about your own fun and nothing else. You
intend to use her all summer and then when it's time to go back to
Toronto you think you're going to leave her cold as if nothing had ever
happened. Well something will have happened, because now I can see it,
the stupid little bitch has let herself fall in love with you too. Maybe you
will be able to leave her and forget her, but the longer you postpone it
the harder it will be, and it'll be a hell of a lot harder on her than it will
be on you. Because women are built that way. It's harder for them to
fall in love and it's a hell of a lot harder for them to fall out of it."

P.L. paused, but only for a moment.

"I'd like to see her get some consideration too," he resumed. "That
means staying away from her. Leave her alone. You're just teasing her,
like a fisherman playing a fish for the fun of it when he has his limit and
knows he'll have to let the fish go as soon as he's caught it."

Rory twisted uncomfortably on the edge of the bed.

"She's probably harmed beyond repair right now," P.L. said. "I suppose you're fornicating like a couple of rabbits every time you find a
bush to lie down behind. Don't you know a man can fornicate and forget, but a woman can't? A man just borrows, but a woman gives and
once she's given she can't take it back."

Outside, the Indian children were shouting, and Rory knew the plane
must be coming.

"Don't you know? Everything you are and everything you represent,
she's trying to forget. She's got a hard enough fight ahead of her. You're
making it a hell of a lot harder."

Rory rose to go, and he did not attempt to reply. They walked down
the stairs and outside and Rory was confused again, because now he was

wondering if P.L. was the fool that he had begun to believe. There was a bitter, patent, irrefutable logic in what P.L. had just been saying.

He could hear the plane coming as they walked down toward the river. Bert Rumsey was coming from the store, not bothering to lock the door behind him although there would be no one there to mind it, and Rory wondered if P.L. had noticed this simple eloquent tribute to Indian honesty. Joan Rumsey was hurrying from the house. The plane circled out over the river and glided down with its engine coughing.

Was P.L. as concerned about Kanina's welfare as he appeared to be, or was he using it as another argument to influence Rory? But it didn't matter what P.L.'s motive was, because the argument was as poignant and damning whether he meant it for Kanina's sake or for Rory's. Probably Rory *was* harming her. Maybe he was even ruining her life in a way not very different from the way in which he had refused to let his life be ruined by her. Or if he hadn't harmed her yet, he would if it went on. For there was no future in it for Kanina. She could only give and get nothing back in return.

The plane came to the beach and the pilot passed a bundle of mail to Joan Rumsey. Bert Rumsey and his company's inspector headed for the store; Mrs. Rumsey, P.L. and Rory walked back through the Indians crowding the bank and headed for the house. They sat on the veranda and she untied the cord from around the mail and began passing out letters. There was one for P.L. Rory noticed that it bore air mail and special delivery stamps, which indicated its importance but accomplished little else, for the letter had probably been waiting several days in Moosonee until there was a plane coming this way to deliver it.

Rory heard the plane's motor start. The pilot was getting ready to take off again. The morning was still cool but P.L. once more was wearing only the khaki shorts; his hairy legs were crossed, his bared toes wiggled childishly. P.L.'s eyes were moving rapidly down through his letter and growing thinner and harder and glassier the farther they got. Then suddenly his forehead and hair line began bobbing violently and he jumped to his feet.

"The stupid bastards! Damn their souls!"

Then he was running madly down the boardwalk and around the corner of the store toward the plane, his short thick body hunched forward so far Rory thought he'd be diving head first any moment into the grass. P.L. began shouting.

"Wait! Wait! Stop that plane!"

"A friend of his must have died," Joan Rumsey said.

"I'm afraid," Rory answered, "that a large number of his friends may have died."

P.L. was waving his arms frantically as he passed from sight behind the store. He reappeared in just a few seconds, racing back up the hill now. His face was pale and he was gasping for breath when he reached the veranda again.

"Rory!" he exclaimed. "Get my packsack . . . . in the canoe. Put it on the plane. He says he can just wait two minutes. And I *must* go on that plane."

P.L. dashed up the stairs to his room and Rory walked down to the canoe. Rory carried the packsack along to the plane and tossed it into the cabin. The pilot was already inside, waiting.

P.L. came around the corner of the store carrying his big suitcase, still barefooted and wearing only the shorts. The crowd of Indians on the bank scattered as he approached them, the men and women laughing but the children running wildly and looking back at P.L. with terror on their small dark faces. He slid down the sand bank instead of taking a path a few yards away, the suitcase falling free and rolling down ahead of him.

"What's happened?" Rory shouted above the noise of the plane.

"The stupid bastards! They were waiting until I got away. Now they have authority from the building superintendent to fumigate the bird room. I was supposed to have ten days' warning but that letter's been in Moosonee a week. They're doing it tomorrow. I'll never make it." P.L.'s eyes were wild and glassy, as close, Rory thought, as a grown man's eyes can come to tears.

"Good luck," Rory shouted back. "And listen, don't worry about it any more. After this, when I see her coming I *am* going to turn around and run like hell."

But the plane was still on the water in mid-stream, still not airborne, when a hand touched his elbow lightly and Rory turned to see Kanina smiling up at him. He hadn't noticed her earlier in the crowd of Indians.

"What's happening?" she asked.

Rory stared at her, too startled for a moment to speak. The plane roared and started its take-off run, its pontoons throwing white clouds of water into the slipstream behind it.

"He just heard about some trouble developing with his research work in Toronto," Rory said. "He's rushing back."

"I can't say I'm sorry. And this alters matters considerably. Do you still want some help driving geese?"

Rory shifted his gaze from the plane back to her. Her arms were raised and she was untying the shawl where it was knotted under her chin. The Indians on the bank above were walking away, ignoring them. The shawl came away revealing her hair; her eyes were lifted toward Rory's, the whites of them very white and the black curving lashes very black. And then she smiled and the dimples came and after that to try to resist was not only futile, it was utterly unthinkable.

"I'm starting for Kishamooskek right now. The canoe's all ready. We'll need a third person anyway to bring back one of the canoes tonight."

Rory could hear P.L. again now: "The longer you postpone it the harder it will be." But they could worry about that when the time came.

So it had happened while the plane carrying P.L. was still in sight, a small dark speck out over James Bay. "The spirit indeed is willing, but the flesh, P.L., the flesh is weak." And who was it who first penned that one? Kanina would know, probably, but he couldn't ask her.

CHAPTER THIRTY-EIGHT

IT was almost noon when they reached the goose camp clearing on the Kistawanee. She was walking across the little beach carrying his pack-sack and he was following with the much heavier packsack of food when she tripped and fell.

"Oo. Ouch!"

Suddenly she was sitting on the sand, laughing up at him.

"What did you do?"

"I stepped on a stone. It twisted my ankle."

"Hurt it?"

"Not much."

He took her hand and pulled her back up onto her feet. She went on walking, limping a little, but she was putting most of her weight on the ankle and Rory knew it couldn't be seriously hurt. Then he acted impulsively.

"Here comes the first-aid corps," he told her. He dropped the pack-sack he was carrying and ran up behind her. "The stretcher bearers have arrived!" He lifted her quickly into his arms and began carrying her up the sand path toward the grassy camp clearing above. She laughed and struggled, her legs kicking. He had one arm under her knees, the other under her shoulders. Then the struggling stopped, she threw one arm around his neck and her soft body melted unresistingly against his.

They reached the top—it was only a few yards—and he did not want to put her down. His face was buried in her hair and his head was giddy with the sweet, ambrosial smell of it. What was the smell? It was so different from the pungent, artificial, drugstore perfumes he usually associated with girls. And then he recognized it, the intrinsic fragrance of the north itself, the smell of balsam—from her balsam-bough bed.

His arms were tiring under her weight but he clung to her, waiting. Her head fell back onto his shoulder and his lips brushed softly across her cheek. Then, when he could hold her no longer, he crouched slowly and put her on the ground and sat beside her, holding her across his lap, their bodies crushed together, her face turned up toward his.

"I love you, Kanina." He didn't want to tell her, but he couldn't keep himself from saying it. And he thought guiltily that what had started as an innocent jest about stretcher bearers had somehow, suddenly, uncontrollably developed into something he had had no intention of permitting. He should have known. He was sorry for it. But it was too late now to turn back.

"I love you, Rory. I don't want to. I've been trying from the first, from that first day on the train, not to let it happen. But I knew a long time ago that it *was* happening. And I knew it couldn't go on, I knew it would have to end when the summer ends, and at first I said 'End it now,' and I tried, but I couldn't."

She talked rapidly, the words tumbling out across quivering lips, her eyes blinking fast against a shining, spreading film of tears.

"Does it have to end when the summer ends?"

"It must end then. I can't go back to face *that* again. And going back with you wouldn't change it. It would only mean that then you would have to face it too. I love you too much for that. I love you too much to bring it into your life too."

Then she cried, with great shaking sobs, and he smothered the sobs with kisses but the tears would not be stopped. She had decided it that way too. Both of them, independently, had come to the same conclusion. He had thought the problem was only his, but she had faced it also, and marriage was impossible, not just for him but for her too. Now the anguish and hopelessness of it loomed over them, more crushing, more appalling than it had before. One thought dominated him. They had no future, for them the future had to be now.

When he had tried to do it before, he could not; today, when he had tried to prevent it, he knew that nothing on earth could stop it from happening. They were as helpless as the plunging water poised on the brink of a waterfall.

They lay back on the grass, pressed close together. Her eyes were closed but she still sobbed softly. She neither helped nor resisted as he unfastened the buttons of her sweater and the waistband of her skirt. For a moment he was surprised at the deep brown color of the skin under her clothing—skin that was always milky white in other girls, no matter how tanned their legs and arms became on the bathing beaches.

They came together slowly and at first he knew he was hurting her because she held her legs stiff and drew back away from him. Then she wilted like a plucked flower in the sun and her body was suddenly soft and unresisting all over. She cried again, passionately, and threw her arms around him and crushed his body violently against her own.

They had a lunch later, much later, but they did not go on across the portage to Kishamooskek. The thought of spending the rest of the day rounding up geese seemed unfitting, almost sacrilegious. And the burning emotion Rory felt was so intense that he thought it must be written plainly across his face for all to read. Jock was too shrewd and discerning; he did not want to face Jock so soon.

So around mid-afternoon they launched the canoe and he turned downstream to take Kanina back to Cape Cree. She sat in the bow as she always had those other times, but now when they smiled at each other there was a tender, tragic understanding, a hopeless blind surrendering that had never been communicated in their smiles before. It was to have been so different, Rory thought. Just a Don Juan and his mistress. A seduction with neither gallantry nor love. And now it had happened. And it wasn't a seduction at all, it was inevitability itself, foredoomed, inexorable, uncompromising, as irreversible as life, as irresistible as death.

Rory felt no remorse. He felt only a hopeless futility, and a searing anger for a society that would force two people to telescope a lifetime of living and loving into one brief fleeting summer.

The summer was indeed fleeting. For a month after P.L.'s frantic and hurried departure from Cape Cree, Rory and Jock were constantly busy trapping and banding geese. They were away from Cape Cree most of the time, returning periodically for supplies but rarely staying at the post for more than one night. A few times when they were working close to Cape Cree, Kanina helped them, but for most of the period Rory and Jock worked alone. After some bungling efforts at the beginning, their goose-driving technique improved with experience and then the trapping went well.

Mid-August was approaching and the brief subarctic summer was waning. Out along the tideflats of the bay the first migrants were pouring down out of the Arctic—*keering* flocks of shorebirds following the coastline south on slender streamlined wings. Back on the muskeg potholes and the sphagnum bogs, the broods of goslings had long since shed their soft yellow natal down. Now the flight feathers appeared quickly in goslings and adults simultaneously, and with faultless timing the old birds regained their powers of flight just as the young ones were flying for the first time.

By mid-August all the geese were flying again and the banding had to stop. Rory hadn't taken time to work out the exact total but he knew that they had placed leg bands on something between nine hundred and a thousand geese. Now the geese gathered into larger flocks and great honking wedges of them flew out to the James Bay coast where they would fatten on the summer crop of crowberries and cranberries for the long flight south in September. The inland nesting territories were abandoned for another year and Rory and Jock followed the big birds out to the coast.

The flocking of Canada geese along the coast was the signal for the *Mooskek-owak* to resume hunting them, and there were plump *niska* breasts in the *Mooskek-owak* cooking pots again where for weeks before there had been only fish.

Rory was back again at Cape Cree, but there wasn't much more he could do. He checked the hunters' kills each day when they brought the geese back to the Indian village, studying stomach contents to learn what the birds were eating and keeping a record of age classes. Almost daily Rory made canoe trips up and down the coast in the vicinity of Cape Cree to study the movements of the geese. Jock was needed at the store now because some of the *Mooskek-owak* families were already picking up supplies and preparing to move inland to their winter trapping grounds, so Kanina frequently made the trips along the coast with Rory.

Kanina and Rory spent all the time they could with each other, both of them knowing that their time was rapidly running out but neither of them mentioning it. Often they were together out on the bay in the big canoe with the outboard during the afternoon, then they would be apart for a couple of hours while Rory examined the day's kill of geese, and then, always, they would meet again for the evening. When the cool night breeze began blowing in off the bay and the moon emerged like a thin white shaving of birchbark in the darkening twilight sky, they would paddle silently up the Kistawanee in one of Bert Rumsey's small canoes. Usually they would go ashore on the little beach behind the island and the embarrassment that Rory had once associated with the spot was only a distant memory, because now their past was dissolved, obliterated, in the bittersweet urgency of the present.

Neither of them referred again to the impossibility of marriage. It was settled, decided, by both, and there was nothing more to be said about it. They yielded freely to the love that had enslaved them, beautiful, tragic, hopeless love; they yielded, uninhibited, uncaring, unafraid, trying to make every hour a month and every day a year.

Often she would cry and Rory would then think guiltily of what P.L. had told him, but both of them were powerless now to end it until the last hour came and there would be no other choice.

Rory noticed that she wasn't wearing the black shawl, flannel skirts, the thick socks or the rubber boots at any time now. Even when he saw her down in the village and she was not expecting to meet him she would be neatly and brightly dressed—a colored skirt and sweater, the beaded moccasins, or sometimes the slacks and the red corduroy jacket, and always a bright ribbon or sparkling clasps in her flowing hair. He knew what it signified. To that extent, anyway, she was defying the conventions of her people; these last days were for Rory alone.

The August days and nights sped by. Now the wind was frequently in the north and northeast, piling great gray sheets of cloud before it, blowing cold and sharp and tangy with the salt mists of James Bay. The nights were often very cool and when they were clear the northern sky would blaze with mauve and green and rosy fingers of the aurora borealis leaping like frenzied ballet dancers across the Arctic horizon. After a night like that of northern lights, the morning landscape would emerge ghostly and frost-covered at dawn.

The Indian camp was bustling and active, a contrast with the slow lazy languid life of mid-summer, because the *Mooskek-owak* families were preparing to move back inland to winter trapping camps. While the men hunted geese along the shore, the women were making snow-shoes, moccasins, parkas and rabbitskin robes. Between goose-hunting forays the men repaired canoes and winter sleds and toboggans. Three or four families with close to two hundred miles to travel to their winter camps had already left, others with trapping territories near Cape Cree would not start out until October. Kanina had made no mention of when she and her parents would be leaving, but Rory knew the Beaverskin trapping territory was more than a hundred and fifty miles inland and they would be among the early starters.

Rory planned on staying at Cape Cree until the first week of September when the Canada geese would begin moving south and the *niska* hunting here on the bay would be ended. He did not know whether he or Kanina would be leaving first.

Planes continued to arrive once or twice a week but there was no letter from P.L. telling whether Turdy and the laboratory birds had survived the fumigation.

Through Jock all the hunters had now learned about the barnacle goose with the yellow neck band, and Rory had asked them to watch for it and refrain from shooting it if it appeared before any of their blinds. But Rory knew the *Mooskek-owak* were mystified by the strange white visitor who caught geese and put bands on their legs and then let them go again. To the *Mooskek-owak* every goose shot meant a day's less hunger next winter. Rory was sure there wasn't a hunter in the camp who wouldn't shoot the barnacle if he got the opportunity.

One evening as they paddled back toward Cape Cree through the chill dusk after a hazy sunless day, Rory said to Kanina: "I've been expecting *man-tay-o* to turn up along the coast somewhere, but there hasn't been a report of him."

"It's a long coast with few people to cover it," she said. "I've been afraid he would turn up right in camp—full of buckshot."

A minute later she asked: "Could he still be in on Kishamooskek?"

"The answer is almost certainly 'no.' But would you like to go up and look?"

"Yes."

"When?"

"I'm afraid it had better be tomorrow."

And somehow Rory overlooked the ominous phrasing of her answer.

They started up the Kistawanee next morning with the outboard on a small sixteen-foot canoe. Joan Rumsey had packed them a lunch. Rory would have to portage the canoe in to the lake and out again that evening, because there was no other canoe cached on Kishamooskek now as there had been for their earlier trips.

They left the outboard by the river and Rory shouldered the canoe and started across the portage with Kanina ahead of him. They came out on Kishamooskek and Rory remembered that other morning, almost three months ago now, when he had seen it first. The lake had lost none of its beauty through familiarity, but it was a changing beauty now with summer's waning. The willows and the aspen leaves were taking on their first soft tints of gold, and the marsh grasses, each sharp spike bending flat before the northern wind, were rapidly turning bronze.

They searched the lake for almost two hours but there was no sign of the barnacle, nor geese of any kind. Most of this time Kanina was silent, her dark eyes heavy and downcast whenever she turned in the bow of the canoe and faced him. Rory felt it too—Kishamooskek did not seem the same with *man-tay-o* gone. And then she told him, and he realized the silence and the sadness had nothing to do with *man-tay-o*.

They had returned to their beach of memories. They had made tea and had eaten Joan Rumsey's sandwiches. They were sitting pressed together, his face in her hair. She whispered it, and her voice was thin and weak and distant although her lips were almost touching his ear.

"This is our goodbye, Rory. I knew *man-tay-o* wouldn't be here, but I wanted to come back to this place, this beach of ours, once more. Father is getting supplies at the store today. I think he'll be ready to leave tomorrow morning."

He had known it must soon come. For days he had been able to think of little else. Yet now, when it did come, it seemed a shocking, impossible, unbelievable thing. Could a love like theirs really end? And then he knew it couldn't end, would never end, as long as life remained in one of them.

They went back slowly that evening and the rosy twilight had faded and it was turning dark when they reached Cape Cree.

"Rory," she said when they stepped from the canoe onto the beach below the Indian village.

"Yes."

"I want to say goodbye now. I want this to be our last goodbye. I don't want to say goodbye tomorrow down here by the canoe when we leave, down here with my parents and everyone else around. Stay away tomorrow, please, Rory. I couldn't speak to you then. Stay away from the canoe when we are loading. Stay away. Make this the end."

And then she was crying again and they were crushed together in each other's arms.

"And don't forget," she went on, her voice tight and husky with sobbing. "You have a job to do when you go back. One man alone . . . . you can't do much, because it is a big job, but try. Do what you can. Change them. Make them see the folly of it. And then someday when there is another girl and another boy and a love like ours it won't have to end like this."

She kept on crying and Rory's throat was too full to let him speak. Then she pushed herself away from him.

"Let's not prolong it," she said. "It will do no good. Goodbye. I love you."

She kissed him once more, a harsh, violent kiss. Then she was away from him, running down the beach, turning up a path that disappeared among clumps of willows.

Rory waited, one minute or many minutes, he did not know, wondering if she might come back, and knowing that she would not.

He had never before felt so alone.

The next morning Rory stood at the window of his room for an hour watching the Beaverskins take down their patched brown tent and load their big canoe. The canoe was loaded to the gunwales with packsacks of foodstuffs, white sacks of flour, bedding and a seemingly endless array of bush-life impedimenta like snowshoes, axes, traps, fish nets, guns, dog harnesses and even a small toboggan. They were almost ready to go when Joan Rumsey called him and the two of them went down and stood beside the store to watch the departure.

Kanina was in the bow and her mother squatted in the canoe's center, her great bulk hidden among the mounds of equipment. Joe Beaverskin came down leading two huskies on their chains and somehow the dogs found room in the canoe too. Then he pushed the canoe off the beach and started the outboard motor.

"Daisy Beaverskin has aged this summer; she isn't well," Joan Rumsey said. "That's why he is using Kanina in the bow." And then after a brief pause: "Daisy might not come back. I hope Kanina does."

The canoe, low in the water, moved sluggishly away. She was gone from him. He would not see her again because he had decided firmly that he would not come back to the bay for another summer, even if the wildlife service asked him to.

She turned once to wave, and then she turned again, facing ahead, facing the endless empty wastes of bush and muskeg that had claimed her again at last after her futile seven-year struggle with an alien world. He saw her reach down. He saw her straighten up and she was tying the black wool shawl around her head. Then the canoe went around a willow point and Kanina Beaverskin, a *Mooskek-owak* once more, was lost from sight in the dying summer's golden haze.

PART FOUR

The Outlanders

THE annual cycle of activity in a bird is controlled by a series of inner urges which leaves the bird little need or indeed opportunity for conscious choices or decisions. The waxing and waning of these urges are linked with the ebb and flow of certain hormones, and the glands that produce these hormones are triggered into their cyclic pattern of hormone production by seasonal changes in the bird's environment, mainly the lengthening hours of daylight in spring and their shortening in autumn.

In spring, as the days lengthen, the hormone output of the sex glands increases and the sexual urge, dormant since the summer before, is revived. With it comes the compulsion to migrate to the traditional breeding grounds of the species where the flocks break up into nesting pairs. In late summer when the mating drive has been fulfilled and the fiery output of sex hormones is cut off, the bird feels a restlessness again, an urge to flock once more with others of its own species. And linked inseparably with this new urge is the desire to return to the species' wintering grounds.

And so it was that the barnacle goose and his Canada goose mate, after a summer of seclusion on Kishamooskek, began to feel an urge to rejoin their kind.

At first that summer the barnacle had been very conscious of the fact that his mate was different from himself, and he had sensed dimly that this difference must also account in some way for the strange inland surroundings to which she had brought him. But his attachment for her, spurred by their mutual courting, had grown steadily through the long hot days of summer and he learned slowly to accept Kishamooskek's calm saltless water and the confining restraint of its marshy and forested shores. There were times still when he yearned passionately for the wildness and freedom of unobstructed sea, but these times became less and less frequent as the pace of their courting mounted.

And then the molt had come, marking the end of the sexual phase of the year's life cycle. Now the courtship displays ceased as the hormone flow that inspired them began to dry up. The barnacle's attachment for his mate remained but some of its fiery fervor waned, replaced now by the new drive, the drive to seek companions, the restless call of the wintering grounds.

There was the brief encounter with the humans when the shiny bands were put on their legs and the yellow streamers were attached to their necks, a terrifying experience while it lasted but forgotten almost as quickly as it had occurred. Then the wing feathers grew in and flight returned. And memories that had been fragmentary and obscure for many weeks in hidden recesses of the barnacle's brain suddenly became vivid and pressing. For now, with the time of migration looming again, the barnacle found himself thinking frequently of Barra, its tideflats, its eelgrass beds and the frothing surf of its sea.

On a cool dark afternoon late in August when the yellowing aspen leaves were trembling crisply in a northern wind, the barnacle and his mate took off and each one knew from the restless build-up of excitement that had preceded it that this was the departure. They climbed high and turned eastward toward James Bay, the yellow ribbons streaming back over their necks. The barnacle watched the island-studded blue of Kishamooskek merge into the haze behind them and he knew that despite all his dislike of it this was now the breeding territory, hallowed by the summer's courtship, the shrine to which inevitably he would return with his mate for the nesting in another spring.

That evening they crossed the coast of James Bay and settled briefly on the water a mile from shore. But the barnacle's discontent remained as tormenting as ever, because this shallow, warm and muddy water, despite its saltiness, failed to satisfy or even diminish his yearning for the sea. They flew again at dusk and joined a flock of Canada geese on a strip of cranberry barrens near the shore. The female gabbled excitedly as they pitched down among the other geese; the barnacle could feel the excitement too, but it was tempered with vague, indefinable doubts and misgivings.

They flew with the flock up and down the shore for a week, feeding, strengthening wings for the long flight. They encountered many more geese, hundreds and then thousands, for James Bay was a gathering ground into which the goose population of the eastern Arctic and subarctic converged. Their own flock grew steadily as newly arrived pairs and families joined them.

The new ones were flying down from the north and it confused and bewildered the barnacle. He remembered his spring flight well. He knew that to retrace that flight to the sea and home he had to start out by following this coastline north. Yet the other geese were flying *out of* this northern land into which his homing urge was pressing him to fly.

Many times each day he looked to the beckoning northern horizon. Finally the lure of it became irresistible and he flew, alone, calling eagerly for the mate to follow. She sprang into the air behind him, her own voice a strident frantic bidding for him to return. She followed him, calling, pleading, until the flock was lost from sight behind them. And then she stopped and circled and would not go on. He circled too, a hundred yards ahead of her, and each of them called loudly and passionately, each bewildered by the other's actions, each unaware of the different migratory tradition that beckoned the other. He waited many minutes, flying far ahead, then circling back. But finally he abandoned it and returned to her. Together again, they flew back to rejoin the flock, talking in soft throaty undertones as they went.

The barnacle knew now he must stay with her. She would not follow him. Now he must go wherever she would lead.

The geese flocks stayed on James Bay another two weeks, their growing restlessness leading them on long flights up and down the coast. But they did not leave the bay. Near the middle of September a strong low-pressure system moved slowly across the Hudson Bay–James Bay region drenching it for two days with warm intermittent rain. When the rain stopped, the wind shifted northerly and the air grew crisp and dry and cold under a clear, blue, sunny sky. It meant that a high-pressure mass of Arctic air was moving in behind the low-pressure system. It meant that for two days, perhaps three, there would be a wide swath of strong northerly winds sweeping down between the two contrasting weather systems deep into the center of the continent.

The Canada geese massed on James Bay did not comprehend the meteorological technicalities that caused it all, but they did know that this was the weather pattern that provided them with a firm, reliable tailwind aloft for the long flight south. For uncountable generations they had been using these continental-scale airflows on their migration flights, the same technique that modern aviation uses and describes as "pressure-pattern flying." The old birds recognized it first, while the last remnants of rain were falling. Around the muddy five-hundred-mile shoreline of James Bay the old ganders were cocking their heads sideways, studying the sky and honking at the thinning clouds. The restlessness spread quickly, bird to bird and flock to flock.

The barnacle's flock was near the southern tip of the bay. There was much chatter among them, much spirited flapping of their big wings, and the barnacle knew that the departure time must be approaching. There was still a high overcast and a drizzling rain over this southern part of the bay when flocks of geese began moving down from the north and passing overhead. This indicated that farther north clear weather had already arrived and the exodus of geese had begun, for geese start their flights only under clear skies, although once under way they may overtake and fly through remnants of storm that lie across their route. They were moving southward in an unending procession of wavering lines and Vs, flying high as waterfowl do on the long flights, their yodeling flight calls floating down faintly to the tideflats and sphagnum bogs below.

The barnacle clung close to his mate, tense and uneasy. A line of blue clear sky crept over the western horizon toward them. The flock's restlessness grew, the old ones running frequently into the wind, their wings flapping, testing the air. They stopped feeding and waited, heads turned toward the sky.

The front, the line of division and conflict between the two air masses, moved across them with a series of quick gusty squalls and patches of fog, and then suddenly the air was cold and dry and a freshening breeze swept down from the north. The front had passed and now they were in the high.

Now the old ones cackled excitedly. Suddenly, en masse, the flock flew, the air rumbling with the beat of their many wings. The barnacle lagged at the rear of the flock. Dark fingers of spruce forest began passing below and his fear of overland flight seized him again. He was flying south when every fiber of him was demanding that he fly north to the sea. Behind him the retreating waters of James Bay were calling him back; ahead of him she called him on and the soft, seductive, eloquent pleading of her voice was again a siren's song that he could not resist. He followed her.

They leveled off and formed their V a half mile up where the north wind blew firmly, unaffected by the ground friction that made it weaker and erratic at lower levels. He took a position behind his mate instead of ahead of her, for now she was the leader. He was flying into a land he had never seen before. He had no knowledge of the goal toward which they were heading. He could only follow.

It had been late in the afternoon when they flew. Far below them the pattern of landscape gradually changed. At first the bronze of dying boglands had predominated, flecked here and there with green lumps of coniferous forest. Then the forest spread out and merged until by dusk, when it turned from green to black in the falling light, it formed a solid fuzz-like mat on the land below.

Throughout those first hours of daylight flight, the dark line of cloud that marked the retreating edge of the storm front was never far away in the east, for they were flying more or less parallel to it. When darkness came, finally hiding it, the storm line was still there, lumpy, black and threatening; if anything, it was perhaps drawing a little closer, for the geese were flying southeastward at a speed much faster than the eastward movement of the storm.

It was a dark night without moon. First the land below and then all but the nearest geese in the flock around him disappeared from the barnacle's view. Now he felt a greater dependence than ever on the female Canada goose ahead of him. He kept close to her, his wings clinging to the turbulent wake of her flight, his eyes straying only rarely from her shadowy form outlined faintly against the gray sky ahead.

It had been dark about an hour when they struck warm eddies of air, and a turbulence began to twist and rock their flight. Then a gray wall of cloud loomed ahead. They dropped below it, for although geese will fly in fog or cloud they avoid it when they can. By dropping they could remain in the cold dry air in which they had been flying, for the old ones knew from many previous experiences with weather fronts that the cold air would be pushing like a long sloping wedge beneath the warm air mass of the retreating storm.

They leveled off a hundred feet below. The warm air and the cloud it contained closed in above them, blocking off the stars. A few minutes later the cloud appeared ahead of them again for its undersurface was sloping earthward along the boundary between cold and warm airs. They dropped once more to a lower altitude and flew on.

For almost half an hour they flew this way, dropping repeatedly to keep themselves below the cloud layer. As they went lower a landscape of lake and forest emerged dimly below. Now the flock was almost on the treetops and ahead of them the cloud merged with a thick fog clinging to the ground. The white wall of it reared up like a chalky precipice before them. The gander in the lead honked a resonant warning and then they plunged into it and the warm mist pressed smotheringly around them.

Suddenly the barnacle could see nothing, not even the mate a yard or two ahead of him. The geese around him began calling bewilderedly to each other and the barnacle could tell from the lack of pattern in the positioning of the calls that the flock was losing its formation. They were wheeling about in confusion, the honking calls sometimes clear and near, at other times some distance away and muffled by the fog. He clung to the faint turbulence of air marking the flight trail of the female ahead of him, sorting out her calls from those of the other geese around them and constantly answering her with his own chattering bark-like notes. Every feather of his body sprang from a nerve ending and he was delicately sensitized to the slightest changes in the pressure and flow of the air around him, but despite this sensitivity it took all the concentration of which he was capable to follow her now in the total darkness that had swallowed them.

The calls of the other geese were faint and distant and then he recognized that they were higher too. The birds were climbing, seeking the safety of height. For a terrifying second or two he lost his mate's trail, then he found it again and detected that she was climbing too, putting more altitude between herself and the trees that must be dangerously near in the blinding void below. And now, with level flight abandoned, it became still more difficult to follow her.

He stayed with her for several minutes, climbing steadily, losing her trail momentarily at times and then picking it up again. Turbulence in the air increased as they went higher. And then a powerful updraft clutched him, flinging him violently upward fifty feet in a couple of seconds. He fought it, regained his flight control, but now the trail that linked them was dispersed and gone, and he knew instantly he would never find it again. He called to her once, a frantic desperate plaint flung out hopelessly into the black maw of the night sky. He thought he heard her answer from far away, too far for him to be certain of its direction. Then there was silence. He was alone.

For the thousands of Canada geese who were caught that night in the frontal band of fog that stretched across northern Ontario, it was a brief and relatively minor hazard. Flocks that hit the thickest zones of fog and broke up as a result re-formed into new flocks when they reached clear air again. Mated pairs that were separated had a good chance of reuniting on the flight south or on the wintering grounds, and if this failed they were sure of finding each other again when they returned to the nesting territory the following spring.

But for the barnacle goose, it was catastrophe. He did not know where the wintering grounds were. Flying over land far from the sea had remained a frightening experience even when his mate and other geese were near to reassure him; now alone it was terrifying.

He flew aimlessly for an hour and then the front moved past him and the fog cleared. Features of the landscape emerged faintly through the darkness below him. He found a lake and landed upon it, staying in its center, keeping fearfully as far as possible from the black encroaching shores.

He should fly on in search of her. He should fly on quickly because she would be flying farther and farther away from him. But fear paralyzed him.

He had faced two conflicting lures—the call of Barra and the sea, and the call of his mate. The choice was easy and automatic while the female was near him, the mere fact of her physical presence creating a bond he was incapable of breaking. But now the bond *was* broken. The mate was gone from him. His yearning for the sea and for the rocky headlands of Barra became an oppressive, agonizing demand.

He fought it for several hours, then finally he turned into the northern wind and flew. He climbed high over the lake's humpy shoreline and headed toward the flashing aurora of the north sky. At dawn the waters of James Bay lay stretched like a taut green fabric below him and he flew on northward without stopping. Somewhere up this long and circuitous coast lay the great sea. And somewhere far beyond that, he had only a vague idea where, lay Barra.

The storm was gone and the sky was clear. The yellow streamer flowing back over his neck gleamed brilliantly in the rising sun.

CHAPTER FORTY

ABOVE the clacking of her loom Mary Macdonald heard the mail carrier's car chugging toilsomely up the sandy *machair* road outside. She stopped pedaling and hunched wearily over her bolt of tweed to stare out through the little blackhouse window. It was September, but late-flowering clumps of primrose still dappled the Barra *machairs* with fading yellow. She lost sight of the car as it passed to the front of the blackhouse, and she listened, wondering if it was going to stop at the letter box with mail for her.

With the loom now silent she became conscious of the other noises around her. There was the rumbling beat of the sea, Big Sammy's snoring in the next room, and the sharp, incessant chewing of rats as they stripped flour paste from the inner surface of the wallpaper.

Mary Macdonald's hair was now white and her face was pallid from working indoors long hours at her loom. Her figure, always plump and formless, had changed little with the years. As a young woman it had made her dumpy and unattractive, but now it was more suited to her years and by the standards of the age group to which she now belonged Mary Macdonald was, if anything, a little more attractive, a little less homely than she had ever been before. She had not grown prettier, but she had at least managed to arrive not greatly altered into a time of life in which the demands were less. Mary Macdonald had begun to look old at thirty; now over fifty, her appearance and her years were beginning to strike a balance again.

The mail carrier's car stopped. She wasn't expecting mail today, so what could it be? Not a letter from Rory, because she had had one from him only two days ago. A month previously she had written to a former teaching friend in Glasgow about the possibility of returning there to teach, but this letter had also been answered and she was not expecting more correspondence on the matter now. The letter to her Glasgow friend had been merely a personal inquiry about teaching conditions there and not a formal request for a job. She had been quite frank and had told the friend that she was unhappy here and was considering leaving her husband, though not until after the winter. She did not say that she was postponing it to look for a goose. The reply she had received about two weeks ago was encouraging—Mary should have little trouble, the friend told her, in finding a teaching position again.

The mail carrier's car wheezed away and Mary rose from her loom and walked out through the middle room where her husband lay sleeping on his bed. In recent months Sammy had been spending several hours each day sleeping like this, snoring hoarsely, because he had little else to do. His only farming activity now was to keep a small flock of sheep to provide the wool for Mary's loom.

Mary went out toward the mail box. It *could* be another letter from Rory. She had had two letters from him since his return to Toronto after his summer on James Bay and there had been a rather strange brooding quality in them with some vague references to what he had called in one letter "the stupid iniquities of man to man." Mary had been receiving letters from him for too long a time to miss the fact that some emotional change or ordeal had come into Rory's life. Maybe he was writing more about this now.

But when she took the letter from the box she saw at once it wasn't from Rory. It bore a Glasgow postmark. She stared at it, her fingers trembling. After twenty-five years she could still recognize instantly the neat, precise handwriting of John Watt.

She walked back toward the blackhouse, tearing the envelope open with clumsy fingers, and then at the door where she could again hear Sammy's snoring she changed her mind and walked down toward the sea. She had no idea what the letter could be about but it had filled her already with a sweet nostalgia and she decided suddenly that she didn't want to read it in *there*.

Mary Macdonald had never been back to Glasgow and she had heard nothing about John Watt since her arrival on Barra. She remembered vividly the letter with which he had ended their engagement and his sudden marriage to the stenographer in the university business office. It had driven her into the marriage with Big Sammy, but the fault was hers, not John Watt's, and any bitterness she had felt for Watt at the time had not endured for long. Now, with a letter from him in her hand again after all these years, Mary Macdonald could feel only a happy tingling excitement.

She walked quickly until she was a hundred feet or so below the black-house and then she could wait no longer. She sat on a rock, hastily withdrew the letter from its envelope, and began to read.

John Watt had heard that she was considering returning to teach again in Glasgow and he was looking forward, he said, to meeting her again. He wanted to help. He was still a professor at the university and if Mary wanted assistance he would be pleased to use his influence in obtaining a teaching position for her.

"I don't know what news you have had of me," his letter went on. "You probably know that my marriage was an unhappy mistake too. I have been divorced and alone for more than twenty years. . . ."

Mary stared at it until the words blurred before her eyes. She read it again. "An unhappy mistake *too*." Why did he say "too"? He had heard, apparently, from the letter she had written to Glasgow, that she planned on leaving her husband. And now the pleasant excitement she had felt at receiving John Watt's letter changed to shock and dismay. She began to wonder if the reason he had given for writing was his whole reason.

But she read on eagerly. He wrote that occasionally in the evening he walked out past the gray stone house where she used to live. The house had not changed. And there were still benches at the same spot in The Green beside the Clyde where they had quoted poetry to each other twenty-five years ago. As she read, the memories came back in a joyous nostalgic flood. How different her life might have been! And now she was shocked at the thoughts that suddenly began racing unbidden and uncontrollably through her own mind. No, she must not let herself even consider it! She was prepared to leave her husband, that much at least she could accept as justifiable, but no more than that. She would still be a married woman, her life would remain circumscribed forever by the marriage vows she had made.

She read the letter again and again, wondering what she could say in reply, wondering if she should reply at all. For the rest of that day and evening she carried it inside the bodice of her dress to keep Sammy from finding it. He would know by the neat distinctive handwriting that it wasn't a letter from Rory.

She wrote a reply next day when Sammy was out. She wrote slowly, composing it carefully, keeping it stiffly formal. She thanked John Watt for his offer of assistance and said she had made no final decision yet about returning to Glasgow. She felt too ashamed to tell John about Sammy or about their home, but she did tell him proudly about Rory, about the love they shared for the barnacle geese and about the one barnacle in particular that she was waiting to search for that winter. She wondered for a long time how to end the letter, and then, hesitantly, she concluded it: "I am looking forward to seeing you again."

Yesterday the thoughts had frightened her and she had tried to suppress them. But now she made no attempt to deny them. A part of her that she had considered dead for twenty-five years was not dead after all, it was only stifled and dormant, and now it had suddenly been fanned into flame. It was the part of her that once, and only once, had known the pain and delights of love.

Mary Macdonald had not played her violin for months but now she felt a desire to play it again. She tuned it and began playing. She was out of practice, her fingers were stiff and for a few minutes she played awkwardly. But gradually some of the old skill returned and soon she felt ready to tackle the difficult Mendelssohn concerto she had always loved. Usually she played to cheer herself when she felt depressed, but now she was playing because the happy buoyant melody of the Mendelssohn concerto seemed aptly expressive of her own altered mood.

The autumn sun leaned farther to the south each day casting vivid pink sunsets over the Atlantic. The gales brought mists and rains and high tides that sent the surf lunging far up among Barra's coastal dunes. The primroses, buttercups and marram grass withered and browned and died.

On a wild night in October when the blackhouse roof was billowing in the gale and back-drafts from the chimney were sending sparks from the stove onto the earthen floor, the barnacle geese returned. Mary heard the first of them as she sat in the kitchen reading by the yellow glow of the lamp on the table. The calls were faint and distant, only snatches of them rising above the roar of surf and wind. She put on a coat and stepped outside to listen. She went around to the seaward side of the blackhouse where the wind blasted her and the salt spray stung her cheeks. For a minute it was impossible to separate other noises from the clamor of the storm, and then as her ears tuned, shutting out the noises she did not wish to hear, she began to detect again the musical bark-like gabble of barnacles out over the sea.

For twenty-five autumns she had heard it now, yet the same old excitement stirred her anew. This time the return of the barnacles meant much more to her than it ever had before. For one thing, Rory's barnacle might be among them, although Rory had said in his letters that its return to Barra was unlikely. And this was the last return of the barnacles she would witness. When the big birds came again another autumn, Mary Macdonald would not be here to tremble at the wild free sound of their night-time cries. But wherever she might be when these first crisp October nights returned each year, she would always hear them again in memory. Most of this Barra life she hoped to forget, but she would never forget the lilting music of the barnacles because it was more than a part of her memory, it was part of her heart.

She stayed there, pressed against the stone wall of the house for an hour. Usually the calls were muffled and distant, but a few times flocks passed close to her and their rhythmic flight chatter came down clearly on the wind although the birds themselves remained hidden in the black void of the sky. Finally she went back inside and to refresh her memory she read again Rory's letter of the summer in which he had described the yellow streamer and how it would appear on a flying or swimming bird. Then she went to bed. Tomorrow at dusk she would walk up to Goose Island Sound and begin the search.

The gale had abated by the following evening but the big green combers were still rolling in off the sea. Mary could hear the barnacles calling faintly out at sea as she crept up the last ridge that hid Goose Island Sound. She peered cautiously over the crest, but she was early and no geese were feeding yet on the eelgrass beds in the sound. She sat down to wait at a spot where the vetches and clover were thick and partially hid her.

Within a few minutes she could see the goose flocks approaching. The first of them came around Goose Island and pitched noisily onto the sound just as the sun dipped like a great orb of molten metal into the sea. Other flocks quickly followed and they began feeding, heads and necks immersed full length, tails pointed at the reddening sky. But there were only a few hundred of them—the vanguard of thousands that would be feeding there each night later on.

Mary watched as the twilight waned. She was half a mile from the main flocks and to check them carefully she would have to obtain a much closer view. She could hide under a blanket down by the shore as Rory used to do, or she could buy a pair of binoculars. There would be binoculars in Castlebay, but they would be very costly, and she discarded that idea immediately.

She crept away and began walking back through the dusk. She would wait a week before checking the flocks again, and next time she would bring a blanket and try to get nearer.

She was back there one week later. She had arrived early, had weighted the blanket down with stones and camouflaged it with a covering of clover and grass. Now she was lying beneath it peering out through an opening she had formed by propping up the edge of the blanket in front of her face.

The geese began appearing as the sun started dipping into the sea. Flock after flock glided in and there were many more of them than a week ago. The full wintering population had arrived and now Mary's search for Rory's goose could begin.

She studied them, bird by bird, seeking the yellow neck streamer that Rory had described, but she discovered quickly that her blanket lookout down here close to the water was not going to permit a thorough search. Her view to the sides was cut off by the blanket and she could see only the relatively small number of geese that were directly in front of her. Next time she must hide nearer the top of the ridge where she would have a view of the whole sound. And now she knew also that she must have binoculars. By naked eye alone she could never be certain that Rory's goose wasn't out there somewhere on the distant fringes of the flock.

For months Mary had been saving a portion of each tweed payment to finance her return to Glasgow and she had kept the money hidden in a jar in one of the rat burrows behind the wall of her room. Sammy had a superstitious fear of the rats, believing they would attack him in his sleep if they were disturbed, so Mary knew it was a safe hiding place.

Big Sammy left the blackhouse right after breakfast that next morning and as soon as he was gone Mary took out her savings and started walking toward Castlebay. The binoculars she bought cost twenty pounds—more than half of her savings. She parted with the money reluctantly, consoling herself with the thought that she could sell them at a secondhand store in Glasgow and get some of the investment back if she needed to.

It was late in the afternoon when she reached home and Big Sammy was lying on his bed waiting for her. He rose when she came in. He was tall and handsome still, his blond hair showing no grayness. He saw the binocular case immediately.

"Whut's thet ye have?"

"Binoculars," Mary told him.

"They ain't nay such thing," he told her. "They be spy glasses, ain't they?"

"That's right," Mary said. "Spy glasses."

"Fer whut did ye buy them? Fer spyin' on people?"

Mary walked past him into her own room and he followed her to the doorway.

"I bought them for spying on geese," Mary said. She sat on the edge of her bed. It had been a long walk and she was tired. She sighed softly. "I didn't tell ye, Sammy, about Rory's goose," she began. "I'd like to tell ye now." Mary told him about the James Bay barnacle and about the watch that she intended to keep for it during the winter.

"I told it tae ye!" Sammy exclaimed. "On the nicht thet Rory was born I told ye. I told ye the barnacles would always watch o'er the bairn who was born that nicht the barnacles came home tae Barra. Und see, one o' them goes tae Canada tae watch o'er him there! I told ye so."

It was twenty-five years ago but Mary Macdonald remembered her husband's quaint and superstitious prophecy.

"I remember ye telling me," she said.

"But ye must never spy on them!" Sammy said quickly. " 'Tis the evilest thing ye can do. They will hate the boy then. They will fill his life with bad luck and turn a' his friends tae be enemies. Aye, ye're crazy! A' the money ye've spent! A'll tak the spy glasses back tae Castlebay in the mornin'."

"Ye'll do no such thing!" Mary said calmly. "The spy glasses are mine and I shall decide what's to be done with them."

Sammy turned away from the doorway. "But A'll nay have ye spyin' on the barnacles!" he said. " 'Twill bring evil tae us a'."

The plank door leading outside thudded shut and Big Sammy was gone.

November passed. A white film of hoarfrost often covered the *machair* in the mornings and sometimes there were thin wet falls of snow that lingered for a day and then melted. On two and sometimes three evenings a week Mary went down to the sound, hid under her blanket before the geese arrived and spent an hour or so checking the flocks. The binoculars made it much easier but the big birds were wary and would not permit an approach of closer than half a mile, so she had to continue using the blanket as well.

Sammy complained frequently but he made no attempt to deprive her of the binoculars. Mary knew that Sammy would be easy to manage, despite his angry objection that day she bought them. Sammy's easy carefree life depended on Mary's tweed money and he was at least smart enough to do nothing that might jeopardize that.

November had almost ended and there had been no sign of the barnacle with the yellow neck band. She tried to select warm evenings for her goose watching but it was always a cold, aching ordeal because she had to lie under the blanket each time until there was enough darkness to let her slip away unobserved. But she kept up the search, because Rory had stressed that the wintering flocks would be moving restlessly up and down the coast, always mixing and changing. The Goose Island flock, though it appeared the same each night, probably consisted of constantly changing birds, so the search could not relax.

And all the time, there were the letters from John Watt. They were coming now about one a week. She carried each one for a day or two in her dress until she had answered it, and then she would reluctantly burn it in the stove. She was afraid if she let them accumulate that Sammy might find them. And she found herself waiting for those weekly letters with a feeling that was both eagerness and shame. A woman in her fifties, she thought, should not feel this way.

But Mary Macdonald could no longer think of her impending move as a return to Glasgow; she could think of it only as a return to John Watt.

CHAPTER FORTY-ONE

WINTER comes early to the far-flung James Bay hunting grounds of the *Mooskek-owak,* turning the sodden land to a frigid steel. Usually it brings deep snow, but sometimes the snow is late in coming, and oddly it is these winters of light snow that bring the greatest suffering, for snow is the protecting blanket that shields the land and its life from winter's harshest punishment.

This year the *mi-kiskaw,* the freezing of the waters, came earlier than usual. On the rambling Beaverskin trapline near the headwaters of the Kistawanee, a hundred and fifty miles inland from Cape Cree, the streams were frozen firmly by the first few days of November. But there was no snow.

The Beaverskins had traveled about half the distance from Cape Cree to the wintering territory in the big canoe driven by the outboard. Then where the Kistawanee's shallow headwater streams began, they changed to a smaller canoe that had been cached at this point by Kanina's parents on the trip out the previous spring. Now they paddled by hand and there were frequent portages, but the load was lighter because most of their supplies were left cached with the big canoe to be returned for after the freeze-up when it could be hauled by sled.

The canoe was crowded and Joe Beaverskin's two dogs were put ashore now to follow along the boggy stream banks as best they could and hunt their own food as they traveled. Frequently the dogs disappeared for a whole day. The canoe twisted through a network of streams and small lakes leaving no trail behind, yet the dogs, miraculous as it seemed to Kanina, never lost them. Often they would make their camp and go to bed with the dogs still missing, but the two ragged and mud-caked animals would be curled up, sleeping soundly outside the tent flap at dawn.

The dogs were typical broad-jowled, thick-necked, northern huskies, a mother and her year-old pup, wild and surly much of the time except for the infrequent periods during which they were well fed when they could be friendly and at times even playful. The mother was Mokwa, which was Cree for "loon," and Joe Beaverskin had given her the name because her howl was high and quavering like the loon's spring call. Her long wiry fur was all white, the only black she carried were her nose and eyes and the scarred dead skin of ear tips that had been repeatedly frostbitten. The pup, smaller and mischievous, was white-furred, too, but he had a black face and muzzle and his ear tips were as yet unfrozen. For a reason that Kanina had never understood, her father had given the pup the English name of Jim.

Kanina had ignored them all summer but now she began to grow fond of them, Jim particularly. Affection, like a full stomach, was something the dogs had not often known. Kanina talked to them, playing with them when they were well fed and would let her. Even on their surliest, hungriest days they began wagging their tails playfully when Kanina approached them.

During the third week after leaving Cape Cree they began pushing up a twisting creek into a region of higher, better drained land where a modest forest of spruce and aspen grew. They reached a tiny jagged clearing and the pole wigwam skeleton on the creek bank told Kanina that this was the wintering place. They fitted canvas tarpaulins over the tepee-shaped framework and banked earth and moss halfway up its sides. From a spruce tree at the edge of the clearing Joe Beaverskin took down a small rusty box-like stove of sheet-metal and several lengths of three-inch stovepipe, cached there the previous spring. He set up the stove on rocks inside and ran the stovepipe out through a hole in an asbestos sheet riveted into the roof tarpaulin for this purpose.

It resembled an earthen mound more than it did a dwelling and it was not a sight to inspire confidence or enthusiasm. This was the *askeekan,* the wintering earth lodge, the only home they would know through the long subzero months ahead.

Her parents began cutting firewood, and balsam boughs for the beds, but Kanina had a different duty to perform and went alone into the spruce forest behind the camp. It was time again to gather the soft rolls of sphagnum moss, because she was not pregnant, as she had hoped she might be. During the last month with Rory at Cape Cree she had feared the possibility of pregnancy. But as soon as she was gone from him she began wishing that another life could begin where theirs had separated, that a part of him could go on living here with her, forever linking them. As they traveled inland, this wish had grown to a fervent hope. And now on her first day in the wintering camp the hope was shattered. Rory was gone. Every part of him was gone. He had left nothing but a racking memory behind him.

When she returned to the *askeekan* the bough beds were laid out on the floor and a fire was going in the small stove. The interior was dark but she could see dimly the quilts and rabbitskin robes on the beds, the black pot on the stove, a sack of flour, a pail of lard, two wooden food boxes, her own linen-covered wardrobe bag. There was nothing more.

Her father was not there but her mother was lying on one of the beds. She rolled over and smiled at Kanina, a wan weak smile, so fleeting that the gaps in her brown-stained teeth were hardly revealed. There were haggard, aging lines in Daisy Beaverskin's face although the hair above it was still jet black; the trip from Cape Cree had weakened her, the woman's old endurance and resiliency were waning.

Two days later Joe Beaverskin left on a trip upstream to check his trapping territory for beaver houses and game signs. He was gone three nights and when he returned his round face with its wide flat nose held no smile of greeting.

"There is little game," he said to them in Cree. "It may be a bad winter."

Kanina knew the main portion of their winter diet had to be game—they called it "country food," for it had to come from the country itself. Flour, sugar, lard, tea, oatmeal and canned milk they had from the Cape Cree trading post, but all this, the "store food," was supplementary. Without a steady supply of country food for the big black stewing pot, the store food could not last out the winter.

Kanina and her mother set nets in the creek and set rabbit snares in the forest behind, because under the *Mooskek-owak* division of labor this was woman's work. But a little exertion would leave Daisy Beaverskin weak and breathing hard. In a few days Kanina was tending the nets and snares alone. The nets produced pike and suckers regularly but there were few rabbits. Daisy was spending more and more time sitting by the stove in the lodge, her big shoulders hunched forward, her puckered lips puffing silently on her little pipe.

By mid-October the mornings would reveal glassy needles of ice along the creek edge. Then a colder night came and Kanina awoke the next dawn with a feeling that something familiar was missing. For a few seconds she was puzzled, and then she became aware that the bubbly murmur of the creek had gone. She looked out and saw that the creek was imprisoned now under a sheet of blue glare ice.

On that first day of the freeze-up they broke the ice with poles and pulled the nets out onto the bank. The nets would be reset through holes in the ice when the ice became firm enough to walk on.

A few evenings later the cold intensified sharply and the creek ice cracked with ringing rifle-like reports as it froze more deeply. "The ice feels cold," Daisy Beaverskin told Kanina. "It is calling for the snow to come and cover it and keep it warm. There will be snow before the dawn."

The first snowfall did come that night, but it was a light fall of only two or three inches and it had ended by dawn. Kanina was awakened by her mother shuffling past her to the *askeekan* door. The woman's big shoulders shrugged as she looked outside.

"Bah! It is nothing," Daisy muttered. "We need the deep snow. And this is only enough to show a mouse track."

But it was enough to make dogsled travel possible and Joe Beaverskin and the dogs set out that morning for the food cache on the Kistawanee seventy-five miles away. He was gone a week and while he was away Daisy showed Kanina how to reset the nets under the ice. It was cold, hard work for it involved chopping numerous holes through the ice with an axe and pushing each net along beneath the ice from hole to hole with a pole. When Joe Beaverskin returned he was in the harness himself helping the dogs haul the toboggan piled with the last of their supplies. The Beaverskins were now as prepared as they could be for *mi-kiskaw* to end and for *pipoon,* the time of winter proper, to begin.

By mid-November Joe Beaverskin had his trapline set along a circular route that covered about forty miles. There was still only a thin dusting of snow on the ground but it was enough to verify his earlier fears. The snow showed few game trails. Most wildlife seemed swept from the face of the land. Only the beaver seemed to have survived and their numbers too were down from previous years. To set each beaver trap Joe Beaverskin had to chop laboriously through the steadily thickening ice, because beavers winter in their lodges and can be trapped only during their short feeding forays out under the ice. He would be away four days and three nights making the rounds of his traps. He would remain at the *askeekan* with the women for two or sometimes three days, and then start out for another circuit of the trapline. He traveled with the dogs and the sled, carrying a small tent and a tent stove which he set up each night.

At the main camp Kanina lifted the fish nets each day while her mother did the cooking and the chores around the lodge. Most of the rabbit snares had been taken up because Kanina could find no trails in which to set them.

For several weeks Joe Beaverskin's trapline produced at least one beaver each time he traveled it. Daisy would remove and stretch the pelt, then prepare the meat for the pot that always sat on the stove.

The days and nights grew colder. Kanina could only guess at the temperature but she thought, even on days when the overcast thinned and the sun shone through, that the temperature stayed below or close to zero. The severest nights were probably dropping to forty and fifty below. With no good fall of snow yet to cover the *askeekan,* its canvas snapped and thumped in the unflagging wind and its interior cooled off quickly whenever the fire burned low. Daisy Beaverskin slept soundly, immune to the cold, wearing the same clothing night and day. Kanina slept in her long-legged and long-sleeved woolen underwear, and she usually awoke shivering three or four times every night and had to build up the fire and warm the lodge before she could get back to sleep.

When she left in the morning to lift nets the cold froze the particles of moisture in her nostrils each time she inhaled, producing a tingle that instantly disappeared again when she exhaled. Her breath hung in a foggy cloud over her head and the moisture from it produced a white rime of frost on her eyelashes and along the rim of the parka that surrounded her face.

The cold continued, the snow stayed away, and one morning two of Kanina's nets were held fast under the ice and she could not pull them free. The other nets had no fish. When she returned and told her mother, Daisy Beaverskin just nodded languidly as if she already knew.

"The ice has given up calling for the snow," she said. "Now the ice is cold all through and it is freezing to the bottom. The nets freeze in and the fish go out to the lakes where there are deep holes and the ice cannot reach them."

Not until then did Kanina understand why her parents had been waiting so anxiously for snow. She had not realized that without a blanket of snow the creeks and beaver ponds could freeze to their bottoms.

When Kanina left the *askeekan* the following morning, her mother told her: "Bring in the nets that are not already frozen in, they will catch no more fish now."

Later that day Joe Beaverskin came in from his trapline and for the first time he brought no beaver with him. "They stay in the lodges," he said. "There is little room now for them to swim under the ice."

For three days after that they had dried goosemeat saved from the fall hunt. And then there was no meat left, there was only the store food —the flour, rolled oats, lard, sugar and tea.

The creek ice snapped and crackled again. "It still calls for the snow," Daisy Beaverskin said. And finally the snow came. For a night and a day and most of another night it fell until its humpy billows lay waist deep. The spruce branches bent earthward under its clinging weight. The creek ice cracked no more. But it had come too late.

CHAPTER FORTY-TWO

MARY MACDONALD had let more than a week of cold foggy weather pass without going back to check the barnacle goose flocks.

Finally she decided she must check them again regardless of the weather, and she set out late on a dark December afternoon when low clouds were racing in off the sea before a cold piercing wind. She lay again under the blanket and waited. There was no sunset, for the sky was mottled with black and gray, but the barnacle geese began arriving on their usual schedule.

At first when the flocks came slowly she was able to check each group as it flew in. Soon, however, they were pouring in faster than she could check them and she began studying the birds on the water instead. She moved the binoculars in a wide slow sweep covering the geese nearest her first, then making a return sweep to study the birds farther away. At the end of each sweep she would put the binoculars down briefly, rub her eyes to rest them, and then begin again.

It was on the second return sweep as she studied the geese far over toward Goose Island more than half a mile away that Mary thought she detected a flash of yellow. It was faint and she had moved the binoculars before it registered on her mind. She jerked them back, but now there was no sign of it. All the geese looked the same and after a few seconds of shifting the glasses back and forth she had lost track of where the yellow flash had appeared. She began to suspect that it had been imaginary.

Now she abandoned the methodical sweeps back and forth and concentrated on the general area where she thought she had seen the yellow. At any one time about three out of every four geese had heads submerged, feeding, and if the yellow neck streamer were actually out there, Mary knew it would be hidden underwater most of the time. Minutes passed. The gray light waned. The tantalizing uncertainty of it left Mary tense and trembling. The yellow she had seen, or thought she saw, was much too indistinct and fleeting to be the basis for any decision, yet the memory of it was clear enough for her to cling to the belief it *might* have been Rory's goose.

The clouds over the Atlantic were thickening and growing darker. She could see a gray sheet of rain moving in over the sea and she knew she should be seeking shelter. But while a chance remained of detecting that speck of yellow again she was held to the spot. If it *had* been Rory's barnacle, it might not return another night. Even if it did return, she might never find it again among the thousands of geese with necks submerged most of the time. And at least tonight she had a rough idea of the part of the sound in which to concentrate her search.

The rain moved nearer. Mary ignored it and kept her eyes on the geese. When she looked again at the sea the rain was a hissing wall almost upon her. Big drops hit first, pummeling the blanket like pebbles, then a few seconds later the downpour engulfed her. In a minute it soaked through the blanket and through her clothes, sticking the underclothing to her skin as though the rain were a cold viscid paste. She lay in a slight hollow because it had been easier to hide herself and the blanket there, and now the water flowed into it, forming a pool beneath and around her. She was trembling so violently with the cold it was hard to hold the binoculars, yet still she searched, watching, waiting. She would stay here, she pledged defiantly, as long as a spark of light remained.

When she saw it again there was no possibility of mistaking it. It was a brief glimpse, perhaps three or four seconds only, but for those few moments she saw it clearly. She was looking right at the barnacle when he lifted his head from the water. She saw the flicker of yellow in the shaky blur of the binoculars' field and instantly she brought her shivering body under control, the trembling ceased, she was holding the binoculars firmly and still. The yellow streamer hanging outward at a slight angle from the bird's neck, just as Rory said it would, was outlined sharply against the gray water. She saw it flutter briefly like a small flag as the barnacle shook the water from his feathers, and then the bird turned and it was gone. The goose plunged his head underwater again, other geese crowded around him and then she lost him and could not find him again.

Suddenly she was trembling more violently than before and she knew it was from excitement and not the cold. She had seen him! She had seen the goose that Rory had held in his own arms on James Bay in Canada's subarctic so far from Barra and this Goose Island Sound.

She looked once more but her eyes were so misted by tears that she couldn't hope to see the barnacle again. It didn't matter because the darkness came swiftly. And there was no doubt now.

She rose from beneath the blanket, cold and stiff and sore. Her sodden clothing clung to her body, the wind pierced it as soon as she stood up and only then did she realize the rain had stopped.

She began walking back, moving with stiff awkward strides which helped a little to keep the cold wet clothing away from her body. But the wind came in gusts and when it blew hard she could not prevent the clothing from wrapping like an icy sheath around her. She tried to walk fast but in the darkness kept wandering off the road and she finally had to slow down. She had walked this two-mile route countless times but never before had it seemed so long. Her teeth chattered violently. Her legs and arms became numb. The last half-mile between the MacNeill's and home seemed interminable. She kept stumbling and falling, and each time it was harder to rise again. When she reached the crest of the last ridge her strength was almost gone and the wind was like a battering-ram against her chest, driving her back before it. She dropped to the ground and started to crawl. Faintly, she could see the dim yellow square of their kitchen window. Sammy had left a lamp lit. She hoped he would be asleep.

She opened the door softly and stepped in. Sammy was in bed, snoring lustily. She slipped past him to her own room, pulled the wet clothing off quickly and rubbed herself dry with a towel. But the cold had penetrated deeply, her body was a livid blue and she could not stop the shivering that still convulsed her. She went to the kitchen and blew out the lamp. Then she went to bed and the shivering persisted for a long time.

Now she began thinking of the barnacle again, and her thoughts were mixed and confused. She was glad she had seen him because he seemed to have forged a new and very tangible link with Rory. The thought that Rory and the barnacle had spent the summer together, that Rory had actually held it in his arms, dominated her thinking and seemed peculiarly moving. Yet she felt a sadness too. Like Rory she had hoped that love would prevail over tradition to hold the barnacle with his North American mate. She was sorry that that strange bird romance on James Bay so far from Barra had had to end this way. And perhaps, she thought, she was a little sorrier than she might otherwise have been because of the fact that love had come once more into her own life.

She would write promptly tomorrow morning and tell Rory about her discovery. She would write to John Watt at the same time because John would be interested too.

The following morning she awoke with a sore throat and a harsh cough that pierced her chest with pain. Her shoulders and limbs ached. When she sat on the edge of the bed her head swam dizzily.

She dressed slowly because it was an effort and went out to the kitchen where Sammy had a fire started in the stove. She sank weakly into a chair by the table.

"Ye're sick," Sammy said.

"Yes, I'm catching a cold."

"Ye were out in the rain last nicht spyin' on the geese again."

"Yes. I saw Rory's goose. I saw the yellow neck streamer very clearly."

"I told ye. I told ye thet ye shouldna be spyin' on them. The rain and now the sickness o' ye, 'tis the geese havin' their revenge."

Mary was too weak and her throat too sore to argue with him. She drank a cup of tea but could eat no breakfast.

"I'll write to Rory and then I'm going back to bed," she told Sammy. Sammy left right after breakfast without telling her where he was going.

She wrote a brief letter to Rory telling him she had seen the barnacle and adding that she had got drenched in a rain squall while doing it. She concluded: "I am catching a cold and feel quite ill. The details about the barnacle must wait for another letter. I am now going back to bed."

John Watt's letter could be written later when she felt better. She marked Rory's letter "airmail" and left it in the mail box outside with postage money beside it. And then weak, dizzy, aching all over, she undressed and went to bed. The rats were chewing spasmodically behind the wallpaper. The ropes that served for springs on her bed cut painfully into the sore throbbing muscles of her back.

CHAPTER FORTY-THREE

IT had been a troubled uneasy autumn for Rory.

He had returned to Toronto in September with a mind rendered tired and sluggish by the burden of the decision he had made. And P.L. had been no help in easing it.

"It's good to see you back," the professor said at their first meeting. And then, immediately, he had begun probing the pain and heartbreak. "For a while," he continued, "I was wondering whether you'd ever get back. I was afraid you'd be shacking up with her in one of those wigwams for the rest of your life."

Rory knew that P.L. was fishing for information. And what Rory wanted more than anything else was a chance to begin forgetting.

"It's good to be back again," Rory said, recognizing it instantly as a lie. They were in Rory's room. Rory went on unpacking his luggage and P.L. puffed slowly on his pipe.

"Well don't be so mysterious," the professor blurted finally. "What did you do about it?"

"It's all over. Both of us agreed that anything else was impossible. I'm going to notify the wildlife service I won't be available to go back there next summer."

"I knew *she'd* be smart enough to see it that way." P.L. blew a thick cloud of smoke and squinted through it at Rory. "But I had some doubts about you."

Rory didn't want to talk about it. It brought it all back too vividly—

the beach on Kishamooskek, the dimples, the hair, the way her sweater clung to her when she raised her arms to untie the shawl.

"How did your problem work out? The birds?" Rory asked.

P.L. was as anxious to talk about this as Rory was reluctant to talk about the other. The professor began talking rapidly.

"I wired the building superintendent as soon as I reached Moosonee on the plane that day. He agreed to hold off the fumigation until I arrived. We had a meeting as soon as I got here and he gave me a week to move the birds out. I told him it was impossible, all my equipment is set up there, the calorimeter, the time switch for the lights. I told him it was developing into one of the most important research projects of its type on the continent. But he wasn't impressed, just kept insisting the birds had to get out. Then I found out what was really at the bottom of it all. A new head janitor . . . . he's got delusions of grandeur . . . . thinks he needs an office . . . . to keep his brooms in, I guess. Last spring he moved into a little room directly above the bird room and I understand he's been complaining to the building superintendent ever since that the noise of the birds is driving him crazy. Stupid bastard. Probably crazy to begin with.

"Well anyway," P.L. went on, "when I learned that was all there was to it, I decided it was too petty a matter to take higher up. Decided I'd take care of it myself. So I told them all to go to hell and I went out and bought the biggest padlock I could find. It cost me fourteen dollars and it's as big as a football. I hired a carpenter one Sunday when no one was around and we bolted a hasp on the door big enough to stop a truck. Now they couldn't get in if they hired a safecracker. Haven't heard a peep from the building superintendent or a janitor since."

Anxious as Rory was to trace the winter movements of the barnacle goose and his Canada goose mate, he found it difficult to concentrate even on this. He had been back in Toronto two weeks before he got around to drafting the letter requesting winter reports of the birds. He described the pairing of the barnacle and the female Canada on Kishamooskek Lake. Then he described the yellow neck streamers and gave the numbers of the aluminum leg bands. He and P.L. had about fifty copies mimeographed and mailed them out to universities, state game departments and game refuges throughout the Mississippi valley. Then they began waiting eagerly for news.

Rory forced himself to overcome the inertia that oppressed him and he began work on his Canada goose report for the fish and wildlife service in Ottawa. It was a big job and for weeks now his room remained cluttered with maps, graphs and notes. University classes resumed early in October, his goose report was slowly taking shape, but despite the concentration it all demanded his mind also remained constantly on Kanina Beaverskin.

Fall changed slowly to early winter. There were no reports yet of the barnacle and his mate. Early in December the winter's first light snow-falls dusted down from the slaty sky. Often, late at night after he had worked several hours on the goose report, he would go out for a walk before going to bed, slipping out of the house silently so as not to attract P.L. Outdoors, alone in the frosty night with only his own thoughts she seemed to come closer. The snow would crunch crisply under his tread and the cold would bite through his clothing and he would think of her sleeping on her balsam bed with only the sagging canvas of the tent roof to shield her from the bitter Arctic air. Often he found himself thinking of the iniquity and injustices wrought by the feeble distorted minds of men. And at these times he hated himself for being a party to those injustices, yet he knew he could do nothing else.

He finished the goose research report, about twenty thousand words of it, in mid-December and mailed it to Ottawa, recommending that the work be continued in the same Cape Cree region another summer. In his accompanying letter he said that "because of other commitments" he would not be available to carry on another summer of the research himself. Cape Cree had become the one spot in the world to which Rory Macdonald must never return. But he wasn't sorry he had gone there, he wasn't sorry it had happened. Some day, years hence, he would forget, but for now he would not want to go on living without those happy, painful, bittersweet memories of Kanina Beaverskin.

Rory had no commitments, he did not even have a spare-time job for the winter, and now that his report was finished he needed one. But events were crowding rapidly and violently into this critical period of Rory Macdonald's life, and his job-hunting was postponed.

The day after he mailed his goose report was a Saturday. He and P.L. were home, and that morning Rory received the letter from his mother telling him she had seen the James Bay barnacle back in Goose Island Sound.

It had been necessary from the outset to take into account the possibility the barnacle might return to Barra and Rory had brought his mother into the project to cover that possibility. But he had done it for scientific thoroughness, not because he had any belief that the barnacle would abandon his mate. Now for the first shocked minute he refused to believe it. But it was only for a minute. He read the letter again and it was admittedly brief with few corroborating details. But she had told him in previous letters that she had bought binoculars and Rory decided there could be no possibility of her having made an error. He did not want to believe it, but there could be no doubting it.

Rory stared out the window. Slowly the implications of it sank in. The barnacle had tried it and had failed and now he was starting all over again, even though it had meant finding his way back across an ocean to do so. And Rory was sorry because he had wanted the barnacle to do what he himself had refused to do.

But slowly Rory's disappointment gave way to a feeling of reassurance. Ever since that August morning when the overladen Beaverskin canoe took Kanina up the Kistawanee and out of his life, Rory had felt an embarrassing guilt whenever he thought of the barnacle defiantly facing a new and forbiddingly different life to stay with the mate he had chosen. And now, here was proof that he had not stayed with her. Now Rory felt more certain than ever that his decision regarding Kanina was the correct and only one.

Rory took the letter in to P.L.'s room.

"The barnacle has got back to Barra," Rory said simply. "My mother has seen him."

He handed him the letter. P.L. read it, his brow bobbing excitedly.

"Well," the professor said, shrugging his thick shoulders, "this *will* be interesting information for the homing and migration investigators. This sort of thing has never been proven before. But the romanticists, and you're one of them . . . . I suppose this is hard to take, eh? All those pretty ideas about loyalty and love until death us doth part. Exploded . . . . gone . . . . all shot to hell. What do you think of it now?"

"I'm sorry," Rory said. "I feel as though that barnacle has let me down. He's proven that geese are as fickle as men. And I expected more from him."

They discussed it for half an hour and then Rory remembered suddenly that in his excitement he had forgotten that the letter also said his mother was sick. He left P.L. and returned to his room. He checked the date of the letter; it was written five days ago. He must write and airmail a reply at once because if she were spending much time in bed she would be getting little care or sympathy from his father. She would need cheering up.

He wrote a long letter and the landlady was calling them for lunch by the time he completed it.

They had finished eating but he and P.L. were still seated at the dining room table when the doorbell rang. Rory went to the door. It was a telegraph company messenger boy.

"Overseas cable for Mr. Rory Macdonald," the boy said.

Rory signed for it and closed the door. He opened the envelope and read it there. Then he went upstairs silently, leaving P.L. alone in the dining room. He closed the door of his room and then let the tears come. Through misted eyes he read the eight words again:

"Your mother died last night of pneumonia. Dad."

CHAPTER FORTY-FOUR

FOR the first crushing distraught minutes Rory had no clear or rational thoughts, and then as the initial shock of it passed and he remembered her letter of that morning, the realization came suddenly that he was responsible for his mother's death. The knowledge was more distressing than the first tragic news itself. Now to his sadness there was added an oppressive burden of remorse and guilt.

He had persuaded her to stay in Barra. And now she had died—looking for a goose. Suddenly the whole barnacle goose project seemed to crumble into trivial insignificance, and it left him with a bitter, harrowing disgust. He had thought it was a scientific problem, but now he saw that primarily it was only a self-indulgent and sentimental curiosity inspired by his childhood nostalgia for the barnacles, made more acute by the hopeless love for Kanina Beaverskin that had come into his life at the same time. He had recognized from the beginning that the barnacle-tracing project had little real scientific significance. That was the reason he had been afraid to write to the wildlife service in Ottawa for assistance and had written to P.L. instead.

Rory lay on his bed and stared at the ceiling and now his eyes were dry. He heard P.L. come up the stairs and enter the other room.

Rory could see it all now in its stark and naked simplicity, shorn of the aura of sentiment and emotionalism with which his romantic mind had invested it. And when all that sentimental effervescence was removed, there was not much left. An Old World goose was storm-blown across the Atlantic; it tried to pair with a goose of another species; migration time came and the Old World goose flew back home. And for that trivial contribution to the science of bird behavior, his mother had died!

He had been away from his mother more than eight years but any effect this should have had in helping him adjust to the fact of her death was more than offset by the tremendous guilt he felt at having caused it. Rory's world seemed to have tumbled in ruins around him but he began at once the process of putting it back together again by going in and telling P.L. After the first expression of sympathy there was nothing P.L. could add. In a couple of minutes the silence was embarrassing to both of them and Rory returned to his own room.

Suddenly he felt a sharp wish that he had Kanina to talk to. No embarrassing silence would come between them, because of all the people he knew, Kanina was the only one capable of understanding the type of person his mother had been.

Rory opened the letter he had written to his mother that morning and began rereading it. "You have done a splendid and thorough job checking the barnacle flocks for me," he had written. "The mystery is answered, although the answer is one I am sorry for, because I expected and hoped that the barnacle would remain with his mate. It is another proof that in scientific research one cannot afford to have preconceived notions about desired or expected results. . . ." They were distressing, hateful words now and Rory could read no farther. He dropped the letter into his wastepaper basket but after a minute he decided that he couldn't destroy it. He picked it up again and put it in a drawer.

Then he wrote a brief letter of sympathy to his father. Sammy would find someone to read it to him.

Rory went back to university as usual on Monday but the guilt feeling lay heavily on him and it was hard to concentrate on lectures. He walked the two miles home, as he usually did when he had time on his hands and the burden of unresolved decisions on his mind. He was early and there was still an hour or more before dinner. He took off his shoes and tie and lay down on the bed. Alone again, the guilt and remorse settled like a black cloud over him, and his confused mind began the task of reassessing a life that seemed suddenly to have acquired a new outlook and a new set of values.

He had killed his mother, yet she would be the last one to expect him to burden his life with a useless penance. She had been as eager as he that Rory's ambitious plans for his future be realized. It was she who had planted the seeds of that ambition and had nurtured them diligently through the years of youth on Barra. So now it had become more vital than ever that he mold that future into something of which his mother could be proud, it was an obligation rendered more pressing by her death and his involvement in it.

He had already overcome one great threat to that future when he refused to consider a marriage with Kanina Beaverskin. And now that the barnacle project had been recognized as a tragic farce, he began to see the new threat being revealed there. It was hard at first even to consider the thought. But it pressed on his mind relentlessly. It would not be ignored. Should he be in biology at all? Was it all a mistake?

His and his mother's love for the barnacles was a childish sentimental thing, he was sure of it now. Did he love everything about biology too much to make a career, a life's work, out of it? Yes, he was too sentimental about it to approach it in the cold pragmatic way one should approach a career. The barnacle episode had proven it. It was a good hobby, but in Rory's case a poor choice as a profession. Play and work do not mix. P.L. was a pathetic and unpleasant example of what this could produce. Rory recognized now that his love for biology could become a handicap, interfering with the advancement that his success-drive, his ambition, demanded.

He heard P.L. come in and enter his room. A few moments later the professor was rapping softly on Rory's door.

"Come in."

P.L., wearing only trousers and an undershirt, stepped in and stood just inside the door.

"I was glad to see you back at university today," P.L. said slowly. "I guess it wasn't easy. But grieving over these things never accomplishes anything."

"That's what I decided," Rory said. "And it *wasn't* easy. I blame myself. I let myself get so excited over that barnacle. And that's what killed her. All for nothing. There was little scientific importance or value to it. We should have guessed he'd find his way back home to Barra."

P.L. was suddenly stiff and frowning. "My God, man!" he declared. "It *did* have value. It has given us an answer to a question never answered definitely before. You're going to write a paper on it for one of the journals, surely?"

"It's not worth it. I'm going to forget about it."

P.L. walked across and settled wearily in a chair. "You're a stupid, erratic, emotional thinker," he began slowly. "You're always loving and hating the wrong people. Loving Indian squaws. . . ." He shrugged his thick shoulders and made an impatient palms-up gesture with his hands. "And now you're hating yourself, for no purpose."

They stared at each other silently for several seconds, then Rory looked away self-consciously and began to talk.

"I'm beginning to wonder," he said, "whether biology is a good choice for me. I'm too much in love with it to work at it. I'd spend my life playing at it, getting nowhere, doing the romantic things, like tracing that barnacle, instead of doing the important things."

P.L. raised his hand impatiently. "Okay, stop right there!" he said. "You've had a bad time the last couple of days, in fact ever since last summer when you met that little brown-eyed wench and had to leave her. You're incapable of deciding anything now. Blaming yourself for your mother's death! Stupid! Wondering if biology is the proper field for you . . . . wondering now, after you have five years of your life invested in it! You love it too much! God, man, you've got to love your work to accomplish anything in it. We need scientists and you'll be a good one. You can't throw it all away now. There's a lot of work to be done in biology, and we're just getting started. . . .

"My work with the sparrows," the professor said hesitantly, "it's getting to a critical stage. More work than I can handle. I have just had another grant approved, enough to finance everything until the research is completed next spring. I was going to hire a student assistant. Well . . . . twenty-five dollars a week, say. Do you want the job?"

Rory knew that P.L. had dreamed up the job as a device to keep Rory in the biology fold. There was probably no grant; if Rory took the job, P.L. would be paying him out of his own pocket.

"Thanks, but no," Rory said immediately. "I'm going to look around in business and see what prospects there are for a career outside biology."

But Rory's decision was far from final and he postponed the job-hunting. For two days he found excuses that would keep him downtown late so that he need not meet P.L. at dinner. He *was* deeply committed in biology to abandon it all now; maybe he should accept P.L.'s offer. On the third day he was still undecided but he was ready again to talk to P.L., and after the day's final lecture he walked down to the zoology building basement. But Rory sensed that something was wrong as soon as he reached the dim corridor that had P.L.'s bird room at its far end. The corridor was silent; there was no chattering chorus of bird chirpings.

As he drew near the door that still bore its red-crayoned sign: "Keep Out, Especially Janitors," he could smell the sharp familiar odor of bird excrement but the silence was an ominous pervading thing. He knocked on the door. There was no answer. It was unlocked so he opened it and walked in.

The room was very cold and it was filled with natural daylight instead of its customary artificial lighting. The three narrow windows near the ceiling which had always been darkened with black paper were wide open. The wire cages piled around the room's three walls were all open and the sparrows were gone from every cage. Rory looked quickly at the cage that stood apart near P.L.'s desk—the cage that had always contained Turdy, the pet robin. It too was open and Turdy was gone. P.L., who usually arrived about this time, was not here. The room, Rory thought, though it was cluttered with books and equipment, seemed filled with a grim and haunting emptiness.

Rory looked around, momentarily startled yet not really surprised. If there was anything to be surprised at, Rory thought, it was the fact that this had not happened months ago. P.L. had had plenty of warning. He saw the overcoat and the vivid sport jacket of green and brown plaid lying in a heap across the desk, indicating that P.L. had already been here.

Rory turned and walked out slowly. As he went back through the door he noticed that the big padlock lay on the floor still intact but the staple through which it locked had been cut away with a hacksaw. This would be an appalling catastrophe for P.L. yet Rory could feel little sympathy for him. It was P.L.'s fault.

Rory stepped outside and he heard the plaintive pleading calls immediately.

"Turdy, Turdy. Here, Turdy. Come now, Turdy girl."

It was P.L.'s voice, but there was a desperate quivering anguish in it that made the voice almost unrecognizable. It came from the side of the building. Rory went around toward it.

He saw P.L. when he reached the building's corner. The professor was lying flat in the snow, in shirt sleeves, hatless, a butterfly net poised over his bald head. About six feet in front of him there was grain and baby chick feed sprinkled on the snow and four sparrows hopped around the edge of it feeding timidly. Rory could see the tiny aluminum bands on their legs. They were apparently all that remained of his hundred-odd experimental sparrows. But P.L. ignored them, for standing in the snow some twenty feet from him, was Turdy, the robin. The red-breasted bird stood with her head turned saucily sideways, staring at P.L. but making no move to come nearer.

"Here, Turdy. Nice girl, Turdy. You can't stay out in the snow all night. You had pneumonia once, you almost died, you'll catch it again. You stupid little bastard."

Rory stood by the corner of the building unable to decide whether P.L.'s actions were pathetic or disgusting. Then P.L. saw him.

"Stay back! Stay back, Rory! Don't alarm her. She's very high strung."

Rory waited. Turdy just stood staring comically at P.L. And P.L. was shivering violently in the snow.

"I'd better get your coat," Rory said, "or *you'll* be catching pneumonia."

"No! No! I came out in my shirt sleeves purposely. Come on, Turdy. Come, girl. This is the way she always sees me—in shirt sleeves. She wouldn't recognize me in a coat."

The bird took two hesitant hops toward P.L. and then stopped again.

"Here, Turdy. Here, Turdy."

And then she flew. She flew in a circle around them first, seeming to revel in her new freedom, and then as she felt the power in wings that had been denied full expression before, she flew higher and straight away across the university campus. P.L. jumped to his feet and began chasing her.

"Turdy, come back here! Here, Turdy."

There was a frantic desperation in his voice, almost hysteria, but he was such a short, ludicrous figure scurrying across the snow in shirt sleeves, the butterfly net waving wildly, that Rory had to smile. Rory ran after him, his long easy strides quickly overtaking P.L.'s.

"What happened?" he asked.

"The janitors, I guess. Stupid bastards." P.L. was breathing hard.

Turdy was faintly visible in the fading light, perched in a bush far across the campus.

"I can't let her get away!" P.L. exclaimed, puffing violently but still running. "She was counting to four again."

Rory slowed to a walk and dropped behind him. P.L., his thinly clad shoulders swaying, ran on ahead. The man was a fool. He should have known it would end this way. He had been bullheaded and childish about it from the beginning. Instead of reasoning with them, he had been belligerent and defiant. Instead of getting it all officially approved at the top, as he could easily have done, he had insisted on handling it alone. He had asked for everything.

Rory left him then and began walking out toward the streetcar stop. He looked back before he left the campus. Only P.L.'s white shirt and butterfly net were visible in the rapidly dropping dusk, but the professor's

voice quavering with misery and heartache came across the campus clear
and sharp still.

"Turdy. Come, girl. Come now, Turdy."

Rory turned away with an irritation bordering on disgust. Was that,
Rory wondered, a picture of his own future as a biologist? He shuddered
at the prospect and he thought that now his decision was made. Any
small doubts that remained were harshly dispelled as soon as he reached
home. Waiting for him on the hall table just inside the door was a letter
from his father:

> Dear Rory:
>
> Peggy Sutherland who used to be Peggy MacNeill is sitting here
> beside me writing my letter to you which I am telling her what to
> write. It is sad for us that your mother is dead but I fear she had
> to be struck down like the Bible says for her sins. She got all wet
> and cold that last night when she went looking for that goose you
> have wrote to her about. Tis a terrible thing that goose and you tell-
> ing her to look for the goose is what made her die. She seen the
> rain storm coming but she stayed out in it to see your goose. I told
> her she must not spy on the geese with her spy glasses or they would
> bring evil upon her but she kept on spying on them. So they brought
> the rain onto her when they knew she was there spying on them. But
> Rory now we know the geese did not want to kill her they just tried
> to make her stop spying. Yes Rory your mother was struck down by
> the God above her for her terrible sins not just for spying on the
> geese. Rory it is hard to tell you about your mother what I have to
> tell you. Before she died when she could hardly breathe no more
> she kept talking and she did not know what she was saying. She
> kept crying and talking to somebody the name of John. And Rory a
> letter came after she was dead. Peggy read it. The letter was from
> Glasgow from John Watt. We do not know who is John Watt but
> he was her lover and she was going to Glasgow, that we know.
> Your mother was an evil woman and unfaithful wife to me.
>
> Your father,
> Sammy Macdonald

Rory read the confused and taunting sentences again and again. There
was no question but that the search for his barnacle had caused his
mother's death. But now the circumstances of her death were over-
shadowed by the mystery of her life. Rory had known for months that
she intended to return to Glasgow but he had never had the remotest
suspicion there might be another man in her plans. It was hard to think
of his mother as having a lover.

But why had she married his father? Who was John Watt? Inquiries in Glasgow would probably produce at least partial answers, but Rory knew he would never launch the inquiries. He had caused her death; he must let the strange secret of her life die with her. But one important fact was clear. His mother too, apparently, had found it necessary to marry someone other than the person she loved.

P.L. did not come in that night for dinner and it was dinnertime the following night before Rory saw him again. In the meantime Rory had applied at the university employment office, had had an interview with an employer downtown and had accepted an evening and week-end job. It was going to be hard to tell P.L.

The professor sat opposite him, a comic childlike figure, eating in silence. Finally Rory spoke.

"Any luck?" he asked.

"She's gone," P.L. answered in a voice barely audible. "The sparrows too, but they're replaceable. Turdy wasn't. Turdy was a genius." Then he lifted his eyes quickly and continued: "But that job, Rory. The offer still stands, of course. I'll be getting more sparrows and start it again. Those janitors can't stop me!"

Rory looked at him, wondering how he could ever have admired the man. P.L. had learned nothing. He was still going to blunder on in the same bullheaded defiant way.

"I have a job," Rory said slowly. "Nights and week-ends for now. I'll finish my year and write off the M.A. but I don't want to work in biology. I'll be joining the firm full-time in June. It's not too late for me to start at the beginning again and build a new career."

"What is it?" P.L. asked him.

"A new firm called Northwoods Enterprises," Rory continued slowly, "a big real estate outfit developing a colony of summer mansions up north in the woods. They say they need a biologist . . . . it's a huge scheme. It'll have its own airport, fifty- and hundred-thousand-dollar homes . . . . no millionaires allowed, only multimillionaires."

P.L.'s brow began bobbing up and down. "What do they want you for?"

"It's virgin country . . . . bush, lakes. Someone in the company decided that being northwoods and all that, they should have a forester or biologist on the planning staff."

"But what in hell do they want *you* to do?"

Rory hadn't intended to go into it in detail. P.L.'s probing questions were embarrassing him.

"They want me to do a wildlife survey and then tell them how to turn the area into streets, lawns, airports and golf courses without disturbing the wildlife. They say the development will have all the luxuries of city life in a wild and undisturbed northwoods setting. I understand *their* idea of an undisturbed northwoods setting is to leave a few trees standing, have tame deer running all over the place, and put in some ponds for swans and flamingos."

P.L. shrugged. "For God's sake! Tycoons think of everything. They need a biologist about as much as they need an astronomer. They're doing it for show . . . . another sales gimmick. So they can advertise 'Hey look, all you wealthy stupid clods! We provide gardeners to manage your gardens, and an expert biologist to manage the natural garden around you.'"

"I know it's a farce," Rory said impatiently. "But it's an opportunity to use my biology to establish myself in the business world. It's a big diversified organization with plenty of opportunity for advancement. Right now they need me as a biologist. They said there would be something better later on."

"Better!" P.L. exclaimed. "Biology has bigger jobs for you fellows to do . . . . pushing back the frontiers of man's knowledge, broadening the scientific understanding of our environment . . . . the foundation our industrial civilization is built on. You *can't* go out prostituting good scientific training, using it to sell real estate for money-mad tycoons!"

"I can. And I am. That barnacle taught me an important lesson. I wasn't meant to be a biologist."

"You've been acting like a neurotic fool ever since you met that little squaw." P.L. had finished eating and he was on his feet, his brow and hair line bobbing angrily again. "Northwoods setting . . . . with flamingos imported from Florida! The stupid bastards! And if you get mixed up with a crowd like that you'll be a stupid bastard too!"

There were moments during the next few days in which Rory questioned the wisdom of his decision. And then he received the news that banished the last small doubts. It was a letter from the Illinois State Department of Conservation. A Canada goose with a yellow neck band had been seen among the thousands of other Canadas at the Horseshoe Lake refuge on the Mississippi in southern Illinois. The goose stayed apart from other geese and appeared unmated, the letter said. There was no barnacle goose with her.

It was a mocking and anticlimactic reminder of the Cape Cree summer and of his mother's death. It opened again the galling wound of self-reproach and regret. He began looking forward to June when he would be able to join Northwoods Enterprises full-time, putting biology and all the heartbreak it had caused permanently behind him.

CHAPTER FORTY-FIVE

ONCE and sometimes twice each decade a mysterious death sweeps across the hunting grounds of the *Mooskek-owak,* cutting the game population to a tiny fraction of what it is in peak years, and starvation stalks the land's meat-eaters. Wolves and foxes grow gaunt and range far in their search for food. Of all the meat-eaters, the *Mooskek-owak* themselves fare best because they can extend their hunt into waters under the ice where there are usually beaver and fish.

But occasionally a winter of late snowfall will coincide with a winter of game shortage. Rivers and lakes, lacking the snow's insulation, freeze deeply and make it difficult to catch beaver and fish. Then the *Mooskek-owak,* too, face famine. Hunger they accept as a part of every winter, but hunger prolonged becomes starvation and it is not easy to say where one terminates and the other begins.

The *Mooskek-owak* who are not far inland move out to the trading posts where they get Hudson's Bay Company credit or government relief. But for families far inland there is a hard decision. It is difficult to travel and hunt at the same time; they cannot set fish nets when they are traveling every day. Often the wintering camp seems to offer the best chance of surviving until the spring geese come and the famine suddenly and dramatically ends. So they wait and hope. And sometimes they wait too long.

That winter the Beaverskins waited. After Christmas Kanina lost track of the days, but many weeks had passed and she thought it must now be getting near mid-February.

It was early morning and she sat on her bed watching her mother prepare the morning meal. Daisy Beaverskin moved slowly, her moccasined feet scuffing the earthen floor, her old vigor gone. Her skirt hung in bulging folds and was glossy with grease. Since she slept in it too, there were tufts of goose feathers from the quilts clinging to the skirt's grease patches. Joe Beaverskin was not there. He had left the day before to hunt and he had not come back to the *askeekan* for the night.

Kanina looked into the pot simmering on the little stove. Entrails and a fish head with glassy eyes still intact protruded from the broth. It was a fish Kanina had netted the day before, the first in four days. A few months ago she would have viewed this with horror but now it seemed unthinkable to throw entrails or fish heads away; now nothing could nauseate her and she waited hungrily. Daisy Beaverskin added three cupfuls of oatmeal for thickening. Kanina watched it go into the pot with a cold clutching shiver of fear but her mother remained stoically indifferent.

"It is the last of the oatmeal," Kanina said.

"Yes, it is the last," Daisy Beaverskin answered.

Weeks before, Joe Beaverskin had taken up the last of his traps not frozen into the ice. He had then helped Kanina reset nets in a small lake a mile below camp where ice could not freeze to the bottom. They had worked four days getting the nets back into the water because it had required digging with snowshoes through thigh-deep snow and then chopping through a yard or more of ice. Kanina tended them with a visit each day while her father went back to hunting.

For six weeks they had had only a fish or two every day and at much less frequent intervals a rabbit or partridge from Joe Beaverskin's gun, to be shared among three people and two dogs. Now for the last week the fishing had dropped to practically nothing, a warning that their small lake was being fished out. There had been no attempt to ration the store food despite Kanina's repeated suggestions that they do so, because Joe Beaverskin, like a losing dice player confident his luck will change with the next roll, went out on every new hunt feeling certain it would produce a moose or caribou that would feed them for the rest of the winter.

Tea, sugar and now the oatmeal were gone. Only a few pounds of lard remained, and six inches or so of flour at the bottom of the last flour sack.

Their stew had cooked and Kanina and her mother were eating when Joe Beaverskin came in. The hood of his parka was ringed with frost and the wide dark face it outlined was solemn and impassive. He carried only a flat dry bone to which a few frozen shreds of meat still clung. Kanina recognized it as the shoulder blade of a caribou from a recent wolf kill. It meant there *was* big game in the region still, but it also meant there were wolves competing with her father for it, and in a land gripped by famine a starving wolf pack is fierce and resourceful competition for the remnant of flesh-food that remains.

Kanina watched curiously as her father laid the bone on the top of the stove. Now her parents stood stiff and unmoving, staring at the bone with eyes that seemed suddenly paralyzed, their breath short and quick and catching huskily in their throats. The bone moistened as the frost thawed out of it. Shreds of meat on it blackened and began to smoke. Then the moisture dried and the bone whitened. Suddenly it cracked with a sharp snap, the crack twisting diagonally across the width of the bone.

The faces of her parents suddenly brightened. Daisy Beaverskin was smiling, showing again for the first time in days the yawning gaps in her teeth. Joe Beaverskin crouched, sighting along the crack in the bone. Then suddenly he was on his feet and grabbing his gun and disappearing out the door.

"What does it mean?" Kanina asked her mother.

"It is a good sign!" Daisy Beaverskin answered. Her Cree words, normally soft and musical, had become strident now with excitement. "It points the way to game. A small crack says the game is distant. A long wide crack means the game is big and fat and is waiting near."

"It is stupid," Kanina said. "How can a bone know where game is?"

"It has the spirit of the animal still in it," Daisy Beaverskin said patiently. "It knows where its brothers are."

"Then why does it point them out to the hunter who wants to kill them?"

"The spirit doesn't want them killed. It always points in the opposite direction to fool the hunter, but the wise hunter knows this and hunts in the direction that is opposite to where the bone has pointed. The white man's schools didn't teach you these things because they are things only the *Mooskek-owak* know."

Suddenly Kanina began to cry softly.

"We have eaten our food faster than we needed to," she said. "It is almost gone. And now we are trusting in signs that are not true. This way we will surely starve."

But Daisy Beaverskin was still smiling confidently.

"There will be much food in the *askeekan* soon," she said. "We will eat moose or caribou three times every day until the *niskuk* fly again."

Joe Beaverskin was back in less than an hour. He walked into camp hastily, snowshoes swishing in the dry snow, a happy grin rippling his cheeks.

"I have found the caribou trail," he said. "It is near and it is fresh, just yesterday he passed."

Daisy Beaverskin turned to Kanina and nodded with shining I-told-you-so eyes. Joe Beaverskin drank several cups of the fish stew and then began hastily preparing to leave camp again. Into his tattered packsack he put two quilts, an axe and cooking pail. He emptied half the remaining flour into a small bag, dropped two fist-sized chunks of lard on top of the flour, and put this in the pack too. He flung the packsack onto his back and picked up his gun. Then he went outside, stepped into his snowshoes and quickly disappeared into the black wall of spruce behind the camp. He did not look back, nor did he say goodbye.

Kanina knew he would stay on the caribou trail for days, for a week if necessary, following it relentlessly, sleeping beside it every night, slowly closing in until he could make the kill. To travel silently he was leaving the dogs and sled behind, and this meant leaving his tent and stove behind too. He would sleep each night in a snow-hole floored and roofed with balsam boughs. He would eat bannock, nothing else, because even if small game appeared he would not risk a shot that might frighten the caribou.

Daisy Beaverskin was jubilant. "Soon we will have much meat," she said. "Soon you will be able to stop lifting the fish nets. Bah! I am tired of fish."

There were no fish in the nets that day and when Kanina got back to the camp in mid-afternoon Daisy took her out and showed her where to dig with a snowshoe for mosses and Labrador tea. Daisy was casual, almost gay about it, but Kanina knew that these were the *Mooskek-owak* starvation foods, the last desperate resort when all other food sources fail.

For four days now there were no fish and they lived on the pasty brownish gruel of mosses thickened with flour and lard. Yellow ribbons of grease twisted through it. It contained fleshy bits of black leaves, bitter and gritty with sand. Without meat, it didn't appease for long and the squeezing pains of hunger in Kanina's stomach were almost permanently with her.

But on the fifth day there was a large pike in one of the nets. The dogs chained behind the camp smelled the fish and whined plaintively when Kanina arrived with it. Daisy knew the meaning of their whining and she came excitedly to the *askeekan* door to meet Kanina.

"We must give some of it to the dogs," Kanina said. "They have had no food for days."

But Daisy shook her head vigorously. "There will be much food for the dogs when your father returns," she said.

The last of their flour and lard went into the fish stew. Daisy put it in without comment. That night Kanina lay on her balsam bed feeling well fed for the first time in several days, but the constant whining of the dogs troubled her and she could not sleep. Her mother was snoring softly and finally Kanina rose and pulled on her moccasins and parka. From the congealed stew she took the head and tail sections of the fish and stepped outside. The cold air cut sharply into her nostrils as she walked around to where the dogs were chained and threw a piece of fish to each of them. They were pathetically small morsels of food, she thought, and each dog snapped up its piece and swallowed it in a second or two. For a moment she was tempted to release them because hunting for themselves they would at least obtain more food than they were getting now. But it was only a fleeting thought, for hunting dogs would quickly kill off or frighten away any game that remained. The dogs stood in the dim light, tails wagging, dark eyes pleading. Kanina could not face them. She turned guiltily away.

She paused at the *askeekan* door, the cold biting through her clothing. Somewhere out there where the jagged forest skyline met the dancing green fingers of the aurora borealis a crucial contest was being decided, a simple elemental contest in which one contestant would have to die that the other might live. This was her father's fifth night on the caribou trail. It was a long time to be in the forest without shelter and with only bannock for a murmuring, pleading stomach. And these muskeg lands hid many skeletons of *Mooskek-owak* hunters who had lost such contests before. Kanina trembled, from cold or fear—she did not know—and went inside and built up the fire and went back to bed.

As soon as Daisy Beaverskin looked at the stew pot next morning she noticed that the pieces of fish were missing.

"You took food in the night," she said, turning sharply to Kanina.

"I took it for the dogs," Kanina said.

Daisy's sharp look of accusation suddenly went but a sternness remained. "It does no good," she said. "A little food only teases them and makes the hunger worse."

Kanina had no hunger pains that day because some fish stew remained. Every hour or so Daisy would step outside and listen, with only a thin tightening of her lips to indicate the anxiety that Kanina knew her mother was beginning to feel. It had been six days now.

Another day dawned. There was only moss for the stew pot once more and the hunger pangs returned. Kanina was chopping wood in the darkening afternoon when she saw her father staggering slowly along the creek ice, his shoulders stooped, arms hanging limply at his sides. Kanina called to her mother. They went out to the creek bank to meet him.

Joe Beaverskin came toward them without looking up. When he started up the little creek bank he stumbled and fell but rose immediately. Kanina ran down to help him. She took the packsack off his back and dropped it in the snow. She took his arm and he leaned against her, a heavy lifeless weight. And then she saw his face and stared at it with a shock that was almost horror. The familiar round plumpness was gone, cheek and jaw bones protruded and his lips were pulled in against his teeth. His eyes were bloodshot and seemed to have retreated into his skull. The skin looked as if it had been removed and shrunken and then drawn back over a framework too large for it. Only the wide flat nose remained the same.

When they reached the top Kanina went back for his packsack. They filed silently into the *askeekan*. There was only a cold mush of moss in the stew pot and Daisy put it on the stove to warm. But Joe Beaverskin did not wait, he dipped into the pot with a cup and began drinking it immediately. Then he unfastened his packsack, took out the bag that had held his flour and emptied it into one of the wooden food boxes. An assortment of bones, shreds of caribou hide and frozen chunks of white entrails clattered into the box. The bones were gnawed and broken. There was half a jaw with the teeth still in it and one black hoof. Here and there were finger-sized shreds of red meat.

"The wolves killed him first," Joe Beaverskin said. "When I got there this was all."

A cold strangling panic seized Kanina. This was the food that was to have fed them until the geese returned again—a grisly mess of carrion that even the wolves would not eat.

CHAPTER FORTY-SIX

THEY were having another thaw. Outside, the sunlight on the snow was blinding and the light even here inside the *askeekan* was bright after the long dark days of what had seemed an endless winter. The first midday thaw had come several days before and now this was the second one. Above the bubbling murmur of the stew pot Kanina could hear water dripping like fairy footsteps outside and occasionally there was a sloshy plop of sun-loosened snow dropping from a spruce branch. It must be well into April, Kanina thought.

They waited without speaking, their eyes returning to the kettle on the stove. Kanina and her father were sitting but Daisy was lying on her bough bed with a quilt over her. Joe Beaverskin dipped a cup into the steaming broth and put it on the floor to cool. It had been boiling only a few minutes and the skunk meat in it was only beginning to cook, but Joe Beaverskin could wait no longer. Kanina dipped up a cupful, let it cool for a few moments and handed it to her mother. Daisy lifted herself slowly onto one elbow, her sunken eyes smiled feebly. The hand that took the cup from Kanina was shriveled so that the fingers looked like brown claws and the veins on the back stood out like twisted blue cords. Daisy dropped the cup before she could lift it to her lips, spilling the broth down her sweater and over the bed quilt. Kanina picked it up silently, dipped it into the stew pot again and this time held it to her mother's lips.

Joe Beaverskin was chewing on a piece of half-raw meat, the first meat they had had in six days—or was it seven?—but Kanina waited for some of the sharp gamy taste to cook out of it before she would eat any herself. Waiting wasn't difficult. The hunger pains had long since left her and there was only a numbing lethargy and weakness in their place. And besides, the stew had a musky unappetizing odor—unappetizing even now despite her starved condition. It was a skunk that had been roused from its hibernating den by the warming sun and Joe Beaverskin shot it near the camp that morning. The animal had released some of its scent before it died and the odor still clung to the meat.

Daisy Beaverskin groaned and Kanina looked at her. Her mother was retching, her shriveled face contorted, as a stomach that had gone too long without food strove painfully now to reject the broth she had just drunk. Kanina reached behind her for one of the empty lard pails and held it under her mother's mouth. Daisy retched again, moaned, and then she vomited.

Kanina's eyes filmed over with tears and she asked herself again the question she had asked many times during these past long weeks of anguish and growing despair. Why was she here? It had all been clear and simple during the early part of the winter before her father's caribou hunt failed and the weeks of starvation began. She was here, she thought then, because she was *Mooskek-owak* and the white race would let her be nothing else. But now for a long time the matter had been clouded by thoughts her mind seemed incapable of developing beyond a nebulous half-formed state. Whatever her original reasoning had been, she had not come back to die a useless martyrdom of starvation. Even those miserable days as the restaurant waitress in Blackwood had had more point and purpose than this. It was not death itself she was afraid of. The starvation pains were gone, her senses were numbed, and if death came now it would come peacefully like sleep in the night. Death's price of pain and panic she had already paid, the rest of it now would be easy. But she did not want to die. There was so much that needed to be done, so much that was apparent only to someone like herself who had lived on both sides.

Of all the emotions that filled the wretched, desperate weeks they had just come through, the one that stood out strongest now in her memory was not the fear, the pain, or the waning hope, it was the amazement, almost disbelief, at the small amount of food required to keep the spark of life aglow. After the unsuccessful caribou hunt there had been a rabbit and some more pike, and some of the strength had come back to Joe Beaverskin's emaciated body. He was unable to go out again on long overnight hunts but he did resume hunting near camp. During the following weeks the stew pot sat empty on the *askeekan* floor for days at a time. They survived on driblets of food, getting the equivalent of a good meal once every four to six days. When they had meat they gathered moss to thicken its broth, but they stopped eating moss alone because without meat it only revived dormant hunger pains and gave no strength in return.

Kanina never saw her parents undressed and there was only the loose baggy clothing as a clue to the withering of their bodies underneath. But in her own case there were deepening furrows between each pair of ribs, hollows in the sides of her buttocks and her breasts were softening as supporting tissue wasted away. Daisy had fared worst and for the last ten days she had lain gaunt and hollow-eyed, rarely rising from her bed.

But now, six days without food this time, they were going to eat again. Most of the musky odor had gone and the stewing skunk had filled the *askeekan* with a rich meaty smell that Kanina found appetizing. After his first impatient sampling, Joe Beaverskin had waited, but now he dipped his cup in once more. Kanina filled two cups, for herself and her mother, and put them aside to cool. She fed her mother first, holding the cup to her lips. Daisy swallowed eagerly but within a few seconds she pushed the cup away, her frail body strained and she vomited.

Kanina sipped from her own cup. The mushy moss slid like jelly down her throat and made her gag. Her stomach heaved uncertainly but after a few seconds it quieted and she tried another sip. The nausea repeated, but again she managed to keep the food down. Only her father was eating without difficulty. He drank several cups in quick succession, then took a bone with lumps of red meat on it and held it in his fingers and chewed on it ravenously.

But Daisy could keep none of it down. Kanina tried many times, giving her small sips of the clear broth only, but finally, wan and weak from repeated vomiting, Daisy dropped back exhausted on her bed.

Kanina and her father rested an hour and then went out together to lift the nets. The glare on the snow forced Kanina to close her eyes the moment she stepped outside. Her father took two pairs of colored glasses from his pocket, put on one and gave the other to Kanina. Not many years ago the *Mooskek-owak* had made their own sun goggles from slabs of wood with narrow slits through which they looked, but in recent years they had been buying colored glasses from the trading posts instead. Sun goggles of some kind were essential to prevent snowblindness during these final glaring weeks of winter.

"Your mother is in a bad way," Joe Beaverskin said when they had put on their snowshoes and started down the creek trail. "Her stomach is angry at having no food for such a long time. Now it needs easy food like tea with milk and sugar and flour in it. And those foods are only at Cape Cree."

They trudged on, the wet snow clinging to their snowshoes adding weight at every step. Joe Beaverskin spoke again.

"In two weeks the break-up will begin," he said. "For two weeks after that there will be too much ice for the canoe but not enough ice for the sled, and we will be prisoners here. If we start now, we will be at Cape Cree in two weeks. If we wait it will be six weeks. Your mother will live two weeks, but six weeks is too long."

Nothing more was said about it. It had been a week since they had caught any fish but today Kanina could detect a heaviness in the first net as soon as she took hold of it. They pulled the fish out onto the ice a minute later; it was a big pike, at least a ten-pounder. In the next net there was another pike almost as large. The two fish represented as much food as they had had in the past month.

They walked back in high spirits and there was no mention again of the trip to Cape Cree. When they reached the *askeekan* Daisy had not moved from her bed and the fire in the stove was out. Joe Beaverskin relit the fire and cut up one of the fish and started it boiling.

Kanina tried Daisy with some fish broth an hour later but she vomited again. Joe Beaverskin watched her, his sunken eyes narrowing, then he rose abruptly, took the second fish and went outside. Kanina heard the dogs begin yapping and snapping noisily. He was feeding the other fish to them and Joe Beaverskin's sudden concern for his dogs could mean only that there was going to be work for them to do.

He came back and stood just inside the *askeekan* door.

"We will leave tomorrow for Cape Cree," he said. "We must hurry to beat the break-up."

Daisy nodded and smiled feebly, but she did not speak.

CHAPTER FORTY-SEVEN

KANINA and her father were up at dawn and began preparing for the departure. Joe Beaverskin tied a snowshoe so that it sloped up against the curved front of the toboggan forming a back rest on which Daisy could partially recline, for she would have to ride the hundred and fifty miles to Cape Cree. They dismantled the *askeekan,* folding one of the canvas tarps and putting it on the sloping snowshoe as a mattress. They loaded the toboggan with the trapline tent and stove, the bedding and cooking pot, and lashed everything on firmly, leaving room at the front for Daisy. Joe Beaverskin's gun was placed under one of the lashings on the top of the load where it would be quickly available if game appeared while they were traveling. Then he harnessed the dogs and Kanina realized now why *Mooskek-owak* dog harnesses were always rope and canvas instead of leather—the starving dogs would have eaten leather harnesses instantly.

Daisy rose unaided and shuffled the few steps to the sleigh. Kanina had not seen her on her feet for several days and was startled by the way the clothing draped like formless sacking on her slender body. She dropped onto the toboggan and Kanina covered her with quilts. Joe Beaverskin stepped out in front to break trail and spoke to the dogs. Mokwa and Jim leaped forward, pushing bony shoulders into their canvas collars and the toboggan began to move, Kanina following at the rear. The long journey had started.

They stopped on the lake and lifted the nets. Again there were two pike, and Joe Beaverskin fed head and tail sections to the dogs immediately. The nets were rolled and added to the load on the toboggan and the journey resumed.

They traveled at a walking pace without talking and without stopping to rest. The sun brightened and they put on dark glasses. Daisy rode facing rearward toward Kanina; she did not speak and rarely moved. By late morning it was thawing again and the wet snow clung to Kanina's snowshoes, doubling their weight. It caked on the bottom of the toboggan making it hard for the dogs to pull. Two hours later, or three hours—Kanina found it difficult to estimate time—Joe Beaverskin stopped and the panting dogs curled up immediately in the snow. Kanina was very tired and she hoped her father was stopping for the day. But he merely cut a pole from the creek bank, gave it to Kanina and showed her how to help the dogs by pushing the toboggan from behind with the pole. Then he snapped his own harness to that of the dogs, leaned forward against the strap across his chest and they were moving again. The sweat was running coldly under Kanina's clothing. Her legs and stomach throbbed with pain.

The sun lowered, the glare vanished from the snow and the afternoon cooled. The melted surface snow began freezing into a crust which broke under their toboggan and snowshoes, making travel more difficult. Finally, when the spruce shadows were long enough to span the width of the creek, they stopped for the night's camp.

Kanina dropped exhausted on the loaded toboggan, but her father, who had been working far harder than she, stepped out of his harness and worked on without rest. He dug a hole in the snow the size of the tent and erected the tent over it. He floored it with balsam boughs and set up the little stove inside. He cut firewood, started a fire and put on the stew pot which still contained some of yesterday's fish. The fish caught that day were to be saved.

Daisy hobbled inside and lay down and seemed to fall asleep immediately. When the fish broth began to steam, Kanina awakened her mother and gave her a cupful, but Daisy drank only half of it, then pushed it away and sank back on her bed. Kanina ate a large piece of fish and it routed the hunger pains from her stomach but the rest of her body remained a vast throbbing ache. It was still daylight but she lay down and wrapped her rabbitskin robe around her. They had traveled about fifteen miles and it was the most exhausting day she had ever endured. And there were at least ten more days like it ahead.

The next day was warmer. The crust on the snow had frozen thicker during the night but by mid-morning when the sun began to weaken it the crust broke under their weight, flinging up jagged knife-like pieces that jabbed their moccasins and cut the rawhide lacing of their snowshoes. Under its crust the snow was sticky and clinging. It packed in icy balls under Kanina's insteps, making the moccasins chafe her feet and she could feel blisters forming. Within a couple of hours, her calf muscles were burning with pain.

She trudged on in a near-blind and aching coma, pushing steadily on the pole against the rear of the toboggan. Dimly through the sun's glare she could see the dogs struggling against their harnesses, and her father leaning into his harness ahead of them all. She began seeing small spots of blood in the footprints of the dogs, yet with paws raw and bleeding from the crusted snow, the dogs were still pulling to the limit of their strength. Kanina knew that, though starved for most of their lives, these northern dogs will work until death drops them in their bloody tracks. There was only one thing worse than being a *Mooskek-owak*, Kanina mused, and that was being a *Mooskek-owak* dog.

Sometimes the toboggan came to a dead stop and it took the full strength of all of them to free it from the clinging snow and start it moving again. Near mid-day Joe Beaverskin stopped and turned, the sweat running down his hollow cheeks. They had not traveled ten miles that day.

"We will camp," he said suddenly. "We must travel at night as long as the thaw lasts."

So they camped again. They ate the last of their fish and went exhausted to bed while the sun was still high in the afternoon sky.

It was dark when Joe Beaverskin awakened them. When Kanina stepped outside, there were waving ribbons of the aurora quivering and glowing in the northern sky, throwing an eerie green light on the snow. The stars shone cold and brilliantly and from their position in the sky Kanina judged the time to be early morning, no more than two hours after midnight.

Before he put the stew pot on the toboggan, Joe Beaverskin scraped up the cold fat from its bottom with the big spoon and handed it to Kanina. She wiped two fingers across the spoon, taking half the fat, and passed the rest back to her father. It was granular and fishy, but it melted deliciously in her mouth. She swallowed it slowly, making it last.

When her mother rose to walk to the loaded toboggan her legs sagged and she sank back onto her bed. Kanina and her father helped her, each taking an arm. The toboggan moved easily now, for the snow was crisp and dry. Hours later the sun rose like an orb of molten copper, and Kanina trudged on, her bloodshot eyes squinting against the snow glare, her stomach and legs burning like fire. Some time well after dawn she became aware that the toboggan had stopped and her father was back beside it snatching for his gun. She heard the gun fire, heard her father's grunt of satisfaction, and then she saw the big black raven dropping and twisting like a falling leaf out of the sky.

It was easier to go on now, knowing that there would be a meal when they camped. By mid-morning the snow had become soft and sticky again. They stopped then and camped, and Kanina waited sleepily for the raven to stew.

They traveled two more nights and before dawn on that second night—
the fifth day of their trip—they reached the Kistawanee, the halfway point
to Cape Cree. That morning when the sun warmed and they stopped to
camp, Joe Beaverskin boiled a small pot of moss and lichen. Kanina had
little desire for food now, but she ate it and drank the water because
she knew she must.

Another night of travel. Another dawn. Another day of thawing sun
and dazzling snow. Jim, the black-muzzled pup, stumbled repeatedly and
Joe Beaverskin finally unhooked his harness and let him run behind.
Kanina tried to recall when they had last fed the dogs; it was four days
ago anyway, perhaps five. Jim staggered along weakly at Kanina's heels;
his eyes were glazing over, he whined steadily. During the brief, infrequent stops Kanina patted his head and whispered encouragement.

As she slept that day, Kanina dreamed that a rope around her stomach
was being twisted tighter and tighter with a stick passed through it. She
was lying in the tent and there was a long procession of white people
lined up outside, taking turns stepping in and twisting the rope tighter.
She recognized Mrs. Baxter, Joan Rumsey's sister at Blackwood, and
then the girls from Park Collegiate—Trudy Brown, Marjorie Ball, and
several others whose names she had forgotten. Dr. Karr, the teachers
college principal, gave it two twists and the rope was cutting deeply into
her stomach and she was screaming with the agony of it, pleading with
them to stop, but still they came, sneering, taunting, twisting it tighter.
There were the boys from the restaurant and the mothers from the
school near Cochrane. And then she saw Rory Macdonald in the line-up
outside, awaiting his turn to twist the rope too.

Rory's tall body stooped to get in the tent door and he was also sneering—and then she saw it wasn't a sneer, it was a smile. He was smiling
because he was carrying the big black stew pot filled with meat. He put
the pot on the stove and then, instead of twisting the rope, he bent down
and kissed her. She threw her arms around him and clutched him to her,
because this time she was not going to let him get away. But he slipped
out of her embrace as though he were a cloud without substance. The
tent flap fluttered and he was gone.

Others came, twisting, twisting, but no matter how much it tightened
the rope could torture her stomach no further, because Rory Macdonald
had filled the pot with meat. It was beginning to boil now on the tent
stove. And soon they would eat.

Suddenly Joe Beaverskin was shaking her awake. It was dark and she
was conscious immediately of the stew pot bubbling vigorously on the
stove. The tent was filled with the steamy aroma of boiling meat. She

rose slowly; her head was dizzy and her legs trembled with weakness. There was no rope around her stomach, but the agonizing pain of the dream was still there. She lifted the lid and looked in. The pot *was* full of meat.

"That's Jim," her father said simply. "Last night he died."

After that Kanina had no more coherent memories, only disconnected dream-like snatches. She had no memory of eating Jim, yet she must have done so, because the trip lasted at least four days longer with no other food. It was an endless tormenting aeon of putting one snowshoe ahead of the other step after step and mile after mile and day after hellish day. She was amazed that her mind could find the will and her body the strength to go on and on without rest, without hope, without end. Even time seemed to be taunting them and standing still. They would pass a point of land and struggle on downriver for what seemed hours and miles, and then Kanina would look back and there would be the same point only a few hundred yards behind.

She remembered the cold crisp nights with their auroras shimmering across the polar sky and brilliant warm days when the snow melted on the river banks and slushy puddles covered the groaning, cracking ice. She remembered Mokwa, the white she-dog, not barking or whining now but just pulling, pulling, in traces that never slacked. And ahead of Mokwa, her father, pulling too, eternally pulling, and sometimes shouting back that the break-up was almost upon them. And Daisy, staring back with eyes that gave no sign of seeing, falling off the toboggan, lying moaning in the snow, being lifted back by her husband, and falling off again until finally, wordlessly, he tied her on.

She remembered the soggy patches of ice where it bent like rubber beneath them, the long detours around cracks where black water rippled and mocked them. And then, not cracks any more but wide yawning gaps of open water where they had to cut trails along the river bank to get the toboggan past.

She did not know when her mother died. She could not even recall whether Daisy was in the tent with them at the last camp, or whether she was a corpse then, tied on the toboggan outside. Her father never told her and Kanina never asked.

Near dawn on a night that had turned very cold, they reached Cape Cree. Kanina did not know they were there until her father began shouting for help. Several men came down to the river bank and it was not until then, when they lifted Daisy from the toboggan, that Kanina realized her mother was dead and had been dead for a long time. Daisy's body was frozen like stone, grotesquely bent, half sitting, half lying, and her shriveled face was coated ghost-like with white frost. Kanina was too exhausted, physically and emotionally, to cry.

She remembered falling onto the toboggan and lying there in blissful, relaxing sleep, yet it couldn't have been sleep either, because she also had misty memories of the excited shouting, the gathering crowd, the lights coming on in the big Rumsey house and then Joan Rumsey with her arm around her, supporting her, saying she must walk and not lie down again. And she remembered saying "no" to Joan Rumsey, saying no she could not go to the Rumsey house, because she was *Mooskek-owak*, she must stay with her people, her own people would care for her. And then, a vague memory of hot broth, tea with milk and sugar, and the repeated vomiting.

It was bright day when next she awakened. She was in a large tent and she was lying on a real mattress on the tent's board floor with several soft quilts over her. It was one of the *Mooskek-owak* tents but Joan Rumsey was still there beside her, not talking, just softly massaging Kanina's hands and arms. Nearby, on another bed on the floor lay her father. He was asleep.

That day and the following night Kanina slept and wakened intermittently, obediently sipping the broth whenever the cup was put to her lips. On the second morning she was awakened by the rumbling and cracking of the Kistawanee's ice. She looked across at her father's bed and she saw that he was already up and gone. The rumbling of the ice lasted an hour and then it mounted into a thunderous roar. Above the ice roar she could hear the shouting and cheering of the usually unresponsive *Mooskek-owak*, for the break-up promised spring and goose breasts for their cooking pots again. Kanina's body tingled with the excitement of it. She rose slowly from the bed and for a few moments her legs sagged weakly and she felt dizzy. Then strength came back and she walked to the door to see the break-up for herself. They had beaten it by little more than twenty-four hours. And then another sound reached her above the clamor of shouting and grinding ice. It was the hammering in the charnel house behind the little white church. They were making Daisy Beaver-skin's coffin.

The mission bell tolled its mournful liturgy. The service in the church had ended and now the silent procession wound among the ragged tents toward the cemetery where grave-diggers had been chipping at the frozen earth since the morning of the day before. The missionary wearing a white cassock, sunglasses and black rubber boots walked in front, slosh-

ing heedlessly through puddles of slushy snow but circling warily around
the snarling dogs. As he walked, he read in a low chanting voice from
the prayer book held out before him. Behind the missionary came the
pallbearers with the coffin, and directly behind the rough plank box were
Kanina and her father. To the rear of them the rest of the cortege was
strung out in a twisting, trudging ribbon of tattered clothes and pinched
faces whose haggardness was only partially hidden by the dark glasses
nearly everyone wore. Every Cape Cree adult was there, including Bert
and Joan Rumsey.

Kanina still felt weak and sometimes her head whirled dizzily. The
service in the church had given Kanina her first opportunity to look over
the other *Mooskek-owak* and most of them bore the sunken temples and
recessed eyes that told mutely of the winter's starvation. Their faces were
solemn but there had been no uncontrolled display of grief. They had
come too near to death themselves to break down now in death's presence.

In the procession behind her Kanina knew there were many hungry
stomachs and anxious eyes that even now would be scanning the sky.
For the air was warm, the wind was from the south, and the *niskuk*
flocks were due.

They walked on. Kanina was tired and she could feel the cold water
leaking through her torn moccasins. And then it came. Like the aromatic
fragrance of the balsam, it seemed a part of the wind itself. It rose
faintly between the tolling strikes of the church bell, it faded, and then it
rose again. Sweet, dulcet, the melody of spring. Geese.

The pallbearers stopped and Kanina, her own eyes searching the sky,
almost bumped into the coffin. Everyone had stopped, every head turned
to the sky, except the missionary in front of them all who walked on
unaware and alone, still reading in a solemn droning voice from his
prayer book.

The gabble of geese came nearer and mounted clearly above the tolling
of the bell. Then Kanina could see them, a large flock, low over the
trees, but well out of gun range downriver. She could see the pain and
yearning on the emaciated faces of the people around her, and she could
see them turning pleading eyes from the retreating geese to her father,
the chief mourner, who stood now with one hand resting on the coffin
but with his eyes following the goose flock, too.

And then: "*Ka-ronk, onka-onka-onka.*" It was not the geese this
time, it was her father.

Downriver the V of big birds faltered. The white-clad missionary now
well out in front stopped abruptly in the middle of his prayer and looked
back, the hand that held the prayer book dropping limply to his side.

The sunglasses failed to hide the look of consternation spreading across
his face. Joe Beaverskin called them again. Several other hunters took
up the call. The geese turned, long necks twisting curiously. Then Joe
Beaverskin ran toward the tent where he and Kanina had been staying.

It was the signal all had been awaiting. The pallbearers lowered the
coffin quickly to the ground and the funeral procession broke up in
noisy confusion as every hunter ran for his gun. The geese came near
and Kanina could clearly see the white face patches. Then the big birds
understood that there was no other goose flock here calling them down
and they veered swiftly away. There were no hunters out yet with their
guns. The geese were getting out of range. Kanina began trembling with
the suspense of waiting.

Then two shots in quick succession and two geese tumbling out of the
sky. Kanina looked back quickly at the tents and only her father was
out. He had got a goose with each barrel of his double-barreled gun.
In a couple of seconds there were others out and more guns were booming, but now the geese were out of range and no more of the big birds
fell.

The men gathered around Joe Beaverskin, laughing, patting his
shoulders. The missionary lifted his prayer book and gave a curt and
commanding cough. They leaned their guns against the tent front and,
leaving the geese where they had fallen, they rejoined the funeral cortege.
The pallbearers lifted the coffin. The missionary resumed his prayer. The
procession moved again. But there was no sorrow now on the hard lean
faces behind Kanina, there was only smiling relief.

Her father spoke quietly to the men ahead who were bearing Daisy
Beaverskin's body. "She was the one who did it," he said. "I was always
lucky when I had her near me."

CHAPTER FORTY-EIGHT

THE barnacle rested, his head tucked under one wing; but it
wasn't sleep and he was aware that the gale was dropping and the sun
was beginning to pierce the sooty overcast. Periodically he lifted his
head to look around him. The other barnacles in the flock were watching restlessly too. The sun came through, the cloud cover retreated east-

ward toward the humpy line of the Hebrides on the horizon and after an hour only a gray-white smudge of it remained, clinging like a tattered bonnet to the craggy crest of Heaval, Barra's highest hill. By sunset the gale had dropped to a hesitant breeze that was soft and warm with the gentle caress of spring.

They took off in the twilight, shaking the salt water from their feathers as they rose from the sea and turned toward Barra for the night-time feeding. The eelgrass beds in Goose Island Sound were thinned out, for now it was March and the barnacle flocks had been feeding there nightly since the previous October. Most of the geese flew in across the sand dunes to the *machair* where the vetches and sweet grass were already turning green. The barnacle with the yellow neck streamer flew inland with one of the flocks and began feeding hungrily.

Earlier that winter he had retained vague and recurrent memories of his James Bay summer, of the mate he had taken in the muskeg lands of that other distant world and of the long wandering return flight that had brought him finally to Barra again. Sometimes during that early winter period he had thought longingly of the mate he had courted on the inland lake where strange forests pressed down dark and hauntingly to the shores. And sometimes then, when a strange goose flock approached, he would search its birds anxiously to see if she were there, returning to him.

But memory in a bird is split into compartments and each compartment belongs to a season of the year, slowly closing when its season ends and opening again when its season returns. And now for several months the sexual phase of the barnacle's annual cycle had been dormant. All memories of the mate and the mating had been forgotten.

But that night as he fed, with the warm softness of returning spring in the salty air, a new emotion began stirring somewhere deep within him. It was a vague restlessness that was not fear, a distant dream-like beckoning he could not identify or understand.

They fed for several hours. Meanwhile, floating down from the night sky, came the tinkling liquid notes of the first migrating shore-birds pushing northward behind the advancing spring. The moon set and one by one the barnacle flocks flew back to the sound to wait for the dawn. And now the barnacle noticed that the new restlessness was affecting the others, too. Occasionally a male would lunge with outstretched neck at another male near him and there would be a brief, violent battle. The sun rose and with a roar of wings the geese took off to fly back out to sea for the day. Flying high above the sea, the barnacle could feel it sharply again—a vagrant, fretting discontent, an impulse to fly on and on into the unfolding spring. But he knew not where.

That night the feeding of the barnacles on the *machair* was hasty and impatient. They flew back to the sound early, and as soon as the flocks had assembled on the water the noisy threatening and gesturing began. Ganders who had fed peacefully together all winter now began pairing off belligerently, buffeting each other with stiffened wings, lunging in and out until the water around them churned white with foam.

But the barnacle with the yellow neck streamer kept aloof, because he could feel none of their belligerency. And then shortly after, a gander near him swam up to another bird and began a display quite different from that of the threatening and fighting males. He bobbed his head quickly, stood erect in the water with chest feathers fluffed out and his neck moving from side to side with a slow swaying grace. There was tenderness and gallantry in it that the male-threat did not possess, and the barnacle recognized it instantly. This was the first hesitant courtship display of a male before his mate, the first feeble symptom of spring's sexual awakening. To the barnacle it was like a key turning somewhere in his brain, opening a compartment there that had been closed for months. And slowly the contents of the compartment spilled out into his consciousness—obscure, murky, disconnected memories.

He remembered her again. She was waiting where the water was fresh and smooth and shallow, where a small cove lay locked between fingers of sand that grew densely with willows, where the horizon was gone because dark trees grew down forebodingly to the edges of the water. He had a vague memory that the place was far away. But he could remember nothing more.

And the barnacle sensed dimly that somewhere here in these developing memories lay the source of the prodding, bewildering restlessness he had begun to feel the night before.

Spring advanced. There were periods when the gales whined in again off the Atlantic, but each time a gale died the rebirth of the sun was quicker and more vigorous and the *machairs* steamed under its growing warmth. By early April the daisies and primroses had begun to fleck the moorlands with color and the trilling song of the skylark poured like liquid music from the sky.

Among the barnacles the courtship fighting and displaying swelled to fever pitch. Mated birds were now in the more intimate and advanced phases of courtship, frequently rising breast to breast in the water, and sometimes treading one another's backs in the symbolic prelude to the copulation which would soon begin. The unmated yearlings had begun to separate into flocks of their own, the males fighting viciously for females and chasing one another in rapid twisting pursuit-flights across the surface of the water.

The barnacle with the yellow neck streamer did not feel as if he belonged to either group. He was mateless here, so he did not belong among the courting adults. Yet he felt no desire to join the yearlings and bachelor males either, because he had no aggressive urge to fight for a new mate. His memory had been sharpening gradually. Now he could see her clearly, a mate like one of his own kind, yet different too because she was brown where he was silver and gray, and the white of her face was smaller. And he could see the place of the mating, too, in sharpening detail—the lake and the marsh with the crescent of beach between them, the islands, and one island in particular that was the focal point of it all because it had the muddy bay where the nesting would be.

Late in April there was a period of two days during which a strong breeze blew down steadily from the north and the air pressure kept rising. The barnacle could detect the rising pressure; it gave the air a firmer property that made flight easier. A high-pressure mass was moving in off the Atlantic and the old experienced barnacles knew that when the center of high passed and the pressure began dropping again there would be a strong return flow of wind from the south. That afternoon at sea there was little sleeping. With heads tilted sideways the barnacles were watching the sky and constantly testing the wind for change.

With dusk, as they flew to the feeding grounds, a full moon rose and the strips of shell sand at the edge of the sea shimmered like silver under its slanting light. They fed hastily, then flock after flock circled noisily up and down the sound, clinging so close to the water that the slipstream of their wings left scudding patches of ripple on the water's surface. Since this was group behavior and not a pairing activity, the barnacle with the yellow neck streamer joined in eagerly. He had attached himself that night to a flock of about fifty adults, all of them paired except himself, and each time the flock flew the barnacle flew with it. The wild darting gyrating flights went on for several hours. The thrill and excitement of it built up until it was a pulsing fire reaching into every part of him.

As the moon neared its zenith the wind strengthened and now it was from the south. For another half hour the barnacles waited as the wind grew firmer. And then the flock took off and this time there was a new and obvious purposefulness in the flight evident in the first few seconds of the take-off. This time it wasn't play; this time they were climbing steeply instead of sprinting off along the water. The sound and Goose Island dropped rapidly away below. They leveled off and turned into the north. The moonlit seascape below softened and dimmed until only the black shadows of the hills and the white strips of beach sand were identifiable. And then the land was gone and there was only the sea below.

The barnacle felt a happy release from the fretting unrest that had tormented him for weeks. For he knew that this was not another dawn flight to the daytime loafing area at sea, this was the springtime departure, the long flight that would take him back to the mate and to the mating territory of hallowed memory.

Daybreak revealed a smooth sea, for the shift of wind from north around to south had flattened the waves. The barnacle's memory was influenced strongly by association and suggestion, and now, seeing the sea emerge below, he remembered again that time a year ago when he had last flown northward like this from the Barra wintering grounds. It had been very different that other time, for the sea was then a berserk fury of towering waves and gale-whipped spray. The great storm had enveloped him suddenly after his flight had started, he had struggled against it until his tired wings could fight it no longer. . . .

Suddenly the meaning of it burst into his consciousness. The strength wilted abruptly from his wings and he dropped behind the flock. That other time when he could struggle against the storm no longer he had turned downwind before it. He had abandoned this northward flyway of his species and moved with the gale out into the open unknown sea of the setting sun.

And now he knew it was there, toward the setting sun, that the mate and the mating place awaited him, not northward where this flock was leading!

The flock was drawing away rapidly ahead of him and the barnacle felt a sudden panicky loneliness. As quickly as it had come, the memory of the mate and the mating place was lost again in his sudden compelling need to rejoin the flock. His big wings sliced the air violently and the increased airflow pressed the body feathers firmly against him as flight speed increased. He overtook them slowly, gaining once more his position at the flock's rear. And then, as soon as he was there and the loneliness was gone, he felt the disturbing unrest again. For now he knew it surely. This flight into the north was wrong. *His* mating flight should lead to the west, away from the sunrise, away from the seas the migrating barnacles knew.

But, though knowing it now, it was hard to act upon, for the lure of the flock was a powerful restraining bond. The crimson of the sunrise faded. The barnacles flew on steadily with the south wind strong on their tails. The yellow neck streamer snapped softly in the airflow over the barnacle's shoulder but he had long since forgotten that it was there. He followed the flock, submissively, not wanting to, yet not able to break away.

By mid-morning they had been flying eight hours and the gander in the lead led them down to the surface of the sea for rest. But there was too much tension and excitement among them to spend long in idle resting. First one pair and then another and another began ardent courtship displays. On the edge of the flock, bewildered and alone, the mateless barnacle watched and the mating excitement seethed in him too, but for him there was no opportunity for release. Suddenly he felt as lonely here amid the flock as he had felt in the air several hours ago when he had dropped behind them. And now the distant lake of islands and the muddy bay of the mating beckoned with a magnetism that nothing would appease or deny.

They flew again two hours later. The mateless one flew with them, tailing the flock as it climbed into a cloudless sky. But when they leveled off and faced the north, the barnacle tilted his wings and turned into the west. He watched the flock fade into a wispy thread, and then a few moments later even that was gone.

His mind now had a vivid picture of the goal toward which he was heading. But the distance and the route that would take him there were lost from his memory. He knew only that here to the west lay the way.

CHAPTER FORTY-NINE

ANOTHER dawn came and the barnacle was still flying over empty sea, and now the rigors of the flight were beginning to leave their imprint. He had started with a body fattened so that it was twenty-five percent heavier than normal. To maintain his powerful forty-mile-an-hour flight his body was converting fat into energy at the rate of about one percent of body weight per hour. He had been flying now for more than twenty-four hours and he could feel plainly the loss of weight, for it made him more buoyant. But with it, flight had become more difficult, not easier, because now the strength was draining rapidly out of him. He began dropping frequently onto the sea for brief rests. The hunger that had started as a chafing discomfort many hours before was now a gnawing pain.

At mid-day he saw a thin white line of ice approaching and soon he was flying over the outer edge of a floe where slushy ice pans clicked and tinkled as they rose and fell on the ocean swells. It meant he was approaching a coast. He was puzzled, because in the dim recollections he had of that other flight there were no memories of a coast as near as this to the Barra wintering waters.

Late in the afternoon he saw mountains lifting faintly over a hazy horizon ahead. Then he began to detect a strange and puzzling feature— a thin shining line of white that hung weirdly between the coastal cliffs and the sky. Drawing nearer he recognized that it was an interior plateau covered with glistening ice. This inland ice mass thrust twisting river-like glaciers down between the coastal peaks to the edge of the sea.

The barnacle's brain had no memory of the landmarks he had to seek and pass on this return flight to the mating place. But once he encountered a landmark his memory had a keen facility for recognizing whether it was familiar or unfamiliar. And this dramatic landfall of mountain and glacier was certainly a land he had never seen before. Somewhere he had gone wrong. This was not the way.

He flew in to a chaotic irregular coast with narrow fiords that twisted inland toward the great plateau of ice. There was much snow here still and the clumps of stunted shrubbery were gray and lifeless. But there were spots where wind had swept the snow away exposing the dry mosses and lichens beneath, and on one of these the barnacle landed and began to feed. It was insipid, unpleasant food, but it routed the hunger pains and put a comforting fullness in his stomach. And well before the dawn he could feel the strength coming back to his resilient body.

Though a bird's memory and intelligence are strangely lacking in some elements, there are other regions of comprehension developed to an acuteness unknown in other animals, including man. One of these seems to be an ability, highly developed in birds that make long migration flights, to detect changes in the height of the sun's daily arc across the sky relative to the height of sun-arc with which the bird is familiar in its home territory. The height of the sun's arc, usually expressed as the sun's altitude at noon, is a measure of latitude, an indicator of how far north or south of the equator the observer is. If an observer in the northern hemisphere moves south it has the effect of bringing the sun higher into the sky; moving north pushes the sun-arc lower toward the southern horizon.

The barnacle still had a clear memory of the sun-arc for the Barra waters from which he had flown some forty-eight hours before. Now there emerged a new detail to add to the steadily developing memory of the mating place he sought. Now he remembered that the sun of the mating place was a higher sun than the sun for the same seasons at Barra.

So when dawn came, he began eyeing the sun periodically to compare its arc here with the sun-arcs he knew for Barra and the distant place of the mating. He determined in a few hours that the sun-arc here was lower, leaning closer to the southern horizon. He waited until noon to be certain of it, feeding and resting intermittently, and then he was sure of what he had to do. There was a languid weakness still in his big wings, but he took off and climbed until the tangled skein of water and ice and craggy shore dropped far below him. And he began following the twisting shoreline southward.

The barnacle did not know that this westward flight had begun farther north than his hurricane-directed flight of the spring before. He did not know that this northern route had brought him to southeastern Greenland instead of the more distant landfall he sought in Labrador. He only knew that, judged against the pattern imprinted from previous flights, the sun's arc now dipped too low in the southern sky. He had applied no mathematical reasoning to the problem, as a human navigator would. He merely felt a need to move the sun back upward to its proper place in the sky. And he knew that to accomplish this he must fly in the direction marked by the sun's noontime zenith.

He had flown about three hours when the coast turned sharply away to the west. His wings were already tired again and he glided down to search for food. To correct the sun's position the barnacle knew he must fly on southward where now once more there was nothing but ice and sea. But his wasted body was in no condition for another long flight. He had to wait.

The barnacle waited six days, feeding steadily night and day on the sparse mosses and grasses under the snow so that his crop and stomach were always filled. The fat built up slowly on his body, much more slowly than usual because it was not nutritious food. With ordinary feeding he would have been back to normal condition in a week, yet now on this sixth day the fat was just beginning to round out his breast again. But much of the old vigor and sureness was back in his wings. And the urge to fly became a demand he could resist no longer.

It was late afternoon when he started and the coast disappeared behind him within the first hour. His flight was firm, his wingbeat unwavering. He did not know he was heading again into mid-Atlantic. He only knew that the sun was misplaced, and flying this way would correct it.

He was still flying strongly when dawn began gilding his neck streamer with a sheen of gold. He had flown all night without stopping and now he glided down and landed on the sea, anxiously watching the rising sun. He had flown perhaps four hundred miles during the night and it became apparent quickly that here the sun was rising at a steeper angle, its arc appreciably higher than the sun-arc he knew for Barra. And now he understood that his southward flight could end, that the next leg of his search for the mate who waited could start from here.

This time he did not need to watch the homeward flight of the petrels to learn the direction of land; this time he knew his flight must be in the direction of sunset. He started flying again in mid-morning, climbing high to reduce the danger of missing landmarks on the horizon. And with the exertion of resuming flight, the hunger pains returned. He flew on into the afternoon with a weakness spreading through his body. His breast muscles and wing tendons were burning again with fatigue.

The barnacle was flying at two thousand feet, an altitude that permitted him to see for sixty miles and overlook ten thousand square miles of sea. It was a clear day but a small black cloud crept over the horizon southwest of him. He watched it curiously, for a speck of black cloud in an otherwise cloudless sky was a peculiarity. For many minutes it did not change. His curiosity intensified and finally he turned toward it, temporarily forgetting the pain of hunger and fatigue that had been racking his body. Gradually he began to distinguish the white island-like speck that sat on the sea beneath the cloud.

It took him more than two hours to reach it for his laboring flight was now much slower than normal. But long before he arrived, the barnacle was remembering the hurricane flight of last spring and the strange, angular, floating island to which the hurricane had carried him. He recognized that this was another of those islands, an island that pitched and rolled and moved slowly across the surface of the sea.

CHAPTER FIFTY

THE weather ship *Talisman* had been patroling for three weeks at weather station Candy, about three hundred miles off the Labrador coast. Spirits were high aboard the *Talisman* because this was the last night on station. Another ship was due to relieve it around noon next day and the *Talisman* was being readied for the four-day run back to New York. It was a steam vessel with oil-fired boilers and after three weeks of slogging around in a circle at half-speed most of the fuel tanks scattered along her double bottom were empty. To adjust the ship's stability and trim for the run home, some of these empty tanks would be filled with water ballast to replace the weight of the consumed fuel.

Early on the morning of the *Talisman*'s last day at Candy, her engine-room crew began flushing out the sludge-like oily residue that coated the empty fuel tanks, preparing them for the ballast water. Dawn was just breaking when the black washings from the tanks began spewing from the *Talisman*'s side into the sea. The oil thickened quickly on contact with the cold seawater and it floated astern in a spreading gluey film. Wave action could thin it out and break it up into smaller patches but nothing in the sea or the air could dissolve or destroy it. The sticky oil film would persist for months, moving hundreds of miles with the ocean's winds and currents, and wherever it traveled it would remain a deadly trap for birds of the sea.

The barnacle rested on the sea nearby and kept the ship in view all night, occasionally making short flights to follow it as it moved slowly away. He slept little because of the intensity of the hunger pains, and he remembered vaguely that the other floating island during the previous flight had in some way provided food. He was afraid to go near, but he could tell from the actions of the fulmars and shearwaters flying close to the ship that there was no food there now.

And then, after the dawn, he saw an activity on the ship that he remembered instantly. Two men came to its edge and emptied the contents of a big container into the sea. The galley refuse floated astern and the circling sea birds pitched down into it and began noisily fighting and feeding. The barnacle overcame his fear and flew swiftly into the writhing knot of birds. He was a larger bird than the others and he fought with them, pummeling them with his wings until they moved back and left the thickest area of feeding to him. He began eating with frenzied haste, and he fed until he could eat no more. Then he flew after the ship which had moved on ahead, and as he came close he saw for the first time the black patches that spread out intermittently astern like cloud shadows on the blue sea. He landed in the sea close behind the ship.

One of the strange black patches was approaching sluggishly. For a couple of minutes the barnacle watched it coming nearer and then he forgot it, for the hunger pains had gone and he felt a need for sleep.

He was awakened by a piercing stab of cold that suddenly spread along his belly underwater. Then he saw that the thin dark scum on the surface of the sea had surrounded him, and its sticky black slime was already penetrating and matting the feathers along his breast and sides.

The barnacle's plumage under normal conditions is a highly efficient insulation against water and cold. It consists of two layers—an outer one of stiff tightly overlapping feathers and an inner one of thick soft down. Near the barnacle's tail is a nipple-like oil gland and periodically the bird presses oil out of this with his bill and spreads it over his feathers. In this way the outer feathers are always kept waterproof, making it impossible for water to penetrate into the soft air-filled insulating layer of down beneath. But oil dumped by ships at sea works swift and violent havoc with this feather waterproofing. It impregnates feathers, gluing and caking them into tarry lumps. Water penetrates to the bird's skin, the essential layer of air insulation is lost, wing feathers often become gummed together making it impossible for the bird to fly.

The creeping spread of water under the feathers of the barnacle's breast and belly left an icy numbing pain. It terrified him for it was like no experience he had ever known. Because of his superb feather waterproofing, he had never actually *felt* water before.

The clinging film on the surface of the sea bewildered him. He plucked at one of the black blobs on his breast and some of it came away in his bill, but most of it remained clotted on the feathers. Then vaguely he became aware that there must be some connection between the black spreading cloud on the water and the icy cold that grasped his belly. He recognized the blackness as a mysterious peril from which he had to escape.

He tried to fly, but the water seemed to clutch at him and all that he succeeded in doing was to pitch clumsily forward so that more of the oil smeared his neck and breast, and black strings of it splashed over his wings. He began swimming toward the line of clean blue water that was moving steadily away from him. Much of his buoyancy depended on air trapped under his feathers and as this air escaped he was sinking lower into the water. His webbed feet paddled violently but some of the power of each stroke had to be used in merely keeping his body afloat.

Slowly he forced his way out to blue water. There, he tried to fly again, but only pitched forward clumsily as he had done before because the oil that clung to his wings interfered with the delicate muscular twisting of the feathers essential for flight. He began preening his wings, running his bill along feather after feather, scraping the black gum away, periodically dressing the feathers with the oily secretion from his own oil gland.

There was little fat covering his breast and this let the cold of the water penetrate deeply into his body. An aching agony reached into every part of him. His normal buoyancy had gone and he had to keep paddling vigorously to stay afloat. The oil was in his eyes, burning them fiercely. It clogged his bill and his throat.

His own natural oil from the gland at his tail helped loosen the gum from his feathers but the struggle to remain afloat was taking most of his energy and it was hard to continue preening wings at the same time. The cold water that clutched at his abdomen was paralyzing him. When the barnacle yielded to its creeping lethargy and stopped swimming, he began to sink immediately. Frantically he found the strength to kick out again with his webbed feet, but the water was still sucking him down, washing over his back, rising up around his neck. Now in desperation he beat the surface of the water with his wings, churning the sea white. He could feel his wings lifting him feebly. His body rose again in the water and his wings began propelling him forward along its surface. Now he paddled violently with his feet, fighting the suction of the water, striving in every way he knew to assist his wings.

Like an overladen aircraft, he plowed along the surface for a long distance, feeling the lightness return to his body as the speed of flight slowly approached. A smooth round swell lifted him and at its crest he struggled frantically, knowing that he must break free and become airborne here because there would not be another opportunity in the dead air of the trough and his strength would be gone before another wavetop could reach him. The far side of the swell began dropping away beneath him. A soft gust of breeze caught his wings, putting an added pressure of lift under them. It was only a fleeting touch but it was enough to turn the balance. The barnacle's body lifted sluggishly. He was flying, skimming along close to the surface, his wings fighting for the altitude he needed to clear the next wavecrest lunging toward him.

The downdraft on the receding slope of the wave pushed him into the trough. He struggled up the slanting surface of the next wave. The crest with a fringe of white on it towered massively over him. He fought to rise over it. The crest came so close that some of its salt spray slapped against him, but he was still flying, and the wave was past, and again a gust of breeze was lifting him, giving him a few more feet of altitude.

He cleared the next wave easily, but his wings were heavy and awkward, and it was impossible for him to rise more than a few yards above the sea. Now he could see the white island again with the black cloud hanging in the air above it, but it was far away and it no longer attracted him, despite the food that it promised. For the barnacle knew that time and strength were running out. He was drawing now on the last of his flight power. And with the strength draining rapidly out of him, the urge to fly west had become a driving obsession. Every wingbeat that failed to carry him westward was a wasted wingbeat.

So he turned away from the ship. He turned in a wide circle because his flight was hard to control and a tight turn might lose him altitude and plunge him again into the sea. He turned until the ship and the rising sun were behind him, and he headed toward an empty horizon. The barnacle had no understanding of what had happened to him but he did realize clearly that he must not land on the water again. The sea, always a friend and protector, had suddenly become a sinister enemy.

The best he could do was to maintain a flight level just a few yards above the highest waves. He did not know how long he had flown when he first detected the glow of an ice-blink rimming the horizon ahead. Now he knew why the water had felt so cold. He was nearing a coastal ice field again.

He struggled on interminably. The white line of the ice was already strong and clear when first he noticed it, but his wings were weakening. He was dropping, slanting downward, and there was no strength left to fight it. There was usually a faint surge of updraft from the crest of each wave and this alone was what kept him in the air. His flight became a struggle from one wavetop to the next. The ice line drew nearer with taunting, despairing slowness.

And then it happened. His tired wings faltered on one of the updrafts, the lift of it spilled out from under his flight feathers and suddenly he was plunging down into the trough with the next wave lunging toward him. The crest of it curled above. The green water reached up and pulled him down and he was in the sea again, rolling over and over.

The wave passed and he began to swim. Instantly the icy water seeped through his matted feathers and clutched again at his belly. He began submerging. He knew he must fly.

He started his wings beating again. His body rose in the water and he began plowing along its surface but he could not break free. For a long time he splashed along this way, half in the sea and half out, his wingtips slapping its surface, a white wake trailing behind him. Sometimes he would be airborne for a few seconds when a wavecrest lifted him but he would always drop back into the sea again, and the splashing sprint would continue.

There were outriders of ice, small isolated pans, far out from the edge of the floe itself. The barnacle saw one and headed toward it. It was a small pan no more than six feet across and when he reached it he was too exhausted to climb onto it. He crooked his neck over the edge of the ice to help keep himself afloat and he rested briefly. He kicked out vigorously and beat his wings again, pulling himself upward with his bill. Slowly he slid onto the ice. Though almost too exhausted to stand, the barnacle started preening immediately.

The nourishment from the morning meal began reaching his muscles and he could feel new strength flowing into them. Later that morning he flew again. His wings were cleaner now after the new preening and he rose easily from the bobbing cake of ice. He flew strongly for more than an hour, passed the edge of the main floe and flew on across solid ice.

But the weakness crept back. He rested, and flew on, and rested again. The sun traced its arc across the sky until finally it passed from view below the horizon of ice ahead of him. He slogged on through the darkness with heavy wings and with senses dulled, knowing only one thing, knowing only that the mate was waiting ahead and he had to drive himself on until he stood beside her.

Another day had come and the coast had been there on the horizon for many hours, beckoning, promising food, yet it still remained distant, as though attached to the horizon and moving away as fast as he could move toward it. His wings were capable now of only a few hundred yards of flight at a time. He would struggle on, low over the ice, and when his wings would beat no more he would glide to a clumsy landing, falling, skidding along on his emaciated breast and belly because the co-ordination required for a controlled landing was lost. He would stand on the ice resting, eyeing the distant coastal cliffs again, his wings trembling like limp rags beside his blackened oil-smeared sides. At times too weak to fly and too impatient to rest, he would struggle forward on foot, clambering over slippery ice ridges, sliding and falling down the other sides.

At the end his wings were paralyzed with exhaustion and he could only walk. He trudged ashore, wending a circuitous way through the jumble of boulders at its edge and leaving a twisting trail of webbed footprints in the snow behind him. He reached a line of bushes and began feeding on their buds. The hunger pains left him. The mate seemed much nearer now.

Komtuk, the Eskimo hunter, stared disbelieving at the tracks in the snow. It was obviously the trail of a goose, but why should a goose be here, *walking ashore* like this from barren sea ice where no goose should ever be? Komtuk followed the trail inland and then he saw the big bird crouched in the willows. The goose sprang into the air with a violent clapping of wings, but the wings seemed incapable of lifting it above the entwining willow canes and the bird pitched back clumsily into the snow. Komtuk raised his gun and fired. He ran forward quickly to where the goose lay quivering in the snow with the red stain spreading outward beneath it.

Komtuk stared, trembling now and breathing hard at what he saw. He had hunted along this coast for twenty years, but this was a goose like no goose he had ever seen in his land before. Yet it wasn't that alone that started him trembling and brought the breath in spasmodic gasps to his cracked lips. For Komtuk was staring at the silver ring on the goose's leg and at the fantastic yellow ribbon around the strange bird's neck.

Komtuk was a religious man and he knew that this was no goose. This must be a spirit from the Christian God's heaven.

He removed his fur parka and spread it on the snow. He lifted the big bird gently and placed it on the fur, rolling the parka corners over it. Then he picked up the bundle and carried it with great care back toward the village and the mission. Komtuk was trembling again and he walked hurriedly.

"A strange one," he muttered. "Yes, yes, a strange one."

CHAPTER FIFTY-ONE

KANINA and her father had no canoe at Cape Cree for they had had to leave it behind at the winter camp. They joined another family for the spring goose hunt and muskrat trapping. This family went down the coast instead of up the Kistawanee, so Kanina had no opportunity to visit Kishamooskek Lake. On their return to Cape Cree Kanina had anxiously questioned the wives of the Kishamooskek hunters about *man-tay-o* and his *niska* mate, but no one this spring had seen the geese with the yellow neck streamers.

By early June the lazy routine of summer living had returned again to Cape Cree. Kanina cooked for her father. Because of the failure of the winter trapping there was little money with which to buy store food, but the spring muskrat trapping had paid for a summer supply of flour and tea. The goose hunt had been good and there would be dried goose breasts until well into the summer. And there were whitefish now each day in Kanina's nets.

But Kanina did not have enough to do to keep herself busy and time became a burden. She had been accepted fully now as a *Mooskek-owak,* but talking to the other Indian women bored her and she found it impossible to find any real companionship among them. Helplessly, inevitably, she began thinking of the books that would still be in the cardboard carton upstairs in the Rumsey house, and of Bert Rumsey's magazines and newspapers. And one afternoon she called on Joan Rumsey.

They had tea and Kanina was careful not to reveal how much she enjoyed having milk and sugar in it again. She did not want Joan Rumsey to know that down in the tent they had no milk or sugar and were drinking their tea thickened with flour.

Kanina stayed an hour. She took a number of magazines and three new books Bert Rumsey had bought by mail order during the winter. Then, hesitantly, the unasked question still tormenting her, she went to the door. And now she knew she could not leave without asking it.

"Did you hear during the winter from Rory Macdonald?"

"We had a letter thanking us a few weeks after he left last September," Joan Rumsey said, "and a card at Christmas. He didn't mention you."

"Thank you for the tea and the reading material," Kanina said quickly and then she walked hurriedly down the boardwalk and away.

At first Kanina had ignored the planes that came once or twice a week to Cape Cree, but now she found herself running eagerly to the river bank with the other *Mooskek-owak* whenever she heard the distant hum of an approaching aircraft. She would stand, silent and staring like the rest of them, as the plane taxied in from mid-stream. She would watch, tense and barely breathing, as the door opened and the passengers one by one stepped down to the float and jumped ashore. And when all were out she would turn and walk back slowly toward the tent village, thinking again that the university year was ended and if he were coming back he should be arriving soon, yet knowing in another more rational part of her that he would not be back, ever, no matter how long she waited.

With her interest in the planes there developed a new interest in her own appearance. She kept her clothes washed and her hair brushed and tied with a ribbon. She began leaving off the black shawl.

Throughout the winter and spring she had got along well with her father, but now, fostered by idleness, some of the old tensions began to return. He complained about the amount of soap they were using, saying it was using credit at the store that should be used for food. Kanina did not try to deny it.

"And why do you no longer wear the shawl?" he asked. "A *Mooskek-owak* woman always keeps her hair covered. The other women are talking about it."

"It is hot and unnecessary and I do not like it," Kanina answered. "I do not care if they are talking."

The difficulties with her father underlined the new problem that had been created by her mother's death. When her mother was alive it had been a natural thing for Kanina to return to her parents, but now living alone in the small tent with her father was an unpleasant arrangement that could not be permanent. She knew she was expected to marry, to bring a new hunter into the Beaverskin tent to support her and to support her father when he became too old for anything but the "women's work" of snaring rabbits and netting fish. There was no place in the *Mooskek-owak* hunting economy for old maids. But the prospect of being married to one of the Indian youths around her filled her with fright and disgust. Sometimes, trembling at the thought, she would look up at the big white house of the Rumseys and wonder if she should go back there to work, as she knew Joan Rumsey would like her to do.

Soon there would be summer sturgeon fishing down the bay and since her father needed money to pay off his store debt, he would want to go. At that time, Kanina would have to decide.

Meanwhile the planes droned in and out of Cape Cree and Kanina still met them regularly.

When she returned the borrowed books and magazines to the Rumseys, Bert Rumsey was there and Kanina learned that he had had an Indian checking beaver lodges on Kishamooskek. His canoe was still in on the lake. She had wanted to look for *man-tay-o,* but she herself could not carry a canoe across the long portage. Now she grasped eagerly at this opportunity.

"May I borrow it? I want to look for Rory Macdonald's geese. I'd need another canoe and outboard to get up the Kistawanee."

Bert Rumsey nodded. "Any time," he said. "Do you want Jock to go along and help you?"

"No. I can handle an outboard now." Then Kanina hesitated before adding slowly: "And I want to go alone."

Kanina felt as a pilgrim must feel when returning to a sacred shrine. Memories, bitter and happy, came tumbling back. There, ahead now, was the goose camp clearing on the Kistawanee where she had turned her ankle on the stone and he had picked her up and carried her and then it had happened for the first time. She cut the outboard and beached the canoe and started across the portage. Every few paces of the trail seemed to have its memory—the logs where he had put down the canoe and rested, the low branches she had held up so that he could carry the canoe beneath, the bird songs she had learned under his tutorship and now once more forgotten. And finally, Kishamooskek, the beach, *their* beach.

Kanina paused at the end of the portage. There were the stakes of Rory's tent still standing in the sand, the black ash of their lunch fires and, protruding through the ash and sand, a charred piece of caribou bone. Even the bone had its memories. She was repeating under her breath the line from somewhere in the poems of Alexander Pope: "How vast a memory has Love!"

The canoe lay overturned on the beach nearby with the paddles beneath it. Kanina launched it and began paddling toward the island with the shallow bay in which they had trapped and banded the geese. As she neared it, she let the canoe slow down until the gurgle of water under its bow dropped to a whisper. She was skirting the willows that screened one side of the little bay. Then she stopped paddling and listened and she heard the geese immediately—the soft throaty gabble of their feeding talk.

Kanina turned the canoe in to shallow water, stepped out carefully and pulled it ashore. She was trembling. Rory was right, the geese had come back!

She dropped onto her hands and knees and began creeping through the dense growth of willows. She heard the goose-talk again, but it started her heart thumping so loudly that after a few seconds she could hear it no longer. Through the green screen of willow leaves she saw a gleam of yellow that flashed momentarily and disappeared. She crept forward another yard or two. She was still well hidden but a broadening view of the little bay began opening before her. Her eyes searched it quickly. She saw the white upturned belly of a feeding goose. She saw the head and neck rise back above water. She saw the yellow neck streamer, faded a little, its ends torn, but still bright and unmistakable.

It was the female, the Canada goose.

Kanina's eyes moved back and forth eagerly, seeking *man-tay-o*. She crept forward again for a clearer view. She could see the whole bay now, the wavelets lapping the sand on the other side, the ranks of sedge and reed bending weakly before a hesitant errant breeze.

Man-tay-o was not there. The female Canada was alone.

She was sure the barnacle had not been shot by an Indian hunter, because this could not have happened without her learning of it. He could have been shot by a white hunter in the south, but it was improbable, for if one were shot, the other would probably be shot with it. No . . . . the thing that Rory Macdonald thought would not happen *had* happened. When the time came for the barnacle to choose between his love for his mate and his love for the sea, *man-tay-o* had chosen the sea.

Looking again at the lone Canada goose, Kanina felt the new bond that now linked them. They had both loved outlanders whose real loyalties lay elsewhere. The circle of events was now complete, they were back where it all had begun, each of them alone again in the muskeg land to which they irrevocably belonged.

Kanina felt like a seeker after truth who had gone to an oracle and been given a sign pointing the way of her future. There were gaps that even love can never bridge. She had known it well last summer when she and Rory had parted, but in recent weeks watching the planes again at Cape Cree she had hoped some magic could change it. Now the hope was gone.

News reached Cape Cree the following day that the sturgeon run was starting down the coast, and Joe Beaverskin immediately began preparations to go. Kanina had no indecision now, she knew she too must go.

They were loading a big canoe in which they would accompany another family when Kanina heard the distant drone of a plane. She watched it approach, angry with herself for the hope and eagerness she was feeling. The plane circled and then slanted down with idling motor to the Kistawanee. It began taxiing ashore. She ran to meet it. The plane door opened and two men stepped down—the pilot and his engineer. There were no passengers.

Kanina turned slowly away and walked back to the waiting canoe. She opened her clothing bag, took out the black shawl, flung it over her head and knotted it impulsively under her chin.

CHAPTER FIFTY-TWO

JULY was hot and humid. The sun's heat seared the pavements of downtown Toronto and flung itself back into the faces of pedestrians like the scorching blast from a furnace door. Rory Macdonald had never spent a summer in Toronto before and he hated it. The bustling offices of Northwoods Enterprises were air-conditioned, but this was a poor substitute for the lake breezes of the northern Ontario bush where he had worked in other summers. And the heat was only part of his discontent.

For six weeks now his name had been listed on the Northwoods Enterprises sales literature as the development's "director of parks and wildlife management." He had visited the site during June conducting what was supposed to be a wildlife survey, but after two days it was called off and he was ordered back to the Toronto office. He wrote a report on his hasty survey, but so far as he could learn no one yet had bothered to read it. At least, none of the brass had ever mentioned it.

The only good thing about it all was the pay. For the privilege of having his "M.A., Biologist" on the sales literature—the M.A. was not official yet, but no one seemed concerned about that—they were paying him ninety dollars a week. But actually he was a glorified office boy running trivial errands for men who smoked cigars and sat behind desks as big as billiard tables.

When Rory's opportunity to get out of Toronto's heat finally came, it was peculiarly galling and taunting. The sales director called Rory into his office one afternoon in the second week of July.

"Mr. Macdonald," he began brusquely, "there's an important job for you now up at the site."

Rory listened eagerly.

"We're getting the odd prospective buyer in there now looking things over," the man continued. "You know that our big sales pitch has been the wilderness character of the development. This is supposed to be wild and remote . . . . untouched wilderness and all that . . . . nature in its pristine glory. For a summer development, that pitch has great appeal. Well, we've bought six tame deer from a zoo supplier. The bulldozers scared out all the wild deer months ago and these things are African deer of some sort, but nobody needs to know that. We're liberating them up there in a couple of days. They're going to be your responsibility."

Rory shifted uneasily on his chair. "What am I supposed to do with them?" he asked.

"Just take care of them, that's all. Keep them from straying away. It's very important that these critters be somewhere out in plain sight whenever any prospective buyers are making a tour of the place. Your job is to chase them out at the right time so they'll be sure to be seen. But don't give any visitors a chance to see them too close. We don't want anyone to realize they're not native deer."

Rory could feel the irritation building up like a cold lump in his throat. "How am I supposed to accomplish all this?" he asked.

"I don't know how," the man exclaimed bluffly. "That's your job. You're the biologist here, you should know how." He waved Rory away. "Get some expense money, catch a train and get up there tomorrow."

Rory was trembling angrily as he walked from the office.

When he reached the boarding house that night there was another letter from the Illinois State Department of Conservation. Rory knew it would be a final report on the female Canada goose and he picked it up indifferently and took it upstairs. He opened it. The letter was brief and he was thankful at least for that. It started with an apology for having been so slow in getting this final information to him, and then it informed that the Canada goose with the yellow neck streamer had left the Horseshoe Lake refuge with one of the northbound flocks during the first week of March.

Rory crumpled it in his hand and dropped it on the floor. Then he lay on the bed and stared blankly at the ceiling. It was mid-July now and the female Canada would be back at the mating territory on

Kishamooskek Lake, alone and probably bewildered still by the disappearance of her mate. And the barnacle, the jilting rogue, where would he be?

I hope you're dead, you bastard! Rory thought. You've caused enough grief for one bird's lifetime.

But probably he wasn't dead. Probably he was back there now on the upper Greenland coast where he was born, back again with the flocks of his own kind. And probably he was mated with a female of his own species, because the fact that he had chosen to abandon his first mate indicated that that first mating would not have been binding enough to prevent him from mating again.

But the barnacle's contribution to Rory Macdonald's life had not been all grief and trouble. Through the barnacle Rory had recognized his mistake in trying to make himself a biologist. There had been many times last winter and spring when he had questioned his decision to abandon biology, but he always ended up by deciding again that he must do it.

And now the question was there in his mind again. The alternative career he had chosen had degenerated to the humiliating point where now he was about to become a zoo-keeper putting on an outdoor sideshow for millionaire suckers. Rory grimaced and shivered. How much lower could he go and still have a remnant of self-respect left? Self-respect . . . . what the hell! The last feeble dregs of his self-respect had gone nearly a year ago. They had gone up the Kistawanee River in that Beaver-skin canoe when he had stood, a coward and a hypocrite, and let Kanina leave him.

He recalled guiltily that he had made a pledge with her when they parted. He had promised that when he was back here among his people he would fight it, he would try to make them see the folly of it. And now, ringing, taunting in his ears, he was hearing again her parting words. "And someday when there is another girl and another boy and a love like ours it won't have to end like this."

It started him tossing miserably on the bed. What had he done about the pledge? Nothing. He had let himself become a God damned zoo-keeper! Well . . . . what else could he do? He had wasted five years of his life in a branch of science that had no practical application; after five years of university training the world of business had no use for him except as a zoo-keeper. He had made his choice. He had chosen the world of business. So this was the only road to the success, the security, the pride of achievement that every thinking part of him demanded.

Rory and P.L. met now only at mealtimes in the dining room and their conversation even there was limited to the minimum that a forced and indifferent courtesy required. They were eating silently half an hour later when P.L. spoke suddenly.

"You look as glum as a tomcat that has just lost a fight."

Win or lose, Rory thought, I don't need any help from you.

"How is the research doing?" Rory asked. P.L. hadn't talked about it for weeks.

"Progressing very well," the professor said. "But the janitors are on my neck again."

Rory stared at him. "Why don't you get this thing properly approved and be finished with this janitor nonsense?"

"I'm big enough to fight my own battles."

"And you're fool enough to be always creating new ones."

"Well I'm not looking for any new battles now. I want to tell you some news."

"What?"

"The zoology department needs two new lecturers for next fall. If I recommend you, you could be one of them. You could go on working for a Ph.D. at the same time."

"No thanks. What in hell would I do now with a Ph.D. in biology?"

"Perfectly happy with the job you have, eh?"

"Yes. It's a big firm, has a lot of important men connected with it. There's plenty of opportunity there. I'm going up to the site tomorrow for the rest of the summer."

"What are you going to do? Interesting work?"

Rory did not answer him.

"Well?" P.L. pressed.

"Sure it's interesting work! Why in hell do you think I'm going!" Rory hesitated again, and then added: "I'm laying out parkland and doing a wildlife survey."

"I thought you did a wildlife survey before."

"Oh go to hell!" Rory gulped the last of his coffee and strode from the room.

As he went up the stairs, P.L. called after him: "Let me know if you change your mind and want that lecturing appointment."

When he had closed the door behind him, Rory stopped suddenly in the middle of his room. For five years he had been looking forward to this time when he could settle down in a zoology professorship. And now he was refusing it—in order to become a zoo-keeper!

Rory was packing, preparing to leave for the Northwoods Enterprises site, when he heard the mailman pushing mail through the letter slot downstairs. He went down, picked up a big brown envelope from the fish and wildlife service in Ottawa and brought it back to his room. He sat at the writing table, opened it and began to read.

It was a report on the banding returns from the thousand-odd geese that he had banded around Cape Cree the previous summer. Of that number, close to a hundred had been shot during the autumn hunting season and the bands turned in by hunters. According to the letter, the wildlife service was highly pleased with his work. Most of the returns were from the Mississippi valley, indicating that most of his banded geese were of the Mississippi flyway population. But some of the geese that Rory and Jock banded along the Otter River had been shot in the South Atlantic states, and this was proof that the breeding territories of the two populations merged in that Otter River region.

"Your work has made a very useful contribution to the management of this game species," the letter concluded. "With this knowledge we are in a much better position to regulate properly the hunting pressure and insure that this fine bird does not disappear from our wildlife scene. For your information, a list detailing the returns is included with this letter."

Rory smiled and for the first time in weeks he felt some pride of accomplishment. Despite the tragic fiasco with which it all had ended, he had at least performed one useful function for biology.

The list of returns was several pages long and Rory began running his eyes down it rapidly. On the third page his eyes stopped abruptly. Suddenly he was sucking in his breath through lips that would not stop trembling.

He read hastily: "508–03723 Barnacle goose, *Branta leucopsis*. . . ." His eyes quickly jumped the data on sex, age and date and place of the original banding. Then he was reading again, his head spinning drunkenly. "Shot May 6th near Makkovik, Labrador, by Eskimo."

Rory stared at it until the words grew misty and disappeared. Shot. Dead. In Labrador.

Labrador!

He was trying to get back to her! He had crossed the Atlantic again. He had almost reached her!

The words came back into focus and he read them again. And then he saw the added notation. "See copy of letter attached."

Rory's fingers trembled uncontrollably as he hastily flipped the pages. He found a typed copy of a letter headed "Makkovik Mission." It had been sent originally to the U.S. Fish and Wildlife Service in Washington, the address all North American bird bands carry.

"Dear Sirs," Rory began to read, "I am a Roman Catholic priest at the above-named mission to Eskimos of the Labrador coast. I wish to inform you of a strange goose that was shot by an Eskimo hunter near here yesterday. No goose like it has ever appeared on this coast before. On its left leg is one of your aluminum bands bearing the number 508—03723. Tied around its neck there is a ribbon of yellow plastic. This ribbon is worn and dirty and I would say that it has been on the bird's neck for some considerable length of time. We would appreciate greatly any information you are able to give us about where this goose has come from and where the above described bands were placed upon it.

"The goose was shot by one of our hunters named Komtuk. The goose was in a very emaciated and weak condition and it is obvious that it has reached this region only after a most tiring flight. Its feathers are heavily smeared with oil and Komtuk reports it was too weak to fly. It had walked ashore from the sea ice. . . ."

Rory's eyes were moistening and it was becoming difficult for him to read.

"I must hasten to inform you that the goose is not yet dead," the letter continued. The mistiness cleared suddenly from Rory's eyes and he read on eagerly. "Komtuk is one of our finest Christian Eskimos and when he saw the strange ribbon and leg band on this unusual goose he thought the bird must be a spirit bird from his God's heaven. He brought the goose immediately to me and he is most anxious that we care for the bird and nurse it back to health. Unfortunately one wing and one leg have been broken by Komtuk's shot. These I have bandaged, rendering them immovable, in the hope that they will heal. I have not told Komtuk of my fears, but I am afraid because of its very emaciated condition this goose will die in a few days."

That was all. Rory looked back quickly to the first page of the letter. It had been written May 7th, more than two months ago.

He resumed packing and his heart pounded like a riveting hammer. He thought he had planned the barnacle tracing project with all the thoroughness possible, but now he realized he had left one serious gap. He thought that determining the barnacle's wintering location would automatically answer everything—the Mississippi valley would mean a permanent mating, Barra would mean separation. He had not considered the possibility of the barnacle leaving her and then setting out to find her again.

And now through a lucky accident he had learned the true story. With revival of the springtime mating urge, *man-tay-o had* set out to find her again. And he had died trying. A broken wing, a broken leg and oil. Rory knew what oil could do to a sea bird. Once feathers were impregnated with it, nothing could remove it until the molt occurred and new feathers grew in. And an oil-saturated bird can rarely survive long enough for the cleansing molt to come.

Rory's train was due to leave in an hour and he had not yet bought his ticket. He began hurrying with the last of his packing.

He wished his mother could know how it had ended. And Kanina too. She loved that bird. She must be told. He would write to the Rumseys and ask them to tell her.

Yet . . . . maybe it hadn't ended after all.

Rory hurried from the house, carrying his luggage. When he reached the station and joined one of the ticket queues, there were only fifteen minutes before the northern Ontario train's departure time. He shifted uneasily from one foot to the other as he moved slowly up the line. There were only five minutes left when finally he stood before the wicket and stared, momentarily speechless, at the clerk behind.

"Where to?" the man asked impatiently.

Rory Macdonald didn't know until that moment what he was going to say. Yet he said it without uncertainty or surprise.

"Moosonee."

It was a wild thought, yet not quite impossible—the barnacle could conceivably have reached Kishamooskek again, and Rory *had* to know. With luck he could avoid Kanina; they were often away at fishing camps at this time of the year.

CHAPTER FIFTY-THREE

IT was early and the morning shadows were still long and cool but Rory was sweating heavily under the canoe when he stepped off the portage onto the Kishamooskek beach. He lowered the canoe to the sand and looked around him. Superficially everything remained the same—the marsh on his right, the blue lake reaching away to the left, and the beach curving between. Even the tent pegs and the ashes of their fires were still there. Yet none of it was the same. It was like a dead body, with every feature still intact, but the spirit and life that had given it reality were gone.

Rory had learned with relief from the Rumseys that Kanina was down the coast at a sturgeon camp. He would be able to have a look for the barnacle and return on the next plane without seeing her.

He launched the canoe and began paddling. Suddenly his throat was dry and he was breathing hard. He beached the canoe on the island and stood silently on the sand where only the narrow strip of willows screened him from the little bay where they had trapped the geese the summer before. His ears were straining to catch every sound.

He waited perhaps a minute, and then he heard the soft guttural gabble of a Canada goose beyond the willows. He listened for the sharper bark-like answer from the barnacle. No answer came. The Canada goose gabbled again. And again there was no answer.

She was alone.

Rory stepped cautiously into the willow tangle. He dropped to his hands and knees and crept forward. Patches of blue water appeared through the screen of leaves before him. And then he saw them, and she was not alone, for the barnacle was there at her side, a beaten, bedraggled effigy of the majestic gander he had been the year before. He was gaunt and thin and the black stains of oil still covered his wings and belly. He had started to molt but the loosened feathers, instead of dropping away, were clinging in ragged tufts to the caked smears of oil. The yellow streamer was still on his neck but it, too, was ragged and smudged with oil. And then he tipped to feed, turning up his belly toward Rory, revealing that one leg was gone. The broken one, apparently had had to be amputated by the Labrador missionary.

But the old love was still there in the shattered crippled body. When his bill came up with food he offered it gallantly to the female and then, in the same movement, he extended his neck past hers and quickly preened her wing.

Despite the labored thumping of his heart Rory felt as though a great smothering burden had been lifted from him. What had seemed for months to be sentimental nonsense suddenly had meaning and serious scientific import again. He felt like someone who had been condemned to serve a harsh, lifelong penance and now the penance had been suddenly removed.

He watched them for a long time, but finally he turned and crept away and it was then that he discovered the soft imprints of her moccasins where the sand was firm and damp under the edge of the willows. The moccasin prints had to be *hers*. They were small prints, a woman's, and no one else but she would be coming here. They were old, their outlines blurred by rain; they had been made several weeks ago.

Rory stared at them, unable to turn away. Last winter he had grasped eagerly at the news of the barnacle's return to Barra. It had seemed to corroborate the inevitability of his own decision. It had given Rory the feeling that he did not stand alone. But now the barnacle was back. Now Rory *was* alone with the decision he had made.

He launched the canoe and started back, his mind reeling with conflict and indecision. But long before he reached Cape Cree the conflict was over.

The following morning he gave Bert Rumsey two telegrams to send out. One was his resignation from Northwoods Enterprises. The other was for P.L. Rory had written: "Leucopsis returned. This deserter also wishes return as lecturer U of T and Ph.D. graduate studies."

Then he set out immediately with an outboard on a large bay canoe. He passed the Kistawanee's mouth and turned it down the James Bay coast.

The barnacle's return had clarified everything, but solved nothing. Everything had changed—yet nothing had changed.

"Sure you could marry her, you stupid bastard. . . ." And he had a vivid mental picture of P.L.'s shaggy hair line bobbing. "But you'd always be the zoology lecturer married to a squaw . . . . frozen at that level. . . ."

The willow point at the mouth of the Kistawanee dropped astern and faded slowly into the low, featureless James Bay shoreline. On the horizon ahead, there was a thin white line of smoke marking the *Mooskekowak* encampment. And now, suddenly, his thighs were trembling like the leaves of the stunted aspens along the boggy shore. For she had said last summer she could not do it, she would not bring it into his life too. Would she say it again?

At one time that question would not have worried him, but now the swaggering self-assurance of boyhood was gone. For the first time since the night with Peggy MacNeill on the Goose Island shieling, Rory Macdonald was meeting a girl with uncertainty and fear.

The wind was increasing. An hour later when he throttled down the motor and turned in toward the Indian camp, his canoe was pitching heavily in the growing sea. He saw Kanina walk slowly down from the tents and across the beach toward the spot where he would be landing. She was wearing the rubber boots, a gray shapeless skirt and the black shawl.

He was close enough now to see her face clearly. And instead of a smile of greeting her face seemed contorted with pain. He waved but she just stood stiffly and did not wave in return. She was sorry he had come.

Then her hands went up to her shawl. She untied the knotted ends. A gust of wind caught it and snatched it from her fingers. The black shawl twisted and whirled as the wind lifted it higher and higher like an escaping shroud. In a few seconds it was gone, high over the spruce forest, lost amid the rising smoke of the *Mooskek-owak* fires.